12/15

Praise for Ark Storm

"A plausible and roomy ecothriller that might presage future events" —*Kirkus Reviews*

"A stunning novel that will shock and awe you . . . a brilliantly crafted ecothriller filled with characters who are authentically good—and bad."

—former secretary of defense William S. Cohen,
New York Times bestselling author of
Collision

"Ecoterrorism on a massive scale meets California hedge-fund glamour! A heart-stopping race against time and billionaire villainy. Top of the list."

—Nigel West, author of *Mortal Crimes:
The Greatest Theft in History; The Soviet
Penetration of the Manhattan Project*

"*Ark Storm* is a winner. It draws you in and thrashes you about like a hurricane. The writing is crisp, the pacing is breakneck, and the characters are vivid. I highly recommend it."
—Douglas Preston,
New York Times bestselling author of
The Kraken Project

"I was going to say that I got blown away by *Ark Storm,* but I'm afraid to! So I'll say that I got caught up in it and loved it."
—Whitley Strieber,
New York Times bestselling author of
The Grays

ARK STORM

Linda Davies

TOR®

A TOM DOHERTY ASSOCIATES BOOK
NEW YORK

ARK STORM

Copyright © 2014 by Linda Davies

All rights reserved.

A Tor Book
Published by Tom Doherty Associates, LLC
175 Fifth Avenue
New York, NY 10010

www.tor-forge.com

Tor® is a registered trademark of Tom Doherty Associates, LLC.

ISBN 978-0-7653-8351-8

Our books may be purchased in bulk for promotional, educational, or business use. Please contact your local bookseller or the Macmillan Corporate and Premium Sales Department at (800) 221-7945, extension 5442, or by e-mail at MacmillanSpecialMarkets@macmillan.com.

First Edition: August 2014
First Mass Market Edition: December 2015

Printed in the United States of America

0 9 8 7 6 5 4 3 2 1

This is for my late brother, Professor John Eric Davies.
You lived so well, died too young.
It's also for his wonderful daughter, Eleanor Beaton.

ACKNOWLEDGMENTS

There are many people to whom I owe many thanks for this book.

My husband, Rupert Wise, has supported me in every imaginable way. He has always believed in my writing and he knew that one day a big story would come along. Like a magician, he guides me to the stories and the stories to me. And he does so much more in helping me craft them. He is an insightful (and brave) critic. He is also an invaluable source of research information with his wide-ranging expertise.

Our children have my eternal thanks for giving it all meaning.

David Vigliano reached out through the ether, summoning my ideas and giving them the oxygen of his faith. The whole crew at Vigliano Associates—Matt Carlini, David Peak, Thomas Flannery, inter alios—have been wonderfully brilliant and supportive both on the business and on the creative side, giving me invaluable editorial input.

My brother Roy, via the website he set up many years ago for me before I even knew that such a thing existed, was the conduit that put David in touch with me. He also is a source of diverse information.

David took me to the fabulous Tor Books. Bob Gleason, editor and writer extraordinaire, you are a genius and I'm not saying that because you spotted me and my book! Tom Doherty, you have created a wonderful enterprise full of talent and energy and brightness. It is a pleasure to know you. Kelly Quinn, fellow Oxonian, you are always cheerful and upbeat, seamlessly professional and never wrong!

Huge thanks to the entire Tor team across sales and marketing and general administration. Without you guys I wouldn't be out there.

I would also like to thank the lovely Hanca Leppink for all her support over the years. Thanks too to Marga de Boer and all the team at Luitingh-Sijthoff.

Yilin Press in China—thanks, guys! My first Chinese translation.

In the writing of this book, I have come across many brilliant and fascinating people who have helped me with research across a very wide range of subjects. I owe you all profound thanks.

Some of you I cannot publicly acknowledge here: the man with the murderous animals—glad you are on the side of the angels! The traveler and his son: I would not wish to bump into either of you on a dark night but your knowledge is impeccable. Mr. Electronica, love the live insights . . .

The scientists and their backers, thank you for sharing your brilliant creation.

Those whom I can thank publicly:

The U.S. Geological Survey, Multi-Hazards Demonstration Project—ARk Storm 1000 scenario, were extremely informative and helpful.

Professor Mark Saunders of University College London gave generously of his time and expertise many years ago when I first explored the idea of writing a novel around the weather.

The wonderful Rupert Allason is always forthcoming with his time and his extensive knowledge.

My brother Kenneth gave me detailed input on Singapore—clubs, restaurants, traffic, and other wonderful local detail.

Marcel Giacometti and Andrew Stuttaford were most helpful with all things financial. Marcel also gave freely of his considerable gastronomic and viticultural expertise.

Dirk Wray was a wonderful source of surfing stories. You big wave surfers are mad!

Doris, Jenie, Andrew, and Tony buy me time to write.

And I thank you, dear reader, for picking up this book.

ARK
STORM

PROLOGUE

What if you could control the weather?

"What if one man could control the weather?"

"Only Allah can control the weather."

"Not true."

Thousands of miles away, in Iran, the ayatollah snorted with derision.

"You think you have the power of Allah, now? You think your billions of dollars make you God? This is heresy."

"Not heresy. Technology. I can make it rain. I can stop the rain. I can harness the power of the storm and I can magnify it. I can bring the Flood. I can wash away hillsides, destroy homes; I can take a swath of some of the most expensive real estate in the United States and I can rain down upon it the wrath of Allah at the infidel."

"You would wage jihad by weather?"

"Does it not say in the holy Quran, *we helped him against those who rejected him. They were surely a wicked people, so we drowned them all.* Is it not a beautiful idea?"

"When will you do it?"

"When the right storm comes. Then I shall magnify it. I will give California the ARk Storm of their nightmares."

1

The wave came silently, like a killer in the pellucid light of dawn. Huge and beautiful and murderous. *Come and get me. C'mon, let's see if you can.* She could see the swell, bigger than those that had gone before. Maybe a twelve- to fourteen-footer, with a likely twenty-five-foot face. Massive. At the outer limits of a wave that she could surf without a Jet Ski tow-in. Her heart began to race as she lay down on her board, reached out long, powerful arms, and paddled hard. She could see the wave in front explode in a frenzy of white water. She could no longer see the monster behind her, gaining on her, rising up behind her, opening its maw, but she could feel it. It raised her up, terrifyingly high. No backing out now. *Paddle for your life, harder, faster.*

She grabbed the board, snapped to her feet as the wave took her, propelled her down its gnarly face. She balanced, knees bent low, arms outstretched, warrior pose, riding it, wild with glee, high on adrenaline. She skimmed down the face, muscling the board against the yank of hundreds of tons of water. She rode into the barrel, into the unearthly blue, into the moment when time stopped and the universe was just you and the barrel and the roaring in your ears. And then time started again and the barrel was closing, just one split second of escape remaining. She ducked right down, shot out of the barrel, flipped up over the back of the wave. Feet still planted on her board, she flew through air, over water, riding the two elements. Conquering them. This time. Her spirit sang and she yelled out loud. No one to hear her. She surfed alone, breaking the surfer's code. Just the woman and the sea with the gulls screaming and soaring and bearing their wild witness.

The gulls watched her paddle round to the quiet water, where the waves did not form up to do battle. They watched her paddle in, walk from the water, sun-bleached hair falling down her back: golden skin, freckle-flecked over the patrician nose, which was a shade too long, saving her from mere prettiness. They watched her glance back at the sea, a look of reckoning, part gratitude, part triumph, part relief.

Always the fear, underneath it all. Only the fool did not feel it. Gwen felt it dissipate as she ran up the beach, board under her arm. Death swam alongside the huge waves, every surfer knew that. It was part of the kick, risking your life. The euphoria of survival was her reward. She felt it sweep through her, filling up the empty parts, washing away the doubts. *Now* she was ready to take them on, to play the games of man. And win again.

2

HURRICANE POINT, CALIFORNIA,
ONE WEEK EARLIER

It had begun like a normal day, then the phone rang. Joaquin Losada in Peru.

"Chica. You up?"

"I am now," replied Gwen, rubbing her eyes, squinting at her alarm clock: 7:00 A.M. She'd been up till three, hit-

ting the tequila with her childhood friend Lucy and her Tae
Kwon Do trainer Dwayne and a few of his fellow ex-Navy-
SEAL buddies who were about to go off on a trip and were
determined to send themselves off in style. The thought
that they would soon be boarding a ship while she got to
remain on dry, unpitching land made her feel marginally
better.

"Switch on your computer. Check the readings!" came
Joaquin's high-pitched voice. It was always high, in a de-
liciously camp way, but this morning it sounded like nails
on a blackboard.

Gwen cautiously swung her legs out of bed, pulled the
alpaca blanket around her, walked through to the sitting
room, and turned on her computer.

"I'm checking," she said, trying to focus on the flickering figures as the screen came to life. She twiddled the
green jade and gold ring she wore on her middle finger,
spinning it round and round in place as she read and then
reread the figures.

"Jeez! These temperature readings are off the scale for
September. Are the sensors faulty?"

"My first thought. Something's been going on here with
the readings for the past two weeks. I didn't say anything
before 'cause it was just too weird, wanted to give it time
to revert."

"And?"

"It didn't revert. The temperatures just keep rising. So,
either the sensors are faulty or the model has a glitch or
we got one hell of a Niño building."

"We did think it was going to be big." Gwen got up,
crossed into her kitchen, filled a mug with water, downed
it. Drips ran down her lips to her chest, dampening her
white vest top.

"Gwen, there is big and there is truly humongous. All
sorts of weird shit is going on here. We've had blasting sun,
high summer sun, and we're just into Spring down here.

We've had torrential rain, and freakish waves. We've lost fifteen sensors in the past fortnight."

"Shoot! And you think waves have smashed them? They're meant to withstand extreme waves."

"Try telling them that. They're at the bottom of the ocean, my guess, smashed to bits. I've been out in the boat looking for them. No trace. And let me tell you, I didn't want to linger out there, but I forced myself to search. Sea has a weird feeling. Strange color, darker than normal, and there's almost an electric feel to it. Hot as hell."

"I know it, like before a hurricane hits." Gwen paused, asked the question that she never wanted to ask, but which hovered between them, always, unspoken, a nightmare subjugated. "Joaquin, it *is* the waves, isn't it? It's not, well, you know . . . ?" Her voice trailed off.

"Sabotage? Persuasion? The Narco Shitfaces? Chica, I hope not. I really hope not, but I don't think so. I'm on the lookout. I'm always on the lookout, but I've seen nothing. No one. They don't know about us. Far as everyone in Punta Sal is concerned, I'm just another dolphin freak cameraman who likes fishing. I go out in my fishing boat, no one gives a shit."

"Keep looking out, Joaquin. I brought you into this."

"Hey, I'm a big boy, and I will look out before you nag the cojones off me, but Gwen, chica, listen up. What's here in my face scaring the shit out of me is the freakin' weather. Something serious is brewing and this is our big chance, Oracle's big chance to predict it." Joaquin's voice had risen what sounded like a full octave.

"Okay. I'm there." Gwen sat down at her desk, looked at the figures again. Numbers don't lie. Logic said it was waves destroying the buoys. She blew out a breath. "So what do we need?"

"More sensors, the toughened ones. More buoys, ditto."

"The expensive ones," observed Gwen, knuckling her pounding temples. "How many do we need?"

"Forty."

"Forty!" exclaimed Gwen, mind furiously calculating the cost. "Jeez, Joaquin, that'll cost nearly half a million dollars. I don't have that kind of money. Fact is, I have almost nothing."

"Then, chica, it's time to quit hiding. You gotta get out there, sell a share in Oracle, raise some serious *plata*, and fast."

3

HURRICANE POINT HOUSE, ONE WEEK LATER,
MONDAY MORNING, 8:00 A.M.

Gwen slid into her Mustang. She turned the key in the ignition, smiled. Thirty years old, the car still roared like a big cat.

She drove slowly down the dirt track, turned onto Highway 1, and snaked along, following the line of the precipitous cliffs. God, she loved this view: the endless blue of the ocean, the serried lines of hump-backed waves, the distant profile of the Big Sur lighthouse, the towering majesty of the Bixby Bridge spanning the canyon below, the parade of cypress trees at Soberanes Point. It was home, had been for a long time, but she had the treasured knack of seeing it with a stranger's eyes and gasping at it.

After about thirty-five minutes she turned inland along the Carmel Valley Road. The sun grew stronger, making her squint, and she nearly missed the turnoff to Laureless Ranch. *"Drive past the ranch house,"* the Big Shot's PA had said, *"and keep going for four hundred yards. You can't miss us."*

She saw what the woman had meant. The square boxlike

two-story granite and glass building looked like an alien spaceship had plucked it from Silicon Valley and deposited it randomly in Carmel Valley.

How the hell did they get zoning, she wondered, stepping from the Mustang. She smoothed down the wrinkles on her black linen trousers, pulled the black tank top down to cover her bare skin, blew out a slow breath. No turning back now. Too much at stake to fail.

She strode up to the locked doors, spoke into an intercom. Aware that she was being monitored by discreet CCTV, she gazed back coolly.

"Gwen Boudain for Dr. Messenger." Her voice was slow, easy, all California surfer girl drawl.

"Come right on in," said an almost robotically metallic voice that miraculously still managed to sound friendly. With an audible click, the doors buzzed open.

A short, middle-aged woman with a thatch of dark-auburn frizzy hair and deep worry lines hurried toward Gwen.

"Hi, Dr. Boudain. We spoke on the phone. I'm Mandy, Dr. Messenger's PA. He's waiting. Corner office. Over there by the ficus tree."

"Thanks," said Gwen. She squared her shoulders, shook back her hair and strode across the office. Her posture, straight-backed, head held high, made her look even taller than her six feet.

She was conscious of heads turning; ignored them.

"Who's the fox?" she heard someone ask.

"That *fox,*" Gwen heard Mandy say, "is *Doctor* Gwen Boudain. And more like a cat, you ask me, with those witchy green eyes."

Gwen stifled a grin, wondered what animal they'd come up with next.

She paused in front of a steel door, knocked hard, walked in. Two men broke off their conversation and looked up speculatively. They were sitting opposite each other across a polished walnut desk bare of all but a phone and a desktop computer. Control freak, thought Gwen immediately, eyeing the man behind the desk. He stood, reached out a hand. Six foot two, the spare frame and hard-planed, tanned features of the athlete and the bright, unwavering eyes of the visionary. Brilliant blue, in his case. Hair shorn to his head—to conceal incipient baldness or just for efficiency and image's sake, Gwen couldn't tell. He wore exquisitely cut gray trousers and a crisply ironed lime-green, open-necked shirt.

"Dr. Boudain! I'm Gabriel Messenger," he announced. No smile, all business. Messenger squeezed Gwen's hand. A bone crusher. Gwen squeezed it right back.

"Dr. Messenger."

He smelled of citrus—some high-end aftershave—and fresh air.

"This is Peter Weiss," said Messenger, gesturing to the other man. Weiss was on the short side of medium, slight in build, with the paunch and hunch of the computer addict.

"Peter is Falcon Capital's uber techie," added Messenger.

Weiss pushed himself up from his chair. If Messenger were day, observed Gwen, this man was night. A hint of a spicy cigar smoke emanated from him. He wore head-to-toe black: t-shirt, shirt worn loose over it, trousers, suede slip-ons. He sported a close-cropped goatee beard, somewhat thin, as if growing it were a struggle. His eyes, redveined and fiercely intelligent, had a feline tilt to them, and his soft, straight black hair made Gwen wonder if he had some Chinese blood.

"Good to meet you, Dr. Gwen," said Weiss, with a warm smile and a gentle handshake.

They moved to a circular table by the window. Messenger bid them sit. Angled blinds cut out the sun's glare.

"OK. Tell us why you're here," said Messenger, squaring

his elbows on the table, leaning toward Gwen, unwavering gaze fixed on her.

His English, spoken with a crisp Germanic accent, made the words come out like a command.

Gwen looked up, smiled at him, turned to include Weiss in the smile. *Let's play.*

"OK, guys, a bit of background about myself and Project Oracle. I'm twenty-eight, a graduate of Ocean Sciences from Stanford. I've just completed my Doctorate in Enhanced Prediction Systems for the Niño phenomenon, also at Stanford. I believe I have come up with a system which will enable users to make a long-range El Niño prediction, longer range and more accurate than current forecasters have access to."

Messenger's eyes flickered with interest.

"You're saying you can beat the market?"

Gwen wondered whether it would sound overly hubristic to claim such a feat, then she reminded herself that these guys were financiers.

"That's exactly what I can do," she declared, flashing them a smile.

"Tell me more."

"Gladly. But on a fully confidential basis only. Here's a non-disclosure and circumvention agreement, standard format. Perhaps you would both be good enough to sign," said Gwen, her normally languid delivery sharpening and speeding up. She handed out two forms. Standard business practice, she reminded herself. No reason why they should see anything sinister in it.

Messenger looked surprised. "I don't make a habit of signing so soon. We might have something similar on our books, or about to come on."

"I doubt it," said Gwen, leaning back in her chair, pausing, hooking their interest as the seconds ticked by. Slowly, she leaned back toward them. "My parents, both marine scientists with PhDs, started to work on this twenty-eight years ago. Four years ago, I personally took over their research. I know what's out there in the market. I've been in this field, one way or another, since I was eight."

Messenger said nothing, just studied her intently. Gwen found herself twiddling her ring, forced herself to stop. Finally Messenger picked up a Montblanc pen, read her document thoroughly, signed. Weiss, mirroring his boss, signed too.

Gwen eased out a silent breath, secured the agreements in her briefcase.

"You're both familiar with the predictions that, sooner or later, an Atmospheric River Storm, known as an ARk Storm, is highly likely to hit California?" she asked them.

"Armageddon by weather," said Weiss. He had a soft, almost feminine voice.

"A catastrophic superstorm," Gwen agreed. "It's been described as Hurricane Katrina pushed through a keyhole. The scenario goes like this: winds of up to 125 kms per hour, rain falling in feet rather than inches, nine million homes flooded, parts of LA under twenty feet of water, one and a half million residents evacuated, four weeks of solid rain, an area three hundred miles long and twenty miles wide under water, innumerable mud slides, God only knows how many casualties, a trillion dollars worth of damage. Basically a meteorological nightmare and a catastrophe for the state of California. Last time something like this hit was eighteen sixty-one to eighteen sixty-two. Witnesses describe a flying wall of water that swept people and livestock to their deaths. California's Central Valley—America's breadbasket, incidentally—was turned into an inland sea for months."

"And it's coming our way, only more intense, thanks to global warming," interjected Messenger. "I've read a bit about it. If the government is correct, it'll hit again, possibly in the next few years. What's that got to do with your Oracle?"

"Everything! Based on my work with El Niño prediction, I would elevate ARk Storm from a theoretical possibility to a probability," concluded Gwen.

The room fell silent. Messenger and Weiss glanced at each other and then back to Gwen. If she had hoped to electrify them, she reckoned she'd just done it.

"That's a pretty big prediction, to put it mildly," said Messenger. "What does your model say that the government's ARk Storm version doesn't?"

"First off, I have an input which they don't. I am the only forecaster using this input. It is one hundred percent proprietary to Oracle. I'll come to that later. Second, my own model is also proprietary. And what it tells me is this: The current Niño we are experiencing will be longer and stronger than the National Oceanic and Atmospheric Administration and the government predicts. The seas off Peru and Ecuador at the equator are warming at a pace I have never seen. That warming will accelerate over the coming months as their summer kicks in. ARk Storms feed off the atmospheric rivers that in turn feed off those pools of warming seawater. So, in my opinion, this Niño is potentially incubating an ARk Storm."

Messenger and Weiss exchanged a long look. What were they not saying? Gwen wondered.

"And when do you think this ARk Storm will hit?" asked Messenger.

"It's September now. Could hit us this winter, or the next. I'm putting my money on one of the two. We're not there yet at anything close to a hundred percent certainty. I reckon there's another push that's needed to bring on a full-scale ARk Storm, but weather variables are so volatile that the push could come in last minute, tip the balance."

"And tell us, Dr. Boudain, why should we take you

seriously? What do you have in the way of proofs?" asked
Messenger, resting his chin on steepled hands.

Gwen held out a memory stick. "Take a look at this at
your leisure. It gives my model's predictions of the past
four El Niños and compares them against the results. The
last two Niños it actually predicted, in strength and duration, over eighteen months in advance. I just ran the numbers back for another two Niños to show how it would have
predicted them too."

Messenger paused a beat, took the memory stick,
palmed it.

"Why didn't it?" asked Weiss.

Gwen shrugged. "I was just a little girl then. My parents
were working on perfecting the model at that time."

"You mentioned you got started on this when you were
eight?" asked Weiss, stroking his goatee.

"Way before," said Gwen. "My parents moved from
California to Peru when I was a year old in order to study
El Niño. Kids and adults alike all knew straight off when
a Niño was coming. The sea got warm. Intoxicatingly
warm, where normally it's cold. My friends and I piled in
for hours . . . we had to be dragged out at meal times. I
found it fascinating. Still do."

"And now you wish to share this with us," mused Messenger.

Gwen gave him a dazzling smile. "In return for a large
investment."

"Who has financed you to date?" asked Messenger.

"I have."

"How, if you don't mind my asking?"

Gwen shrugged. "It's no secret. I made a decent bit of
money from surfing endorsements, modeling, that sort of
thing."

"You're a surfer?" asked Messenger, face opening with
curiosity.

"I am."

"Pro circuit?"

"Yep. But my thing was big waves."

"How big?"

"Big enough to give you nightmares."

Messenger grinned for the first time. It transformed the hard-planed face, revealed a kind of locked-down charisma.

"Is that why you stopped? I take it you did. You spoke in the past tense."

Gwen blew out a breath. The question, the only question, she dreaded. For a second, as she blinked, the images spooled behind her closed lids: the red car hurtling off the road, rolling over and over, coming to a final stop, bursting into flames. Another car, real or imagined, driving victoriously from the scene. She stared across the table at Messenger, meeting and holding his gaze.

"No. I stopped because my parents were killed in a car crash in Peru, and I decided I needed to do something more meaningful with my life than pose in a bikini." She swallowed, her mouth dry, longed for a glass of water.

Messenger nodded slowly, eyes somber. "Hence Oracle."

"Hence Oracle," she replied. She felt a spurt of gratitude toward Messenger. No sympathy. She hated sympathy.

"Why now?" Messenger asked.

Gwen leaned across the desk toward him, eyes narrowing.

"Because something out there is destroying my sensors and my buoys. My assistant reckons it's giant waves, because the survivors are giving readings which are off the charts; because half of me is shit scared and the other half is electrified. Because something huge is coming and I need the money to predict it properly. The question you guys need to answer is, do you want to be part of it, do you want to anticipate it or just run for the hills when it hits?"

4

Special Agent Ange Wilkie sat demurely in the gray skirt suit she wore in a doomed attempt to blend in and enjoyed the floorshow. Her new boss strode into the conference room declaiming to his team, shirtsleeves rolled to his elbows as if ready for a fight. With his musical, rich tenor voice and obvious passion he sounded like an old-style, hellfire preacher.

"To those of you who might be tempted to think that we have the insider traders running scared after our successful prosecution of Raj Rajaratnam and his merry band of tipsters, remember this: no amount of money is ever enough. Human greed has not gone away. Many of those in the corrupt networks of tipsters and traders are already supremely wealthy and privileged, with, you might think, little to gain and everything to lose by breaking the law.

"Raj the Rat was a billionaire. Still not enough for him," thundered Commissioner Troy Bergers. He paused, leaned his muscled arms on the table, dropped his voice, eyed each of the ten people in the room in turn, made them all feel special. And meant it.

With his extravagantly broken nose and pugnacious manner, Bergers had a gladiatorial air and would not have looked out of place in the Coliseum in a leather skirt. Agent Wilkie pondered her boss. Preacher, fighter, Holy Warrior? She narrowly suppressed a giggle, glanced round to check—no one had noticed. They hadn't. They only had eyes for Bergers.

It was obvious his team adored him. He was one of those rare people who, via some indefinable quality, made you feel safe. You felt damn lucky to have him on your side. There was integrity and honesty in his eyes, but also a determination to do the right thing, come what may.

But Ange had heard he could play the political game too, that he was wily and sly when he needed to be. Ange was thrilled to have been seconded onto his team. What Bergers didn't fully realize yet was that he had acquired himself a fellow zealot. Ange tuned back in.

"To bring these people down," Bergers declaimed, "we need to understand their mentality. We need to get under their skin. They combine greed with a sense of invulnerability. They are the elite. They are the privileged. No one can touch them. Or else they think they are the small, invisible cog who just happens to have access to price-sensitive information. Too small for anyone to bother with. And they want a taste of what the big guys have."

Bergers was on a crusade, and looking round. Ange saw that everyone in the room joined him in it. A company of zealots, she mused. This was gonna be fun.

"But for all of them," Bergers continued, "it's not just about the money. It's about winning the game, it's about being the player left standing with the biggest pile of chips on the table. And make no mistake, insider trading is not an isolated aberration. We pick up unusual trading patterns preceding thirty percent of mergers and acquisition activity. It's rife, people. It contaminates the financial system. It is my intention to eradicate it. Zero tolerance. It starts here. I have brought in two extra FBI agents from the New York and New Jersey field offices: Special Agent Wilkie and Special Agent Rodgers."

Ange and her colleague, Pete Rodgers, smiled and raised hands in greeting.

The table smiled back at the tall, handsome woman whose crisp red bob and mischievous grin made her look much younger than her forty-four years, and her younger, wearier and barrel-like male colleague with pallid skin and deep dark rings under his eyes. His thick, dark hair with the premature streaks of gray at the temples earned him the nickname of *Rac*, short for *raccoon*, care of Agent Wilkie. Rodgers was thirty-three, but the birth six weeks ago of his and his wife's first child and the sleepless nights that followed made him feel ninety.

"They are targeting Ronald Glass," continued Bergers. "You might remember him from the Raja file. His name cropped up again and again, but we had no hard evidence on him. Special Agents Wilkie and Rodgers are here to change that. Judge Bustillo has approved a workplace wiretap—"

"Yay!" called out one listener. Handclaps rang out.

Bergers smiled, revealing predatory-white teeth. "And Special Agents Wilkie and Rodgers will have the enviable task of listening to his calls all day long."

"Why're we so keen on this one guy?" asked another of the team.

"Because I think the very well-connected and exceedingly ambitious Mr. Glass is part of a much bigger network. He's a corrupt modern-day Samson. We bring him down, offer him twenty years inside or the opportunity to cooperate, we bring down the whole corrupt temple."

Amen to that, thought Ange.

5

HURRICANE POINT HOUSE, CALIFORNIA

Hurricane Point House was built, totally illegally, without permit, but with love and passion and whatever materials came cheaply to hand, at the beginning of the twentieth century by two naturists wanting an escape from the world.

They were shortly joined by a fellow traveler who built his own illegal house fifty yards away. Over a century of occupation had granted legal status to the houses, and Gwen Boudain and her elderly neighbor, Marilyn Shanahan, were the current happy incumbents and owners.

Both houses were to be found at the end of a private dirt track, a hundred feet back from the sea. Like most of the structures in Big Sur, they blended into its landscape. They were single story, spacious but not enormous, built of rugged wood and stone, weathered by the elements. A low, jutting roof soared out over large French windows that gave onto a deck of gray wood.

Below the houses, a hill of grass and scrub fell away fairly steeply to the sea. At the ocean's edge the land was pared down by the force of millennia of crashing waves to bare black rocks which formed a low cliff, about ten feet high, keeping the sea at bay.

On a wild night Gwen would imagine the storm-driven waves leaping over the cliff, roaring up to the houses, sweeping them away into blue oblivion. It had never come close so far, but as she had just said in her meeting, the weather was getting wilder, and if the dreaded ARk storm ever did come, she and Marilyn would be on the front line.

To the right of the houses, the meeting between land and sea was gentler, with a wide, long beach sloping down to the waves. It was the view and this beach, effectively private, which had drawn the naturists and which Gwen loved with a passion.

Gwen's golden Labrador, Leo, was waiting as she pulled up on her stony drive. Gwen had rescued Leo from the pound when he was just ten weeks old. He'd been hit by a car. The vets didn't think he'd survive. He did, and for that as well as the glint of comradeship in his eye, Gwen had adopted him. He had repaid her with a loyalty that went beyond dogged.

"Hey, Boy, whaddya say to a run?"

Leo yelped his agreement, tail whirling like helicopter blades.

"OK, OK, give me a minute."

Gwen pulled off her clothes, threw them on her bed, and changed with a sigh of relief into shorts and a tee.

Barefoot, shadowed by Leo, she walked out onto her deck, skipped down the steps, and broke into a run.

She followed the hill down to the beach, aimed for the harder sand of the seashore. She ran with her dog through the shallows, kicking up droplets of water. The sun beat warm on her shoulders, but a fresh onshore breeze cooled her. She ran off her tension, reveling in the feeling of movement as her body sped across the sand. Thirty minutes later, she turned and walked back, thoroughly purged and starving.

She quickly checked her neighbor's house. Marilyn was away for a week's visit to her sister in Sacramento, and Gwen was checking up on her house as they always did for each other.

Back in her own home, she took a quick shower, muttering darkly at the lukewarm trickle of water that seeped from the showerhead. Then she fed Leo and dug around in her freezer.

"Pepperoni pizza! Feast time, Leo."

She popped it in the microwave and five minutes later sat down on her deck with a cold beer, feeding slices of pizza to herself and peeling off a few spare pepperoni circles for her dog. She stared out pensively across the sea. She imagined mile after mile of ocean stretching from here to the cauldron of the equator where something truly terrifying was brewing.

6

Gwen tried not to check her e-mail every ten minutes. She ran, she swam, she longed to surf, but the next morning a flat sea set in, offering nothing but pretty views and wave-lets she wouldn't deign to ride. Her next best distraction, Dwayne, her Tae Kwon Do trainer, was on his cruise in Mexico teaching a boatload of seniors dirty fighting instead of putting her through her paces. After three days when she had heard nothing from Falcon Capital, she was in need of major distraction. The sea relented.

She woke to the roar of surf. She sat up in bed with a smile. Her bleached linen curtains wafted in a breeze carrying the smell of brine and white water. Naked, she wrapped herself in her Peruvian alpaca blanket and stepped out on deck. She gazed at the sea for a good five minutes. Surfable, she thought, eying the waves. Medium-sized and ragged, workable.

She fed Leo, grabbed an apple, and selected her board from her storeroom: a six-foot-two-inch swallowtail, right for the conditions. She secured it between the driver's and passenger's seats, sticking out over the backseats, and drove off. She could have surfed alone on the beach at Hurricane Point, but she didn't want to push her luck twice in one week, and she needed to stock up on provisions in Carmel, so she headed for the little seaside town and some company.

She parked on Scenic Road, grabbed her board, and walked over to the path that snaked along above the sandy beach. A hundred yards away, powerful waves broke with a roar. A good fifteen-foot face and pumping. Just inches above them, rising and falling with the waves, flew a pelican patrol.

The sea was empty of casual swimmers, but a phalanx of wet-suited surfers rode the waves with varying degrees of fortune. There were plenty of people walking or just sitting on the beach, gazing out at the churning water.

For a good five minutes, Gwen studied the waves. She knew this beach well, had surfed it many times, but the sea always had her surprises, particularly for the unwary. Fools rush in, thought Gwen, watching a couple of muscled college boy dudes do just that.

When she had a feel for the waves and the set patterns, had spotted an oddity or two, she pulled off her shorts and tee, wiggled into her wet suit, and worked through her stretch routine, a quick three minutes' worth; then she trotted across the sand, board under her arm, into the water.

It took her a few minutes to paddle out, duck-diving the waves as she did so before she got out to the lineup.

Most of the other surfers greeted her with a wave and a shout.

"Hey Boudy!"

"Hey guys," she called back, waving. The surf community. Nothing like it. Once you were in, you had to do something truly loathsome to be out.

Her regular surf buddy, Jordan, paddled up.

"How's it hanging, Boudy?"

"Just peachy, Jordie. Catch any good ones?"

"Oh yeah. A real big set came in first thing. Woke me up."

"Another one's coming. Get ready."

From habit, Gwen picked the last one in the set. She lined up her board, paddled, snapped to her feet, and rode all the way into the beach.

She paddled out again, watched one of the college boys riding in. He was standing in the barrel almost as if he were just out on the street waiting for a cab. Alert but relaxed too.

In no particular hurry. Then she watched him skim out, almost effortlessly. He paddled back out.

Gwen eyed him critically. A stranger. He had nice style, she was forced to admit. Tanned and ripped too.

She turned away, focused on powering her way back out beyond the break point. She got an hour's worth of good rides, caught a good wave, the second best of the day. Rode it in.

Jordie walked out of the shallows with her.

"I'm done, you?"

"Yep."

Jordan hip-bumped her. "How about a coffee, my place?"

Gwen hip-bumped him back. "Not today, Jordie." She grinned. "Not tomorrow either, 'fore you ask."

"Can't hang a guy for trying."

"Hell, I'd worry if you didn't." She walked up the beach with her board, wondering whose eyes she felt on her as she walked, determined not to turn to check.

She secured her board and crossed onto Junipero Street, heading for Bruno's Market & Deli. Outside she was ambushed by the smell of toasted sandwiches. Weak with hunger, she ordered a toasted BLT, and almost swooned with joy as she made her way round the aisles with a shopping cart, munching en route.

She somehow amassed two hundred dollars' worth of supplies, including a case of Stella Artois, four bottles of local wine, a selection of healthy staples, pastries for tomorrow's breakfast, and enough fresh produce to keep her going for a few days. She cleaned out her wallet. God, she really, really needed Falcon to come through.

Preoccupied, bag-laden, Gwen didn't notice the eyes watching her from the car that edged by slowly and then fell in behind her, veiled by the two innocent cars sandwiched in between, as she drove away.

7

Singing along to Jason Mraz, who lilted out from the water-proof radio, Gwen took her desultory shower. She wrapped herself in her tattered toweling robe when the phone trilled. Unknown number. She nearly didn't take it.

"Hello?"

"Dr. Boudain, good morning. It's Gabriel Messenger. I'm sorry it's taken us a while to get back to you. We closed a big deal this morning. Now it's out of the way I can focus on Oracle. We'd like you to come in again. We've got some questions for you."

"Sure. When were you thinking?" asked Gwen, mani-cally twisting her jade ring.

"How soon can you make it?"

She wanted to say now, right now. Prudence prevailed. *Don't be easy, Gwen.*

"Tomorrow, round noon?"

"Make it eleven."

"See you then."

Gwen hung up, did a major happy dance round her room. "Yessss!" She punched the air. "They're on the hook, Leo. And tomorrow I am gonna reel them in."

8

Gwen rang Joaquin in Peru.

"Hey, *flaco,* go buy yourself a beer, a new sweatshirt."

"Beer is on my list, *flaca.* What's wrong with my sweatshirt?"

"It's lonely. You're the only gay guy I know with an unfilled wardrobe. Listen, we got funding!"

"Awesome!"

Gwen laughed as Joaquin belted out a glorious roar.

"How is it over there?" she asked when he'd calmed down.

"Well, last night eight tiles blew off my roof, two days ago a coupla surf tourists drowned getting suckered by a rogue wave forty feet high at least, we lost five more sensors and buoys and the sensors we have left are all still screaming their warnings. I daren't go out deep to check on the far offshore sensors, three of which I think have gone psycho. We got hit with three humongous thunderstorms in the last week, and I don't fancy getting my ass fried or drowned."

"Jeez. Stay close to shore Joaquin. We'll worry about those deep-water sensors later. As soon as I get my money, I'll order all the new kit and we can review things then."

"Move it, chica. This thing is changing week to week. We need the sensors, like, now."

9

Gwen made another call. She needed sunshine and celebration. Lucy Chen, bond salesperson, best friend since they'd met at age eight sitting on neighboring desks at middle school, answered with her usual prescience and the smooth jazz voice that beguiled a legion of brokers.

"Boudy! You got news?"

"And then some! Falcon want to invest! And they want to offer me a job. They say they need weather expertise and I have it, so would I come on board."

"Awesome! Boudy! Well played. Please say you didn't accept straight off."

"Luce, I am not an idiot. I've brought their proposal home."

"Right. I am ditching the date, coming over tonight. We need to talk strategy. Just do me a favor. Don't cook. Let's hit Carmel."

"I could be insulted but I'm too happy. You're on. My treat."

Gwen found Lucy cruising the shops on Ocean Avenue. She'd already acquired three large, tony shopping bags.

"Candlesticks. Just gorgeous. And alpaca blankets," said Lucy, holding them up like trophies. "I have a weakness."

"You 'n' me both," said Gwen, giving her friend a giant hug. She grabbed two of the bags. "Here, let me lighten your load."

Lucy rolled her shoulder. "Thanks."

"You OK?"

"Shoulder's playing up. Took a fall at the dojo the other day. Don't bounce like a fourteen-year-old anymore."

"Who does? But fourteen-year-olds can't drink and we can. Follow me, there's a great new bar by the water."

"As long as the wine is excellent and chilled. We have a deal to celebrate!"

Gwen's eyes shone. "And we shall!"

They walked in, snagged a corner table overlooking the beach.

"Let's order first, then talk," said Gwen. "I am ravenous."

"When are you ever not? How you're not the size of a horse, I don't know."

"I ever stop exercising, I probably will be."

"Now that is what I call a view."

Gwen, consulting her menu, did not look up. "Isn't it great? I love this time of evening, sun going down, sea all golden."

"All golden all right. And ripped."

Gwen peered up. "The sea? *Ripped*?"

"Over there," said Lucy, pointing with her chin. "The dude with the blue surfboard."

"Hmm," mused Gwen. The college boy with the seriously chilled surfing style.

"You know him?"

"Dropped in one of Jordie's waves the other day. No etiquette."

"Who needs etiquette when they look like that?"

Gwen watched him as, only partially shielded by his car's open door, he dropped his trunks and pulled on shorts.

"You might have a point," she said, grinning.

The surfer emerged from behind the door, pulled on a t-shirt and flip-flops. A friend called to him and together they made their way toward the café.

"Bottle of the Hawke's Chardonnay, please," Gwen asked the hovering waiter. "We'll get round to food."

The waiter, with the speed of the best of his tribe, glided

away and back with the bottle, opened it, let Gwen sample and approve it, poured out two glasses, then intercepted the surfer and his friend, giving them a table on the other corner.

The surfer looked up, saw Gwen. His eyes narrowed, then he broke into a cocky smile.

"Oh no," said Gwen. "He's coming over."

"What is your problem, girl?"

"He's a surfer."

"Boudy, this is crazy. When are you going to get over Brad?"

Gwen shrugged. "Brad is dead and buried far as I'm concerned. And there's no law saying I have to like surfers."

"No one with a pulse would not like that guy."

The surfer stopped before their table, gave them a dazzling smile. Gwen took him in at a glance: jaw-length tousled brown hair, aware honey-colored eyes harboring some private joke, and curving, sensual lips. But he wasn't a college boy, she noted. His eyes had deep grooves around them, cut by sun and surf and life. He must have been over thirty, but he had the body of a college-boy athlete still. Six-four, powerfully muscled, not in a showy gym way, but what looked like real, working muscles; a natural, unposed masculinity. Most working men didn't have the time to nurture a physique like that. She wondered what he did.

"Evening, ladies," he said in a low-slung voice with a hint of a rasp.

"Good evening," hummed Lucy.

Gwen growled something inaudible.

"We meet again," he said to Gwen.

"If you can call sharing the ocean *meeting*," drawled Gwen, as if she were quite bored.

The surfer smiled off the barb. He nodded to Lucy. "I'm Dan Jacobsen."

"I'm Lucy, and this is—"

"Boudy, if I heard right."

Oh God, thought Gwen, he'd heard them.

"Gwen," she said archly. "Boudy to my friends."

Lucy gave him an apologetic look. "Don't mind her. Low blood sugar."

"How d'you get to Boudy from Gwen?"

"Boudicca," said Gwen. "Lucy here gave it to me as a nickname when I was eight, 'cause I liked to fight. It kind of stuck."

"Boudicca, Queen of the Iceni tribe, kicked the Romans' asses in Britain, for a time anyway," he noted wryly. "Yeah, I've heard of her."

"And she looked like a warrior queen, did our Boudy," added Lucy.

The surfer looked Gwen up and down. Slow, incendiary.

"Still does," he said. "See you on the waves, Boudy."

Gwen shook her head, watched the man walk away waving a farewell. He had just the slightest of swaggers, and, like most surfers, a tinge of arrogance. Gwen glowered at his retreating back and took a fortifying glug of wine.

"So, changing the subject before you kick my ass," said Lucy. "Falcon Capital. Tell all."

Now Gwen smiled. A dazzler. "Get this! They want to put ten million in, for a twenty percent stake. They want to employ me full time. Apparently my expertise will be 'useful,' to them. Salary of one hundred and fifty thousand dollars a year!"

"You happy with the equity, giving so much away?" asked Lucy levelly, unimpressed by the dollars.

"It's for Ten. Million. Dollars. Luce! Ten Mill! No more posing in swimsuits. And Oracle gets all the funding it needs. And boy does it need it. Yeah. I'm happy. Plus, I get to keep Hurricane Point House. Do every last damn repair it needs. Get a power shower!"

"No."

"What d'you mean *no*?"

"The Oracle money stays in Oracle. It ain't fungible babe. Be real careful with compliance stuff. Separate bank accounts and all. You need a signing-on bonus. Do up your house with that."

"Lucy, I don't want to screw them," said Gwen, twisting her jade and gold ring round and round in place.

Lucy reached out and grabbed Gwen's hand. "Cut the ring-twiddling shtick, will you? Know it gets on my nerves."

Gwen stuck out her tongue, felt about fourteen. "It's my ring and I'll twiddle it if I want to."

Lucy gave an exasperated sigh and released her friend's hand.

"Listen, Boudy, they're freaking venture capitalists. They'll be screwing you, and so well you'll just sit there and say, *more,* and that's kind of fine, up to a point, but please, please don't ever hold back on screwing them when you get the chance."

"So, I screw them back. OK. I get that."

"They'll respect you for it in the morning. I promise. The last thing you want to be is easy in their world. So, your golden hello . . ."

"Please don't tell me that's like a golden shower."

Lucy burst out laughing. "Shower of cash, babe. Ask for $100k. And listen, if they want you, they'll pay for you. $100k is peanuts to Gabriel Messenger, a few minutes work."

10

The two men spoke in hushed voices in the crowded Bar Agricole in the financial district of San Francisco. Angled together they could hear well enough but nobody else could. In the packed bar, late on a Friday night, alcohol flowing like water in all but their glasses, no one paid them any heed, which was all part of the plan. In their dress-down Friday uniform of casual trousers and polo shirts, they looked like just another pair of still-prosperous but market-weary traders letting off steam before going home to their wives in Marin County. Braying laughs and tall tales were all the white noise they needed.

"We have a problem," said the tall one, known to his associates as The Man. No one was quite sure who had coined the moniker—some thought The Man himself, for there was a self-celebrating machismo about him—but whatever its provenance, the name suited him and it stuck. The Man toyed with the condensation that slicked down his chilled glass, as if what he was about to say had really no import at all. He looked up, met the other's eyes.

"Contagion of an earlier leak," he said deliberately. "Thought it had gone away for good. Raised her pretty little head in town last week. Been making noises about a *guy getting rough, blacking her eye, losing trade. Guy was drunk, talking all kinds of crap.*"

The other man sucked in a breath. "Shit."

"Potentially. Not the kind of thing the Boss would like." He gave the shorter man a contemptuous look. "You and your drinking . . . Can't hold your drink, shouldn't drink.

Plain and simple. You shouldn't drink anyway. Double bad whammy."

"Does he know?" The shorter man felt a stab of fear and his sweat glands seemed to have suddenly opened. In seconds, rivulets of sweat were soaking his back.

"Not yet. Maybe never. Just a little trickle now. Not sure where it will go." The Man leaned back on the banquette, long legs stretched out before him. He radiated power and confidence. He almost seemed to be enjoying this.

"Trickles can turn into torrents," said the sweating man, replaying his words to himself with a nervous laugh. "We know that better than any."

The Man sat forward, complicit once more.

"We will do when the timetable starts."

"Oh, it's started. It's running. It's why we need to plug the trickle. And soon. We can put it down to expenses, can't we?"

The Man gave him a long look, made him sweat a bit longer. He drained his water, got to his feet. "Funds are there. Don't think the Boss will even notice. I'm on it. Count yourself lucky." He leaned over, bent in so close he could smell the other man's sweat.

"Don't fuck up again," he said slowly.

"Thank you. Thank you. And I won't. I promise."

"Promise your God," said The Man, lip curling with contempt.

He slipped from the bar, already planning how he would do it. The how and where, the ruse and the trap. Seventeen Mile Drive. Perfect for both. Those seventeen gilded miles, nothing bad could ever happen there, could it? All milk and honey and money, the glittering houses in their manicured gardens, eyes focused inward, never outward on the dark beyond the security windows, oblivious to the lonely wood, the precipitous cliffs, the pounding surf.

11

Just over two weeks later, with all the documentation finally agreed to by her lawyer and Falcon's, and with a cool ten million dollars sitting in her new corporate bank account and another hundred thousand dollars in her personal account, Gwen drove off for her first day at Falcon Capital.

She still couldn't quite believe the ten million. She'd gone from almost cashless to rich overnight and it didn't feel real. It felt like there was a catch somewhere, some hidden cost. She mulled it over as she drove, making herself crazy. *Jeez, it's not a gift horse, stop gouging at its mouth,* she told herself. *It's a legacy,* she settled on, *her parents' legacy to her.* That made sense, made her feel better, made it seem real and justifiable.

A few miles short of the turnoff for Laureless, she saw something approaching at high speed in her mirror. Seconds later it zoomed up behind her; a red Ferrari. Gwen blew out a breath as it swerved around her, seemingly inches from her bumper, and with an impatient roar accelerated away.

"Moron," murmured Gwen.

The Ferrari, hot to the touch, was parked in the car park at Falcon House, flanked by two Porsches, an Aston Martin, and two seriously high-end motorbikes. Venture capital evidently paid seriously well. Gwen grinned at a VW Beetle parked incongruously between the two Porsches. There was also a high-tech road-racer bike. Someone liked to stay fit.

In through the security, into the blasting air con, and

then Messenger came striding to meet her. The bone-crushing handshake, she was ready for this time; the probing gaze she returned.

"Dr. Gwen! Good to have you! Welcome to the Lab." Messenger was in an ebullient mood. "Come. I have an office for you." He led her through the plant-filled central atrium to a glass-walled office, one in a row of three. The two flanking hers seemed to be empty.

Her office was a good size, well appointed, with a gleaming Apple computer atop a polished wooden desk that still smelled faintly of beeswax.

A ridiculous image of Messenger polishing it while sporting a frilly apron popped into Gwen's head, making her smile. Messenger was sweeping his arm round her space like a proud homeowner showing off his castle.

"Settle in," he declared. "Buy those sensors. Buy all that shit," he added, in what Gwen would come to recognize as one of his oft-used Americanisms that sat ill with the crisp tailoring and European old-world manners.

"We're all rather keen to avoid getting swept away," he added, a shaft of seriousness cutting through this new bonhomie.

"You and me both," said Gwen, dumping her bag and taking a seat behind her desk.

Messenger nodded, one arm braced high on the door jamb, his long body slanting across the doorway like a barrier, head tilted, analyzing her.

"So, what's with the jeans and the cowboy boots? Dress down Monday?"

Gwen smiled. "Every day's dress down for me. I don't do suits."

"Do you *always* wear jeans?" asked Messenger, bemusement in his eyes.

"I'd rather drink Cloudy Bay than wear Calvin Klein," replied Gwen.

Messenger laughed. "Well, if I had to make the choice

I'd be with you. My wine cellar is a thing of beauty, but, and *please* don't take this the wrong way, you'd look sensational in a suit."

Gwen raised one eyebrow. "I'd look like a transvestite!"

Messenger barked out a delighted laugh. Gwen got the impression he held himself in pretty tight, didn't toy with humor too often. Maybe the business of making a fortune was just too serious. Far as she was concerned, the higher the stakes the more you needed to cut loose.

"Instead you just look like you've swaggered in from some old western town to sort us all out. All you need is a pair of six-shooters."

"Am I the sheriff or the bad guy?" asked Gwen.

The gaze deepened. "Who would you like to be?"

"Oh, I'd be the sheriff I guess. A sheriff with a cause."

"And what would be the cause?"

"Oh, that one's easy," replied Gwen. "Justice."

"Knock, knock," said a voice. A muscle-bound man, tanned leather brown, with an entirely bald pate stood behind Messenger.

"Am I interrupting? I can come back. . . ."

As if remembering himself, Messenger straightened abruptly.

"In you go," he said, stepping aside. He nodded to Gwen and strode from her office. Again Gwen got the impression of control and beneath it something much more interesting struggling to breathe.

"Randy Sieber," announced the bald man. "Head of Security. I got your pass."

He handed Gwen a hard, laminated, credit card–sized pass with her name, her photo, and a bar code on it.

"So this gets me in?"

"And out."

"Whoa, am I locked in?"

"No. There's a safety button you can push on the inside of the doors. That'll get you out if the card fails. But you need to use the card, saving an emergency. You also need to input your own special PIN in the keypad on the main door." He gave her a yellow Post-it with a seven-digit code made up of numbers and letters.

"Memorize that and destroy it."

Gwen glanced at it, balled it up, and threw it into her trash bin.

Sieber's eyes opened wide. "You're meant to memorize it!"

Gwen grinned, recited the code.

"Shit! You've got a memory!"

Gwen smiled. Sieber reached down, took the Post-it from the bin, and shredded it systematically.

"Security," he intoned, with a mock-serious finger wag.

"Why the PIN and the swipe card?" asked Gwen, watching him drop half of the shreds into her bin and pocket the other half.

"Registers the timings, is all."

"My own personal timings. OK." So Messenger liked to keep tabs, did he? Gwen filed that away.

"Talking of timings, don't try to come in too early," said Sieber. "Not before eight. If you see a red light blinking outside by the key swipe, it means the alarm is running. You have to wait until either Dr. Messenger or I come along and deactivate it."

"I'll try to remember that," said Gwen. "What happens if I forget?"

"If you swipe your card and enter your PIN, you'll be admitted through the main door but you'll be stuck there in the air lock between the first and second doors. Held captive," he added with a grin that bordered on malicious. "Cops'll get here all fired up. I'll get here all fired up." Sieber eyed her, unblinking. "You'll *upset* people."

"Well, I sure as hell wouldn't want to do that," said Gwen, masking her smile as the sarcasm soared straight over Sieber.

"Card gets you in the gym too," said Sieber, looking enthusiastic now. "That's inside the old barn. State of the art." The security man gave Gwen an appraising look. "Look like you work out."

"Now and then."

Sieber nodded his approval. "Cupcake Café's in the smaller barn. Waitress who doesn't stop talking and a chef who never says a word if he can help it, but the food's great and it's free."

Gwen smiled. "I'm sold." She nodded to the stairs. "What goes on up there?"

"My office. All the comms. Nothing *you* need worry about. Think of it as a Chinese wall."

"Separating me from what?"

"Just keeping Falcon's material locked up. Our projects are valuable. Intellectual property. It's—"

"I know what it is. It's why I'm here," said Gwen, thinking, *shit, that sounded pompous.* Had corporate life infected her already?

Sieber held up his hands. "Cool. That's cool. Just telling you."

He looked like he enjoyed *just telling.* There was something of the overly dominant about his gaze, the thrust of his chin. Gwen shrugged. She didn't have to like everyone.

"And I've got a document here. You need to read it real carefully and sign it. I'll witness it."

Gwen took it. CONFIDENTIALITY AGREEMENT was highlighted in bold along the top. It was three pages long. Most of it was taken up with the dire legal consequences of repeating to any third party outside of Falcon Capital any facts relevant or pertinent to the business conducted in said Company. It also prohibited discussing individual deals with other Falcon employees unless they had a direct role to play in the deal or investment. That was fine by her. More than fine.

Gwen looked up at Sieber. "Basically, shut up or else?"

He barked out a laugh. "Hole in one!"

"No, please do *not* shut up," cut in a friendly voice. "I need to hear all about Oracle." A smiling, ferociously tanned woman stood before her, almost Gwen's height thanks to vertiginous heels and a towering bun perched on her head from which a bleached lemon frizz seemed intent on escape. The woman stuck out a skinny hand. The red-tipped nails stuck into Gwen's palm as they shook.

"Mel Barbieri. Head of PR."

"There *is* only you," remarked Sieber. "So you're head of yourself."

"Profound," retorted Barbieri. "Now scoot off and do something all secretive and leave us to talk."

"Gwen Boudain," said Gwen. "But I'm a tad confused," she added. "Randy Sieber wants my silence and confidentiality, and you want me to talk."

"Trick is," said Barbieri, "knowing when to talk and when to shut up."

"Thing is," said Gwen, "I don't like publicity. Fact is, I hate it. I want my work here kept under wraps, totally."

"But that's crazy!" exclaimed Barbieri. " 'Scuse my saying and all that, and you've just joined us, but I gotta tell it as I see. Why would you bury yourself under a bushel? We need to build a profile so that if and when we sell out, you've already got yourself a brand name."

"First," said Gwen, "let's not get premature. No one said anything about selling out, OK? Not on the table as far as I'm concerned and I'm the majority shareholder here. Second, and please don't take this personally, while I can see the need for PR in certain cases, it adds nothing to my work, to the perfection of my model. It can only be a distraction."

Gwen expected the other woman to defend her turf vocally, but instead, disconcertingly, Barbieri just looked at her speculatively.

I've overdone it, thought Gwen, overplayed my hand. "Look," she said, placatingly. "I used to have to do publicity, surf publicity, modeling in a bikini and all that shit?"

Barbieri tilted her head, looked interested.

"I'm a serious academic now," said Gwen, trying the feminist angle. "I don't want to go down that road again."

Barbieri shook her head, but there was just a hint of understanding in her eyes.

"All righty. I can see your point, sorta. But no one's asking you to pose in a bikini here. . . ."

"Call it burnout," said Gwen. "And let me move on, would you?"

"Sure," said Barbieri. "You're the talent. You call the shots."

"Thanks," said Gwen, pasting on a smile. "Well, I'd better get to it."

Barbieri nodded, walked slowly from Gwen's office.

Gwen watched her go. Close, she thought, too close. She'd have to work hard to keep Barbieri in line, and stay, where she wanted to be, in the shadows.

12

THE LAB, CARMEL VALLEY

Some time later, not straightaway—she knew how to be discreet—Mel Barbieri checked her reflection in the compact mirror she kept in the desk drawer, tried in vain to tuck the escaped tendrils into her bun, gave up with a humph, and headed to Messenger's office.

She stood outside chatting with Mandy, waiting to be noticed. No one interrupted the boss when his door was closed. Messenger might not have appeared to be working—he sat, long legs braced on his shredder, staring out of his window—but Mel knew that was what he did for a good few hours every day. He sat and he thought. She could only assume it was about work, cooking up another brilliant trade or investment, but for all she knew, he could have been brooding about the family he no longer saw.

After five minutes, he swung round on his swivel chair, frowned at Mel as if trying to place her, then beckoned her in. It looked like he was coming back from a long way off.

"What's up Mel?" he asked, leaning forward, arms crossed on his desk, the busy doctor asking his patient her symptoms.

Mel had a random desire to peel off her shirt and ask him about her rotator cuff. She quickly subdued it.

"Interesting, our new recruit . . ." She threw out her gambit.

"In which particular respect?" asked Messenger, glancing at his wall clock, a look Barbieri saw. She got to the point.

"No PR. That's why. Nada. No photo, no write-up. Nothing to even keep on file. Premature, she called it. She was adamant, tried to backpedal, but she was still adamant."

Messenger leaned back in his chair, eyed Barbieri with interest. They all competed for that look, some got it regularly. She got it rarely. The job of the unsung. Now she felt the glow.

"Interesting, potentially, but she's just come on board. PR right now *is* arguably premature.

Mel shook her head. "Nah. It's more than that. She dressed it up saying she'd done enough posing in swimsuits, just wanted to get on with her job, but I didn't buy it."

"And your theory?"

"I almost got the impression she was running from something. Just a look in her eyes, just for a second, and then she covered it up, all California surfer drawl. All cool. Only it wasn't. I saw fear in her eyes."

13

THE LAB, CARMEL VALLEY

Gwen devoted the entire morning to shopping and modeling. She rang her suppliers, ordered buoys and sensors, and begged and cajoled them to expedite the order with express delivery to Joaquin Losada in Peru. She went online and purchased megabytes of input data she hadn't previously been able to afford. She played with her model, broadening it, deepening it, running the new data over past Niños, checking how well the new statistics and her evolving model predicted them. Glorious what a fat bank account could achieve.

At 1:00 P.M., stunned by all her new data, she stood and stretched. Her t-shirt rose above the low-slung waistband of her jeans revealing the corrugated muscles of her stomach. She looked up, arms locked overhead, as she heard someone whistling surprisingly tunefully. She recognized the song: "Losing My Religion" by R.E.M. Then the whistler came into sight: Peter Weiss, ambling by. He glanced at her and shyly away.

Gwen took her pass and headed out with a plan to grab some fresh air and to check out the gym and the Cupcake Café.

She walked round the building. A repetitive thwack, thwack, thwack led her to the far side of the old barn. There on a clay court, clad in immaculate whites, Messenger was playing tennis, but this was no casual knockabout. The bout looked gladiatorial, the standard near-Davis Cup. Messenger played without a shirt, and his brown, lithely muscled body glistened with sweat under the broiling sun of an unseasonably hot fall day. She felt sure he hadn't seen her as she stood and watched. Every fiber of him was focused on the ball and on his opponent, a man his size but perhaps twenty years younger. The match seemed almost perfectly balanced. But while the opponent seemed focused, Messenger burned with an intensity that was almost frightening. He seemed to want to exterminate his opponent. He played every stroke as if it were match point at Flushing Meadow.

Riveted, Gwen watched. Finally, she saw Messenger race from one side of the court to another, take a ball on the volley and shoot it to the far right corner of his opponent's court just out of reach.

Messenger straightened, arms and racket erect, in a victory spasm that was almost sexual.

Feeling suddenly voyeuristic, Gwen turned quickly, headed for the barn. As she did, she noticed a worn-looking man emerge from the trees. Something about him jarred. He looked out of place, and he seemed to be in the grip of some powerful emotion, almost vibrating with it. Gwen could see it in the tension in his face, the fisted hands. A kind of fury and grief. Gwen watched him approach Messenger, who was striding off the court, flush with victory. Messenger halted. His face hardened. He walked toward the man, jaw jutting.

"Get off my property now. I am asking you nicely. If you do not I will get my security to bodily remove you."

"You're good at that, aren't you, bodily removals. Or should I say disposals," said the man, refusing to be cowed.

As if alerted by some sixth sense, Randy Sieber strolled

out of the barn in his workout kit. He approached the man, took his arm with surprising gentleness.

"Come on, Mr. Freidland. This isn't helping you. Please."

The man looked up at Sieber, at his muscles pumped and slick with sweat. Physical frailty met outrageous vitality, but it seemed to be Sieber's gentleness that won. The man gave him a faint smile and nodded. He started moving back the way he had come, Sieber walking with him, but he turned and shot a last look at Messenger.

"I'm not finished with you," he said in a rasping voice. "I won't be. Until I've proved what you are."

14

THE LAB, CARMEL VALLEY

Gwen headed for the barn, mind racing. *What you are? Bodily removals? Disposals?* Sounded like Messenger had bought some company or other from the old guy. Clearly they knew him. Had Messenger fired him, slashed and burned through the employees, creating something lean and mean and worth more? Or was that the domain of corporate raiders, not venture capitalists? Disconcerted, but not enough to lose her appetite, Gwen swiped her card, entered her PIN, pushed open the door to the barn and walked into the café.

"Gwen!" called out Peter Weiss. "Come join us."

Weiss was sitting at a long table alongside the picture-perfect jock who'd preened past Gwen's office a few times that morning and whom she had affected not to notice. Opposite, seemingly forming a little unit of their own, was a conspicuously attractive young black woman with a medusa-like headful of long braids; a huge, NFL-type with shorn fair hair and an uncertain smile; and a short, wiry, intense looking man with spiky black hair. They all wore identical-looking shirts, save the color, respectively pink, blue, and white. Gwen wanted to ask them if they'd got a three-for-one.

She mosied over.

"Hi, I'm Gwen Boudain," she said, smiling down. The trio stayed sitting, chorusing out their names and hellos—friendly from the men, Jihoon Lee and Curt Cuchinski, faintly hostile from the woman, Atalanta Washington—but the jock leapt to his feet and stuck out a hand.

"Kevin Barclay," he announced. "Good to have you on board," he added, as if he were some kind of skipper. Gwen took in at a glance the immaculate khakis, the crisp white shirt, sleeves rolled up as if ready for business, the sporting tan, not too dark, not trying too hard. From his artfully layered brown hair to the tip of his Tod's loafers, he spoke East Coast Privilege. The ever-so-slightly constipated Boston accent sealed the deal. He was good-looking, as a young Rob Lowe, in the way that would enslave teenage girls, and his cocky eyes said he knew it.

Gwen took his proffered hand, shook it with a smile whilst telling herself A) not to leap to conclusions and B) not to be so judgmental. She was behaving like an animal happening onto a strange pride on the savannah, quietly analyzing everyone: friend or foe, prey or predator, carnivore or veggie. She suppressed a smirk and sat down opposite Peter Weiss.

"We were just taking a bet on which of the grunts would be fired first," announced Barclay, nodding at the trio opposite. The two men gave an infinitesimal cringe; the woman looked openly furious.

"Good for the digestion," murmured Gwen.

Barclay laughed. "It's not personal. Two of the three always get fired. Natural selection."

Gwen cocked her head. Maybe her savannah analogy was not so far-fetched.

"This some sort of tradition?"

"It's how Dr. Messenger staffs up his analysts," explained Peter Weiss, Barclay's note of pride absent from his voice, clearly not quite so enamored of the dog-eat-dog school of business. "Hire three or four every year, cull all but one at the end of the year. Sometimes cull them all."

"That's how Peter and I came up, through the ranks," intoned Barclay. "Proving ourselves, no cutting in solo," he added, veiling the barb with his Harvard smile.

Weiss laughed. "Ignore him. He's just jealous."

Gwen wondered whom else her rival-less entry had annoyed. She shrugged. Their problem.

"That's more your vice, Peter," Barclay replied with the smooth delivery of the truly annoyed. "So, join our bet?" he asked Gwen.

"Real kind. Think I'll pass."

"No biggie. I'm putting my money on you, Curt," he said, nodding at the NFL type. "Atalanta, nobody with a brain would let you go," he added to the black woman.

Gwen felt her rush of fury, and her impotence as Atalanta literally bit her lip and shook her head.

A young, smiling, and pretty waitress sashayed up, breaking the simmering tension.

"Hello new girl. Welcome to the Cupcake Café. I'm Narissa and that sad sack back there in the kitchen is Luke."

Gwen glanced at Luke. Longish dark hair, red-and-black bandana round his head, watchful brown eyes. He eyed her back, frowning like a workhouse matron confronted by another starving orphan.

"Lasagna's on today and it's real good," said Narissa.

"Sounds great. I'd love one."

Narissa balanced a heap of emptied plates, and with a

communally contagious glancing at their watches, Barclay and the trio got to their feet and flocked away.

Weiss poured Gwen a glass of water from a jug on the table. "Don't mind Kevin. He'd bet against the sun rising then paint the windows black," he said in his almost mesmerically soft voice. "Can't help himself."

"That so?" remarked Gwen levelly.

Weiss was silent for a while. He seemed to be gathering himself. He turned to Gwen.

"I'm sorry about your parents."

Gwen's eyes flared in alarm.

"Dying in a car crash," said Weiss, shooting her a quizzical look. "What did you think I meant?"

"Nothing, nothing," Gwen said quickly. "It was just the way you said it, as if there were something else."

Weiss nodded slowly. He kept looking down at his empty plate. "There is," he said quietly.

Gwen felt her heart begin to pound.

Weiss looked up. "We're more alike than you think," he said slowly.

"Meaning?" Gwen knitted her fingers in her lap, began to twiddle her ring compulsively.

"I don't have parents either. Lost them both."

"My God! How?"

"My mom killed herself," said Weiss, eyes locked onto Gwen's as if daring her to look away from his grief. "My father used to beat on us both, for years. Wore her down so much till there was nothing left. She'd left her family, her homeland, everything to marry him, and this is what she got in return. So, when he finally took off, she was left with nothing, in a way. So she killed herself."

"She had *you*," answered Gwen.

"And she left me too."

"Where's your father?"

Opposite her, Weiss sat motionless, head bowed, as if trapped in his pain, unable to move under the weight of it.

"I have no idea," replied Weiss. "Haven't seen him since I was sixteen. Never want to see him again."

"I get that," said Gwen. She reached out, took Weiss's hand, gripped it hard. "I am sorry, Peter."

His eyes moistened. He nodded. "Just wanted you to know that you weren't alone, you know." He gave an almost helpless shrug. "That shit happens."

15

SEVENTEEN MILE DRIVE, BIG SUR,
MONDAY NIGHT

The girl ran through the darkness. This was like something out of a nightmare, only it was real. Her heel broke on the rough trail. She kicked off the other one and ran on. The man followed. He seemed to have all the time in the world, as if he knew he would catch her. It had started so well.

The flash car shouted money, the crisp shirt and suit murmured class. Some tony husband cheating on his wife, looking for fresh meat, for something quick, and paying well for it. He had paid her straight off, four hundred dollars, told her all he needed was an hour but that he had a thing about the forest, could they park and do it there, *make me feel like I'm a teenager again*, he had said with a winning smile. And she had stepped into his car and into the nightmare.

He had driven to Seventeen Mile Drive. Ritzy, she had thought. Then, as advertised, he had turned off into a forest, parked. He took out a silk scarf, reached across, kissed her, then tied it round her mouth. Then as she struggled with the locked door, he took another, grabbed her hands, and bound them behind her back.

"Get out," he'd said as fear exploded in her stomach. His voice was different, his eyes were different. He seemed amused, but didn't share the joke with her.

"Go on. Run. If you want."

And run she did. Spurred by terror. She ran as fast as she could with her hands bound behind her. She could hear him, keeping pace. Now he accelerated. In seconds, he caught her, pulled her down. She saw he wore gloves, and she whimpered into her scarf.

He reached his hands around her neck. She pleaded with her eyes, with all the voice she could summon.

He smiled again. "You want to ask why? There's a time to talk. And a time to stay silent. You didn't know the difference. Good-bye."

She struggled, she tried to scream out, but he was too strong, too big. There was nothing she could do. She saw the fireworks as her brain, starved of oxygen, began to shut down; then there was nothing.

16

THE LAB, CARMEL VALLEY, TUESDAY

The next morning, Gwen parked and stepped from her Mustang. She reached into the passenger seat to grab her laptop when a roar made her straighten up with a frown. A motorbike sped up, braked at the last minute in a cloud of dust. The leather-suited rider swung his leg off and parked his bike. He pulled off his helmet.

"Dr. Messenger," said Gwen coolly, brushing the dust off her t-shirt. "Didn't have you down as a motorbike man."

"My car's in for valeting. The Beamer can match it for speed. Runs like silk. And looks like a work of art."

"Vorsprung Durch Technik," said Gwen before she could stop herself.

Messenger frowned. "I like technological capability," he replied, not letting the humor breathe today. "Especially when aesthetically pleasing. The BMW satisfies both criteria," he added.

And people too, wondered Gwen. Form and function. Everything had to do its job, and prettily. He was no exception in his immaculate, body-molding leathers, which appeared to have been hand-tailored for his tall, lean frame. Gwen reckoned the consistently exquisite tailoring was not personal vanity, merely the appropriate adornment for a well-formed machine. He wouldn't put crap in his car, so why on himself? It was a curiously egoless kind of vanity. The man was distant even from himself.

"How's Oracle coming along?" Messenger asked as they walked into the Lab.

"Sensors and buoys are all ordered. Should be in Peru by the weekend, and now that I can afford more data I am playing with the model a lot, refining it, trying to increase the accuracy."

"Good. Keep at it. Don't try," he intoned with a sharp sideways look at her. "Succeed."

Gwen laughed. "Sounds like a business-school mantra."

Messenger said nothing, his displeasure evident in the way he studiously ignored her as he walked on ahead.

Two hours later, Messenger strode into her office, in bonhomous mood this time. Maybe he'd pulled off a good deal, made another few millions in the meantime, mused Gwen.

"Play backgammon?" he fired off, bracing his arms on her desk, leaning toward her. His lips curved in a smile, but his eyes were narrowed in speculation.

Gwen eyed him back, wondering if this were some sort of code.

"Sometimes," she replied cautiously.

Messenger clapped his hands together. "Excellent!"

He wheeled round, strode to the atrium, called out.

"Tournament time! Let's ramp it up today. Since I, and Falcon Capital, have just made a killing in the markets this morning—"

"How much?" called out Kevin Barclay.

Messenger paused.

"Not a great deal. But not bad for a few weeks' work."

"And?" prompted Peter Weiss.

"Thirty-eight million dollars," announced Messenger, to whoops all round. "So I'm feeling generous. Let's call it fifty thousand dollars to the winner!"

Gwen watched in what she feared was openmouthed amazement. Messenger's words set off a feeding frenzy. Mandy let out an alarming war-cry whoop, while Barbieri and the grunts, chattering excitedly about Falcon's killing, rushed from their offices, pulling chairs with them. Weiss and Barclay, with practiced fluency, inverted the smooth wooden tops of what Gwen had thought of as five oddly placed occasional tables to reveal the backgammon boards on the reverse. Randy Sieber, as if again displaying some sixth sense, though more probably alerted by Mandy's war cry, which could have pierced steel, appeared at the door at the top of the stairs, closed it smoothly, and trotted down, muscular legs bulging through the tight trousers of his suit. Mandy scurried round with a cowboy hat in which were crunched little pieces of paper.

"Doctor M., Weiss, Kevin, Randy, and Gwen, lucky dip. Pick your opponents," she instructed. Excitement had raised the pitch of her metallic voice, making it sound to Gwen only marginally better than nails scraping down a blackboard.

"Let's rock and roll!" bellowed Mandy. She pointed a remote and a pounding rock anthem by Foreigner boomed out.

"This is surreal," murmured Gwen, picking her paper.

"Looks like you and me, Atalanta," she called out with a smile. Atalanta said nothing, just gave Gwen an appraising glance as they took a table and laid out their pieces. She pushed back her black braids with a long, manicured finger, all cool elegance, just a tad too studied to be natural, thought Gwen. Pose, not poise. Underneath all that polish the woman was nervous.

The atmosphere in the office had gone from businesslike to electric. Pieces clack-clack-clacked and slammed down, dice rolled and clattered on the wooden boards punctuated by hisses, curses, and *Yesses!* as they fell, dispensing their random fate.

"What's the deal here?" asked Gwen above the throbbing bass. "This all feels just a tad gladiatorial."

Atalanta frowned at her, as if conversation were not done.

"It's all part of Dr. Messenger's metrics," she answered, winning the opening throw.

"Metrics?"

Atalanta cocked her beautiful head and looked at Gwen like she were an imbecile. "You don't know what metrics are?"

"So shoot me. Just tell me first."

The hint of a smile played round Atalanta's eyes. "Testing yourself. Measuring yourself. Improving. Competing."

"What, like *every day in every way I'm getting better and better*?"

"Ridicule it all you like, it's how the office works."

"Part of all this survival-of-the-fittest stuff? Part of weeding you guys down to one at the end of the year? Or to none?" Gwen added with a sweet smile.

"Exactly. And you're immune due to your fancy model. Lucky cowgirl in your jeans and tee. So go ahead, scoff all you like, but don't mind me if I focus on my job. I wouldn't mind getting a quick fifty K. But it's more than that. You can't afford to lose around here. You think this is just a game, but it all gets marked down on your record, how you play, win or lose, your attitude, the whole deal. . . ."

Phew, thought Gwen, a touch of paranoia, maybe? She looked around. If so, they all seemed to feel it. All the players were concentrating with a kind of joyless determination, even those who were trying hard to affect an image of relaxation. All so desperate to win, to shore themselves up, to stay in the game and have themselves a bite at the cherry that was Silicon Valley, to get their share of the money that on occasion flowed just like milk and honey, even if they poisoned it with their own fear and greed. And you, Gwen, she asked herself. Are you so pure?

She glanced at Messenger, the puppetmaster, felt a quick stab of shock as she saw his eyes on her, watching her as she had watched everyone else. She met his gaze until he looked away. Was this some kind of game for him? He seemed to be enjoying himself, eyes flickering round the players with a slight smile of amusement. Uncomfortable, she turned back to Atalanta.

"Is Dr. Messenger married?" she asked, twiddling her jade ring.

Atalanta spluttered. "What? You want the position?"

Gwen let out a throaty laugh, garnering a scowl from Mandy, who was locked in what appeared to be mortal combat with Jihoon.

"I'm just wondering how any wife could put up with this?"

"Word is she didn't," replied Atalanta. "Hightailed her bony ass back to Germany with their three sons."

So that would explain the lack of photographs on the desk.

"So, enough talk. Ready to play?" asked Atalanta testily.

Gwen stifled a smile. So let's go up a few gears. See what happens.

"Oh, yeah," she drawled. "I'm ready."

Gwen beat Atalanta with brutal efficiency. The dice

ran well for her, but Atalanta was cautious, conservative, hadn't learned, despite the aggression she wore like a badge, that sometimes attack was the safest way. As Gwen got up, Atalanta glared at her with a new and deeper hostility. Gwen gave a low chuckle, moved round to watch the other games.

Mandy was playing a wild game against Jihoon. A few lucky throws spurred her on to wanton play. She popped three Tums during the remaining five minutes of the bout, scenting the air with peppermint as she chewed furiously. Ruthlessly, Jihoon dispatched her.

Peter Weiss was playing Randy Sieber. The security man leaned forward over the board, shirtsleeves rolled back over bulging forearms, eyes locked on Weiss as he threw, as if he could win by intimidation. Peter Weiss affected blithe indifference. He lounged in his chair, as if he were in a late-night bar shooting the shit with his buddies. A faint, almost feline smile played on his lips as he watched Sieber roll and play. Then, in competition with the booming music, perhaps to drown it, he started whistling quietly, almost under his breath. R.E.M., "Losing My Religion" again. This seemed to infuriate Sieber, who flicked angry glances at him. Unsurprisingly, thought Gwen, feeling a flash of sympathy for the security man. Weiss ignored him. Still whistling, dressed as always, in his head-to-toe black, he made his moves with rapid precision, slamming his pieces down, wiping Sieber's from the board.

A gaming ninja, thought Gwen, eyeing this new, martial side of his character with interest. He was obviously an expert compartmentalizer. He kept his pain locked away. He'd let it out to make her feel better, she acknowledged with a pang. She watched him, willing him on, but feeling too her usual sympathy for the underdog. Sieber didn't stand a chance.

Weiss played with the speedy confidence and studied disdain of the regular winner. Glancing in amusement at

Sieber, he smoothly and professionally moved all his pieces off to victory while Sieber was still evacuating his last eight pieces from the far quadrant of the board. Weiss got up before he'd finished, a deliberate if casual insult. Sieber swore at his departing back.

Gwen moved on to watch Kevin Barclay lose to NFL Curt with a throaty "*Goddamit*," the Harvard charm not quite so bulletproof. Curt met Gwen's eyes with a conspiratorial nod of triumph.

Messenger walked up to Gwen, smiling easily. He stood close enough for her to smell the lemony cologne. He glanced down at her with a look of complicity she did not wish to buy into.

"Enjoying your little experiment?" she asked sharply.

Messenger raised a quizzical eyebrow.

"Throw scraps to the sharks, watch them fight."

"It's interesting, is it not?"

"If you like that sort of thing."

"I do. Human nature. The human brain, emotion. Backgammon is a good tell."

"A tell?" asked Gwen.

"It reveals character, the aspects we normally hide. Did you win?"

"Yes," replied Gwen, conceding Messenger's point in the smile of triumph she was unable to hide. "I did. But why tell me, if you are using this as some kind of assessment? Am I immune?" she asked, thinking of Atalanta's words.

"No one's immune. But you knew anyway, didn't you? Your question gave you away, but I saw it in your eyes before that. I saw you watching everyone else, assessing."

Gwen shrugged. "Guilty," she replied, wondering what other means he would use to analyze her.

"Time for Round Two," he declaimed, moving away.

Ten minutes later, Gwen beat Curt in the semis, noting that he was a gracious loser, the only one she'd witnessed today. Only Weiss and Messenger were still playing, locked in a long drawn-out back game, Weiss a few throws ahead of Messenger. He wasn't whistling now, noted Gwen.

Messenger for the first time played with a kind of rigid concentration. Then, as if the tension finally got to him, he pulled off the wedding ring he still wore and spun it compulsively on the wooden board as he considered his moves. Gwen gave a slight jolt. He had her nervous tic, only worse. She could see the irritation in Weiss's eyes and his struggle to mask it. He wasn't slouching anymore. Gwen could smell his desire to win; it was there, veiled by the habitual whiff of the spicy cigar smoke, pungent and male. In eight well-played moves, Weiss won.

Messenger jumped to his feet, shook Weiss's hand warmly.

"Good job, Peter. Nice game!" Messenger seemed genuinely delighted by his protégé's triumph, Gwen was pleased, and surprised, to note.

Weiss looked ecstatic. He beamed up at his boss, and Gwen saw in his look the delight of a son praised by a beloved and admired father. Messenger was a substitute and, evidently, a hell of a good one.

Gwen wished, protectively, that Weiss would veil his feelings for his own sake. His delight was too naked to share with an office where most everyone seemed to wear a bit of a mask.

"Looks like you and me, Surfer Girl," said Weiss, sauntering over and patting Gwen on the back.

Gwen gave a smile of relief. His mask was back on. "Bring it on, Techie Boy," she replied, patting him back.

The game played out, almost perfectly matched; both Gwen and Weiss rolled well and played better. Weiss was guarded, Gwen aggressive. Playing it safe bored her more than losing. Fifty thousand dollars was on the table, but Gwen tried to ignore it. She felt sure that, like the booming music, it was designed to distract.

It all came down to the last two throws. Weiss was behind Gwen. He needed to throw two successive doubles, three or above, to beat her. And he threw double six, followed by double four, to general uproar.

"Hell! What were the chances of that?" cried Barclay, frowning with indignation.

Gwen laughed. "One thousand, two hundred and twenty-five to one, actually, lucky bastard'!" Messenger turned to her, whipping out his phone. He tapped out a few numbers, then gazed down at Gwen.

"You just worked out those odds in your head?" he asked, eyes wide with unmasked admiration. It was as if he were seeing her properly for the first time.

Gwen looked around. Everyone was watching her. Weiss, his victory forgotten, looked furious.

Gwen wished she could hit the rewind button. "It's no big deal," she said with a shrug. "The numbers just sort of arrange themselves in my head. It's almost involuntary."

She heard Atalanta mutter something and realized that she'd just made it worse. She got to her feet, stuck out her hand.

"Well done, Peter," she said. Slowly, he reached out, shook her hand, and silently pocketed the check Messenger wrote out to him. Mandy clicked off the music, and Gwen walked back to her office through the suddenly silent room.

Rule number one on the savannah, she told herself, *don't be conspicuous.* Do well, but not too well, unless you're ready for the knives. Judging by the looks sent her way, there was a point at which "survival of the fittest" gave way to "kill off the competition."

17

The room smelled of sweat and dust baked on the halogen strip lights. A fan turned listlessly in the ceiling, cutting the silence with a soft whirr. Gwen faced off to the man. He paced round in a circle; she paced with him, keeping the distance between them, eyes fixed on his. Six foot five, two hundred and fifty pounds of lethal African American. His hair was cropped short. Tattoos bulged on both biceps. He started to dance on his feet, taunting her.

"C'mon! You are rusty! Take one, give me your best shot, go on."

His eyes twinkled, mocking her, his usual mix of charm and provocation. He always read her so well, always knew how to get the best out of her.

Goaded, Gwen kicked out, but Dwayne Jonson merely spun out of range, muttering profanities of contempt. They sparred on, Tae Kwon Do, which Gwen had practiced for fifteen years now, overlaid with strategic dirty fighting, something she'd done, courtesy of Dwayne, for four years.

She got in two good kicks to Dwayne's thigh, one of which dead-legged him. He was delighted. The more she hurt him, the bigger the smile. But he dished it right back at her. He got in a few blows to her shoulder and hip; she would sport the bruises for at least a week. She loved this, a good, clean, open fight, a vent for her aggression, her competitiveness. And more. It made her feel armed.

"You are useless, girl!" opined Dwayne when he'd landed another blow on Gwen. "Drop. Gimme ten. No, gimme twenty. I go away for three weeks and you let yourself go, like this?"

"Been busy, Dwayne," retorted Gwen, deciding not to

tell him about her new job. There'd be an inquisition. Instead, she dropped into the press-up position, pumping out twenty, her fifth set of the session. She straightened up. "So, how were the seniors?"

"They were cool, Boudy. Now there's a buncha gray old ladies in Florida with bricks in their handbags you don't wanna mess with."

Gwen laughed. "I'll bet."

"Told 'em the best form of defense was don't get in the situation, but if you got your back against the wall and the shit's coming down—"

"Hit someone with a cliché. . . ." drawled Gwen.

"Yeah, funny," boomed Dwayne, suppressing a grin.

"I just love the image, you and your ex-Navy-SEAL buddies and the blue rinse brigade."

"Last time we were on a boat we were sailing for Iraq. Lemme tell you, the *Caribbean Queen* gave us a cabin each, fresh food, not rehydrated rations, and no incoming. What's not to like?"

"Just don't go soft on me, Dwayne. Who else is gonna keep me in the game."

"Well, I guess that would be me. Wanna do some dirty fighting yourself?"

"Always," replied Gwen.

"C'mon then, take me down. Surprise me."

"Sure, just let me get some water," said Gwen. She turned as if to grab her bottle, then ducked, rammed her shoulder into his lower stomach and chopped at the back of his knees.

Dwayne went down laughing and cursing.

"That was low, you cheating little . . ."

"Now, now Dwayne, watch that potty mouth," laughed Gwen. "You did say dirty."

"Yeah, but there are *rules*."

"Yeah, the only one that matters is *Stay Alive* I remember some big, scary guy telling me."

"Well, he don't know shit," declared Dwayne.

They sparred for another half hour, then, dripping with sweat, Gwen pulled on a hoodie, stretched out for five minutes, and waved a cheery good-bye as Dwayne's next client arrived, a reedy-looking schoolboy of about fifteen.

Dwayne would give him moves to sort out the bullies, thought Gwen, giving the boy a broad smile and a wink that brought on a ferocious and achingly sweet blush.

"Next week," called out Gwen.

"Stay alive," called back Dwayne.

Planning to, thought Gwen, peering through the darkness of the lot, walking to her Mustang, sliding in, wishing that her car's roof was up. Quickly she turned the key in the ignition and pulled out. She always reversed into parking spaces, another of Dwayne's lessons. Always be ready for a quick getaway.

She suppressed a shudder. Falcon had made her think of the past more than she wanted to, had brought back the fear, made her look over her shoulder again, made her imagine eyes in the darkness, watching her, cars pulling out onto Highway 1, staying on her trail. Paranoia, she told herself as she drove down the track to Hurricane Point to her cottage, where no lights burned. She should put the deck light on a timer, she thought. A job for the weekend.

She stepped out into the night, inhaled the clean air, the damp oregano wafting in the sea breeze. Home. Her refuge. Quickly, she let herself in, locked the door, and fell to her knees to hug Leo. She breathed him in, doggy breath and warm fur. She held him and he nuzzled her. Her pulse slowed and she got to her feet.

She pulled the curtains, fed Leo then fed herself. She sat on the bleached canvas sofa, listening to Jack Johnson crooning away her tension, tray on her lap, eating pizza, a Jack Reacher novel clasped in one hand ratcheting up the tension. But that was OK. It was someone else's fight. Someone else's terror.

She finished off dinner with hot chocolate and macadamia-chip brownies made by her neighbor, Marilyn. Everything was fine, she told herself as she snuggled down in her bed, duvet and her parents' alpaca throw keeping her warm against the chill wind blowing in from the French windows she had defiantly opened. A pane of glass wouldn't have stopped them anyway. . . .

18

LIBERTY STREET, JUST OFF WALL STREET,
NYC, WEDNESDAY MORNING

Ronald Glass had two near-misses that day. Ignorant of both, he would have what he considered to be a fulfilling day, an eighty-five percent day. It started routinely. His town car dropped him off at eight fifty. At his desk in his corner office, twentieth floor of the Newman Brothers building, view of the Fed just down the street, he scrolled down his iPad, checking his diary as his PA, Romula, brought him a skinny latte.

Gallery Klesh had an opening that night. The catalog was in his desk drawer. He reached into the pocket of his custom suit, pulled out his key, opened the drawer, flicked through the glossy pages, seeking first the photo of the artist. He smiled; he might just do himself some acquiring. The art was a touch gloomy, but good enough. The bio of the artist made it collectible. She'd gone to the right schools, made all the right declarations, her love of chiaroscuro, of darkness and light, of the seen and the unseen.

The catalog was entitled WHAT LIES BENEATH. *The artist, beneath him,* thought Ronnie with a smirk.

As a bet, she and her art were good enough, and a hell of a lot more fun than the markets, arguably more predictable too. And he had wall space, thanks to the new condo; he had the funds, thanks to his last, and highly secret trade, and he had the itch, that acquisitive urge that was half caveman, half sophisticate. *Fill the cave, fill the cave.* Grinning, he gave his groin a speculative jiggle.

He glanced up. Romula was occupied at her machine, eyes down; the associates were laboring away in their cubicles; no one was loitering, waiting their moment with their co-department head. Him, Ronald Glass. His much hated co-department head, Greg Kriedwolf, was fishing for business in Houston. *May he not find it,* wished Glass.

His fingers slid deeper into his desk drawer, probing. He found the envelope, taped to the bottom of the drawer above. He pulled it down, snuck a quick look. Almost empty. He pocketed it, rose to his feet, turned down Romula's offer of assistance—some things you just had to do yourself, no matter how elevated you were.

"Back in ten," he announced. He headed for the john, snorted the thin remains of his stash, binned the baggie, then headed for the elevator. It was walled with mirrored glass, giving him a full view, front and back. Alone, he straightened up, eyed his reflection. Not bad for thirty-five. Still trim, thanks to three workouts a week and an appetite depleted by coke. A tad short, but, as his father-in-law was fond of saying, he was plenty tall when he stood on his wallet. The two-thousand-dollar Armani suit made him look enough like a sophisticate to impress the city's maître d's, but the luxuriant black hair, rolling down over his collar, and the rapacious brown eyes, which flickered constantly as if looking for his next mark, made him look more like a used-car salesman or a bookie.

Glass fingered his hair, pulled out his cell phone.

"You around? Need a coffee. There in five." He spoke in staccato bites to his subordinates, but he could waste his words when he needed to, with new women, with the CEO.

He strode across the marble foyer and out into the heat. Ninety-five and seventy percent humidity. He pulled on his shades. They fogged in a second. He toyed with calling his driver, Alfonso; rejected it. No witnesses. No honor, some of these drivers never knew when to keep their mouths shut. He walked down Liberty, took a right on Broadway, building up a sweat, wondering if it had all been such a good idea. Aiming for casual, he sauntered into Zuccotti Park. Eyes raking the park for his dealer, he didn't see the athletic blonde striding out behind him, didn't see her clock the dealer, veer away into Starbucks on Broadway, where she stood in line, looking through the window, watching.

Glass's dealer handed him the Styrofoam cup. He made as if to take a sip, talked a while, reached into his pocket for the tightly bound wad, shook hands and palmed it to his man.

"See ya."

"Next week?"

"Most likely."

The two men peeled away from each other, slowly, all casual, two Wall Street types, one dressed down, but still Brooks Brothers' smart.

The blonde, now with a coffee of her own, a real coffee, followed again at a distance, wondering at Glass, at his sheer imperviousness, wondering at her own luck. She had staked out the bank every day for a week and no sign of the man, now here he was, up to no good. She smiled, lucky for her, unlucky for Dirty Ronnie.

A van with blacked-out windows was parked outside the entrance to Newman Brothers. Glass paused. No one and nothing was allowed to park outside. Then he saw the dogs emerge from the building, the two German Shepherds with their handlers. The antiterrorist bomb-sniffing dogs. *Well, they would be allowed,* figured Glass. He watched the dogs disappear into their van, helpfully emblazoned with a BEWARE, DOGS! strip, then he crossed Liberty and strolled on into his building. One more call, then he could get on with his work.

"Glass here. Need a suite. Tomorrow night."

He got it. He rang his wife.

"Kimberly, honey? Got to fly to Houston tomorrow. Kreidwolf's digging up a deal and they need me there. Yeah, I know we were, and I'm *reeeal* sorry, honey. Take you to dinner there next week. Promise."

He hung up. Done. His wife had been an art cutie, worked for one of the top galleries until he collected her, gave her a penthouse and a kid. She was old England, one of the founders with an illustrious name and a devoted father who had enough edge and connections to make life uncomfortable if he upset his baby girl, so Glass, a liar of the highest order, made sure to keep her sweet.

"Just missed the dogs," said Romula.

"No bombs today?" asked Glass, with a wry smile.

"They did sniff around in your office a bit, must have taken a leak they spent so long in the John, but no, Ronnie, no bombs."

He wished she wouldn't call him *Ronnie*. One bang and he was forever *Ronnie*.

A gent Ange Wilkie walked back toward the SEC building at the World Financial Center, just off Fulton Street and West. Too impatient to wait for a face-to-face, she pulled out her cell phone and called her boss.

"Why do dogs go into investment banks?" she asked Troy Bergers.

"This some kind of a joke? I hate to imagine the punch line."

"No," laughed Ange. "I'm serious. Is it a petting thing, a stress relief thing?"

"You really want to know?"

"Yeah. I do."

"Why?"

" 'Cause I just saw two German Shepherds come out of Newman Brothers."

"You stalking our boy again?"

"Er, yeah."

"Excellent! Banks'll say it's to sniff out explosive materials."

"And?"

"Drugs."

"Really? Well, hot damn. Our boy is a lucky sonofabitch."

"Now, now, agent. Mouth. Why?"

Ange told him, concluding: "Think about it. We could bust him. I'm sure he has coke."

"I could care less what he shoves up his nose. We want him on the insider trading. Cool it, Ange."

"I know. I'd just like to see the look on his smug pug face if he was cuffed and roughed."

"Take a rain check. That day will come."

Zealot to zealot, they smiled down the line to each other.

"He doesn't have any idea, does he, how close he came. He'd lose his job for sure."

"None of us know how close we come," reflected Bergers. "The tile blowing off a roof in a storm; the psycho walking down the street just as you duck into a doorway; the cab losing control and mounting the sidewalk, you delayed round the corner 'cause you stopped to stroke a stray cat. . . ."

"The people who missed their train, were late for the office on Nine-eleven . . ." Ange added, nearing her office, glancing at the ghosts of the Twin Towers opposite.

"Exactly."

"But you're talking about blind fate. This is fate with a vision. Right here, right now, we are molding Ronald Glass's fate. He just doesn't know it."

"You're molding it, Angie, from where I sit. You're on a crusade."

"Just call me Nemesis!"

19

THE *SAN FRANCISCO REPORTER* OFFICES,
BRANNAN STREET,
WEDNESDAY AFTERNOON

Dan Jacobsen walked past the oval stretch of scrappy grass known in San Francisco as South Park, obeying the summons that had been issued earlier that morning. It was lunchtime, the sun was shining, and scores of trendily dressed men and women, many seemingly teenagers, sprawled on the grass with takeout lunches. More drifted past him, exiting the renovated lofts surrounding the park, blinking like moles. Jacobsen had no desire to eat or drink, but he detoured via a coffee shop, bought a takeout and a Danish.

The condensed ten-square-block had once housed immigrant families, printing plants, and a flophouse. Now it was home to high-end restaurants, coffee shops, and a flourishing interactive media industry of Web site developers, interactive game makers, and CD-ROM publishers. Known as Multimedia Gulch it was also home to the *San Francisco Reporter,* one of the few original tenants who still remained.

Nodding to the security guards, Jacobsen walked up the stairs, swung through the glass doors, and headed up to the corner office on the first floor. He paused outside, next to the desk of a harassed-looking woman with glasses and a deep worry frown, gazing unblinkingly at her screen.

"Delivery," he said with a smile.

The woman looked up, beamed as Dan handed over the takeout coffee and Danish.

"Hey Dan. Thank you! I *needed* this!" She took off the lid, inhaled, swigged with the thinly concealed urgency of an addict. She always did need her coffee. Her boss took the view that lunch was for wimps. And for networking, which of course exempted him from his own adage.

"Go right on in. He's on the phone. He's always on the phone so what the hell . . ."

Dan smiled. "Thanks, Maisie."

Without knocking, he pushed open the door, walked in, nodded to the man on the phone, made himself comfortable on the sofa. While the other man paced and talked, he took out his cell, played a game.

After two minutes, having made his point, the other man finished the call, edged back onto his large desk, stretched out his spindly legs, and regarded Jacobsen with a look of arch speculation.

"What have you got for me, Jacobsen?" he asked in a clipped, tight voice.

Mack Stackridge, the editor, universally known as MackStack, was not liked by his staff, but he was respected, grudgingly. He was lauded in the profession as a man who got the stories, the scoops, and the back stories that no one had thought to get. He was creative, he was devious, and he was ruthless. It was all about the story. He was tall, thin, avian with his hooked nose and quick, predatory eyes, always probing, always seeking the angle.

"Let's just say I've laid the foundations," replied Dan. "Now we wait."

"I'm not a patient man."

Dan gave a bitter laugh. "I've noticed."

"Do what you have to. This is what you were trained for. Don't disappoint me, will you Jacobsen?" the man asked softly.

20

THE LAB, THURSDAY MORNING

At five after nine, Peter Weiss sidled into Gwen's office. Gwen smelled the waft of the exotic cigar smoke that seemed to impregnate his being before she saw him. She was head down, scribbling some figures on a notepad.

"How's it going, Surfer Girl?"

Gwen regarded him quizzically. After a day to cool down, he'd apparently forgiven her. "Radical, Techie Boy! What can I do for you?"

"Dr. Messenger requires your presence."

Messenger was sitting behind his desk as Gwen walked into his office. He leaned back in his chair and studied her as if there was something he could not quite figure out, something that wasn't quite conforming to his expectations.

"It's our resident supercomputer," he said, breaking his slightly uncomfortable silence. "Please," he gestured grandly, "have a seat."

Gwen gave a brief smile, took her indicated seat at the round table where Kevin Barclay sat, flicking glances at his BlackBerry, fingering it briefly, now joined by Peter Weiss.

"Something puzzles me," Gwen said, twiddling her jade ring round her finger.

Messenger sat forward. "I like puzzles, ones I can solve anyway."

"How can you make thirty-eight million dollars in a few weeks doing venture capital?" she asked. "I thought the payback was years."

"It's not ven cap, that's why. I play the markets. Peter and Kevin are tasked to help me. We seek out value, aberrations. Sometimes we get lucky."

"I'd rather call it smart," chipped in Barclay, laying his BlackBerry on the desk with a clatter.

"And I'd call that hubris," retorted Messenger. "Smart still needs luck for the timing to work if you're running short-term positions, which we were."

Barclay shrugged an elegant Brooks Brothers' shoulder. The man was like a walking fashion plate.

"Close the blinds, would you, Kevin," said Messenger.

A flash of irritation swept Barclay's features, quickly replaced by his customary, bulletproof Harvard charm. He got to his feet.

"Sure. Happy to."

Quickly, efficiently, he let down the blinds on the two large windows.

Gwen watched, puzzled.

"What's with the blinds?" she asked.

"Protection," supplied Barclay.

Gwen raised an eyebrow.

Messenger bridged his arms on his desk and leaned toward Gwen. "Against a low-tech attack. Used to be the case that one of the most effective ways of stealing information was to record a view of a meeting from a covert place or safe room across the street focusing on the lips of the speaker, then taking the recording to a reliable lip reader in order to transcript the detail. It's still done, according to Randy. It's cheap and effective, so now we normally shut blinds and remove conference phones from meeting rooms."

"What about bugs then?" asked Gwen, feeling like she was stepping into a new and not altogether appealing world.

"Randy sweeps for them. Rest assured. We aren't bugged, though there're many who would like to." Messenger snapped back in his chair. "Let's move on. You'll have met Kevin Barclay by now," he said.

Gwen nodded. She'd seen him preening in his Porsche, checking his hair in the mirror before he went into the Lab, and eyeing himself in the gym when he bench-pressed, in her view, a desultory weight. And losing at backgammon. She suppressed a grin.

"We've lunched at the Cupcake," she said. "But not talked business."

"Time you did. There are synergies between your work and his, and Peter's."

Gwen raised an eyebrow but said nothing.

"Why don't you explain, Kevin," said Messenger, folding his hands in his lap and sitting back.

"I play the markets. I'm a mini hedge fund," said Barclay, a tad grandly, thought Gwen.

"Dr. Messenger's told me a bit about Oracle and your Niño predictions. I want to know more," added Barclay.

How many people know about Oracle now, thought Gwen. The risk expanded exponentially with each additional person who knew. She glanced at Messenger. "This is confidential information."

Messenger nodded. "We all know when to keep our mouth shut, Dr. Gwen. Why are you so protective? Mel told me you don't want any publicity."

Gwen felt the tension knit her shoulders, then magnify within the room. She paused, considered her answer, tried, and failed to resist the temptation to attack. She eyed the three men before her.

"We wouldn't want to be premature, now would we, guys," she drawled.

Messenger blinked. Peter Weiss coughed out a laugh. Barclay mimed a poker face. "Never happened yet," he said.

Gwen breathed out a low sigh as the tension evaporated.

Messenger eyed Gwen coolly but with a hint of reluctant admiration, as if to say *Round One to you*.

"You can speak freely here, Dr. Gwen. We all know when to talk and when to keep our mouths shut. You're protective of Oracle. I can see that, but you need to share now. Oracle isn't just yours alone anymore."

No, and that was the hell of it, thought Gwen. Time to play for the team. She had no choice but to trust them. Liking the other players didn't come into it. Weiss she liked for his gentleness and a hinted-at vulnerability. She didn't know yet if she liked Messenger or not. He made her wary. He was a spectacle, a force of nature like a hurricane, best admired from a distance. Barclay was a jock and a poser, and Gwen had the feeling that under the charm lay a jerk, and a ruthless one. She put aside her latent dislike, for now.

"OK. Everyone knows we're moving into a Niño cycle right now," started Gwen. "But where I differ from the market is that I think this Niño will become much more powerful. I'm predicting a Mega Niño. That in turn could incubate an ARk Storm."

"Goddamn!" exclaimed Barclay. "So you're saying there's an ARk Storm coming sometime soon."

Gwen shook her head. She'd have them running in the streets if she weren't careful.

"No, that's not what I'm saying. The likelihood of one hitting has gone up because of where I think this Niño is going, but I don't think the current conditions together are enough." They could well go that way, thought Gwen, but she didn't want to say it until she was certain.

"So, financially speaking, you're saying that it's not the time to short California property casualty insurance companies?" asked Barclay. "Or to go long wheat and orange juice futures?"

"Not unless something else kicks in to gee the system up even more," answered Gwen.

Barclay nodded, gave a pained look.

"This is *good* news," said Gwen, puzzled.

"Barclay, you are such a troll," said Weiss. He turned to Gwen. "He's getting greedy. He wants to set up a monster trade, short the prop casualty companies, make a killing."

Barclay laughed. "You innocent. I'd buy put options, get me a massacre!"

21

CARMEL VALLEY VILLAGE

Gwen needed a change of scene, a break from a world of dubious metrics where disasters were a commodity to be parlayed into a fortune. She headed for her car and drove to Carmel Valley Village in search of lunch. She found to her delight something called Roy's Deli and came out hugging a brown paper bag of supplies: a huge BLT on crisp french white, dripping with mayo; pink lemonade to wash it down; a coffee and brownie for dessert.

She walked back to Carmel Valley Road, crossed over, and found herself the perfect spot. She was far enough away from the road to hear only a dim roar of traffic, she was shaded by an enormous sycamore, and she had the panorama of the valley stretching out before her to the hills shimmering blue in the distance. Nearby, a swath of wild oregano baked in the midday sun, releasing its tangy scent into the slight breeze.

For half an hour, Gwen lost herself in the pure pleasure of eating, uninterrupted, and just letting her eyes close. . . .

She opened them abruptly, aware of scrutiny. She leapt to her feet. She felt the sweat of fear and adrenaline break out. She turned three-sixty, doing a rapid inventory. Behind her, no one. In front, perhaps twenty meters away, an old man walking up the path toward her, eyes on hers.

It was the same man who had confronted Messenger at the Lab. He stopped ten feet away. Gwen stood, hands loose by her sides, calculating. From this close she could see his gray stubble, the deep grooves in his face, the unkempt hair, the weary eyes. He was disturbing, but nothing about him spelled *threat*.

"You work at Falcon," he said in his raspy voice.

"How would you know that?" asked Gwen. Had he noticed her that day? He had seemed so focused on Messenger, as if seeing only him and Sieber.

"I've seen you, driving that old Mustang."

"*You've* been following me!" exclaimed Gwen. So she hadn't been imagining it. She gave a brief, mirthless laugh of relief. This guy, whatever his strange agenda, was no threat to her, wasn't even in the league of the others.

"What of it? You should know something about the people you work for."

"So you're doing me a favor, are you?" asked Gwen, narrowing her eyes.

"I've tried to tell the others. Those new kids. They wouldn't listen."

I'll bet, thought Gwen. Wouldn't look good on their record.

"What have you tried to tell them?"

The man paused, glanced at his feet, uncertain now that he had found someone willing to listen.

"Messenger," he whispered, looking up to meet Gwen's eyes. "He's a murderer."

Gwen studied him, gauging him. Was he mad? Should she walk away, or was there just a kernel of something she should listen to? Pity and instinct and her own inveterate curiosity made her stay.

"Did you used to work there?" she asked.

"My son," the man replied, his face gentling as he sensed the sympathy in his listener. "My son, Al, worked there. Until four months ago. Then Messenger killed him."

Gwen blew out a breath.

"How did he die? Your son?" she asked softly.

"Road accident," said the man bitterly. "That's the word the police used. *Accident.*"

Gwen froze. The man didn't notice. He was locked in his own personal agony.

"Was a hit 'n' run. He was cycling back home from the Lab. Messenger ran him down. He took that Ferrari of his and he ran down my boy."

Gwen could feel her heart pounding. So the Ferrari owner was Messenger. He certainly drove like a maniac. She could attest to that.

"But why would Messenger *do* that?" she asked.

"Have they told you about Paparuda?"

"*Paparuda*?" Gwen shook her head. "There's a lot of secrecy in the Lab."

The man barked out a bitter laugh. "They have a lot to hide."

"So what is Paparuda?" asked Gwen. "And what does it have to do with the death of your son?"

"It is something people would kill for. Have killed for."

Gwen felt questions bubbling up. "And? Are you going to tell me what it is?"

"Not here. I don't want anyone to see us together. For your sake and mine." He seemed quite sane now. Scarily so. He fished a tattered business card out of his pocket, handed it to Gwen.

"If you want answers, ring me, we'll meet up somewhere we won't be seen, and I'll tell you what I know."

Gwen took the card, watched the man hurry off into the trees and out of sight. Her t-shirt stuck to her sweating chest and her heart still felt as if it were racing as she walked down the path and back to her car.

22

THE LAB

Gwen gave a little gasp when she swung round the corner and saw Messenger in her office, sitting at her desk. He was spinning his wedding ring on the polished wood, staring at it contemplatively.

"You look startled, Dr. Gwen." He caught his ring mid-spin and slipped it back on his finger.

"Just coming back down to earth," said Gwen breathily. "I was miles away."

"Thinking of Oracle?"

"As always," replied Gwen, summoning a smile to gild her lie.

"Know any of the government techs involved in Project ARk Storm?" Messenger asked, getting up from Gwen's desk, taking his time. He moved past Gwen so close she could feel the heat from his body. She let out her breath, sank into her chair. She found herself hugging her handbag to her chest like a security blanket. She dropped it on the floor, swiveled in her chair to look up at Messenger, who was leaning against her doorjamb in his casual and wholly proprietorial way.

"As it happens," she answered, channeling her natural drawl, "I do. One of their chief meteorologists was my prof at Stanford."

"Friends?"

"Yeah. She's a surfer too."

"I'd like you to pay her a visit. Get an update."

"Sure, I can do that, but with a view to what? Their Web page gives a pretty good update of their thinking."

"There's the stuff they put out in the press conferences, then there's what they really think but don't want to share with the public in case they scare the shit out of them. Privately, they might be on the same page as you. Be nice to get confirmation."

"I'll see what I can find out. Hi Mandy."

Messenger turned around.

Mandy was standing patiently outside the office.

"Sorry to interrupt," she said with a little shoulder shrug, "but Sheikh Ali rang when you were grinding that poor pro into dust out there on the court. Went through to voice mail. Didn't sound urgent but I thought you should know."

Messenger straightened up as if someone had just flicked a switch. He gave Gwen a backhanded wave as he strode off to his office.

"Who the hell is Sheikh Ali?" asked Gwen.

"You don't know?" asked Mandy tinnily.

"Er, no, should I?"

"He's Falcon's major investor. He backed Dr. Messenger just after he started out in this business. He'd seen the doctor's blogs on investments on the Internet. Got in touch and offered him money to manage."

"Wow! Just out of the blue?"

"Yep."

"Dr. Messenger must have written a killer blog."

"Oh, it was. And get this. He wrote it during his down time, during his shifts when he was on call at the hospital, but there was nothing happening."

"Stop!" Gwen held up a hand. "Dr. Messenger is an MD?"

"Well, yeah."

"I thought it was a DPhil, like mine."

Mandy vigorously shook her head. "Everyone thinks that, but no. He was a real medical doctor. Brain was his thing."

"And he gave that up to be an investor?" asked Gwen.

"Let me put it another way. He gave up a half a mil a year and four sleepless nights a week for a few hundred million and a life."

Gwen blew out a breath. "Wow again."

Mandy laughed. "Yeah, wow again. And look, I can see you thinking what a waste of all his doctoring and all that baloney, but he paid his dues, over and over, let me tell you. He saved plenty of lives. He'd done his giving back, before he got his getting."

"Didn't say he hadn't."

"Didn't need to. In your eyes." Mandy laid a freckled hand on Gwen's shoulder. "Piece of advice. This place is a money machine. Lean and mean. Check your moral qualms at the door, honey."

Not trusting herself to speak, Gwen nodded mutely.

"How d'you know so much?" she asked after a pause.

"I was his nurse. We paired up for most surgeries. Then he started Falcon, he asked me to join him, and before you ask, honey, I'd paid my dues too, needed time off my feet and on my ass plus enough dough to buy me a home."

Gwen raised her hands. "Truce!"

Mandy laughed and bustled out of her office.

Intriguing, thought Gwen, getting up to fetch herself a coffee, eyeing Messenger in his office as she passed, wondering how much else she had yet to learn about Falcon, its backers, and about Messenger himself. How many personae did he keep in that pared-down frame? The Healer, the Investor, the Murderer?

23

Special Agent Ange Wilkie walked through the streets of lower Manhattan, reveling in air—hot, humid air, but still air—and sounds and life: a couple chatting on their stoop; an old man with his aged dog, both limping down the sidewalk; the smell of frying garlic wafting from the Italian restaurant she just passed; a noisy game of basketball played under blinking neon. Anything but the life she had been listening in to, the sterile, avaricious, to her meaningless life of Ronald Glass. She had listened in for over twelve hours today. Her share of eight, and an extra four.

When she went to ask her partner if he wanted her to grab him his customary corn beef on rye, a giant Coke, and a Danish for lunch, she found Pete Rodgers, now known throughout the building as Rac, asleep in his office, headphones still attached, head on his desk, snoring loudly enough to drown out whatever detritus of a life he was listening to. Sleep was in short supply at home, especially at night, which as far as Ange could gather, baby Rodgers had switched with day.

So she'd woken him, told him to go home. Meekly, sleepwalking almost, he had gone and she'd listened in to his share of the intercepts.

Ronald Glass ringing his dealer; Ronald Glass ringing his wife, telling her he'd be flying to Houston, that he'd see her the next day; Ronald Glass hustling a deal; Ronald Glass potty-mouthing his colleagues; Ronald Glass booking a Manhattan hotel suite; Ronald Glass assuring the gallery owner in Manhattan who rang to remind him that the opening night of the hot new exhibition was tonight *and to please, please come* 'cause *he'd simply love the stuff and the artist herself too—so talented—so eminently collectible.* The artist, or her work, wondered Ange.

And here it was, the focus of what she had pretended to herself was just a random walk; Gallery Klesh on West Twenty-first. Ten thirty and still the art lovers were tilting their heads and scrutinizing, still with glasses of what must have been warm wine in their hands, while the odd rebel stood on the sidewalk, cigarette in hand, gesticulating with the grand abandon of alcohol. Ange, sporting her blond wig once again, allowed herself a quick glance, walked on by.

Five minutes later, on the other side of the street, she approached again. A Persian cat crossed the sidewalk in front of her, paused as if debating whether to cross the street. Ange bent down, ruffled the luxurious fur.

"Hey, pretty thing. How ya doing?" she crooned. In the shadow between a Range Rover and a Hummer, she glanced up, saw a man emerge from the gallery, arm draped across the shoulders of a young, spectacularly pretty redhead with tumbling hair and a slightly stumbling walk.

"Exquisite rendering, simply exquisite," gushed Ronald Glass. "So, honey, *Shibhaun,*" he added deliberately, as if to say he would never forget her name. "I have a suite at The Carlyle. What say you we go and celebrate your sell out?"

The woman's reply was inaudible, but it was clear to Ange that Ronald Glass was about to collect.

A business trip, he had told his wife. Yeah, it was business, of a kind: a few thousand dollars for a soul. You bastard, she murmured, watching him slide with the redhead into an idling Town Car. Just give me time, she thought, and I'll collect you too.

24

Gwen didn't go out of her way to avoid her colleagues, and neither did they seem to avoid her, but either way, she had little contact with them over the next week, which was just peachy, far as she was concerned. She wasn't worried by the odd flashes of animosity, just wasn't interested in playing their *metrics,* nor in fielding questions about Oracle. Messenger, she just wanted to avoid until she could get her head around Freidland's accusations, not that she knew how she would manage that. Even Peter Weiss, after the intimacy of his revelations about his parents, kept his distance. He seemed hugely preoccupied with some highly secretive project he was working on, at all hours it seemed from the bags under his eyes.

Mandy popped in every day, like a mother hen, checking up on her, making sure she was settling in. Gwen wondered whether she had children; she seemed the naturally maternal type. The way she buzzed round the office and all the staff made Gwen wonder whether Falcon was all the children she needed. On Wednesday morning, Mandy had come in with a plate of home-baked brownies.

"Eat them, take them, please, else I'll feed my fat ass."

Gwen laughed and took two. "Share them round. The grunts look underfed."

"I've already given them a ton. I made three dozen. Get into the manic baking phases sometimes. Calms me down, I suppose."

"There are worse habits," said Gwen, taking a bite of brownie, swooning. "These are delicious!"

Mandy smiled. "Thanks, honey. You are the sweetest thing."

On Thursday, Mandy came in with an envelope that she presented with a small bow.

Raising an eyebrow, Gwen pulled it open, pulled out a stiff invitation.

FALCON CAPITAL'S ANNUAL PARTY. GABRIEL MESSENGER AT HOME, SEVENTEEN MILE DRIVE, MAP ON REVERSE.

She could imagine Messenger living there, with his private equity millions, ensconced in some uber-contemporary cliff-top palace.

"Two weeks Sunday. Hope you can make it," said Mandy.

"Sure," said Gwen, figuring it wasn't something she could really get away with missing. "I'll be there."

"Goodie. There's always a killer BBQ, and Dr. Messenger gets out his finest wines. There's a fleet of cars made available, so no one needs to fret about drinking and driving."

Should be interesting, thought Gwen, a party full of tanked-up colleagues.

The day rolled on; Gwen did her job, drove home to her own world. Her deck light—she'd attached a timer to it the past weekend—glowed out into the night.

It didn't shake the paranoia. She still had a sense of being followed: her back tingled, she felt that animal awareness—a few times as she took a lunchtime run, one time as she drove home—then she quickly told herself not to be so ridiculous. Peru was a long way away, a long time ago, and, if anyone were following her, then it was Charles Freidland. He'd already admitted as much.

She got to Friday afternoon without incident. As planned, she ducked out early.

"Where're you off then?" asked Mandy, tailing her as she walked to the exit.

"I'm meeting an old buddy who heads up the ARk Storm Project."

"Are you now?" asked Mandy, freezing in place, hand planted on Gwen's arm.

"Dr. Messenger asked me to, so like a good little girl I am doing his bidding."

Mandy cackled. "I'd say it's been many years since you were a good little girl, if ever. Look, do tell all when you get back. I am just dying to hear if we're all gonna be swept away in our beds at night."

"Count on it," replied Gwen, swiping her pass and pushing her way out through the heavy glass door, resolving to tell Mandy with her Cheshire Cat curiosity and love of gossip as little as possible.

25

STANFORD UNIVERSITY, FRIDAY AFTERNOON

Ninety minutes later, Gwen walked the cool halls of Stanford University, her alma mater. She felt like she was coming home, to the familiar, the safe. She headed toward the lecture theater, her heels clicking out a tattoo on the stone floors.

She saw her friend at once, deep in conversation with a tall, well-built, tousle-haired man in chinos and a loose blue shirt. Even from behind, he looked vaguely familiar. She walked closer.

"I am really sorry, Dr. Riley," the man was saying in a low, beguiling voice. "I've just got a few more questions. My misguided editor sent me to do a piece about a local pol, can't keep it trousered. Was doing a mea culpa press con and I had to be there. Shot out of it, but hit Friday traffic. Reckon I missed the first fifteen minutes."

Gwen spied Riley giving the speaker a dazzling smile.

"Think no more of it. I have time. Got a former colleague swinging by, but she can listen in. It's her field, so she might get bored, but what the hell. Hey, speak of the devil! Boudy, Your Blondness!"

Gwen grabbed her friend, stepped into a hug. Over Riley's shoulder, she saw Daniel Jacobsen grinning at her.

Gwen released her friend.

"How are you, Riley?"

"I'm good. I'm excellent. Was just explaining to my new friend here that—" Riley paused, eyed them both.

"You two know each other?"

"Barely," replied Gwen.

"Yet," replied Daniel, "something I would like to rectify. Looks like fate's given me a helping hand."

Riley laughed. "Too bad for me. Come into my office, kiddos. I'll play mama."

As they walked along the hallway, a short, wiry man came barreling round a corner, head jutting forward pugnaciously. Faced with the trio of Gwen, Dan, and Riley walking three abreast, he came to a halt with an audible exhalation.

Dan stood back to let him pass.

"Nice to see someone has manners," the man declared, aiming for humor, missing it. Deliberately, thought Gwen.

"Who's that?" she asked as the man stalked out of earshot.

"Jon Hendrix. My new co-head of Hazards," replied Riley, spitting out the words. "As of two months ago. Can you believe it?"

"Why?" asked Gwen, turning and frowning at the retreating man.

"Why indeed? They say I run on a short fuse, but that guy, Hendrix, has a temper like an angry rattler."

They reached Riley's office. She gestured to them to sit, closed the door behind them. "Two minds are better than one is the official line."

Dan guffawed. "Two minds equal paralysis and constant conflict. There can only ever be one leader."

"My thoughts exactly!" declared Riley, beaming at Dan. "The politicos put Hendrix in to *balance* me," she added with some bitterness.

She spun round to her windowsill where a coffee percolator hissed softly. She turned back.

"Coffee?" she asked brightly.

They nodded. Riley poured, sat herself at her desk, smiled across at Gwen.

"So, Mr. Journalist here has some more questions about ARk Storm. Mind listening in, Boudy? It'll be a tad basic for the likes of you."

Gwen shrugged. "Sure. I got time." So he was a journalist. Didn't look like her idea of one.

"Basic?" asked Dan.

"Boudy here is a hotshot Doctor of Meteorology. With a rocking invention to her name."

"Is she now? I'm impressed."

"I can see that," replied Riley tartly. "So, what can I tell you about ARk Storm?"

"Assume I am an ignoramus. I find that always works best," replied Dan.

Gwen gave a smirk despite herself. The guy was funny.

He placed a small black box on the table. "OK with you if I record this?" he asked.

"Sure," replied Riley. "You doing an article for the *San Francisco Reporter,* or is this general background?"

"MackStack, my editor, has tasked me with keeping up-to-date on ARk Storm. He wants me to write articles every so often, today being the intro, future ones if the situation warrants."

"Fair enough," agreed Riley. "I want this info disseminated. It could help save lives."

Daniel nodded, hit a switch on his recorder, glanced at Gwen, sat back and listened.

Riley took a slug of coffee and pushed to her feet. "So, ARk Storm 1000. A for Atmospheric, R for River, K 'cause if it hits we are all gonna need our arks. One thousand because that is the scale we're marking the biggie at. All other Atmospheric River Storms are graded down from that."

"Let's start with talking me through an Atmospheric River," said Daniel. "Is it what it says on the label?"

"Yes and no," replied Riley, beginning to pace. "Imagine going for a walk out there," said Riley, gesticulating at the window. "Take a look up at the sky. It might be a clear day but up in the atmosphere there could be a giant ribbon of moisture, hundreds of miles wide, transporting more water than the Amazon River. Atmospheric rivers play a key role in the global water supply. We'd be even more of a desert here without them and the skiers can thank them when we get massive dumps in the Sierras."

"They sound kinda friendly," observed Dan.

"They can be," declared Riley, pausing, locking on to Dan, her eyes intense. "But they can also be murderous. That's where ARk Storm 1000 comes in. It is basically a scenario put together at the behest of the US Government's Hazards Unit. That's me and my team." Riley scowled. "And Hendrix. It is not a prediction. It's a what-if, but like lots of what-ifs, it could happen." She looked away, resumed pacing. "So we ran a model, patterned it on the mega storms that rocked California in 1861–62 for forty-five consecutive days, and turned the Sacramento and San Joaquin valleys—a region around three and a half million acres incidentally—into a lake! The storms wiped out nearly a third of the taxable land in California, leaving the state bankrupt."

"Holy shit," exclaimed Daniel.

"Quite," replied Riley.

"So we took data from the storms here in '69 and '86, stuck them back-to-back, and came up with the ARk Storm 1000 scenario." Riley took a glug of coffee, set down her cup atop a precarious-looking heap of papers. "Let's start with the Pineapple Express," she declared, smiling with a teacher's pleasure at a keen student. "It's basically an atmospheric river that kicks off around the equator near Peru and Ecuador. This atmospheric river then flows north like a fire hose. On the way, it embeds itself into much broader atmospheric storms we call 'extratropical cyclones,' or ETs. They are the wintertime analogue to hurricanes, but have a different structure. Hurricanes get their feed from ocean surface heat, but ETs gain their energy largely from pole-to-equator temperature contrast. ARs are the business end of ETs. So they come rocketing up the Pacific, slam into the west coast like a hurricane." Riley semaphored the storm with her hands, making flowing and slamming motions.

"Just imagine fifty Mississippis racing through the air and you get the picture. And when they hit the mountain, they dump their load. We're talking so much rain it looks like walls of water falling through the air. We're talking rain falling in feet instead of inches. This could last more than a month. The storm system just sits there off the coast and the 'storm door' doesn't close. There'd be major landslides across the state, one point five million people would need to be evacced out, nine million homes flooded out, damage around one trillion dollars." Riley gave an ironic smile. "Welcome to ARk Storm."

"Yeah, well, I might just hand in my notice and move to the Rockies," said Daniel.

"And miss the biggest weather event for two hundred years or more?" Gwen asked him.

"Some things are meant to be missed, like wrestling with crocs or riding forty-foot waves." He gave Gwen a knowing look.

"You saw the YouTube of our Boudy on Mavericks," mused Riley.

"I watched it and I bowed down in awe."

"Yeah, well, you only live once," said Gwen, twiddling her jade ring.

"And die young, you make a habit of that."

Gwen looked up, met his eyes. "True for too many."

"So, this thing is basically a hurricane of water hitting the West Coast; I get that. But where's the history, besides 1861–1862? I thought the West Coast got to avoid the wilder weather."

"What do you mean?" asked Riley.

"Well, first off, there's never been a hurricane hit the West Coast," observed Daniel.

Riley arched an eyebrow. "Get Boudy here to take you home. Give you a bit of historical perspective."

Dan's eyes widened. "Yeah, I'd really like that, but I can't see how that is connected with a hurricane; well, I could but that might earn me a slap."

Gwen laughed. "It's where I live that's relevant. On Hurricane Point. The Esselen Indians named it that, way back. So Riley and I reckon they knew something we don't. There *have* been hurricanes that hit this coast, just not in living memory of whitey."

"OK, I can buy that. I'd like to see it sometime, Hurricane Point."

"Free country," shrugged Gwen. She turned back to Riley.

"So what d'you reckon? Is this thing gonna hit anytime soon?"

"That's the big question isn't it? Which comes first? The San Andreas Quake or ARk Storm? Both have about the same probability of hitting. Historically speaking, we can expect one in the next hundred or two hundred years."

Gwen smiled. "And gutturally speaking?"

Riley laughed. She glanced at Dan. "The woman's teasing

me. For a scientist I go a long way on gut hunches. Too far
for some."

"They're mainly right too," added Gwen. "The woman's
a genius."

Riley flushed, batted the compliments away.

"And?" pressed Gwen.

Riley looked from Gwen to Daniel and back again.

"What?" asked Gwen.

"I'm just wondering if I can trust Mr. Golden Eyes here."

Daniel looked at Riley for a beat. A different, serious
light showed in his eyes, as if the bravado and joshing were
a mask. Interesting, thought Gwen.

"You can trust me," Daniel said simply.

Riley eyed him, head to one side. "You know, I think I
can, but you rat me out and the whole of California's scientific community will be closed to you."

"I don't need threats to keep my word," he replied, just
the hint of an edge to his voice.

Gwen filed that away. There was something of the ren-
egade in Daniel Jacobsen, just a feeling she had of a streak
of well-veiled larceny, but there was clearly a keenly felt
sense of honor too. Just like you, said the voice in her head,
only you've hidden the larceny so well you've almost forgotten you have it.

"OK," Riley was saying. "Turn off your recorder. This
is all off the record. What I am about to say does *not* appear in your article. Are we clear on that?"

Daniel held her gaze. "Crystal. None of what you are
about to say will appear in any article I write."

Riley nodded. She turned to the coffee machine.
"Empty. Darn. Come with me, Gwen."

Dan watched them, surprise mingling with relief as they
walked together from the office. He reached down to his
ankle holster, removed the Kevlar knife. He leaned forward, long arms resting on his knees. His fingers ex-

tended under Riley's desk. His knife found a small object, a GSM listening device the size of a matchbox stuck to the underside of the desktop. He worked the knife under it, removed it, folded his fingers round it. Seconds later it was in the pocket of his chinos.

He probed under the desk again, found the remotely activated store-and-forward device. Quickly probing with the knife, he removed that. It was about the size of an iPhone. A legitimate object to have in his pocket. He quickly secreted it there, then pushed to his feet.

When Riley and Gwen came back, he was gazing out of the window, hands in pockets.

Riley was speaking. He turned, looked down at her, stepped from one compartment in his mind into another.

"Just let me brew up," said Riley. She poured a jugful of water into the percolator, set to grinding beans and filling the funnel with economical and well-rehearsed gestures.

Dan nodded, watched her thoughtfully. Only when three new coffees were poured and Riley had inhaled the steam, taken a long sip, closed her eyes for a second of bliss did she speak.

"This is not me speaking as the voice of ARk Storm," she declared. "This is a personal hunch. Also clear?"

Gwen and Daniel both nodded.

Riley dropped her voice, leaned across her desk toward them, eyes bright.

"I think ARk Storm *is* for real. I think that freakin' Pineapple Express is gearing herself up to deliver us a monster. We're not there now. It'll take something extra to kick this one into the catastrophe zone, but hell, we're so close, and weather dynamics are so volatile. My colleagues think we're in the clear. Hendrix, damn the man to hell, thinks I have target fixation. I disagree. I've been looking at weather patterns worldwide. I have a real bad feeling."

"What'll it take to kick it there?" asked Gwen, thinking of the story told by the sensors in Peru.

"Could be any little thing. Chaos theory. Butterfly flaps her wings and empires fall."

26

HURRICANE POINT

Each shaking off a feeling of oppression, Daniel and Gwen walked into the sunshine.

"She's pretty intense, your friend Dr. Riley," Dan observed.

Gwen squinted, pulled on a battered pair of Aviators. "Often the way with brilliant scientists."

"OCD?"

Gwen frowned.

"Obsessive Compulsive Disorder?"

"I hate labels," said Gwen.

"But something's there," probed Dan. "And I would bet she's somewhere on the bipolar spectrum too. She was an inch short of manic today."

Gwen looked levelly at Dan. "You a psychiatrist?"

"Nope. Just an observer of human nature." He said it with slight self-parody, but Gwen could sense it was the truth. There was a deep shrewdness in his eyes.

"You'd have to ask her," she murmured.

"A loyal friend. I like that." Dan gave her a crooked smile. "So, you gonna show me Hurricane Point?"

"What, you need your hand held?"

"You offering?"

Gwen laughed. "How'd you get here?"

He nodded to his car.

"The Batmobile?"

"Yeah, I like fast cars, and I like 'em black. So shoot me."

"The thought occurs. It's a long drive."

Dan shrugged. "And?"

Gwen paused. She had nothing planned. She could show the guy the Point, send him on his way. What would be the harm?

"OK. Wanna follow me?" she asked.

"With pleasure."

A short two hours later, finally freed from Friday afternoon traffic, they stood fifty feet above the Pacific, listening to it roar. The scent of wet herbs wafted up on the air so strong you could taste it.

"Hurricane Point. Nice." Daniel turned to look at Gwen, standing just feet from him.

"More than nice. It's home, and I love it."

"I can see why. Let's just hope it doesn't live up to its name."

"Let's hope," agreed Gwen, suppressing a shudder. "You ever been in a hurricane?"

"Used to live in Florida, hurricane central. I remember when Hurricane Andrew was heading for us. All these hurricane warnings came: *get out, get out.* My parents figured it wasn't going to be so bad, reckoned we'd all stay put, and the warning guy said, *fine, just get a pen with indelible ink, and write your name and social security number on your forearm. And your kids' forearms. Then we can identify their bodies when the storm's done.* We got out. But I tell you, when we came back after the storm, saw what it had done . . ." Daniel shook his head. "Like a war zone."

"Did you rebuild?"

Daniel shook his head. "My Ma'd had enough. Broke her heart. She couldn't face that again. We went to Denmark."

"As in Europe?"

"Yeah."

"Why?"

"No hurricanes."

Gwen laughed.

"My father is Danish," he continued. "My middle name is Soren."

"Ah, OK. Makes sense. But where'd you get the tan from, and those eyes?"

"My ma's got Spanish blood in her."

"Not a bad combo."

"Easy, Boudy. That almost sounded like a compliment."

"Unintentional."

Daniel eyed her, openly speculating. "Surf's up, Boudy. Got a spare board?"

"You want to surf with me?"

"I'll start with that."

Gwen eyed the waves. She needed to surf, could do with the distraction. Again she asked herself, what could be the harm?

"Maybe we can catch a few waves. But cut out the Boudy-this and the Boudy-that. Only my old friends call me Boudy."

He smiled. "What do your lovers call you?"

Gwen gave him a dazzling smile right back. "I leave them speechless."

"I can believe that."

Gwen had to admit, he surfed with a certain style and bravado. He whooped with joy when he caught a good wave, or when she did. His joy was contagious and soon Gwen found herself forgetting Freidland and his son, and Messenger, and all her suspicions and her fears, and just living in the moment.

She laughed out loud, turning three-sixties, pulling

stunts, rewarded by handclaps and whoops and more of
the same from him, many of which ended in a pile of
spume and human limbs, from which he would invariably
emerge with a smile. Gwen hadn't had so much fun in
months. He was the dream surf partner. Technically strong
and watchful, not greedy with his waves. Every inch the
gentleman, damn him. It was much easier being angry
with him.

Reluctantly, they left the sea as the sun began to dip.
Reality began to intrude. Gwen wanted to keep it at bay
just a while longer.

She smiled up at him as they carried the boards back to
her house. They peeled off their wetsuits. Gwen almost
gasped as she saw a vicious scar that cut down Daniel's
ribs.

"Where's that from?" she asked.

"Long story," he answered. "Got a hose?"

Gwen recognized a subject change when she heard one.

"Over there."

Together they hosed down the boards then stacked them.
Daniel grabbed the hose and turned it on himself. He stood
there, eyes closed, utterly unself-conscious as the water
cascaded down his tan body. God, scar or no scar, he was
beautiful, thought Gwen. He *was* ripped, with the long,
muscled body of the best surfers. Muscles that didn't just
look pretty in the gym but could generate real power. For
a fugitive moment, Gwen just watched. Then she headed
in to her house, brought out a towel for him.

"I do have a shower inside," she said, handing him the
towel.

"This is just fine," he said, vigorously rubbing his
hair.

"I don't know about you," said Gwen, not giving herself time to wonder if this were wise, "but I am starving.

If I snagged a coupla pizzas from the freezer, would you like one?"

"I would fall down on my knees."

They put away two pepperoni and cheese, washed down with two Coors, talking easily, laughing. Leo, Gwen observed, was a quick convert to Dan. He planted himself at Dan's feet and gazed up adoringly until he got a ferocious back rub.

Gwen sat back, relaxed. She would forget, then every so often, she would remember.

"What's on your mind, Boudy?"

She sighed. "Is it that obvious?"

"It comes and goes, likes clouds across the sun."

"You're a romantic, Dan."

"I know trouble when I see it. Am I wrong?"

She shook her head. "No. You're right. I just can't talk about it."

"If you need to, I can listen well enough."

Gwen smiled. "Thanks, I reckon you can."

Daniel got to his feet, cleared the dishes, washed them and stacked them in the drainer.

"I'd best be going," he said.

Gwen nodded. "I think that's wise."

"Maybe this isn't." He pulled her in, eye to eye, bent his lips to hers, kissed her slowly at first, and as she responded, faster and deeper. Their bodies pressed together and Gwen could feel his muscles hard against hers.

To her intense frustration, he was the first to pull away.

"Hell of an afternoon and evening, Boudy."

She nodded, catching her breath.

"I do believe I have left you speechless!"

"With outrage! Not awe."

"Felt like it," he said, with his infuriatingly cocky grin.

He grabbed his keys off the table, and with a jaunty wave, he was gone.

Long after she'd heard his car fade away into the night, Gwen stood on the deck, her dog standing sentry at her side. The cool air was moist against her skin, raising goose bumps. The moon shone palely above her, haloed by a shimmering meniscus. She gazed out over the mass of the ocean, wondering what was there, what was coming her way. An ARk Storm? A murderous boss? The long arm of the Peruvians. Paparuda? Whatever the hell that was. . . . She had the feeling she sometimes got in the barrel, when her exit was closing.

27

HURRICANE POINT,
FRIDAY NIGHT/SATURDAY MORNING

Gwen slept badly, haunted by images of Messenger's Ferrari closing on the cyclist, striking the killer blow, then speeding off into the night. She pushed herself from bed, blowing out breaths of panic. She was going to have to do something; she just had no idea what. Run then think, she decided.

She was just lacing up her trainers outside on her deck when a throaty roar had her jogging round to the front of her house. She stood, hands on hips, as Daniel Jacobsen emerged from his Cougar.

He was carrying a bag from Bruno's Deli. She could smell the croissants. He lifted up two coffees in a carry tray and smiled.

Gwen dropped her hands from her hips. It was impossible to be annoyed with this man. And that should have also annoyed the hell out of her.

"I come bearing breakfast. It's Saturday morning. Don't tell me you have to be somewhere."

She smiled back. "Not for a while. But you'll have to run with me first. Pain, then pleasure." A lie, she thought; she loved to run. From the look of his body, he did too.

"Have to be barefoot for me," he said, indicating his flip-flops.

"We could swim. Sea's calm."

"I have no trunks."

Gwen grinned. "My cottage was built by naturists. You'll thrill their ghosts."

"Yeah, and hopefully not the sharks."

"I'm sure you'll just stun them."

"Swim it is, then. You're going to thrill the ghosts too?"

"Tempting, but no."

The water was cold enough to give her a blood rush. It would have been bliss to swim without a swimsuit, thought Gwen, to feel the cold, salty water sluice over her.

"What the hell." She wriggled, pulled off her suit, balled it up, and hurled it up onto the sand. She grinned at Daniel. "Even."

She struck off at a fast front crawl. Daniel matched her stroke for stroke. She wondered how long he could keep up the pace. She glanced at her watch. They swam out beyond the gentle swell, a safe distance from the cliffs. Gwen found her rhythm, gliding through the water, falling into an almost mesmeric state. After half an hour, she turned around. Daniel turned with her, swam alongside, even when she upped her pace for the last quarter mile.

Time to get out of the water. She was too cold and too hungry to be coy. She strode from the waves. Daniel emerged with her. Neither of them said anything. Gwen felt an almost magnetic yearning to turn to him, somehow managed to stop herself. They grabbed their towels. Gwen secured hers round her body, was peripherally aware that Daniel did the same, waist down. She turned to him. Saw the same look in his eyes she felt in hers.

"Er, well, I think we've earned our breakfast," murmured Gwen.

Daniel just smiled.

"You going to tell me about that scar?" asked Gwen as they jogged up the hill to get warm.

"If you tell me what's been bothering you."

"You won't be able to help," said Gwen. She glanced across at him. "I don't mean that in an offensive way. It's just . . ." She shrugged.

"I didn't take offense. Like I said to Riley, I can keep my mouth shut."

"I'll keep it in mind."

They took turns in the shower, Dan insisting Gwen go first. When she was done, Gwen heated the coffee in her microwave, laid out plates, squeezed some oranges. Dan emerged from the shower and walked up to Gwen, smiling at her, smelling of soap. And of man. Gwen swiveled, grabbed a tray, thrust it at him, a necessary barrier.

Together they carried breakfast out onto the table on the deck.

Gwen sipped her coffee. "So, Daniel, the scar . . ."

"Do you really want to know?"

"I do."

He nodded, looked out across the huge blue sea. "Before I became a journalist, I was in the military. I joined up the minute I graduated Harvard. It was 2005. Nine-eleven had a big impact on me. I lost my uncle. Fuck of a way to die. It wasn't about revenge, joining up—well, maybe a bit, at first. It was more a feeling that enough words had been spoken. *I wanted to do something.* I had skills they could use. They did use them, but I wanted to see the front line too, go where the rest of the platoon went. Iraq and Afghanistan. Wrong place, one day. Big IED. Shrapnel everywhere. Scar." He turned back to Gwen.

"Is that why you left?"

"My best buddy died. I was inches from him. I'd done three tours. Reckoned it was time to quit while I was still walking unaided."

She wanted to say *wow,* she wanted to kiss his lips. Her cell phone rang. Lucy. Shit, she'd almost forgotten.

"Boudy, running late," breathed her friend. "Can we meet at twelve instead of eleven thirty?"

"Hi Luce, no prob." She clicked off the call, turned back to Dan.

"I have to go out."

He got to his feet, walked round to her, drew her up and in. His kiss was pure temptation. They both broke away.

"See you round, Boudy." He picked up her shopping list, scrawled down a number. "In case you want a swim buddy again."

Gwen watched him go. She could pretend she didn't want him, knew it was one battle she was going to lose.

28

A SUPER-YACHT, MOORED OFF SAN DIEGO,
SUNDAY AFTERNOON

Sheikh Ali Al Baharna sat in his stateroom aboard his two-hundred-and-eighty-foot yacht, *Zephyr,* currently moored off San Diego. The yacht was all sleek modernism, but the Sheikh could have stepped forward from any of the past fourteen centuries. Part of it was the *juhayman,* the facial attitude of his Bedu forbears, one of harshness, of disapproval. In company, he had to remind himself to wear his Western mask. Part of it was his clothing: he wore the traditional flowing white *kandoora*, and the *ghutra*, the white headdress, secured with a black *akal*. Part of it was the timeless scent that clung to him, the oil-based *oud* of his perfume, narcotic almost. It mixed with the spicy scent of the *bakhoor* frankincense which glowed in a *mabkhara* burner in the middle of the room.

The detritus of a game of backgammon lay before him and his guest. He took a sip of cardamom-flavored coffee served in a small golden cup. He was an elegant man. His moves were graceful as he waggled his hand, signifying to the uniformed waiter who hovered with the ornate golden Arabic coffeepot that he wanted no more. Three cups a day. Never more.

He laid down his cup on a mahogany side table and lounged back on the sofa. His unusually tall body was lean, the result of self-deprivation and a punishing exercise routine. He looked more like his Bedu forebears than did many of the modern Arab merchant princes, whose bodies, genetically long inured to a minimal diet in the deserts, had grown fat with the plenty brought by oil. Those close to him knew the asceticism wasn't born of vanity, but of *al-jihad al-akbar*, the greater jihad, the internal jihad sanctioned by the Koran. He waged his own internal war against the temptations of the flesh.

This was a war of many battles, and during his young manhood, when he had studied Politics, Philosophy, and Economics at Oxford University, he had lost those battles. He had drunk alcohol with women who were free and with women for whom he paid. He had taken drugs. He had forsworn his five-times-daily prayers. He had been the despair of his father, who feared Allah and the wrath of the ruling Al Saud family perhaps in equal measure. With good reason.

Sheikh Ali and his father were Shia Muslims, from the Eastern Province of Saudi Arabia, where the country's huge oil wealth gushed from the ground. His father had built the family fortune from modest means. He had been a driver for Aramco, the state oil company, and had quickly seen the opportunities for supplying the burgeoning oil industry. The ruling Al Sauds were keen to throw a few carrots to the Shia, who, despite being in the majority in the Eastern Province, were in the minority in Saudi as a whole and were routinely discriminated against by the Sunnis. So the Al Saud, ever pragmatic, keen to stabilize the Eastern Province, had granted the substantial trading concessions which allowed Sheikh Ali's father not just to prosper, but to build over his lifetime an empire. On his death, his eldest son, Ali, had taken over his mantle and, with shrewd investments and some spectacular insider trading, had magnified the fortune.

He had also come back to the ways of Allah. Three things had wrought this: the first was the Iraqi invasion of Kuwait and with it the arrival of half a million infidel Crusader American troops in the Holy Kingdom of Saudi Arabia; the second was the realization that the Al Saud were, despite their prodigious wealth, never going either to defend the purity of the Kingdom and Islam, or enfranchise the Shia in the Eastern Province. The third thing was meeting the radical preacher, Sheikh Haider Al Jibrin, in San Diego, when Ali al Baharna went there to do his Masters in Economics.

And so merciful Allah had brought him back to the holy life that was real life. For many years now he had been following his path, still waging jihad, internal jihad, he was keen to remind his friends and acolytes. Only the chosen few knew the true extent of his wider jihad.

His eyes might have suggested it. They had a distant focus that seemed to see paradise, and they shone with an unflinching certainty that his was the way, his was the right and the just path, no matter how many innocents were slaughtered along the way.

His own private library might have revealed some of his philosophy—it was a history of armed struggles from the War of American Independence to the Partition and the emergence of Pakistan as a separate nation. History was littered by precedents, by terrorists and freedom fighters becoming legitimate. He liked the quote that *treason doth never prosper, what's the reason? For if it prosper none dare call it treason.* The same would be true of jihad. Once the Holy War had been won, the warriors would be hailed and sanctified as the legitimate government.

And thanks to the only vice he could not conquer, his desire to make money and more money still, though he had more than he could ever spend in a hundred lifetimes, he could prosecute that Holy War, arm the warriors. To cover his tracks, he was careful never to meet with the Jihadis in public. He had no need to. His money met them and spoke for him. And if the price of waging jihad was consorting with infidels, it was a price worth paying. They were tools. To be used and eliminated if and when necessary. So he drank his coffee and he smiled his smile.

"What news on Project Zeus?" he asked, a faint rolling of his "r" giving his otherwise Oxford-honed English an exotic lilt.

"We're testing it," answered his guest with just a flicker of caution. Sheikh Ali, despite his approval, both explicit and implicit, always made him feel uncharacteristically hesitant, as if every question might be a trap.

"And?"

"We are perfecting it."

"What you are trying to say is that it is not perfect yet. That you are not ready to push the button, as it were, yet."

Hesitation. The trap. Truth the only way out. "Correct."

"So what's delaying you?"

A sudden and most unfortunate death, thought the man. He said, levelly: "I feel Zeus isn't giving us all it could. It's done well, but I think it could do so much more."

"So rectify it."

"I'm planning on that. I'm planning on drafting in our new recruit to assist."

"Which new recruit?"

"A woman. A specialist in weather prediction. In storm prediction. She says that a Niño is coming, and with it might come a superstorm."

Sheikh Ali's eyes widened with interest. He leaned forward, popped a date into his mouth, chewed reflectively.

"An oracle."

The man laughed. "You're psychic! That's the name of her model."

Sheikh Ali waived off the compliment with a sweep of his arm. You didn't need to be psychic when you had informants.

"Can we trust her?" he asked, the veneer of charm falling from his eyes, revealing a flash of what the other man knew to be there, just preferred not to see.

"Sure we can. She's what it says on the label. Academic, loves surfing. Dead parents, killed in car crash in Peru. And it's her subject. She's a resource we'd be foolish not to use."

"Fine. You trust her, so let's use her. Let's speed this thing up. I'm keen to get a return on my investment."

The Sheikh waited until his guest had departed. He waited until he heard the roar of the helicopter blades, until the sound had dissipated over the limpid ocean. Then he moved from the stateroom into the privacy of the office that adjoined his bedroom. There, looking like the modern businessman he was, he made a call. Unlike many but not all modern businessmen, he used a cell phone with hardware and software encryption. He was sophisticated, he took no chances.

He used a Telsey encrypter, a Spanish system known to have no back door or remote access. The system used a rolling code algorithm, which made it very difficult to intercept. But not impossible. Certain top level decryptors used by various agencies in the US could on occasion break it, although breaking it once on a single conversation did not mean that they could break it again. Much depended on luck.

But the Sheikh believed it was secure. He did not tolerate mistakes. In himself. In others. The Telsey was his favored encrypter of the many he owned, protecting his conversation, he believed.

He dialed The Man's encrypted phone, established the two-way encryption, then began to speak.

"The pretty meteorologist," he murmured, "is about to be inducted into the inner sanctum. She may be trustworthy, she may not be. Power corrupts, but so do secrets. I want an insurance policy taken out on her, to ensure she knows when to stay silent, to ensure she plays by the rules. Find out who she cares about. Her parents are dead, but there must be someone she loves. Identify them in case we need to use them for purposes of encouragement."

"Full Pattern of Life study?"

"You're the security expert. Do what is necessary."

The Man smiled his dazzling smile. He would enjoy this. "I'll need four of your men; I'll add in one or two women I use occasionally, for blending-in purposes. I'll put together a full surveillance team, establish her exact routine, lifestyle, connections. I'll run it for three weeks, give or take."

"My men are yours. For as long as you need them. I have plenty well trained up onboard. We cannot afford any more mistakes. Another body might attract undue attention, might deflect us from the path."

"Don't worry. No one's found the other body. We're clean."

No, thought Sheikh Ali, neither he nor the infidel circumstances forced him to use, would ever be clean. No amount of blood could ever wash away the old sins. Expiation was all he could hope for. A partial balancing of the scales.

29

EARLY TO MID FALL

In the Northern Hemisphere, the leaves had turned. They decorated the trees with their glorious array of red and russet and bronze and gold. From San Francisco to Hurricane Point and beyond, occasional mists drifted in on the morning air, hugging the contours of the parched land, which sucked up the moisture, dampening the golden soil to a dark terra-cotta. The air temperatures, usually at their warmest in September and October, were beginning to dip, but the sea temperatures lagged behind, holding onto the last heat of summer, only slowly, reluctantly giving it up.

The NOAA predicted it would be a bumper year for hurricanes. They advised residents of the US Hurricane Belt to lay in supplies: plywood to board over their windows, bottled water and canned goods, and to confer with vulnerable neighbors, ensuring they too had supplies.

In the Southern Hemisphere, the sea temperatures rose, slavishly following the air, absorbing the heat that pounded from the equatorial sun. The incipient Niño sucked in its fuel. The sea levels dropped in the west, rose in the east. Warm surface water surged eastward along the equator. The growing Niño prepared to go supercharged. The children on the Pacific coast of South America felt it first, as always, playing in the warming water, but it wouldn't be long before the whole world would feel it too. Then it would bring not innocent pleasure, but devastation. High in the air, two and a half kilometers up, flowed the atmospheric rivers. The Pineapple Express, racing up from Hawaii, began to fatten as water evaporated from the warming ocean. Like a fire hose, the water raced north, toward California.

And the humans, even those living below the fire hoses, remained largely oblivious to the movements of the fates above them. They skirted round one another, some resisting falling in love, some hurtling into it, some just luxuriating in lust; they plotted fifty new ways to enrich themselves; they plotted wars; they plotted murder and the silencing of threats, and they plotted jihad and ancient revenge for the centuries-old sins of the Crusaders. They all played on, getting nearer every day to the intersection point, some aware, some unaware, none wholly conscious of what they would unleash, and where it would leave them.

30

THE LAB, MONDAY MORNING

Gwen flicked through the paper. She paused as she recognized the byline. Curious, she leaned back, sipped her coffee, and read.

THE SAN FRANCISCO REPORTER
A Different Kind of Shake Out?
BY DAN JACOBSEN

Would you rather die under tons of falling rubble or be washed to your death by a ten-foot wall of water? Not a question any one of us wishes to entertain, yet here in California you are about as likely to be hit by an ARk Storm as by the "shakeout quake." Yet few of us have ever heard of an ARk Storm. It is the big quake that is the stuff of our nightmares, but now we have a new nightmare scenario lurking on the horizon.

What is an ARk Storm?

An ARk Storm is a kind of supercharged West Coast Winter Storm caused by Atmospheric Rivers dumping huge rainfall as they make landfall. Every winter season several ARk Storms make landfall and dump heavy rains. *The* ARk Storm 1000 is the big one that threatens to hit every one to two hundred years or so.

A team of 117 scientists, engineers, public policy and insurance experts under the umbrella of The Multi-Hazards Demonstration Project have worked for two years to create the hypothetical scenario of what such a storm could be, and what damage it would wreak across the State of California.

ARk Storms take their name from what's known by researchers as "Atmospheric Rivers," a term coined as a result of last-generation satellite imagery that shows these bands of moisture flowing several kilometers above the earth. ARs are giant ribbons of moist air, at least 2000 kilometers long and several hundred kilometers wide. They flow in the lower troposphere, normally about ten kilometers up, where winds with speeds in excess of 12.5 meters per second can carry as much water as the Amazon River.

Most people looking up on a clear day would never think that just a few miles above their heads a huge river of moisture hundreds of miles wide could be coursing through the atmosphere.

In an ARk Storm 1000 scenario, this river, described by the head of the ARk Storm Unit as "like Forty Mississippis," races from the tropics toward the west coast of the US, then hits, and keeps on hitting. The Storm Door opens and fails to close. The rains start and a biblical scenario plays out.

The ARk Storm 1000 would be predicted to come ashore at 125 mph in Los Angeles County. This is a storm so intense it has been described as "like Hurricane Katrina pushed through a keyhole." It would cause widespread flooding in the Sacramento-San Joaquin Delta. Fifty levees could be breached. Some one and a half million residents in inland and delta regions would be forced to evacuate. The model estimates that up to one quarter of all homes in California would have flood damage to the tune of 400 billion dollars. Because the flood depths in some areas could realistically be of the order of ten to twenty feet, without effective evacuation of up to one and half million people there could be substantial loss of life. High winds would cause further damage of around five billion dollars. Huge waves would damage coastal property. Landslides would be extensive, causing around one billion dollars worth of damage. The overall cost, adding in economic disruption to the State of California, is estimated to be in the region of one trillion dollars. That is four times as much as the shakeout earthquake. And only around 12 percent of California property is insured.

Has such a storm happened before?
Major ARk Storms have hit California on a regular basis. The last huge one was in 1861–62 when it rained continuously for forty-five consecutive days. Witnesses describe a "flying river" washing away livestock and

humans. That storm caused flooding of biblical proportions, turning the Sacramento and San Joaquin valleys—a region around three and a half million acres, incidentally—into a lake. That storm bankrupted the state. And it gets worse. . . . The geological record shows six megastorms more severe than 1861–62 hit in California in the last 1,800 years. There is no reason to believe such events will not recur.

What caused the 1861–62 ARk Storm?

The atmospheric mechanisms behind the storms of 1861–62 are unknown; however, the storms were likely the result of an intense atmospheric river, or a series of atmospheric rivers, striking the US West Coast. With the right preconditions, just one intense atmospheric river hitting the Sierra Nevada mountain range east of Sacramento could bring devastation to California.

Can we predict an ARk Storm?

The Hazards team's answer is: "*to some extent.*" Unlike for earthquakes, forecasters have the capability to partially predict key aspects of the geophysical phenomena that would create changes in the days before an ARk Storm struck. They concede though that "enhancing the accuracy, lead time, and the particular measures that these systems can estimate is a great challenge scientifically and practically."

So what can we do to prepare?

The whole ARk Storm Project has been undertaken to enable the State of California to prepare an emergency response plan. We can only hope that it gives us notice.

When might it hit?

The most senior scientist for the Hazards Project notes the coincidence that California's last big ARk Storm occurred in 1861–62, very close to the last big Southern San Andreas big earthquake in 1857. It appears that both events occur with a frequency of about two hundred years. Which begs the question: Which one will go next?

Gwen finished her coffee, folded her paper thoughtfully. Yeah, hell of a way to go, drowning in earth, or drowning in water. Involuntarily, she shuddered.

31

THE LEE OF THE SIERRA NEVADA, CALIFORNIA

Gwen brewed up a second cappuccino from the machine. She spun in her chair and gazed pensively at the clear blue sky. She wheeled round as approaching footsteps rapped out. Gabriel Messenger strode into her office with the Monday morning enthusiasm of the workaholic. Gwen took a bolstering slug of cappuccino.

"Dr. Messenger. Good weekend?"

"Won a tennis tournament at Pebble Beach, so yes, I did. Get your bag."

"Why?"

"We're going on a trip."

"Where to? And, forgive me being repetitive, but why?"

Messenger handed her a sheet of paper.

"You want me to read the *weather* forecast?" asked Gwen.

Messenger nodded.

"Sun. Zero chance of rain. Light breeze. Are we going on a picnic?" Gwen asked as Peter Weiss joined them with a nod and a smile.

"You ask a lot of questions, Dr. Gwen."

"I'm a querulous academic."

A helicopter flew in. Gwen, Messenger, and Weiss scurried under the blades, hopped in. Gwen gazed out, curiosity bubbling. No one spoke, so she just sat back and enjoyed the ride.

Soon they were flying over the rolling brown and green hills of the Diablo Range. Weiss ignored the scenery. He spent the entire trip busily tapping away on his laptop. Gwen had never seen him this intense. She tried to angle a look at the screen to see what he was up to, but he seemed to be shielding his laptop so she saw nothing save a haze of light.

They flew over what Gwen reckoned was Fresno, then approached the Sierra Nevada. Gwen was surprised to see a large, dense gray, mid-level altocumulus hovering over the valley in the lee of the mountains. Where had that come from? she wondered, thinking of the zero chance of rain forecast.

They landed beneath the cloud on a large, scrubby plain. Led by Messenger, they hiked a few hundred meters away from the helicopter. Gwen suddenly had a mad fear that she was being walked to some isolated spot where she would be shot. Al Freidland's ghost, she thought, hovered over her. She began to sweat lightly.

"Hot isn't it, under all this sun," remarked Weiss, smiling up at Gwen. "Could do with some clouds. Whoa, look, there is one, right above!"

Gwen felt her unease deepen. Weiss and Messenger were grinning at what was evidently a private joke.

A low, droning sound made her look up.

"There they are!" said Weiss, rubbing his hands together, looking suddenly like an excited schoolboy. All three of them craned their necks, looked up.

Gwen spotted two small airplanes, which seemed to be orbiting at opposite ends of a huge loop above them, not just going round and round on one altitude, but going higher and lower through the cloud, appearing and disappearing, the sun glinting on their wings.

"What the heck are those planes doing?" asked Gwen.

"Drones," replied Messenger. "Unmanned Aerial Vehicles."

"Drones as in the things they send in to bomb the bad guys in Afghanistan and Pakistan?" asked Gwen.

"Exactly, just smaller, less expensive, and they're not carrying bombs."

"So what are they doing?" asked Gwen. "Hey," she wiped her face. "It's raining!"

Messenger and Weiss both let out whoops. Weiss started dancing, stamping round in a circle, bending down then straightening, raising his hands to the sky, fluttering his fingers. Gwen wondered if he were manic-depressive. She'd felt the depression, now she saw the mania.

Weiss paused, eyed Gwen, exultant.

"Exactly! It's raining. Remember the forecast? Zero percent chance of rain?" he asked, his usually soft voice several decibels louder.

Gwen nodded, wiped her face as the rain began to pelt down.

"Welcome to Project Zeus," said Messenger, gesticulating at the sky.

"This is you guys?" asked Gwen, disbelief warring with the rain sluicing down her face. *"You made it rain?"*

Messenger and Weiss nodded. "We made it rain."

32

Back in Messenger's office, with the door closed, they sat round the table. They were soaked. And exhilarated. Messenger had turned off the air conditioning and opened a window. The balmy air drifted in with a whisper of birdsong and the tang of eucalyptus baking in the sunshine.

Gwen turned to Messenger, who had a seemingly permanent smile fixed to his lips.

"Am I dreaming?" she asked. "Tell me if I just imagined the rain."

"It's true, Gwen," he said, using her name. He never used her name without affixing *Doctor* to it. Gwen recognized a new intimacy, was not immune to it.

"It rained. We made it rain," intoned Messenger, voice low as if imparting the secrets of the confessional. "We can create rain where there is none. And where there is rain, we can make more of it. Or if we choose, less of it."

"You can stop the rain too?" Gwen asked, glancing between Messenger and Weiss. "What are you, shamans?"

Messenger gave her a wry look. "In our own way."

"This is cloud seeding?" asked Gwen.

"Not even close."

Gwen got to her feet. She had too much pent-up energy, too many bubbling questions to sit still. She braced her hands on the table, leaned toward the two men. Her hair fell forward like two heavy curtains. The rain had turned it into tendrils.

"All right. Put me out of my misery. Tell me what this is, how it works!"

Gone was the surfer drawl. Gwen's words tumbled out

as an academic's curiosity combusted with a child's fascination at the magic of the world.

Messenger laid a hand on Peter Weiss's shoulder.

"Weissy, why don't you tell Gwen? You've put in some serious hours on this. Go on."

A strange cocktail of emotions seemed to play across Weiss's face. He looked thrilled, he looked cautious, then there was a glimpse of something far away, as if he were making some kind of hidden reckoning. Finally, he nodded.

"Sure. Happy to," he added, as if none of his conflicts had just played out.

He looked up at Gwen, practically cricking his neck as she towered above him. He stood, gaining a few feet of height and distance, then leaned back on the windowsill, making her wait.

Messenger, still sitting quietly at the table, flicked his gaze between his protégés.

"OK," Weiss declared at last. "You know all about the freshwater pipelines in the sky, how they're fed by the sun's action on the sea . . ."

Gwen nodded.

"Well, each year, the sun desalinates half a million cubic kilometers of water, which becomes atmospheric water vapor and is transported by those pipelines in the sky. What Zeus does is to hook into the earth's electromagnetic field and open the water valves in the pipelines. Our technology replicates the sun's natural ionization of the atmosphere and creates rain clouds."

"How?" asked Gwen.

"Ionizers—basically a machine the size of a microwave cooker. We set them on masts, or, much better, we send them up in drones. That way, we get them right up into the cloud zone, anywhere between a few hundred meters and several kilometers from the ground. Then, from here, based on Zeus's proprietary weather models, we program the ionizers to emit just the right quantity of short-living ions over the appropriate time period and circulation pattern to charge the natural aerosol particles. That's where we do our shamanistic dance, with the computer model," Weiss added, picking up his laptop, cradling it to him like a beloved infant. "All in here. Priceless."

"I'll bet," said Gwen. "Then what?"

"We enhance the growth of ice particles," replied Weiss, gently laying down the laptop on the table. "Then those babies fatten up by merging with water vapor, which then condenses and drops fast enough to turn the ice to rain before it hits the ground." He made pitter-patter motions with his fingers, grinning now. Then he sat back, arms behind his head, a vision of sheer delight.

"In other words, we make clouds, full of rain, ready to drop it just where we want it," concluded Messenger.

Gwen's head spun. "OK. I get the science. Your ionizers attract dust particles, which in turn grab water vapor out of the atmosphere. These particles bond with the water. If you ionize the atmosphere sufficiently, you get rain. This is the stuff of dreams. Too good to be true. There must be a catch."

"Well, you do need the right conditions," conceded Weiss, bringing his arms down, reengaging. "Humidity needs to be thirty percent minimum. You can't do this if there's insufficient water vapor to attract."

"OK. Got that. What kind of area are you talking about?"

"Guess."

"No! I don't wanna guess. This whole thing is crazy. I'll be way out. Just tell me."

Weiss laughed. He was relishing this, Gwen realized, empowered by the secrets he guarded.

"The answer is, we don't know yet, exactly," cut in Messenger. "It's a function, given the necessary thirty percent humidity threshold, of how many drones, how many ionizers, and how much computing and human brainpower we can throw at it."

"We know it's a minimum of several hundred square kilometers," declared Weiss. "We've achieved that with geostatic ionizers on masts. But with drones and mobile ionizers . . . we think it could be tens of thousands of square kilometers, given the resources. Perhaps as many as ninety thousand," he mused, a faraway look in his eyes.

"Holy hell!" exclaimed Gwen.

"Quite," agreed Messenger.

"So, you use the atmospheric humidity generated from the oceans, I get that too. But how far inland can it work?"

"Hundreds of kilometers, maybe three or four hundred," replied Weiss. "Even further inland if the humidity in the atmosphere is more than thirty percent."

"And it rains down."

"Or snows. We can do snow too," said Messenger.

" 'Course you can," said Gwen, shaking her head in amazement. "This thing's a miracle. Think what you could do! This could bring water to drought lands, to starving communities. This is a life changer, a game changer."

"And it's cheap," added Messenger. "One of our sites with twenty-five emitters, costing six hundred and twenty-five thousand dollars, has produced over one hundred million cubic meters of water in the past year. That's the same volume of freshwater as a one-point-two-billion-dollar desalination plant consuming a hundred and twenty million dollars' worth of fossil fuel per year and costing three hundred and twenty-five million dollars a year to operate."

Gwen threw up her hands.

"I'm speechless. This is the stuff of science fiction."

Messenger smiled. "People said that about planes, cell phones, the Internet."

Gwen shook her head. "No, this is bigger than that. This is like being God." And Weiss was the Gatekeeper, thought Gwen. The computer model was God. Messenger was the High Priest. And she was an acolyte and didn't give a damn. She was beyond grateful to get the chance to see this.

"Thank you, thank you for showing me this," she said.

"Pleasure," replied Messenger with a munificent nod. "But this wasn't just an idle demo. We need your input. You're a trained meteorologist."

"And?"

"We can make it rain. You've seen that. We want you to work some more on the model so that we can make even more rain. Specifically with the drone-based ionizers."

Messenger got up. He took a key from his trouser pocket, unlocked his desk drawer, and pulled out a laptop that he handed to Gwen.

"Have a look at Zeus. The model is downloaded onto this laptop. You can take it to your office, work on it there."

Peter Weiss gave a small gasp.

He was surprised, Gwen supposed, that she was being trusted with something so enormous.

"You will make no copies," said Messenger, "and the laptop itself cannot leave the Lab." He gave her an unblinking look, half caution, half threat.

"I wasn't planning on stealing Zeus," asserted Gwen.

"I'm sure you weren't," replied Messenger, "but other people might not be so trustworthy. For your own safety, it's better it stays right here."

"I'll hand it right back to you when I'm done at the end of the day."

"Good."

"So you want more rain," mused Gwen, moving on. "At the risk of sounding simplistic, wouldn't you just turn up the ionizers, emit more ions?"

"That's only part of it," replied Messenger, "but the

other parts relate to picking the optimum prevailing humidity, atmospheric pressure, factoring in all the wind speed and direction permutations, the rotational height and flight pattern of the drones, how many drones to use, for what duration . . ." He paused, frowned. "As you know, the interplay between variables creates multiple outcomes. We want you to have a look, have a tinker, see if you can improve the theoretical yields."

We want you to play God, thought Gwen.

"OK. I can do that. Then what?"

"Then we make it rain," replied Messenger. "Harder and faster."

Clasping the computer to her chest with one hand, Gwen walked to the door, paused, her other hand on the jamb.

"I'll get started after lunch. But what about the inventor? Can we work with him, or her?"

"You won't be able to do that," said Messenger stiffly.

Gwen tilted her head. There was a wicked undertow swirling round and she felt stuck in it without understanding it.

"He's dead," said Messenger.

"Oh no!" exclaimed Gwen. "Old guy? Old age?" Suddenly she felt she had to know more.

"Jeez, Gwen, do you never ease up," asked Weiss with a flash of irritation.

Gwen shot him a look. "Rarely."

"Not old age," said Messenger. "Car accident. He was killed in a hit-and-run."

Gwen felt a roaring in her ears. Al. Zeus was Paparuda.

33

Gwen locked the laptop in her desk, then locked her office door. She crossed the Lab and flashed her pass at the reader by the exit. The door clicked open and she walked out. Now she understood the security, the clocking in and out. If Zeus worked, it would be worth billions of dollars, maybe tens of billions. Governments, individuals, would kill to get their hands on it. It occurred to her that maybe they already had.

She headed quickly for her car, drove out of sight, dug into her wallet, hauled out the tattered business card. She called the number, waited, heart sounding out her anxiety like a drum.

"Hi, Mr. Freidland. Gwen Boudain. We met the other day. Could I come and see you?"

Gwen made the short drive from Laureless to Meadow Place in the Carmel Valley. Was it somewhere along this route that his son, Al, had been run down, knocked off his bicycle, and killed?

Charles Freidland's house was a single-story structure of stone and Spanish tile overlooking the green expanse of the Garland Ranch Regional Park.

Freidland opened the door.

"Park the car in my garage. It's too noticeable."

Quickly, Gwen did as she was told.

Freidland closed the garage door, reappeared at an inner door that led straight into the house.

"Thank you for seeing me, Mr. Freidland."

He nodded. "Ms. Boudain. Had a feeling I would be. Come in, please."

He led her into a sunny room with soft terra-cotta sofas, warm wood side tables, and photos in plain wooden frames. Gwen studied the baby, the boy, the man. Al, tousled-haired, smiling back at the camera, the same light warming his crinkled eyes. Always smiling. Gwen felt a yank of emotion, swallowed before speaking.

"He was a lovely looking boy. A handsome man."

Freidland bowed his head, looked back up. "He was." He paused a moment. "Er, would you like a coffee or something?" His usual rasping voice was softer on his home base.

Gwen didn't want to put him to any trouble, but thought it might settle them both.

"Sure, thank you. If you're having something . . ."

"Tea. Spent three years in England when Al did his undergrad at Cambridge. Got a taste for it."

"Bright boy. Tea'd be great. Thanks."

Freidland gave her a measured look. "Al was more than bright. He was a dreamer, but he had the brains to make those dreams real. He thought up things no one else did, then set to making them happen."

Gwen nodded, chastened. She followed him into a small, neat kitchen. "Like Paparuda?" she hazarded.

"Like Paparuda." Freidland occupied himself with making tea. Gwen saw his hand shaking as he poured the boiling water into the pot.

"So, they told you about Paparuda?" asked Freidland as he sipped his tea in the sunny room.

Gwen took a deep breath, conscious that she was totally and irrevocably breaching the terms of her confidentiality agreement. Necessary larceny.

"Messenger and Weiss just treated me to a demo. It's unbelievable."

Freidland smiled wistfully. "Paparuda. It means *rain dance* in Romanian. My grandfather was Romanian," he added. "It was Al's dream. Bring water to those who don't have it. Grow more food, use the water from up in the atmosphere without having to desalinate the ocean by burning fossil fuels. I bet Messenger didn't tell you all the social implications."

"You could say that."

Freidland laid down his teacup with a clatter on the wooden side table. He leaned toward Gwen, resting his palms on his knees.

"For starters, there is no shortage of water in the world. We have one point three billion cubic kilometers of water. But, for our needs, it is either in the wrong form or in the wrong place. Paparuda can deliver freshwater to the right place in a way that no other technology offers."

Gwen listened as Freidland spoke. His eyes gleamed.

"Let's just start with man-made desalination. Global annual desalination is twenty-two cubic kilometers of water. This burns up forty billion dollars in fossil fuels and belches out four hundred million tons of CO_2; the sun does half a million cubic kilometers of desalination and it doesn't cost a cent! What Al wanted to do, as well as commercially exploiting Paparuda, was run a parallel program financed out of the profits, and they would be huge, of the commercial side." Freidland paused, narrowed his eyes, spoke more slowly. "Over one point four billion people live in water-challenged areas where the future use of current groundwater is untenable. In many impoverished communities, on the coast but also up to a few hundred kilometers inland, Paparuda could provide desperately needed water, both for farmers and for drinking water for communities."

Freidland sat back, drained his tea. For a few moments his eyes drifted off, then he seemed to gather himself again. Gwen could see that the conversation, the emotion of it, was taxing him.

"I'm sure this is what they fought about," he continued. "For Messenger, Paparuda was a license to print money.

For Al, it was a green dream. Brilliant and simple, like all the best inventions are. Inexpensive too."

"But worth a fortune," stated Gwen.

"Almost priceless," said Freidland, his voice low with reverence. He gave a weary smile. "Forgive me. I tend to get carried away."

"There's a lot to get carried away about," said Gwen softly.

Freidland nodded. "Now it's your turn. Why don't you tell me why you're here?"

Fate, thought Gwen. Fate with a sick sense of humor. Fate that seemed intent on using her.

"Something this big . . ." she began. "I can see why someone might contemplate killing to get control of it. But there's still a heck of a leap between a motive and acting on it. I want to know why you think Messenger killed your son. And what proof you have."

Freidland nodded.

"And what'll you do in return?"

"If you convince me of his guilt, I'll try and help you prove it."

34

CARMEL VALLEY

"OK. Here's what I know," started Charles Freidland. "Back in June, the week before he died, Al went to this big conference at Half Moon Bay. Told me all about it when he got back. How it was full of all these venture capital hotshots congratulating themselves on their latest Learjet."

"I'll bet," murmured Gwen.

"He said he'd heard something that really worried him. He wouldn't tell me the whole story, but what I got was that Al bumped into a lady of the night one evening; she was real upset, he comforted her, sort of thing he would do. Anyway, Al says she told him that some guy had got tanked up, told her something crazy about Paparuda. Al refused to believe it was true, wouldn't tell me what it was, even. Just that he had to talk to Messenger first, and only then, when he'd given him a chance to defend himself, would he tell me."

"But he never got to tell you?"

"He didn't. It happened like this. Monday morning he goes to work aiming to confront Messenger. He rang me at five thirty, said he was just about to come home. Then five minutes later, he rang me back, said Messenger had called him in to a meeting. Said he'd ring me when he got out and head home and we'd grab a pizza." Freidland paused, looked at his empty teacup. "One hour passed, then Al called. He sounded upset. He said he and Messenger had had a major blowup. Said he'd tell me when he got home."

He raised his eyes to Gwen, who saw the tears falling freely now. "Only he never did get home. A car hit him on Carmel Valley Road, knocked him from his bike, drove off, leaving him in a coma. He died three days later." A hard look came onto the old man's face and he brushed his tears away. "Police said he had no rear light, said there was fog, it was dark. Well, it *was* dark and there was a light fog, but when Al left home that morning he had a light on the back of his bike. I watched him cycle away and I saw the light. One of those ones flashed on and off. I *saw* it!"

"And you think Messenger removed the light?"

Freidland nodded. "Then he followed him and ran him down."

"And do you have any proof that Messenger did this?"

"Two days after Al was knocked off the bike, police said Messenger's Ferrari rear-ended a garbage truck at an intersection."

"And you think this was some kind of deliberate collision to remove any evidence from the Ferrari?"

Freidland nodded. "I do."

"It's a stretch," said Gwen.

"Maybe. But enough stretches and you get there. All that stuff at the conference, the last-minute meeting, the delay until it was dark, the fight about something—must have been about Paparuda—the destruction of evidence . . . kinda mounts up."

"And you told the cops all of this?"

"I did. They claimed they did a thorough investigation. They looked for the motorist. Came up with nothing. Concluded it was a tragic accident. Case closed."

Gwen blew out a breath. Her heart was racing, she could feel it banging away. Her skin felt hot. The images came, uncontrollable now. The man and the sunny room receded and she saw the red car, spinning and rolling, bursting into flames, immolating her parents.

She felt a hand on her arm, and started. She focused on the man bending over her.

"My dear, are you all right? You're pale, you're shaking. Can I get you something?"

"Whisky," Gwen managed to say.

She took a long glug, felt the heat roar down her throat and into her stomach. She let it warm her. Crazy to think she had gotten over it. Some things you just never did.

"What is it?" repeated Freidland.

Gwen drained her whisky, took its secondhand courage.

"It's lightning. Striking twice. Once now, once four years ago." She gave him an apologetic smile. "It's a long story."

He gave a soft laugh. "I have an abundance of time."

Gwen nodded. "OK. Here goes . . . My parents were working on a great innovation, not on the scale of your son's but big enough. It's to do with predicting El Niño."

Freidland nodded. He moved from Gwen's side and took a seat opposite her on a snug armchair. He leaned forward, eyes fixed on hers.

"They were doing it for the intellectual curiosity, sure, but also because if you could predict El Niño better you could save lives. You'd have time to lay in supplies in remote areas, to prep for flooding, to prep for drought, even to plant more drought-resistant crops. But, here's the thing, you could also make a killing on the markets. Think about it . . . if you had advance warning you could go long or short, play all sorts of futures markets—wheat, orange juice, weather futures themselves." Gwen's eyes slipped away from Freidland to another sitting room, in her family home in Punta Sal in Peru. She spoke, looking out of the window, seeing only Peru: the desert plains, the dunes stretching down to the sea, the endless blue . . .

"Four years ago, I'd come to visit my parents in our family home in Peru. It was remote, up near the border with Ecuador, not far from the equator. Hemingway used to fish for marlin there. Nobody much went there. A few tourists, lots of fishermen. A few small-scale suppliers. Of coke." Her eyes snapped back to Freidland, as if to check he was keeping up. His eyes were riveted on hers. She looked away again, drawn back to the images that haunted her.

"Don't ask me how, but word filtered out about what my parents were doing. One day we were paid a visit. Big black Hummer. Narco car. They didn't feel the need to be subtle. The trafficantes are often protected by the army. They're sometimes members of the army, or terrorists who are looking to fund their cause, with enough cash to pay off the cops and the army too. So the guys came in. Three

of them. Two henchmen and the big narco himself. Carlos
Ramirez. Living the cliché, big-ass gold watch, mirrored
shades, the hard look, the face frozen into contempt for
anyone and everything. Save money." Gwen got up, began
to pace.

"He had heard about my parents' work. Wanted to buy
them, basically. Wanted to hire them and buy their
research so that they could predict El Niño for him, or La
Niña. Useful knowledge for planting all his coca crops,
and for trading the markets. This man was not some
jungle narco. He told us, so proudly, he'd been to the University of Miami, worked in an investment bank for five
years before taking over the family business. He told us
how he loved to play the markets. How my parents' research
would help him play them even better."

Gwen paused in front of the sofa, sat down abruptly.

"He offered them one million dollars. Non-negotiable.
Take it or leave it. They left it."

Gwen hugged her knees.

"One week later, when I was surfing, my parents were
out picking up groceries in the local town. On the way
back, their car veered off the road, onto the sand, rolled,
burst into flames. Burned them to death. Police said it was
an accident. There were no witnesses, officially. Unoffi-
cially, I found one. A little girl who'd been out with her
mule, also heading for the market. She was coming in from
a village, must have been hidden by the dunes or else the
narcos would have obliterated her too. She told me there'd
been another car, a big black car that had driven up, pushed
my parents' car off the road, made it crash, then disappeared." Gwen closed her eyes.

"What did you do?"

She opened her eyes. "I've never told anyone. You're the
first. What could I do? If I went to the police, the narcos
would go after the girl, kill her. And do you think I would
have got any justice there? Me against Mr. Big?" Gwen

demanded. "I did all I could. I took all my parents' research and laptops and I got the hell out of there. I went home to California, started my Doctorate at Stanford, secretly carried on their work."

Freidland nodded, eyes soft with sympathy. "They never came after you?"

Gwen shook her head. "No, they didn't. But I've never shaken the feeling that someone is out there . . . watching me. It seems to have gotten worse lately." She blew out a breath. "It's all this, I suppose—you, Falcon, knowing what I know. It's making me paranoid."

Freidland bowed his head. "I'm sorry. For your loss, for all of it, for bringing you back into it."

"Kismet. My fate."

"So what are you going to do?"

Gwen gave a bitter laugh. "What can I do? I would love to run, to just forget all of this. Doesn't seem to work though. I still get the nightmares. You know it's funny, Gabriel Messenger said I looked like a gunslinger coming into the office to sort them all out. I asked him if I were the bad guy or the sheriff." Gwen's eyes drifted off again. "I told him I was the sheriff on the trail of justice."

Freidland gave a wry chuckle.

"Freaky, huh?"

The old man came over, squatted arthritically beside her. He reached out, grabbed her hand.

"You can just pretend you never met me. You've suffered enough. Nothing will bring Al back."

"No, it won't, nor my parents, but if I can help you get the murdering bastard who killed your son, if that is Messenger, then I will. It'll even the scores, just a little bit. And it'll keep Paparuda out of his hands too. Shit, can you imagine what the wrong person might be able to do with rainmaking technology?"

"You'd have to be truly evil to abuse it."

Gwen laughed. "And?"

Freidland gave a sad smile. "I take your point. Another reason to walk away."

"And to stay. Messenger would never suspect me. I'm just a querulous academic. I can ask questions, snoop around. I'm inside, in the perfect position to snoop. Messenger trusts me."

Freidland squeezed her hand. "Be careful, please."

Gwen squeezed his hand back, got to her feet in one fluid, decisive motion.

"Oh, I will. I've no intention of dying for a long time."

Hidden in the base of the carriage lamp that hung from the ceiling, the voice-activated listening device fell dormant. Over the past hour, it had relayed every word to a secure office where a digital recorder saved it all and stored it, awaiting the man who would come and listen to it all.

35

THE LAB

Gwen drove straight back to the Lab from Freidland's house, giving herself no time to stop and think. Just act. Inquisitive academic, surfer girl . . . she got to play snoop, veiled by airhead. And, she'd make it work, she thought with quiet fury. For the ghosts of her parents and for Al Freidland. For her own sake too.

Remember, said the voice in her head, *how Messenger likes head games, how he likes to read people.*

She felt light-headed, emotionally exhausted, but in

some strange way armored by her resolve and by a kind of mastered terror. She just hoped her armor was Messenger-proof. She flashed her pass, entered her PIN, and strode into the office, raising a hand to greet Mandy, who scurried across her path like a black cat.

Mandy opened her mouth to speak, but Gwen's determined stride brooked no interruption, and Mandy must have seen something in her eyes, so she just mouthed a silent "Hi" and went on her way.

The phone rang just as Gwen walked into her office. She checked the number, grabbed up the handset.

"Joaquin, what's up?"

"The good news is I got your new sensors, chica, and the new buoys. I've spent the past three days getting them into position. I gave them a day to settle; I've just looked at the readings they kicked up. I've checked, then triple-checked them. They should have hit your screen an hour ago. I take it you have not seen them."

"I'm looking now."

Gwen eyed the new readings marked in green, scrolled down to the conclusions.

She swore under her breath.

"I've never seen sea temperature readings rise so fast," she murmured. "And the colorscope results have moved onto a whole new stratum. You know what this means, Joaquin?"

"A mega-Niño. Wild weather, wilder than we've ever seen."

"It's the butterfly flapping her wings, Joaquin."

36

THE LAB

Gwen stilled her breathing. She was good at it, bringing down her pulse, slowing her breath, using less oxygen, calming herself. It was a survival skill for all surfers of big waves. A multi-wave hold-down was not uncommon, and it could keep you underwater for several minutes. If you could hold your breath when you were getting the shit kicked out of you, you could sure as hell master your breath, and your nerves, during a conversation in an office, reasoned Gwen. She pushed to her feet. Showtime.

"Dr. Messenger, I've got kind of bad news," said Gwen, standing in his open doorway.

"What, your model doesn't work?" asked Messenger, looking up from his computer screen, eyebrows pinched.

"Oh, it works all right. It's what it's telling me that's the problem. My sensors have been picking up extreme readings. We have checked and triple-checked them. They are accurate. We've got a mega-Niño brewing up, so fast and strong that as far as I can tell, no one else is onto it."

Messenger jumped to his feet. "Mandy," he called out. "Get Peter and Kevin in here now."

Messenger turned back to Gwen. She felt his gaze, intense as always. She met it, steady-eyed.

"Come in, please," he said, gesturing to a chair, pulling it out for her, old-world charm ascendant.

"Thank you," replied Gwen, sinking down elegantly into the seat, flicking a smile at him. She could do charm too.

Weiss and Barclay hurried in. Weiss was carrying his laptop, as always. Barclay brandished his iPad.

They all sat round the table. Messenger turned to Gwen.

"Tell them what you just told me," he said urgently, as if the flood were coming even now.

"Oracle is predicting a mega-Niño," said Gwen. "It's brewing up as we speak. To put it in context, the last mega-Niño hit in nineteen ninety-seven. It caused twenty-two thousand deaths worldwide and cost thirty-three billion dollars in flood and drought-related damage."

"Ugly," proclaimed Barclay.

"It gets uglier. A mega-Niño means superfuel for the Pineapple Express. A warming sea causes more evaporation, giving a massive boost to the water vapor in the atmospheric rivers. These rivers are the ammunition, if you like, for an ARk Storm."

"And what's the detonator?" asked Messenger.

Gwen smiled. God, he was quick. In another world, she would have liked him.

"Pole-to-equator temperature differentials," she replied. "And get this. A mega-Niño causes global weather chaos. It is more than possible that it will ramp up those differentials, in layman's terms, detonating an ARk Storm."

"Shit!" said Weiss, eyes going faraway. "The ARk Storm cometh. What would it look like?" he asked, eyes snapping back to Gwen.

"Read the article in the *San Fran Reporter* this morning!" instructed Barclay, pointing at a folded paper on Messenger's desk. "That describes it pretty well. Scared the shit out of me!"

Thanks, Dan, thought Gwen; an element of scaremongering to generate interest was a common journalistic tool, but then some things we should be scared of, she reckoned, remembering Riley's words.

"Think of forty Mississippis slamming their way across the Pacific, hitting California."

Weiss paled. Barclay's eyes, flickering in thought, came to rest on Gwen with a kind of awed speculation.

"How sure are you, Gwen?" asked Messenger.

Gwen held up her hands. "I cannot be one hundred percent sure, obviously. All I can say is that the chances of an ARk Storm have increased dramatically."

Messenger nodded. "Timing?"

"It's a winter phenomenon, so sometime in the next two to four months, I'd say."

"And the market view differs to this?" queried Barclay.

"Yes," answered Gwen. "The prevailing academic opinion is that an ARk Storm is a possibility, not a probability, let alone a high probability."

"Sure, academic opinion, gimme the *market* opinion," pushed Barclay. He leaned across the table with the controlled aggression of an interrogator.

Gwen paused for a moment, registering that she did not *have* to reply. When she did, her voice was coolly impassive. "There is nothing like Oracle out there, so the market opinion will follow the consensus academic opinion as broadcast by the ARk Storm Project on its Web site."

Barclay's mood changed with the rapidity of a spoiled child granted the toy he'd screamed for. He leaned back, grinning. "So Oracle beats the market. I'm loving it!" He tapped away on his iPad. "You want me to buy some puts?" he asked Messenger, glancing across at him. "I've already prepped a short list of companies with the most exposure."

Gwen stared at Barclay in disbelief.

"Good anticipation," replied Messenger, rising to his feet. "Give me ten minutes. I want to check Falcon's liquid funds." He eyed each of them in turn. "I don't need to tell you we have an information lockdown on this."

"Wait a minute," said Gwen, jumping up, slamming her hands on the table, locking eyes with Messenger. Outside at her desk, Mandy shot Gwen a worried look.

"We need to start warning people," argued Gwen. "I need to talk to my friend at Hazards so the whole ARk Storm Project can be alerted."

"We alert no one," said Messenger.

"What, we just sit on this information?" asked Gwen, fury building, voice rising.

"Until I say so, yes we do. We need to get these trades on ahead of the market."

"What, you mean benefit from my inside knowledge, from Oracle's predictions?"

"Of course. Why would I not act on that?" asked Messenger, visibly impatient.

"But isn't that insider trading?" asked Gwen.

The German burst out laughing. "Welcome to the world. Private equity is legalized insider trading. That's why we all do it!"

37

HIGHWAY I

Not trusting herself to speak, Gwen marched out of Messenger's office, stormed across to her own, grabbed Messenger's laptop, and marched back.

Messenger looked up in surprise as she walked back in. He stared at her, mouth set in disapproval.

"Here, lock up your baby," she said, handing over the laptop.

"Where are you going?" Messenger asked, glancing at his watch.

"Surfing! I've had enough of the Lab for today, and if you or anyone else has a problem with that, too bad." Without waiting for an answer, Gwen turned and stalked out. Tapping on his iPad, Barclay followed her.

"I hope I did not make a mistake there," Messenger said to Weiss, eying Gwen through his window as she threw open the door to her Mustang and jumped in.

"She's a scientist, not a money person," said Weiss softly. "She's ill at ease with the commercial imperative. I was too, way back when. Give her time. She'll get over it."

"She'll have to, won't she. If she wants to survive."

On Highway 1, Gwen made a call.

"Hi, Dan, Boudy here. Look, you once said you were a good listener. I could really do with some of that now. . . . I'm heading to Hurricane Point. . . . I'll be there in thirty minutes. . . . OK, great . . . see you then."

Gwen ended the call, turned off her cell. She felt as if she were on a collision course with fate. Fury, as it always did, made her reckless. Bring it on, she thought, accelerating along the coast road, hugging the contours as hundreds of feet below her the waves smashed into the cliffs.

38

THE SECURITIES AND EXCHANGE COMMISSION REGIONAL OFFICE, NYC, LATE MONDAY AFTERNOON, EARLY EVENING

Agent Pete "Rac" Rodgers sat at his desk, headphones clamped to his ears, elbows braced, chin in his hands, listening to the stream of verbal diarrhea that was Ronald Glass's life. He was onto his fourth Red Bull. Domenica had kept him and Marlee up most of the night, and he found himself fantasizing about an all-white hotel room with blackout drapes, empty of everything save a big soft bed and him. He felt like he could sleep for a week.

Abruptly he sat up, knocking over the thankfully almost-empty Red Bull. He listened to the clip three times, then halted the recording and pushed himself stiffly to his feet.

He rubbed his back like a pregnant woman. He was carrying too much weight and he knew it. Damn-all he could do about it. He'd given up cigarettes nine months ago, soon as Marlee told him she was pregnant. He'd replaced nicotine with sugar, and he and his wife had grown large together.

He barreled into Wilkie's office. She was standing, back to him, headphones clamped to her ears, looking out the window. She was barefoot, doing perfect calf raises, like a ballerina warming up. She had a ballerina's calves too—muscled and lean. Rodgers knew she did aikido, was some kind of black belt, and it showed in the parts of her powerful body that the suit did not conceal. A blond wig lay coiled on Wilkie's desk like a dead animal. One of her disguises. She wasn't pretty, her features were all a tad large for that, but she was handsome with her open face, ready smile, sharp gray eyes, and her striking red hair.

In her customary skirt suit—gray, anonymous-looking—she could have been any one of the thousands of PAs and lower-ranking executives who thronged Wall Street and its environs, but to anyone who looked closely enough, or who knew what they were looking for, she stood out. It was partially the stance. Even at rest, she stood like a sprinter on the blocks, leaning forward slightly on the balls of her feet, keen eyes focused on some finish line only she could see, and with an awareness that took in faces and memorized them, and names and bytes of information that would have defeated a lesser brain. The woman was encyclopedic; she was also one of the most energetic people Rodgers had ever met. He wished he could borrow some, just for a day.

As Rodgers reached out to tap her shoulder, Wilkie spun round in a perfect pirouette and beamed at him, pulling off her earphones.

"Saw your reflection," she said with a grin. "No, actually, I felt your presence with my finely honed skills. What's up Rac?"

Her partner grinned.

"We got Ronald Glass at it! Well, the foreplay, not the act. But it's a start!" The mantle of exhaustion lifted and Rodgers' dull eyes managed a sparkle. "Picked up a reference to *personal cell phone*. Come 'n' listen."

Wilkie followed Rac into his tiny office. "Hit it."

The disembodied voices drifted through the room.

"Hi. It's me," said an excitable female voice.

"Call me on my personal cell phone," snapped Glass.

"Sure thing."

The recording ceased.

Wilkie studied her manicured hands. "The insider trader's mantra. Call me on my fuckin' personal cell phone." She looked up at Rodgers. "He's dirty."

"Just a few weeks since we got the wiretap. Think how much went down before."

Wilkie grimaced. "And the woman calling Glass, the one who no doubt gave him a big, juicy insider tip on his personal cell? Any ideas?"

"Unregistered cell phone," replied Rodgers. "Pay as you go. She'd have trashed it after the call."

"Profile?"

"Blue collar. Sounds like fuckin' Minnie Mouse," observed Rodgers, sliding into his chair, swiveling round to face Wilkie, who stood alert and straight, gazing down at him, her gray eyes cool and clear. No red veins for her. "Got access to some valuable info. Probably a PA somewhere. I'll get the accent people to run her voice."

"Good one," said Wilkie. "I want to bring this bastard down, and all the crooked little shits he runs with."

"You sound like Bergers: *eradicate the contamination*!"

"I'm a woman on a mission."

"All we can do is do what we're doing."

"And pray for a lucky break. Wait for Glass or one of

his tipsters to get just a bit too greedy. Then they'll mess up." Wilkie gave a nasty smile. "Wouldn't it be nice to tap that bastard's cell phone."

"Nice if we could tap his home too."

"I don't think we'd ever get Judge Bustillo to agree to that," said Wilkie.

"What would it take?" Rodgers asked.

"Evidence of terrorist activity. National Counterterrorism Center can get NSA to tap whoever the hell they like. Find some terrorist crap, and we're sitting pretty."

Rodgers screwed up his face, gave her a wry look. "Dream on."

39

HURRICANE POINT HOUSE,
MONDAY AFTERNOON

Daniel found Gwen on her deck, attended by her dog, who stood to meet him, alert, head raised. Dan trotted up the stairs with the fluidity of movement of the truly fit. He was wearing a suit. It should have looked incongruous with his tousled hair, but he wore it with a casual ease that only made it more elegant. He took Gwen's face in his hands, kissed her lips lightly. Pulled back to study her.

"I've dragged you from work," said Gwen.

"Praise the Lord!"

Gwen laughed. The man was a tonic. She watched him bend, ruffle her dog's neck.

"Let's sit down," she said softly.

They sat at her table, looking out to sea, an endless, innocent blue today, the blue of the cloudless sky. Out of a brilliant blue sky . . . she could never think those words without thinking of Nine-eleven. The terrorists had hijacked blue skies forever, it sometimes seemed to her. Her mind was jumping, spinning. She brought it back under control.

"It's pretty wild, what I'm going to tell you," she started, eyes fixed on his, looking for any flicker. "Riley trusted you. Something tells me I can, even though I don't know you well. But you need to tell me if you don't want this laid on you. Someone's dead. I don't want either of us to be next."

Dan raised his eyebrows—not in a disbelieving way, more in an interested, speculative way.

"Gwen. You can trust me. Want to shake on it?"

"All right," replied Gwen, eyeing him, seeing something flit across his eyes, a kind of concern.

They reached across the table, out on the deck, clasped each other's hands. Gwen felt it, the surge between them, knew he did too. For a while, they just sat there, holding onto each other; then, Gwen released him and began to speak, telling him about Charles Freidland, about Paparuda, about Zeus, about ARk Storm and Messenger's prospective insider trading.

Dan listened without interrupting, a frown etched between his eyes.

"What have you walked into, Gwen Boudain?" he asked when she'd finished.

"That's what I'm asking myself. But I'm in now."

"And walking away, just pretending you've never heard any of this, isn't an option?"

Gwen shook her head. "Not again."

Dan grabbed her arm as she made to stand up. "Not so fast. What do you mean *again*?"

She sat down. "I ran away once. From Peru." Quickly, clinically, she told him about her parents. Telling him was much harder than telling Charles Freidland, and that had been hard enough.

Dan listened, face largely impassive. His eyes narrowed as she described the car crash and the little girl's story, but he did not touch her, his eyes did not soften with sympathy, and for that she was grateful. She didn't want sympathy, not from a man she was involved with, cared for. Sympathy undid her.

How did he know, she wondered? How did he always seem to know just the right emotional note to hit?

She finished speaking, got up quickly before he could say anything. She walked into her kitchen and began to brew up coffee. Grind the beans, spoon them into the plunger, boil the water.

Dan stayed outside, sitting at her table, gazing out into the deep blue. He didn't move, but Gwen could sense a kind of contained tension to him. After a few minutes, he got up and joined her in the kitchen. He kept his distance though, leaning against her worktop.

"You've had some stuff . . ." he said softly.

Gwen smiled. "A bit."

"You were right to run."

"I should not have run. I should have got justice for my parents."

Dan took a step closer, said softly, "Yeah, right. Getting yourself killed would avenge their murder."

Gwen couldn't speak. She shrugged in a gesture of utter helplessness. She saw Daniel move, then stop himself. She stood, just looking at him, seeing in his eyes a strange kind of fury. She got the feeling it was part to do with her, part something else altogether. So many secrets in his eyes.

She blew out a breath, poured him a coffee, passed it to him with a steady hand. By some kind of silent accord they both moved together, walking outside, sitting again at the table overlooking the vast blue.

"You think they ever came here, came after you?" Dan asked, bending his head to the mug, blowing gently on his coffee.

Gwen shook her head. "I looked over my shoulder for the longest time. I upped my fight training, got taught some dirty stuff from my trainer—he's an ex-Navy SEAL," she added, looking down to sip her own coffee, missing the flaring of his eyes.

"Now's the danger time, I think," she said. "No one knew I had taken on my parents' work. Just Joaquin, my assistant, and everyone just thinks he's a wildlife photographer. He is, he just works with me too. Lucy knows, my closest friends know. Now Falcon knows and Messenger knows. The more people know, the bigger the risk."

Dan nodded. "Let's hope your narco gets whacked in some turf battle. What's his name?"

Gwen told him and added, "In my saner moments, I don't think he'll come after me. Doing a hit in California is not the same as in Peru. He won't own the cops, or the judiciary. It's not so easy here."

"It's easy if you have the will, the money, and the manpower," said Dan absently.

Before Gwen could ask him what he meant, he spoke again.

"So what about your boss? The intriguing Gabriel Messenger. You think he's a killer?"

"I think he could be. There's certainly enough motive, with Paparuda."

"Is that for real?"

"My reaction too. But yeah, I've seen it! They made it rain down on me."

"It's biblical!"

They drained their coffees, walked back into Gwen's kitchen. They put down their cups. They both leaned back against Gwen's faded wooden work surface, legs cocked, arms resting lightly on the wood, inches apart, flicking glances at each other. Anyone looking in from the outside might have thought they were discussing what movie to see that night. Anyone inside would have felt the tension stretching between them, joining them, filling the kitchen.

"So what's your plan?" asked Dan. "I see it churning in your eyes. You've got a kind of square-jawed determined look on you."

Gwen smiled and said sadly, "You sound like my mother. *Gwen and her plans* . . . I always have a plan. Like I can control life!"

"Yeah, well, you're not the only one who harbors that particular illusion."

Gwen studied Dan. "Not you. You seem to have emerged from life fully formed, shit together, no cracks or chinks."

Dan raised his eyebrows. "I have my chinks, my cracks."

"Then you must cover them with some extra special armor."

"If I do, it's probably called denial. We were talking about your plan. . . ."

Gwen shrugged, realized she wasn't going to get any more out of him by probing.

"All I can think of is to stay put and to try to find out if there is anything to Freidland's allegations," she said. "Also, if I'm on the inside I can hopefully persuade Messenger to let me go to the ARk Storm team with Oracle's predictions. Either way, I *will* go to them sooner or later." She straightened up, paced. "That's if I haven't gotten myself fired. I kind of stalked off earlier."

"I can imagine you in full stalk. But I'm sure Messenger'll get over it. You probably just came over as a naïve academic. That's a good act to cultivate."

"Oh I am, trust me." Gwen paused as an idea popped. "That venture cap conference at the Ritz-Carlton in Half Moon Bay I mentioned . . . I think I might go to the hotel, ask around, see if anyone knows anything about someone from Falcon getting wasted, and even what they said."

"Great idea. Mind if I tag along?"

"Now why would you do that?"

"Call me helpful."

Gwen raised a cynical eyebrow.

"OK then. Call it a ruse to spend the night with you at a swanky hotel."

Gwen laughed. Dan had done it again, fractured the gloom, made everything light. My God, this man was something. . . .

"Why the need to spend the night there?" she asked. Everything seemed to be accelerating around her. She wanted to slow it all right down. Get it back under control.

"Hookers will hit the place on Friday night, not during the day. And don't take this wrong, but they'll probably be more eager to talk to me than to you."

"You might have a point."

"So Friday night?"

Gwen hesitated.

"You got a better idea?"

Gwen looked at him thoughtfully. Honey-colored eyes holding hers with a smile and a challenge. She felt the yearning pulse through her body like a fever.

"Maybe not," she murmured.

40

THE SUPER-YACHT, *ZEPHYR*, MOORED OFF
SAN DIEGO, MONDAY EVENING

The man stepped from the helicopter, ducked under the blades, straightened up on the spotless deck. He was met by two of the Sheikh's men, dark skinned, clean-shaven, no doubt so as not to attract undue attention when they went ashore. They would be hajis at the very least, the designation given to those who had done the pilgrimage to Mecca at least three times, and who almost invariably sported the full beard of Islamic men, but they were probably also Jihadis who wished to disguise themselves.

They looked him over with their dead eyes, no smiles, no word of greeting. The men, and the team of others like them, posed as the sailing staff in their white polo shirts emblazoned with ZEPHYR and their silent, soft-soled deck shoes. The yacht swarmed with them, padding about like assassins.

One soft-shoe led him, the other fell in behind. The man paused, gathered himself for just a moment.

He always felt, despite himself, despite who he was, what he had become, that he was somehow diminished alongside the Sheikh. Part of this was the money, the towering billions; part was the entourage, the men with the dead eyes; and part of it was the knowledge that the Sheikh despised his weaknesses as the ascetic loathes the voluptuary. Even though he had made such progress, traveled so far. It never seemed to be far enough.

He was led into the glittering stateroom, rich with the scents of cardamom and coffee, oud and bakhoor. The polished wood gleamed in the low lights, and in the distance, through the huge windows, he could see the lights of San Diego flickering like distant beacons.

And there was the Sheikh, rising from the twenty-seater horseshoe-shaped leather sofa, resplendent in his white kandoora. He wasn't wearing the ghutra, the headdress, today, just the *taqiyah*, the white skullcap.

With a nod of his head, the Sheikh beckoned him. He moved forward over the artfully scattered Persian carpets.

"*Asalaam aliekum,* my brother," the man intoned warmly.

"*Wa aleikum asalaam,*" replied the Sheikh, resuming his seat. "What can I do for you?"

The man gasped at the breach. Normally the Sheikh, in the tradition of his region, would have spun out the niceties, offered refreshments, bided his time before they got down to business. Was something wrong? He felt his jaw clenching involuntarily. He blew out a slow, silent breath and took a seat opposite the Sheikh, fifteen feet away, separated by a Persian carpet and low intricately carved wooden tables—made from old Omani doors, the Sheikh had told him during a loquacious moment.

"I have good news for you," announced the man. "Zeus works! Falcon staged a major trial of the mobile unit this morning, in what had been a cloudless sky, zero chance of rain. And it rained. It rained half an inch." The man's eyes glowed. No matter what the Sheikh did with it, Zeus was an astonishing achievement.

"Excellent!"

Approval, radiance. The man basked, felt the glow of reassurance.

"You will be well rewarded. Be sure of that."

"You are very kind, Sheikh Ali. And there's more. Another investment is bearing fruit."

"Tell me."

"Oracle forecasts the Niño phenomenon. Apparently, the one we are into at the moment will intensify into a mega-Niño."

"And what does that mean?"

"Floods, landslides, wasted harvests around the world, drought in some places."

"More little local catastrophes. I am weary of them."

"And storms, Sheikh Ali. It will bring large storms. Perhaps the storm you have been waiting for, right here in California."

There was a pause. The Sheikh's eyes flickered with calculation.

"You think these storms will be big enough for us to use?" he asked. "You think we can *crrrreate* an ARk Storm from one of them?" The Sheikh was trying, and failing, to keep the excitement from his voice.

"The forecaster used an interesting choice of words. She described the warming water as ammunition, the pole-to-equator temperature differentials as the detonator. . . ."

The Sheikh laughed. "She is indeed an Oracle! And we shall provide the spark."

The other man was silent.

"What, my friend, are you developing a conscience?" asked Al Baharna, leaning forward, eyes narrowing.

"I cannot afford one; besides, it's too late now." Too late for him to change his mind. Any weakness would be punished by a slow and painful death at the hands of the dead-eyed men hardened by years in Lebanon and Iraq. So he was committed, on a path of his own. The man gazed out of the dark windows, wondering what it would look like, the ARk Storm, the ten-foot walls of water slamming through the air. Forty Mississippis drowning them. He fingered his collar, suddenly feeling short of breath. He would be long gone, he reminded himself, hiding somewhere dry. As the vengeance of the holy rained down upon the infidels, money and the rewards of jihad would rain down on him.

"It is too late, my friend. Much too late. So, when do we light the spark?" asked the Sheikh, dragging him back.

"Forecaster thinks the Niño will develop into a mega-Niño over our winter."

"Two to five months from now," mused the Sheikh. "Are we ready?"

"We're still perfecting our model, trying to get it to produce more rain. The forecaster is being most helpful with this."

"I should meet this helpful Oracle," mused the Sheikh.

"It can be arranged." They'd have to make sure she behaved herself. She was too valuable to risk allowing her to make an enemy of the Sheikh.

"Is there a problem?" asked Al Baharna.

"No problem. I was just thinking it wouldn't harm to have more drones and more ionizers," improvised the man.

The Sheikh threw back his head and laughed for a few, seemingly uninhibited moments. The man wondered what on earth he had said that was so funny. The Sheikh leaned forward, eyes still creased in mirth.

"Ah, the drones. I do love the drones. Buy them immediately. Buy as many as you need. Ionizers too."

"We've got plenty of space in our hangar."

"Then fill it. Build in redundancy," intoned the Sheikh. His smile faded. He rested his forearms on his knees.

"It is fitting, as well as amusing, do you not think, that we shall be using drones to bring death to the Americans, after they have dispatched so many of my brothers with their drones and their Hellfire missiles?" His eyes went distant, perhaps, thought the man, seeing in the desolation of the desert the streak of white, the explosion and the fireball, the immolation.

"Like Anwar al-Awlaki," the Sheikh added softly, almost to himself, "whom I met so many years ago here in San Diego." He turned his eyes, narrowed, almost black, back on the man, who, despite himself, shuddered.

"It does have a certain symmetry," the man managed to admit. "I'll get onto it."

"It reminds me of one of the things that Bin Laden used to say," mused the Sheikh, fingers toying with his close-shaven beard. "He might have been Sunni, but his insight was unparalleled: 'We love death. The US loves life. That is the difference between us.'"

41

Sheikh Ali watched the man leave, then he strode from the stateroom to the small office that abutted his bedroom. His kandoora, fiercely starched, made a crisp thwacking sound like a flag snapping in a stiff breeze.

Using his BlackBerry, he dialed a number from memory. Again, this call was protected, this time by a software-installed encryption system, Cellcrypt. This was not as secure as the hardware systems he preferred, but the man he was calling did not have those systems. And Cellcrypt was good enough. Of that the Sheikh was confident. The man might be an ayatollah, in theory a man of God, but he was also the head of Iran's state-funded terrorist organization—a rogue breakout from their intelligence division, VEVAK—a cunning opportunist who would forgive no mistakes.

The Sheikh listened to the dial tone, smiling. He was looking forward to the call, to the advantage it would give him. He did not much like the ayatollah. He knew that the Iranian, as did many of his countrymen, regarded the Gulf Arabs as little more than camel drivers, peasants compared to the scions of the ancient civilization of Persia. He knew that the Iranian bitterly envied the Saudis their oil-based and US-endorsed ascendancy. Iran had its own oil wealth—just under three million barrels a day—but channeled much of these revenues toward weaponry and nuclear programs, toward maintaining the Revolutionary Guard and with it their hold on their own volatile country, and toward funding terrorism—Hamas, Hezbollah to name but a few.

And it was here, reflected Sheikh Ali, listening to the clumsy connection go through, that their interests coincided: to wage jihad against the Western secular materialists who threatened their religion and its place in the Middle East and in the world; to elevate the status and reach of their Shia brethren, particularly in Saudi and Bahrain; and, in the ayatollah's case, there was a third agenda; to raise Iran back to the status it had enjoyed for centuries as the hegemon in the Middle East.

The ayatollah picked up with a curt "Yes?"

"*Asalaam Aleikum.*" Peace be upon you.

"*Wa Aleikum Salaam. Wa rahmatullahi wa barakatu.*" And upon you the mercy of Allah and his blessings.

"My brother, I have something for you," intoned the Sheikh.

"Tell me."

"The rain of Allah is a much-blessed thing, is it not?"

"You rang me to discuss the weather?" asked the ayatollah, voice dripping the disdain of the righteous.

"No. To discuss jihad," the Sheikh replied.

"I am listening."

"What if one man could control the weather?"

"Only Allah can control the weather."

"Not true."

The ayatollah snorted.

"You think you have the power of Allah, now? You think your billions of dollars make you God? This is heresy."

"Not heresy. Technology. I can make it rain. I can stop the rain. I can harness the power of the storm and I can magnify it. I can bring the Flood. I can wash away hillsides, destroy homes, I can take a swath of some of the most expensive real estate in the United States and I can rain down upon it the wrath of Allah at the infidel."

"You would wage jihad by weather?"

"Does it not say in the holy Quran, *we helped him*

against those who rejected him. They were surely a wicked people, so we drowned them all. Is it not a beautiful idea?"

"When will you do it?"

"Within the next six months. When the right storm comes, I shall magnify it. I shall give California the ARk Storm of their nightmares."

42

THE SUPER-YACHT, *ZEPHYR,* MOORED OFF
SAN DIEGO, MONDAY EVENING

Sheikh Ali hung up, then he took a key from his pocket, unlocked his desk drawer, selected one of his stock of prepaid, disposable phones, charged and ready for one sole use.

He smiled to himself. Jihad, then money. Time to put in a call to his broker. He did a quick calculation. It would be the next day in Singapore, lunchtime, not that it really mattered. The broker would take his calls any time, day or night, and did.

Marcel Caravaggio was fifty-nine, a nomad. Swiss German by birth, Swiss Italian by blood, American by education, French by MBA, citizen of the globe by financial reach. He was of middle height, dark, a *bon viveur* waging war with his waistline—winning, for the most part. He played tennis five times a week to a surprisingly high standard. The excellence of his shots meant he had to run less than weaker opponents, and his cunning meant he normally beat his peers too. Marcel had an expensive young Singaporean wife, second version, and an expensive divorce behind him to the first version, so when his cell phone chimed just as he was walking onto Court One at the Tanglin Club for a prelunch game, he took the call, even though he didn't recognize the number.

He set down his tennis racket when he heard the Middle Eastern voice, signaled to his partner to give him five. He dropped his gym bag, fumbled for pen and paper.

"I would like you to put on a trade for me," intoned the Sheikh. "Please take out six-month put options on Californian Real Estate Casualty Insurers, or on any insurers heavily exposed to California."

"How big?" asked the broker, jamming the phone between his ear and collarbone, pen poised.

"How much cash do I have in my accounts with you?"

The broker answered from memory. "Two hundred and ten million dollars in cash, another nine hundred million in liquid investments. But that'll kill the market."

"Then put on as many trades as the market will bear. With the utmost discretion," added the Sheikh, in the soft voice that the broker recognized as his own code red on the threat level.

"Got it. You want me to do it now?"

"I want you to do it now."

"Can I spread it over the next three-four weeks? Big puts all taken out right now might attract attention."

Silence for a few beats. "Yes," murmured the Sheikh, "and we would not want that. Fine. Spread them, but within the month."

"How about I sell some tailored shorts too, with a view to closing them off in six months? Mix it up a bit."

"Do it."

"Consider it done."

A brief grunt of response, and the line was cut.

Caravaggio, well rewarded, knew better than to ask the underlying reason for the trade. Better not to know. He played his match. He won, ate lunch at the club, wagyu steak, medium rare, fries; no Chambertin, Napoleon's favorite wine, to his own, self-imposed chagrin. He needed his mind as clear as it got. Then his driver took him back to his office just off Clarke Quay. There he drank the espresso his secretary made him, lit up a Cohiba IV, and started his research. Clouds of aromatic smoke suffused his office. From time to time he would circle his cigar through the air to see the contrail it made, studying it thoughtfully like an ancient alchemist conjuring spells from smoke. He *was* conjuring, seeking the best way to extract money from the uninitiated.

One hour later, he had identified the companies with the most exposure, and he began with his customary delicacy to put on trade after trade after trade.

This was a multitiered process which involved considerable skill and investment. One of his best investments was his spectacularly curvaceous mistress, Jeannette, a rising star at CFLT private banking in Hong Kong. Jeanette's creativity in hiding trades was unmatched. She inherited the larceny from her Chinese Father, a legendary loan shark, and her curves from her Colombian mother. Marcel had proved an able student.

The concealment began with the third layer, the trash layer. This comprised four different Hong Kong–based but mainland China-financed private banks. Marcel had visited them, hand-selected them, satisfied himself of their discretion—reinforced by four separate pieces of information about the broker in charge at each, which would ensure a level of loyalty above and beyond the normal corporate requirements. Next layer up sanitized the trash so that it had only the faintest potential whiff of financial skulduggery about it. The four trash banks would issue the trading instructions to the Hong Kong branches of a selection of international banks. Those perfectly respectable financial names would then use their own nominee accounts to instruct the final layer. This layer completed the sanitization process, gave the trades the patina of respectability that would help to veil them and to stall any investigators in the unlikely event it ever came to that. The broker liked state-owned banks for this. The final tier of trades would be funneled through another selection of respectable, unwitting banks in New York. By the time the actual trades were put on, there would be a trail of over fifty nominee companies concealing the originator.

Marcel had set up encrypted contact with four chief brokers at his trash banks using CryptoPhone, a German system that offered mid-level encryption. It was quite commonly used commercially, so would not attract undue attention to itself. He dialed the first one. When Xu Ling answered, three letters appeared at top left of screen and a box that said RESPOND. Marcel typed in the letters, hit SEND. Xu Ling did the same in reverse, then the two men spoke. Marcel described the trades, adding *"ultra high discreet"* at the end of his instructions. Xu Ling knew the protocol. It had all been well worked out in advance.

Twenty minutes later, Marcel had spoken to all four trash bankers. He had given all four specific instructions re the trades and the necessary secrecy, but slightly different timelines to enter the market. He sat back, lit up another Cohiba, and began to add a few personal trades of his own. For this, he started off with three different Singapore nominee companies, confident of his security since Singapore had possibly the best banking secrecy laws in the world, unlike his birth home of Switzerland, whose banking secrecy now resembled a mouse-addled cheese.

He recognized the whiff of insider trading in his client's instructions, could not resist its lure.

43

The Sheikh's family cell rang. Another phone, also encrypted. Cryptophone, as favored by his broker and by many VIP families. Combined with clever use of veiled speech, it was a very effective tool.

He checked the number; his brother, Nasr.

They each set up the encryption, exchanged greetings, spoke for a while about family, and about the riots that had recently taken place in the Eastern Province; Saudi's Shia Arab Spring, brutally suppressed by the Al Saud family so successfully that it didn't even make the world's media.

The Sheikh wondered whether a warning was premature, decided it was better than too late.

"Tell me, brother, is your eldest son still studying in California?"

"He is. Los Angeles."

"A dangerous place for the infidels and the holy alike. It's a shame you can't lure him back."

"He's nineteen. He does what he wants."

"Their corrupt ways don't bother you?"

"Of course they do. But he'll come back, in all senses. We both went through the same phase, if I remember. And you still like San Diego. Don't pretend you don't."

"I do. But I think I shall avoid it."

"Why?"

"Because of the corrupt ones. Because, as the sun rises each morning, be sure that the wrath of Allah will rain down upon them."

The brother was silent for a moment. "When should I invite him home for a visit?"

"Oh, anytime over the next two months would be good, but be sure to get him home for Hussein's birthday. The celebrations will be extra special this year. His grandfather's too."

"Then that is what I shall do. Thank you for the advice."

"*Habat hoboob al jenna*. The winds of paradise are blowing my brother . . . what better place to be than home."

44

NATIONAL COUNTERTERRORISM CENTER,
TYSON'S CORNER, VIRGINIA,
TUESDAY EVENING

At Tyson's Corner, a fifteen-minute drive from Washington off Route 66, lay an urban sprawl of anonymous-looking concrete and glass buildings. They looked from the outside like commercial offices. But behind the concrete walls, heavily fortified to prevent electronic eavesdropping, they contained highly restricted classified spaces. Entry was gained via retinal scanners, electromagnetic key fobs, and backed up with personal PIN numbers.

The complex looked like a wasteland in some ways. Cars busied back and forth—black Escalades with tinted windows seemed to be the car of choice—before disappearing into underground car parks. No pedestrians attempted to cross the roads, or were seen anywhere. Employees drove the ramps to the basements, swiped their fobs, entered their PIN numbers at the security check, and gained admittance to one of the myriad buildings in the burgeoning secret world of US counterterrorism.

CTC was the agency of choice, but in the era of budget cuts and financial crises, the tens of thousands who labored inside the fortified walls felt under increasing pressure to justify their existence.

Chief Andrew Canning, the man who felt the pressure most keenly, beckoned the young and brilliant Arabist into his office.

"Sit, please," he told the woman, eyeing her speculatively. She was attractive, fit, with none of the pallor he might have expected in someone who must have spent half her life in an office translating intercepts.

Canning's two assistants, Frank Del Russo and Ol Peters, stood by the door, as if ready to repel any sudden attack.

The Arabist stuck out her hand, shook Canning's firmly. "Pauline Southward, sir."

Canning nodded. "Ms. Southward." He turned to his assistants.

"Ms. Southward has come over from Fort Meade to brief us. Told her boss she has what she believes to be a live one." He turned back to the woman. "All right Ms. Southward. Tell us what you got. And it better be good. Pulled me out of a dinner party. Mrs. Canning's not best pleased." Canning felt a little dyspeptic. He needed to hear this, but he needed to eat too. There were so many false alerts, analysts with target fixation seeing smoke in dusty breezes, that he was beginning to feel like a fireman called out on hoaxes: relieved that there was no fire, but some small part of him secretly hoping that there was.

The analyst gave him a bright, professional smile, devoid of warmth. CTC had a reputation for arrogance. She saw it in the eyes of Canning's two aides: built, confident, languid with entitlement. They would regard her, an employee of the National Security Agency, as a mere functionary, a troglodyte who never got to see the light of action, while they, either CIA or FBI—probably CIA, ex–Marine Corps, thought Southward, rapidly profiling them—were the glory boys.

"Sorry about that, sir. It *is* good, or perhaps bad would be a better way to describe it. Yesterday, over at NSA, we picked up an intercept. It's been working its way through the system since then. Got to me an hour ago. Sheikh Ali Al Baharna. We have a FISA Court Warrant on him, which allows us to intercept as many of his comms as we've managed to track so far. We also listen in to some of his close family members, in this case his brother, Nasr. The call was encrypted, suspicious enough in itself." Southward paused, gave a crisp smile. "But we broke the encryption."

Canning nodded, awaiting the punch line.

"We believe Sheikh Ali is behind many of the suicide bombing attacks in Israel. We believe he pays bonuses to the families of the martyrs depending on how many Israelis die. We've long suspected it's only a matter of time until he sets his sights on the US. He spends a lot of time here. He's here now, in California. As you know, he's a Saudi, a Shia from the Eastern Province. In this call, he's talking to his brother, Nasr, asking him if his eldest son is still in California. Nasr says that, yes, his eldest son is studying in Los Angeles. The Sheikh tells him: *A dangerous place for the infidels and the holy alike.* The brother asks why and the Sheikh says this:

Because as the sun rises each morning, be sure that the wrath of Allah will rain down upon them.

Nasr asked when he should invite his son home for a visit. The Sheikh said that the celebrations of Hussein's birthday might be extra special this year, as might be his grandfather's. He suggested he come home then."

Canning snorted. "Hell of a lot of use that is. How many Husseins are there?" He made no effort to veil the contempt in his voice.

Del Russo and Peters looked down at the Arabist dismissively. They'd been yanked out of the dinner party's catering kitchen, halfway through a spectacular beef Wellington.

If she were rattled, Southward didn't show it. She smiled.

"I believe it's code," she replied softly. "I think the particular *Hussein* is the Prophet Muhammad's grandson. His birthday will be celebrated this year on Saturday, the twenty-fourth of November in the festival of *Ashura*. As you know, Islam follows the Lunar Calendar, so birthdays, feast days, and so on change every year. For Shia Muslims, it's a major festival marking Hussein's martyrdom. While the Prophet Muhammad's birthday falls January twenty-ninth. *Milad un Nabi*."

"Your hypothesis," mused Canning, leaning back in his chair. He still looked skeptical, but the contempt had gone from his voice.

Southward shrugged. "Sure. We've already searched for any Husseins connected to Sheikh Ali, come up with several, but none stand out. This is the best hypothesis we've got."

"Their voices, when you listened in. You think this is for real, or just Jihadi posturing?" Canning asked.

"Jihadi jive talking," cut in Del Russo, with a satisfied smile.

Southward didn't condescend to look at him, she replied to Chief Canning.

"I've heard the Sheikh's voice announcing a one-hundred-thousand-dollar bonus to the families of the *Shuhada'*, the suicide bombers, for every dead body in the bombings. He said it in code, but I interpreted it, I knew what he meant. I've listened to over a hundred hours of his voice. I know the posturings, and I know when it's for real. This, I am sure of it, is for real. *The wrath of Allah will rain down*, some aerial attack. Could be planes crashing into their targets. Or dropping bombs."

"How the hell would they get hold of bomb carriers and bomb loads?" asked Del Russo.

"What if they managed to turn one of our own, or more than one?" posed Southward.

"What, our own Air Force attack us?" asked Canning scowling.

"It's an avenue, sir. Another is a private plane. The Sheikh has resources; we believe he has at least four billion US dollars in liquid investments, some of that earned by shorting the Dow pre-Nine-eleven. It would be nothing to him to buy a couple of private planes, kit them out."

"You're very well informed, Ms. Southward," observed Canning.

"The Fusion Group sends me the briefings they collate. I read them, well, some of them. All the ones relating to Sheikh Ali."

"Target fixation," murmured Del Russo. Southward again ignored him.

Canning sat back, massaged his temples. They got so much intel coming at them like flak. What to prioritize, what to ignore? Even with the monstrous resources at his disposal, they had to prioritize. Only time would vindicate, or hang him.

He eyed the woman before him. He'd read her CV in the car on the way. She was brilliant, one of the top Arabists of her generation. Ambitious, keen to make her career, keen to prevent an atrocity. Her clear, bright eyes looked back at him. He saw in them utter conviction, a conviction that he, these days, overburdened, sometimes lacked. Hoax or fire? He went with his gut.

"OK, Ms. Southward. We'll run with your hypothesis. We'll explore both ideas. Maybe this is a Shia version of the Sunni's planned *second wave* post-Nine-eleven."

Canning turned to his aides. "You'll remember Khalid Sheikh Mohammed, with a little persuasion from the boys in Guantánamo, disclosed that he had been planning to attack the Liberty Building in LA. We arrested all the plotters, foiled the attack, but we've all been wondering when the next would come. This might be jive talking, but it might be real. We cannot afford to discount it. Get it typed up, Ol, circulate to Category A. Frank, get a list of all private airfields in California. Have every last one of them checked out. Discreetly."

Both men straightened, ready for action. Now that their boss had spoken, all their languor stiffened into resolve, observed Southward, amused but also relieved. From the moment she had listened to the intercept, her spine had been tingling.

"One question, sir," asked Peters. "At what stage do we consider bringing Ali in? I mean if he's here in the US now . . ."

"Reality is, we'd upset our allies," replied Canning. "We cannot afford to piss off the Saudis without a damn good reason. Even if Baharna is a Shia not a Sunni. Plus, some proof would be good. We have nothing concrete. We have suspicions, but Ali Al Baharna always speaks in riddles, as you know. All our suppositions are extrapolations. He cannot be arrested for mouthing veiled threats without there being evidence to back up the threats. As far as the world is concerned, he is a legitimate businessman, vastly successful. And that part is all true. So we keep doing what we're doing." He turned to Southward. His craggy face had softened a fraction, as if he had eased, just a fraction, the barrier of his cynicism. "And you guys at NSA keep digging. We all keep digging until we expose him for the Jihadi you believe him to be."

"One more thing, sir," murmured Southward. "He signed off his call to his brother saying: *habat hoboob al jenna.*"

"And?" demanded Del Russo with a defensive jut of his jaw.

"Oh, sorry, I thought you'd know what it meant," replied

Southward with a sweet smile. "It *is* rather well known. It means: *the winds of paradise are blowing*. It's what the suicide bombers and the Nine-eleven hijackers signed off with."

45

Special Agent Rodgers, sporting a broad grin, shuffled into Ange Wilkie's office. His partner was sipping one of the toxic-looking green smoothies she put away every day.

"What's up Rac? Someone give you a present?"

"They got a hit on Minnie Mouse's accent. California. San Jose," announced Rodgers.

Wilkie slammed down the smoothie. "Excellent! Silicon Valley. I like this one."

"Me too. So what next?"

Wilkie tilted her head to one side, pondering. "Let's assume there's some kinda local connection to Silicon Valley, or California. . . . Let's look for an unusual trade that has something to do with either."

"That's a tad wide. . . ."

"We narrow it down," replied Wilkie. "We look for an announcement, a price-changing one. Then we check out the trades that went down just before."

"Big ask. I'll get on it."

"You 'n' me both. As luck would have it, I've got a contact down there. Bond salesperson. Real smart," declared Wilkie.

"How'd you rub shoulders with one a' those, Wilks?"

"Aikido contest. She's a third dan black belt. We were up against each other in the national finals three years back. We've stayed in touch. She's smart and she's straight."

"No shit. Who won?"

"Come on now, Special Agent Rodgers. D'you have to ask?"

"So she beat you. Cool. Glad someone can."

"Get outta here before I force-feed you my smoothie."

Rodgers backed out, arms raised in surrender. Chuckling, Ange scrolled through her contacts. God, she loved this job, loved her colleagues—some of them at least, Rodgers and Bergers chiefly—and she loved searching for the trail of guilt, sniffing round randomly at first like a loosed bloodhound, then homing in on the scent and following where it led. They followed lots of scents, lots of trails, waited for them to intersect. That was the moment of bliss. The intersection point. She had no husband, no kids, just a feral cat who showed up sporadically like the Casanova he was. And she was cool with all that. She had freedom, she had purpose, and both sustained her.

She found the contact she wanted, put in the call, hoped the contact would remember her after a silence of years.

"Lucy Chen," purred the voice.

"Hi, Lucy, it's Ange Wilkie here."

"Hey, Wilks!" exclaimed Lucy with the instant recall of the best brokers. "You calling to fix up a rerun?"

"Anytime, just not soon. You got a minute?"

"Shoot."

"I need some help. I'm looking for any big announcements coming out of Silicon Valley, or California in general, over the last few days. Something price changing. And/or, and I know this is a long shot, any unusual trades being put on."

"Why? What's up?"

"You know I can't answer that."

"A girl's gotta ask. The more I know, the better I can help you."

"Look, all I got is this: A blue-collar type, female, in California, is tipping off a white-collar type, male, in NYC. He came onto our radar back when we got Raj Rajaratnam. Supposition, no hard evidence. We're looking for evidence. What we can be pretty certain of is that the guy'll be hiding behind nominee companies for the trades. We have no idea what the tip is or what the trades it generates will be, just that she called in with it this past Monday. It's possible there'll be a California connection to the trades, but then again maybe not."

"Bit of a needle in a haystack," observed Lucy drily.

"Does anyone ever search for a needle anyplace else?"

Lucy laughed. "Touché. I'll see what I can do. Let me have a trawl and a think."

Lucy had contacts. Lucy had admirers. Lucy was owed, and there was a sizeable community out there who would be happy to have Lucy Chen in their debt. The power of charm.

46

Dan Jacobsen looked round the office, scarcely masking his distaste. The place was a friggin' gallery of black-and-white images, all featuring MackStack posing with the powerful—a president, four movie stars, three sports stars—basking in their reflected glory, unaware that his own was a leasehold, merely the trappings of an office that could be snatched from him at any time by the capricious billionaire owner of the *Reporter*. And he didn't even know it. Power corrupts, image blinds . . . Dan eyed the man slouching against the power desk of pewter marble.

The editor wore his usual black trousers and crisply ironed shirt. He had a shirt fetish, had hundreds of hand-tailored ones, which he and only he would iron. No maid or laundry service ever got it right.

"What have you got for me, Daniel?" MackStack asked silkily.

"I'm playing it straight here; I've got what you read. Nothing more," Dan replied levelly. He walked to the window, looked out, wanted to step right through the glass and out.

"Listen up, Jacobsen," said Stack, straightening up, walking to the window, standing shoulder to shoulder with Jacobsen. The journalist had four inches and sixty pounds on the editor, who disdained all forms of physical endeavor, save sex, but felt safe, sublimely cosseted and enthroned by his editorship,

"I know there're more stories you can get rooting around with the ARk Storm people," Stack whispered with a sickening complicity. "Stories they don't want the public to get. Stories of thousands of bodies rotting in the waters, in the ghettos, in the badlands, where the voters don't vote. Make Katrina and the New Orleans rescue look fuckin' textbook. No way they could get to everyone, or evac everyone out. So there'll be a certain minimum collateral damage they'll be prepared to accept. This is the shit they'll be discussing behind closed doors." He moved away, perhaps finally detecting the energy and the revulsion pumping from his journalist, who stood still, superficially unmoved.

Stack moved behind his desk, sat, spoke to Jacobsen's back.

"Added to which, I am gunning for that bastard Gabriel

Messenger. Christ, the guy's a number. The custom house on Seventeen Mile Drive, the Ferrari, the backgammon tournaments, the tennis . . . In love with himself!" he spat. "I'll just bet there's some dirt there. No one's that good without pushing the envelope, and my gut tells me he's pushing it right over the edge. There's at least two good stories going begging. So why do we have none of it?"

"I am using my journalistic skills, old school journalistic skills, legal ones," replied Dan, turning to face him.

"You mean that you are not using any of your considerable technical skills?"

"Using listening devices to get stories, like *News of the World* in the UK, who incidentally had to shut down when they were caught. . . . That would be illegal, would it not?" observed Dan. He stood, hands in his pockets, and he smiled, the same smile that had been on a number of occasions the last thing the recipient had ever seen. The editor remained oblivious.

"Don't get cute with me," snapped MackStack. "There's a queue round the block who can out-write you. You're here because you can write, granted, but equally because you have skills that any editor would kill for. In-house skills."

Dan walked forward, leaned over his editor's desk, palms planted on the polished wood. His shirtsleeves were rolled back. The editor, in an instinctively male atavistic way, looked at the bulging forearms, felt the first flicker of uncertainty.

"You know what?" suggested Dan, voice low. "Why don't you just round up that queue and go and have a group jerk off. Get them to do your dirty work."

MackStack laughed. "Nice try. Do your job, Jacobsen. While you still have it."

47

The Man listened to the recordings, care of his remotely downloaded store-and-forward device. Freidland was paranoid, though as was true for many paranoiacs, he had good reason. The Man would not have put it past Freidland to sweep his house for bugs, and so he had chosen a device that did not emit a signal that could be intercepted or tracked. It could be detected by very high-tech scanners that flooded the room with radio waves and analyzed the bounce-back patterns, but he doubted that Charles Freidland would have the seventy grand to spend on that or would know where to go to get hold of one.

The beauty of this device was that he could connect to it remotely at a safe time of his choice then download an actogram—a graphical picture which showed when conversations were taking place. This allowed him to download and listen to only parts of the actogram that were clearly conversations, not vacuuming or washing up. It was a time-consuming process, but it was a necessary insurance policy, one he was to become very glad he had taken out.

He had also—cleverly, in his mind—downloaded via the wireless LAN in Freidland's house. As it worked over the GSM system, it could be monitored anywhere in the world. If he'd been forced to use Bluetooth or the radio link, its range would have been only fifty meters for Bluetooth and about five hundred meters for the radio link. He smiled to himself. The beauty of technology.

He sat in his office, swigging black coffee, putting in the hours. He couldn't afford not to. The CDs which housed the recordings were stacked in a cascade system, allowing for days of recordings to be saved. When one was full, the next in the cascade took the recordings. He hadn't listened in for over a week and now he paid the price: hours of recordings to listen to.

He sat up sharply when he heard a familiar name. He listened to the woman's questions, to the man's answers, listened to the woman as she made her bold and oh-so-foolish declaration, unwittingly tightening the noose around her own elegant neck.

The Man looked at his watch. Morning in the Middle East. If Sheikh Ali were there. With his fleet of boats and planes he could be anywhere.

He rang, waited, completed the encryption process while the Sheikh completed his side.

"Yes," said the lightly accented voice a little while later.

"We've got a problem."

"What kind?"

"Freidland's been talking."

"Old man's crazy."

"He's convinced someone he's not."

"Who?"

"Someone who works for Falcon. The forecaster."

"The Oracle?"

"Correct."

"She knows all about Zeus. Deal with her. Immediately."

"I have to be careful. As you said a few days back, the body count is climbing. We don't want to attract attention. I need to make it look like an accident."

"Do that. But if it looks like she's going to talk to the cops, the press, anyone, then kill her as soon as possible, accident or no accident, just silence her."

"I will. I'll stick close, keep an eye on what she does, who she talks to."

"Don't make her suspect you."

"Don't worry. She has no idea who I really am, no reason to suspect me."

48

Gwen stood outside on her deck, gazing into the night, looking for the solace it normally offered, waiting for an elusive calm to descend. She felt exposed, swimming in a sea of lies. Not drowning. Not yet. She blew out a heavy breath. Leo trotted out behind her. She reached down to stroke him, noticed that he was standing alert. He started to growl, a low rumbling. Leo never growled. Maybe at skunks. Only at skunks, and from a safe distance.

"What's up boy?" Gwen asked, her neck tingling. Leo kept up his growling, eyes staring into the darkness.

Gwen felt a raw, instinctive fear. This was no skunk. Someone was there in the darkness, beyond her line of vision. She could feel an alien presence, almost as keenly as Leo now that he had alerted her. She imagined someone there, eyes fixed on her. Behind her, the house was all lit up, illuminating her and her dog like figures on a target.

She wheeled round, grabbed Leo's collar, pulled him into her house. Leo did not stop growling as she closed and locked the door behind her, pulled shut the curtains she rarely used, closed and locked all the windows.

Shit, shit, shit. She never felt scared here. Cursing, she called Daniel on his cell. It rang and rang. No answer.

49

Gwen left the Lab at three. The weekend couldn't start early enough for her. On Tuesday morning, Messenger had forgiven her outburst, handed back the laptop with a sardonic raising of an eyebrow. She reckoned she'd managed to act the distracted and naïve academic as the week wore on, tapping away on the laptop, playing with Zeus, getting into the guts of the model, trying to offer up more rainfall. But she found out no more about Gabriel Messenger.

She hoped to rectify that this weekend at the Half Moon Bay with Dan.

She parked up outside her house, changed into her running kit, and set off with Leo. She walked down the hill, her dog windmilling his tail in sheer joy. No growling today. Had she imagined the threat last night? Had it just been a skunk or a fox? Lit by the sun the sloping grass, the cliffs, the sea beyond all looked peaceful, devoid of threat.

It could all change in an instant—she knew that—like a quiet sea ravaged by a rogue wave, like one car slamming into another.

One hour later, pouring with sweat, purged, Gwen knocked on Marilyn's door.

Her friend pulled open the door with a smile. It seemed to Gwen that in the few weeks since she'd seen her, the old lady had become a tad more stooped. But the pale blue eyes were still as sharp and as warm as ever.

"Well *hi there* absent friend," said Marilyn in her soft voice, pulling the door open, standing back to allow Gwen in.

"I have been, haven't I?" said Gwen. "I'm sorry. It's this job. When I get home I tend to just flake."

"That's all right, honey, long as it's going well. Sit." Marilyn gestured to a sagging but comfy sofa adorned with hand-embroidered cushions that sat in the kitchen, always for others to sit in while she baked and fussed around them.

Gwen knew the drill. She sat. Marilyn poured them both glasses of her homemade lemonade, then pulled out a straight-backed chair and lowered herself into it.

Gwen drained the lemonade with a sigh of bliss. "Still OK for Leo to come to you for a sleepover?" She'd rung to ask a few days ago.

Leo was already lying by Marilyn's feet, as if he too knew the drill. Marilyn bent stiffly to ruffle the dog's ears.

" 'Course! He's good company."

Gwen wondered whether to tell Marilyn about last night's fears, decided not to frighten the old lady so baselessly.

"So, where're you off then?" asked Marilyn.

"The Half Moon Bay hotel."

"Nice! With that very fine young man you went swimming with?"

The naked swim; Gwen almost blushed. "Yes, actually. God Marilyn, you didn't look, did you?"

Marilyn planted her hands on her hips. " 'Course I did. Don't get to see sights like that at my age. Fine-looking man. Didn't even need my telescope."

"Marilyn!"

The old lady laughed in delight. "You go to that ritzy hotel with that handsome man and you have yourself a good time. " 'Bout time you did."

"I don't know about that."

"What's to know? You're both young, free, single I assume?"

"All true. And he is gorgeous, funny, intelligent, kind, a good surfer."

"And your problem is?"

"He's just too perfect. He arrived in my life like that"—
Gwen clicked her fingers—"like magic. One day nowhere;
next day, in my life."

"Sometimes fate offers us a gift," said Marilyn softly.
"And the grateful and the wise take it."

Gwen got up, walked over to Marilyn, and kissed her
cheek. "You could be right," she said, musing silently that
all gifts, even from fate, still had a price.

50

THE RITZ-CARLTON HOTEL, HALF MOON BAY,
CALIFORNIA, FRIDAY EVENING

The hotel was a huge crescent topping the high, wave-cut
cliffs. Gwen and Daniel, driving from opposite directions,
arrived within ten minutes of each other.

Gwen was sitting in the lounge drinking a chamomile
tea when Dan walked in, long and lean in his jeans, an
overnight bag slung over one shoulder.

"Hi." She got to her feet.

"Hi back." He kissed her, a quick flutter of lips to lips.

"Sorry I didn't get here first. Was in San Fran doing an
interview and the guy turned up forty minutes late. Threw
out my timing."

"No problem. It was good to just sit and people-watch
for a while."

They walked through to Reception.

"I booked two rooms, with sea views," said Daniel to
the receptionist.

Gwen filed that one away, gave him serious brownie

points. They each handed over their credit cards for an imprint.

"When d'you want to meet up?" asked Daniel, outside Gwen's door.

"Give me twenty."

Unpacked, changed, made up, Gwen twirled before the mirror. The red jersey dress fit closely over her body, flaring out from the hips. She wore nude-colored heels that put her at a good six four. She spritzed on some scent, tossed back her hair, and went to answer the knock at the door.

Daniel stood there in chinos and a blue shirt. He just looked at Gwen.

"Wow! Gwen, you take my breath away."

Part of her wished he'd said it in a flippant way.

"You're not bad yourself," she managed.

He smiled. "Let's go hunt."

It was ten fifteen when three women who just might have been hookers sashayed into the wood-paneled Eno bar. Gwen, lounging on a leather banquette, sipped her champagne. "Coming in, behind you. Three possibles."

Daniel gave them a quick glance. "No."

"No?" whispered Gwen. "Why not? They look like hookers in those minis and heels, all those erupting boobs and makeup and hair."

Dan smiled. "They're just girls out for a party. The hookers at a place like this don't look like hookers, else they wouldn't get in."

"But those hooker look-alikes do?"

"Because they're not. Because the doorman knows they're not."

"You know your subject."

He laughed. "I just notice stuff. Hookers have never done a whole lot for me. I like more of a challenge," he added slowly, eyes on hers, his own challenge unmistakable. Gwen felt the heat. It radiated out of her. She could feel his too, as he sat, just inches from her, carefully and cleverly keeping his distance.

"I can believe that," said Gwen over the rim of her glass.

"Now those two over there," said Daniel, glancing at two nicely turned-out women in pencil skirts and silk blouses. "They get my vote."

"So what now?"

"Stay here. Try not to get picked up."

"What, I look like a hooker?"

"No. You look like a goddess. That'll do it."

Gwen watched him saunter over, introduce himself with a smile. He had them laughing straight away. Gwen sipped her champagne, then glugged it as the minutes passed. Still the women laughed and tossed their hair and seemed to be on the verge of eating out of Daniel's palm. She felt a twist in her stomach, recognized it, angrily, as jealousy when one of the woman evidently gave her phone number to Daniel, who input it into his cell. Then he raised his hand in farewell and walked back to her.

She drained her glass. "And?"

"Yeah, nice girls. Very helpful."

"I'll just bet they were."

"What's that mean?"

"Scored the brunette's phone number, didn't you?"

Daniel chuckled. "Daisy, that's her name by the way, gave me Rochelle's phone number, Rochelle being the best friend of Elise, the lady who Daisy recalls had a problem with a drunk guy at the conference."

"She remembers! That's great. The conference was months back."

"True, but it was a big deal for these girls, all those big swingers in town with their ample wallets and sense of entitlement. She remembers."

"What about Elise?" asked Gwen, thawing. "Any leads on her?"

"Daisy says she hasn't seen her in an age."

"So we start with Rochelle."

They stood outside, a cool breeze whispering over the ocean. Dan dialed the number.

"Hi, Rochelle, your friend Daisy gave me your name. No, that's fine, I'm not looking for company. I just want to talk. My friend, female friend, and I just want to ask about the conference here a few months back. A friend of ours was here and, well, long story. We'll pay for your time. . . . No, there is no problem, at least none involving you. . . . Five hundred dollars? Rochelle, come on . . . three hundred it is, ten minutes of your time'll do it. . . . We're staying at the Half Moon Bay Ritz-Carlton. Great, see you at noon tomorrow. We'll be in the Conservatory Lounge."

He clicked off. "Done."

"Well done, by the sound of it. So, I guess that means we're off duty now?" mused Gwen.

"I guess it does. There's a jazz club inside, and if I'm lucky they'll play something slow. Like to dance?"

51

THE RITZ-CARLTON HOTEL, HALF MOON BAY, CALIFORNIA

Nina Simone sang "Wild Is the Wind." Gwen stood eye to eye with Daniel. Their bodies touched, molded to each other. They swayed together, not speaking. Gwen felt as if every nerve ending were supercharged. She had that heightened sense of reality she felt after riding a huge wave. Jumping in, taking the risk, riding it with utter concentration and at the same time complete abandonment to a terrifying physical force. Beauty, danger, and thrill all mixed. There was an air of contained violence about Dan, a dark intensity she had just glimpsed. She could feel the power in his body. She wondered how it would feel to unleash both in her bed.

"Er, Dan," she said, pulling back from him. "You've either got skills to die for or your phone's vibrating."

"Damn!" Dan hauled his cell phone from his chino pocket. He read the message, swore.

"My editor. Mack the Fuckin' Stack," he added, somewhat bitterly, thought Gwen. "I have to call him. Urgently, it says."

Gwen held up her hands. "Do what you've got to do. I'll just quietly self immolate here."

He grinned. "Never heard it called that before."

They walked out into the hallway.

Dan's face hardened as he put in the call.

"Yeah, Mack. Hell of a time."

Gwen watched as Dan grabbed the hotel pen, scribbled on the notepad.

"OK. I'll do it. I'll make sure I fly to San Diego too next private weekend I need."

He finished the call, turned to Gwen. "I have to go. I am theoretically on call. As is my colleague Sam Sanderson. He just had the brains to fly to San Diego. So I'm the idiot in the wrong place at the wrong time."

"Ooh, I don't know," said Gwen, snuggling closer. "Felt like a pretty right place to me."

Dan laughed. "To me too." He kissed her lightly. "To be continued."

"What's the story, anyway?" asked Gwen.

"Body's been found. Seventeen Mile Drive."

52

After a fractured, frustrated night with little sleep, Gwen woke late. She stretched, slipped from her king-size Egyptian-cottoned bed and wandered through to the marble bathroom. Pure luxury, everywhere she looked. She pulled on the heavy cotton-toweling robe and padded across the thick carpet to the minibar. Knocking back a bottle of pineapple and mango juice, she saw a piece of paper protruding under her door.

"Boudy, got back at four. Dirty and p'd off. Didn't want to contaminate you. I'll knock on your door at eleven thirty."

"You're punctual," said Gwen as she opened her door two hours later.

"Military habits die hard."

He looked tired, thought Gwen and weary. "Bad night?" she asked.

"A young woman, buried in a deep grave, dug up by a mountain lion then found by a hiker and his Weimaraner. And I'm tasked with grubbing round, getting the story."

"And?"

"Nothing yet. There'll be a press con when the cops figure out who she is. No one's been reported missing, which means she's one of life's forgotten people, few or loose bonds, not missed." He rubbed a hand over his face. "Not much of a life. Worse death."

Gwen didn't ask more.

Dan's cell phone trilled. He frowned at it. "Rochelle.

Please don't cancel," he said to the ringing phone. He answered it.

"Daniel here." His frown faded. "No. No problem. Early's great. We'll be right down."

53

"Rochelle?" asked Daniel, holding out his hand. The girl nodded, shook it tentatively. She wore skinny, faded jeans and white Converse sneakers, with a white tee. Her face was pale, un-made up. She was thin—not trendily thin, but druggie thin, underfed thin, nerve-wracked thin, one or all three, thought Gwen. Her fair hair was lank. She looked uncared for, lost. She looked about sixteen, thought Gwen with a flash of anger. She should have been at home, eating apple pie, fussed over by Mom. She offered her own hand.

"Hi, I'm Gwen."

Rochelle took her hand, sat back down at her table, tucking her hands under her thighs.

"Would you like coffee?" asked Dan.

"What I'd really like is lunch," Rochelle replied. "I'm kinda hungry."

"Me too. Good idea," said Gwen.

"And my cash. Please," added Rochelle.

Gwen handed her three rolled hundreds under the table.

Rochelle checked them and pocketed them.

A waiter appeared and all three of them ordered burgers, fries, and Coke. When the waiter disappeared, Dan turned to Rochelle.

"Thanks for meeting us."

She shrugged. "Three hundred dollars and lunch for a bit of talk is a no brainer."

"So this big conference," said Dan, "the venture capital one, back in June. You were there, right?"

"I was. Lots of the girls were. Place was full of guys with a ton of money, away from their wives, looking to party." She spoke impassively but a film of disgust clouded her eyes.

"We heard talk that your friend Elise was with some guy who got wasted—"

Rochelle cut in. "They were all wasted, seemed like. But, yeah, she was with this drunk guy. Very drunk guy."

"We've heard he said, or did something out of the ordinary, in a business context," said Dan.

"Something about Paparuda?" prompted Gwen.

"All that shit with the weird name? Yeah. She told me bits of it."

"Could you please tell us whatever you remember," nudged Dan.

Rochelle pulled her hands from under her thighs and picked at her nails. She looked up. "I remember it all 'cause it was kinda crazy. Elise says she went to this guy's room, that he seemed OK, but then he started drinking more and shouting and ordering, do this, do that, getting rough, hitting her and stuff. She wanted to get out. He wouldn't let her. She got him talking, thought it'd maybe calm him down. She asked him what he did." She paused as the waiter delivered their cokes. She took a long sip through the striped straw, looking suddenly like the child she was.

She looked up, flicked her glance between them.

"So Elise said he started talking rain, 'bout how he was going to make it rain. And this is the crazy bit. Sounds like one of those God freaks. He said it would soon be time to get into your ark, that he was going to *make* it rain. That he was going to make an Ark Storm, whatever the hell that is."

Gwen held her breath, let it out silently. "*Make* an ARk Storm?"

"Yeah. And that she'd better believe him and get the hell out of California 'cause it was going to rain like hell. And that *he* was going to make it rain." She looked up as their food arrived.

"And that's it. She must've believed him 'cause she did just that. After she told me all this crap, she just upped and left. No one's heard diddly squat from her."

"Did she tell you his name, assuming he told her that is," asked Gwen, heart pounding.

"Men often give the wrong name," snorted Rochelle. "They don't want a whore finding out who they are, stalking them. But he did give her a name, for what it's worth; Haas, Hans, some foreign shit like that."

"Hans?" queried Gwen and Dan in unison. Dan glanced at Gwen but she shrugged. "Did she tell you what he looked like, this Haas/Hans?" Gwen asked Rochelle.

The girl shook her head. "Just that he had these intense, kinda crazy eyes."

"Nothing else?" asked Dan.

Rochelle shook her head. "Na. Just that he was crazy and scared the shit out of her."

"So how'd she get away?"

"When he went to the can, she ran for the door, got out, ran down the corridor. He chased her, she was shouting, then this guy came out of his room, stopped the crazy one. They musta known one another, Elise reckoned. Anyway, she got her chance. She bolted. The nice guy came after her, bought her a coffee, comforted her. I think she told him what she told me. She said he was sweet, was a good listener. That's all I know. End of story. She got out. She was lucky, I reckon."

54

Gwen and Dan sat huddled at their table after Rochelle had left. They stayed silent as the waiter cleared the detritus of lunch. Background Muzak tinkled.

"Who the hell is *Haas or Hans*?" Gwen asked herself aloud. "I don't know anybody going by either name."

"Haas could be a fake name," hazarded Dan. "Just as Rochelle suggested. Or Hans could be a real, and incidentally, a German name."

"Intense, crazy eyes. That description could fit Messenger all right," said Gwen. "Maybe Hans is his middle name."

"That's easy to find out. I'll get onto it in a bit."

Dan braced his elbows on the table and leaned across to Gwen. "Let's assume, in the absence of any other ideas, that it *is* Messenger. The thing that's really freaking me out is the suggestion you can *make* an ARk Storm!"

Gwen lowered her voice, even though no one was near.

"If the ionizers were correctly positioned and programmed, if there were enough of them and they were all sent up on drones, and a big enough atmospheric river storm roars in, then I'd have to say, yes. It is theoretically possible you could make an ARk Storm. The ARk Storm 1000. Clearly someone, and we have to assume it was Messenger, believes that they *can* do it. *Intends* to do it. And here's the thing," added Gwen. "Monday, Messenger comes to me, gives me a laptop with the Paparuda model loaded onto it, asks me to play with the model, see if I can get it to yield more rain."

"Shit!"

"Yeah, shit. It is quite possible that I have helped him."

"But why? Why the hell would someone want to make an ARk Storm?" Dan peered intently at Gwen, seeking the answer in her eyes.

"Three reasons. Because he's crazy, because he can, and to make money."

"How d'you make money out of this? Riley said an Ark Storm could cost the state of California a trillion dollars."

"Exactly. He'd short the companies that insure property against severe weather events like this. Even better, he'd buy put options. And he'd go long on wheat, orange juice, all that kind of thing."

"And I thought I'd seen evil," mused Dan, eyes looking away.

"Comes in many guises," said Gwen.

Dan looked back to her. "You're very well informed, on the financial front."

"We discussed it at the Lab. One of the traders has it all planned out, with Messenger's backing. How to make money out of my prediction of an ARk Storm."

"And scores of people would die, hundreds of thousands would lose their homes, harvests'd be washed away. . . ."

"Yeah, but Messenger would make out like a bandit."

"There must be easier ways to make money, legally and illegally," said Dan, frowning. "There's something we're not getting here."

"The mania of the scientist testing his invention?" suggested Gwen.

"Have to be one hell of a mania."

"Evil, then."

"Messenger strike you as a psychopath?"

Gwen fell silent. "He's an extreme person. He seems to live on the edge—fast cars, fast bikes. He likes playing head games. He seems to be holding himself in so tight, like he's afraid of his shadow." Gwen shrugged. "Does that make him a psychopath?"

"Not that, but the hidden stuff could. They're not easy to spot. They wouldn't have a head count if they were."

Gwen's mouth felt dry. She drained her Coke. "No, I guess not."

"And, if he thought someone, say Al Freidland, had heard about his plans, from Elise, say, and was threatening to blow the whistle on him," suggested Dan. "That would be ample motive for murder, especially if he's ready to fill the morgues just to line his bank accounts."

"Ample motive for murder," agreed Gwen. "Add to that, with Freidland dead, he gets sole charge of Zeus. Gabriel Messenger gets to play God."

55

THE SECURITIES AND EXCHANGE COMMISSION, NYC, MONDAY, NOON

Ange Wilkie was prowling down Liberty Street, hunting lunch, when her cell phone rang. She groaned, saw Lucy Chen's name displayed, and smiled. She took the call.

"Lucy! What's up?"

"Old Chinese proverb I want to share with you," purred the voice, sounding ever more like the cat who got the cream.

"I'm listening."

"Proverb says, sometimes if you have really nice, really helpful friends, you just might find that little needle hiding in the haystack. . . ."

Ange felt her blood quicken. "You're killing me, Lucy. What you got?"

Lucy laughed, but when she spoke again her voice was all business.

"Unusual activity. Conducted by nominee companies. I asked some of my buddies. We can all sorta sniff out insider trades, at least some of the time 'cause they basically justify trades for which we, the uninitiated, can see no justification. They're the kind of trades that give you pause. Some of the time it's that the guy on the other end takes a different angle on the same info you have. Other times he just has different info. *Inside info.* So my buddies and I got together at Bar Agricole and had a good old root around." Lucy paused for effect.

"I'm biting . . ."

Lucy laughed.

"So here it is. A series of put options on three California property casualty insurance companies. Quite a collection, far as I can gather. They've all been put on over the past week. Add up to a nice chunk a change. Thing about these trades that stuck out is that they are very specific and counter to the general market trend at the moment. My buddies and I could see no reason why someone would take such a position. And, the even odder thing is that the position is not company specific, but sector specific."

Ange nodded furiously. "How big were the trades?"

"Big. All I know."

"Any idea who did the trades?" Ange probed, standing like an island surrounded by rushing lunch hour bodies who flowed around her with varying degrees of grace and fury. She was impervious to all but the voice on the phone.

"Nominee companies. Their identity I cannot tell you. I don't know myself. And my sources wouldn't tell me. Client confidentiality. Could get themselves fired."

"Fair points. Lucy, this is awesome! I owe you. Big time!"

"I'll remember," purred the voice. Always nice to have the SEC on side."

Ange chuckled. "One last question. What does it mean? Why would someone put on those trades?"

"It's basically like selling something short, only with leverage. It's like a bigger punt."

"I get that. But *why*?"

"I mentioned the trades were sector specific, not company specific. That means whoever put them on thinks the sector as a whole is gonna get hammered. That means big, and I mean real *big* insurance claims are expected. Big enough to move the price substantially." Lucy paused. "This is where it gets really weird. I was wracking my brain trying to figure out why the price would move against prior market expectation. Here's your menu; the Big Earthquake, catastrophic fires, though it's getting to be the wrong season for California wildfires, or the new big one there's been talk of recently, the ARk Storm—basically a huge winter storm bringing in biblical floods. Google it," added Lucy. "There was a big article about it recently in the *San Fran Reporter,*" she continued. "Scared the hell outta me. Anyways, someone, maybe several someones, clearly think one of those three is on its way. Oh, and this I forgot to mention. These are six month puts, meaning the players think it will hit within six months. Which kinda rules out fires. So take your pick. Quake or flood?"

Ange forgot lunch. She wheeled round so fast she nearly took out a Starbucks-carrying jock. With a quick apology, she speed-walked back to the office.

"Keep him there! Cuff him if you have to!" she called out to Bergers' PA, Bret, rushing past her boss's office to collect Rodgers. She found him, head on his desk.

"Rac! Wake up!" she hissed. "Come with me."

"Hm, this good?" he mumbled.

"Red hot! C'mon." She pulled him to his feet, marched back to Bergers' office. Bret niftily stepped out of their way.

"A word, sir?" asked Wilkie, managing to pause at his open door.

Troy Bergers forked his tuna salad into his mouth. He eyed them as he swallowed.

"Come in. You look happy. What you got?" He nodded to his chairs.

Rodgers sat down. Wilkie paced.

"The woman who rang Glass who then did the 'call me on my personal cell phone' insider shimmie?"

"Yeah?"

"Agent Rodgers got the accent people on her. They came back with California. Silicon Valley area. So I call a contact, ask about any unusual trades going down San Fran way."

"Needle in a haystack," grunted Bergers, "though the look on your face tells me you found it."

"Contact found it. Or something that sure looks like it. A series of put options on California property casualty insurance companies. Described as "big" in size. All in the last week."

Bergers laid down his fork, dabbed at his lips with a napkin, then trashed the lot. "Who did the trades?"

"She couldn't tell me. Didn't know herself. Said her sources wouldn't tell her. Client confidentiality. Could get themselves fired and all that. Nominee companies, of course."

"OK, I get that. But it's a bit of a stretch to think this is an insider trade. First, why would someone put on those trades?"

"Asked her that. Only reasons she could think of was the Big One, the mega-earthquake, or the ARk Storm."

"*ARk* Storm? What the hell is that?" asked Bergers with a frown.

"Catastrophic superstorm," answered Rodgers. "Basically washes away California. Read something in National Geogr—"

"Guys!" exclaimed Bergers, cutting him off. He threw up his hands. "You're trying to tell me that someone knows this earthquake or this storm is coming, your California woman, and she tips off Ronald Glass and some seriously huge hitter, who then buy the puts. That's crazy! How can anyone forecast a quake or the weather like that?"

Wilkie gave a moue of defeat. "I know it's a stretch; thing is, taking out a put like that—a six-month one, incidentally—it's very specific. It suggests inside info."

"Yeah, from God. It's probably some weird hedge. Nothing more. Get outta here and lay off the drugs."

56

CARMEL, MONDAY MORNING

Gwen clocked into the Lab at five after nine on Monday morning. She forced a breezy smile, aimed for a loose stroll as she headed for her office. She greeted Mandy, Kevin Barclay, and Mel Barbieri, all hogging the coffee machine with Monday morning yawns. Peter Weiss shuffled past, Beats headphones clamped to his ears, whistling in time. R.E.M. again. He raised a hand in greeting, secreted himself in his office, back-kicking the door closed, able to whistle, Gwen supposed, to his heart's content without risking violent attack.

Gwen sat at her desk, turned on her computer, wondered how she could keep up her act.

She buried herself in the sensors and their latest readings. Still the seas warmed. She felt sure an ARk Storm was getting closer. Maybe *the* ARk Storm 1000. She could almost see it, speeding across the oceans on the Pineapple Express. How much longer could she keep silent?

Her cell trilled at eleven.

"Lunch today?" asked Dan, unusually curt.

"Sure," she replied.

"Same place we met?" he asked elliptically.

"Sure. Twelve thirty?"

"See you then," he confirmed and hung up.

He didn't sound his usual self, thought Gwen, perturbed.

He was waiting for her at a corner table of the seafront café in Carmel, nursing a San Pellegrino.

He greeted her with a distracted kiss.

"Went to a press con this morning, Monterey cops," he said by way of hello. "The body they found when we were at the Half Moon's been ID'd. Elise Rochberger."

Gwen gasped. "Rochelle's friend. The hooker the man calling himself *Haas/Hans* roughed up?"

"Yeah, roughed up, and quite possibly killed."

"Unless you believe in coincidence."

"I don't," said Dan, eyes hard.

57

HURRICANE POINT, MONDAY EVENING

Gwen reckoned there was no alternative but honesty. Up to a point. She knocked on Marilyn's door, called out to her neighbor.

"Gwen, come on in," called out Marilyn. She was bent over the oven, in the process of retrieving a heavy dish.

"Shepherd's pie," she announced, placing it on a heat-proof slab on her wooden table.

"Care to join me?"

Gwen smelled the vapors drifting across the kitchen.

"Try keeping me back!"

They blew on the steaming meat and potato, then Gwen set to some serious eating. Lunch with Dan was more talk than food. Elise's murder had obliterated her appetite.

Gwen finished with a smile of delight. She was just about to launch into her warning when Marilyn spoke.

"Glad to see you got the electricians in at last."

"Say again?"

"The work's started on your house. Good to see."

"No."

"Whaddya mean no, it must be—"

"Sorry, Marilyn, to cut in, but no, no work has started."

"But I saw the man letting himself into your house. Surprised him actually. I'd driven out, two minutes later realized I'd forgotten my pocketbook, came back, drove past, saw him going in, white electrician's van parked outside. Vale Electrics it was called. Anyways, I slowed, said *hello* and it was good to see him starting, how I was always afraid the house would burn down and all. . . . He was real friendly. What's wrong?"

"He wasn't an electrician. I haven't arranged anything to be done to my house yet. I haven't had time."

"Then who was he?"

"That's the question. Look, Marilyn, something's going on. The less I tell you the better, but, fact is, you're in danger just because you live next to me. I want you to go and stay with your sister again."

Marilyn pushed her plate away from her. She clasped her pale, veined hands together and gripped tight.

"What are you saying, Gwen?"

"Last week, Thursday night, I felt sure there was someone outside my house, watching me. Leo went on alert.

Now this. Someone has effectively broken into my house in broad daylight."

"Why would they do that? Were you burgled?"

"Not obviously. I'm going to go back and have a thorough check after we've finished up here. There's something going on with a deal at Falcon. Two people are dead. I have no proof that there's a connection, but my handsome friend and I are convinced there is and we are trying to prove it. In the meantime, please Marilyn, go away somewhere safe. If not to your sister's, then let me treat you to a cruise."

Something in her words must have struck a cord because Gwen saw fear mixed with the outrage in Marilyn's eyes.

"What, just up and leave?" asked the old lady, taking a long gulp of water, swallowing awkwardly.

"I have to get you out of harm's way, Marilyn. Please. I cannot lose anyone else. I cannot lose you."

Marilyn nodded, looked resolute. She reached across the table, grabbed Gwen's hand, gave it a squeeze.

"All right. I'll ring Belinda later. Tell her to expect me."

"Good. Soon as possible."

"For how long?"

"Until this is all sorted out. I have a feeling it won't be long." Gwen had that sense of events accelerating, sweeping all before them, almost too fast to step out of the way.

58

HURRICANE POINT

Back home, Gwen took her cordless phone, walked out onto the deck, leaned against the rail, and called Dan.

"Someone broke into my house."

"Are you all right?" he asked sharply.

"Fine. I was out. I just—"

"Stop!" Dan said sharply. "Save it till I get there. Just got to make a quick detour. I'll be there in an hour. Lock your doors. Bolt them from the inside."

Gwen waited. She hated waiting. Darkness fell. After forty minutes, Leo started to growl. *Shit! Enough of this,* swore Gwen. Marilyn was alone, with no dog to protect her, and she had witnessed and spoken to whoever had broken into her house. She was in danger now! Gwen grabbed her Maglite—flashlight-*cum*-weapon—called to Leo, and ran from her house. She ran full-pelt down the hill to Marilyn's house, where the lights still burned. Her flashlight wobbled in her hand. The battery was old and the light was faint, all but useless. She heard Leo yelp, then when she ran toward the sound she collided with someone in the darkness, someone big and solid. She lashed out with fist and feet and flashlight, connected with flesh, heard a grunt, then she was violently shoved, falling hard on her back, knocking her head as she hit the ground, winded. She tried to jump up, to suck in breath, but it took seconds and by the time she was up, the man, it had *not* felt like a woman, had gone. Leo ran up to her, limping badly, licking her face.

"Marilyn. Go to Marilyn," she rasped, still short of air.

She knocked violently on the locked door, called out. Marilyn appeared moments later, looking ghostly in a billowing white nightgown.

"Gwen! Are you all right? What's happened?"

Gwen hurried in with Leo, locked the door behind her. She brandished her flashlight. "Marilyn, I'm just going to check your house. Stay here with Leo." Gwen moved quickly through the rooms.

"No one's here," she reported back.

"Why would you think there was?" asked Marilyn, her voice tremulous.

"Leo growled. I ran down here, collided with someone. I think he was here to go after you. It was right by your house."

"Well holy hell!" Anger mixed with fear now.

"I think he's gone now. And it seems he was alone. Look, Marilyn, I want you to pack and leave. Now. Don't wait till tomorrow. Just drive out of here. Stop at a hotel, motel. Wherever you need. I'd say stay the night with me, but I'm not sure my house is safe."

59

HURRICANE POINT

Gwen saw off Marilyn, watched her taillights disappear up the dirt track, then she went back up to her own house. She'd left it unlocked, wondered whether the man had come here. Again she checked rooms, heart racing, flashlight aloft. But her house was empty and undisturbed, far as she could tell. Minutes later Dan's Cougar roared up.

Gwen unbolted, unlocked her door and let him in.

"Just passed your neighbor," he said. "Nearly sideswiped me. Woman in a hurry."

"With cause!" exclaimed Gwen.

Dan raised a finger to his lips. He pulled her close, kissed her hard, then whispered in her ear.

"Come outside with me."

Raising an eyebrow, she followed him out. They stood on the deck, leaning against the wooden rail, gazing into the darkness. The moon was full but the sky was cloudy; stratocumulus scudded across the curve of the sky at great speed switching the moonlight on and off like a lamp. When exposed, the moon was circled by a white corona.

It should have been beautiful. Gwen could smell the salt of the ocean and the sweat of her own fear.

"What do—" Dan paused, took hold of Gwen's arms. "You're trembling."

"Something else happened."

Quickly, Gwen told him about Leo growling, her flight, her collision with the man in the darkness.

"Fuck! You see him?"

Gwen shook her head. "He was big, built. That's all I know. He grunted when I kicked out so he'll have a good bruise where I hit."

"He could have killed you."

"He didn't try. I got the feeling he didn't want to. He ran off quickly enough."

Dan nodded, face grim. "What about Marilyn?"

"I think he was about to go in there and I disturbed him." Quickly, she filled him in on what Marilyn had told her about the electrician and his van. He nodded, taking it all in, the crease between his eyebrows deepening, with anger or just concentration Gwen couldn't tell.

"Nothing stolen?"

"Not a thing. No trace anyone had even been in."

"A pro then. And he might have been after Marilyn if she ID'd him earlier in the day."

"Anyway, as you saw, she's hightailed it out to her sister's in Sacramento."

"So now we just have to worry about you. First thing, don't say anything you wouldn't want the bad guys to over-hear in the house," said Dan.

"Why?"

"If nothing's stolen maybe something's planted."

"A listening device?" guessed Gwen, voice rising with outrage.

"Exactly. I've got a sweeper here." He pulled out a foot-long rod that looked like a radar gun.

"Called Palladium. We keep it at the *Reporter*. There's a lot of people'd like to steal our stories or ID our sources."

"And you can just walk out with it?"

"My Ed, the truly loathsome but sometimes useful MackStack, has one at home. Tad paranoid but with what he's seen and heard I can't blame him. He lives fifteen minutes from me." Dan shrugged. "He owes me."

"OK. Sweep away."

He turned to move. Gwen followed him. He paused.

"Do something for me. Come in with me, put on some music, not too loud, anything."

Gwen eyed him. "Sure. But why?"

"Can I explain everything later? Sooner we get this done, the better."

"OK," replied Gwen, not exactly happy, wanting to know, impatient as always, but she was out of her depth here and Dan seemed to know what he was doing. The crooked smile was gone, replaced by a hard seriousness she had rarely glimpsed in him. He stood there in his jeans and t-shirt, hair tousled. Despite all that was going on, she wanted him, wanted to reach out, kiss his lips, take his hand. . . .

Instead, she followed him back into her home, put on Jason Mraz, and watched him.

Dan dropped to his knees beside the closed door. He took out what looked like a small medical microscope with a tube and an inner light, put it to his eye, and peered at the lock. After about a minute, he straightened up, put his finger to his lips as Gwen opened her mouth to speak.

Next he pulled out a pair of headphones and, radar-gun-like scanner in hand, began to move around her sitting room. He regularly got down on hands and knees, fingers probing under tables, inside and under lamps, in her desk drawers, behind her TV, under the sofa, under and in almost every object in the room. It was oddly intimate, and utterly thorough, this silent probing. The man clearly knew what he was doing.

After forty minutes, Gwen saw him pause then move toward her desk. Carefully, he picked up her table lamp. He turned to her, pointed to it, and offered her his headphones.

She slipped them on and heard a high-pitched wailing sound. Dan took back the headphones and continued his search for another five minutes. Then he removed his headphones and gestured outside.

He replaced his kit in the briefcase and followed her out onto the deck. They leaned back against the table, a foot apart, looking out to sea. Every so often the moon would emerge, the crests of waves silver, then disappear behind the clouds again, drawing darkness down upon them.

"First off, your lock's picked," announced Dan.

"How d'you know?"

"Tiny scratches. The usual key wears deeper scratches into the lock over time. A picker will leave tiny, faint scratches. You've got that."

"Bastards," hissed Gwen.

"There's more."

"Something to do with that wailing banshee sound in the headphones?" asked Gwen, glancing across at Dan.

"Ghost on acid is how I think of it. It screams like that near a bug. The closer it gets, the more it screams. You're bugged. Light fitting."

"Shit! Let's get rid of it!"

"No. We're safer if we leave it. Whoever's done this is highly sophisticated. We don't want to alert them that we're onto them. Might make them take a more serious step, plus, we can use their bug to plant misinformation."

"How d'you know they're sophisticated?"

"Because of the device," replied Dan. He got up and started to fidget with a loose shard of wood on her deck rail.

"And?"

"It's a GSM device molded into the base of the light—with dental paste, I reckon. It's the kind of device that belongs to the Specialist Surveillance Equipment category," he held up his hand, "which, before you ask, means it is generally only released to governments and law enforcement agencies and those with special connections. In other words, Boudy, it's a high-tech attack."

Gwen got up, dragged her hair back into a ponytail. She was too agitated at that point to ask him how he knew so much.

"I hate the thought of someone listening in to me, to everything I do or say in my own home."

"It stinks. But you've no real choice."

Gwen nodded. "So we leave the bug, so Messenger, assuming it is him, doesn't know we're onto him?"

"Yeah. And that way we can plant false leads, cover you, make you continue to seem like the innocent academic."

"Assuming I want to continue this charade."

"Do you?"

"Fuck yes! Someone was on his way to attack Marilyn, broke in here, may or may not have killed Al Freidland and Elise, probably did—"

"All good reasons to walk away."

"Not again. I won't pretend I'm not frightened, but fear keeps you alive, gives you an edge. I want to catch this fucker. However sophisticated, however scary they are."

Dan nodded. "You think it *is* Messenger?"

"Who else?"

Dan nodded. "All points to him. He has the funds to get hold of this stuff and the people to do his dirty work."

Gwen gave a savage smile. "Hey, seeing as I have to live with a fucking bug, let's return the favor."

"What, bug Messenger?"

"Yeah. I'll get into his office, or wait, even better, there's a Falcon party he's hosting at his home this Sunday. I'll go in, plant something then. He'd probably speak more freely at home too."

"True. Less likely to run bug sweeps at home as well."

"Question is," Gwen asked, giving Dan a long, level look, "is where can we get hold of a bug?"

"I think I can answer that."

"Thought so. And, for that matter, how d'you know all this stuff? You're very teched up for a journalist," she remarked.

"Hey, I'm not the enemy here," replied Dan, frowning. "Besides, you'd be surprised how much journalists know about this stuff, as you call it."

Gwen blew out a breath. "Sorry, I'm rattled. I get bitchy. But I'd still like to know how come you do know all this stuff? You looked like a pro in there, Dan. This is clearly not some one-off."

"I was in the military, Gwen," replied Dan by way of answer.

"So I recall. But I didn't think they taught you about bugging." Gwen pondered as Dan stayed silent. "Unless, of course, you were in Intelligence, or maybe even Black Ops, I think it's called."

"If I were I couldn't tell you anyway."

"So were you?"

Dan laughed. "As it happens, no. I was just your regular Marine Corps kinda guy. But I've been around people who were, picked up a thing or two."

"But then you'd have to say that, wouldn't you."

"So why'd you ask?"

"To see if I could spot a lie."

"And could you?"

"No. Which either means you're telling the truth or you're one smooth bastard.

60

Chief Canning sat at the head of a long oval table so highly polished that he could admire his bald pate in the reflection. Streamlined. He liked streamlined. Efficient and fast.

"Sit," he told the assembled team of four. The Arabist, Pauline Southward, bidden by him from her office at Fort Meade, walked in, made it five. She was sporting a battle-red suit and a beige silk shirt. She looked martial, and delicious. Canning's assistants, Del Russo and Peters, both jumped up to bring in another chair for her. Moira Zucker, a new recruit to the Sheikh Ali team, eyed Southward through her red-framed glasses. Her look was half quizzical, half hostile.

"OK," said Canning, stifling a smile of amusement. Southward with her prim prettiness, her fit body and razor mind was converting his cynics, some of them anyway, he thought, noting Zucker's reaction.

"Let's start with the intercept known as Project Oscar; the threat to rain down the vengeance of Allah on the State of California. Do we have anything?" Canning asked.

The roomful of officers shook their heads. The room hummed with murmured nos.

"Nothing. No further intercepts picked up," said Southward. "Not relevant to this anyway."

Zucker leaned forward, spoke in a gravelly voice, the legacy of throat polyps that she wouldn't have dreamt of removing. She could have earned a decent living wielding a late-night phone line.

"Before Nine-eleven there was stock market activity. A

big short was taken out on the Dow. If there were to be an attack, a major attack somewhere in California, the Dow would plunge again," she declared. "Since you pulled me onto the team last week, I've been searching for any suspicious-looking big shorts on the Dow. Anything out of pattern. Hell of a lot of stuff to wade through. Nothing leaps out so far." Zucker was a treasury specialist, financially sophisticated. Increasingly finance was an essential tool used to track terrorists, to follow their networks. *Follow the money.* It told its own tale, very often labyrinthine, and it was Zucker who picked her way through the maze.

"Someone's always shorting the Dow," replied Chris Furlong, at fifty-three the oldest officer present. Furlong wore his world weariness like a badge.

"A big short, coming out of the Middle East," countered Southward. "That would narrow it down."

"Big short is good, Mideast is irrelevant," declared Zucker. "Trades can come outta anywhere."

Southward shrugged, like the barb was nothing to her.

Canning spoke. "I'll talk to SEC. See if they got anything. Ms. Southward, you talk to your colleagues at NSA. Get them to input into the software the word *short* and *Dow*, see if anything comes up."

Before Southward could reply, Del Russo interjected.

"Might try *short* and *NASDAQ* as well," he said. "Worth trying a number of indices."

"Good point," noted Canning.

Zucker twisted her face and gave Del Russo a "duh" look, like he were stating the blindingly obvious. He stared through her till she looked away, then turned to Canning.

"Thank you, sir."

So Del Russo did have a brain, thought Southward, not just a lantern jaw.

After the meeting wound down, Canning rang the head of the SEC, asked her about any big shorts on the Dow.

"Sounds like a long shot," she replied, "no pun intended." "But I'll ring all the district commissioners. See if they have anything."

Ten minutes later, the head of the New York Office of the SEC rang.

"Chief Canning, Troy Bergers here. You want to know about any big shorts?"

Canning popped a Tums. His dyspepsia was playing up again. Counterterrorism wasn't the most restful of postings. For thirty years, since he entered West Point as a skinny teenager, he'd never done restful and his digestion bore witness. Now he was a desk warrior, but his purview was still life and death, albeit at one remove.

"I do," he replied chewily.

"Listen up. Two of my people have been looking at an insider trading ring. In connection with that, they dug up the fact that a series of shorts have been put on."

"On the Dow?"

"No. Much more specific. On the three big California property casualty insurance companies. And it's not actually shorts, it's more specific still. Put options. Six-month duration."

Canning felt a roaring in his ears. On his hoax/fire spectrum this one had gone to ignite. He managed to keep his voice impassive. "Is that so? Who's behind these puts?"

"We don't know that yet. We've got as far as a series of nominee companies. We'd dearly like to find out who is behind the nominees, but we don't have the evidence of criminal activity we need to justify a court order."

"Maybe we can help with that," mused Canning, thinking, *more than one way to play that one*. "Can I have one of my people call you?" he asked. "Moira Zucker. She might help bust through the nominee walls."

"Sure. Tell her to ask for Special Agent Ange Wilkie."

"Will do. You know any more about these puts?" asked Canning. He got the sense that Bergers was holding out on him.

Bergers pondered. All this earthquake or ARk Storm stuff sounded like Wilkie and Rodgers' overactive imaginations. They'd sound like a laughing stock. He knew better than to share that.

"No, that's all I know at this moment in time."

"If you find out anything else, let me know. Or, put it another way, if you could find out more, we'd appreciate it."

"See what I can do."

Canning called Del Russo, Peters, Furlong, and Zucker into his office as soon as he hung up. Luckily for her, Pauline Southward hadn't yet left the building. Canning's PA, Brad Cooper, known as Coop, located her as she was about to get in her car, told her to get back upstairs. She hurried in, took a seat.

"SEC came up trumps," declared Canning. "We have the equivalent of three sets of interesting shorts which have recently been put on."

"So someone, several someone's, have shorted the Dow," said Southward, feeling the quick burn of adrenaline.

"That's what I asked, but no. Better than that, or perhaps I should be saying, worse than that. They've bought put options on California property casualty insurance companies. On all three of the big ones."

Zucker yelped.

"Shit!" exclaimed Southward.

Canning gave a grim smile. "I think *shit* covers it."

"Who bought the puts?" asked Zucker.

"They don't know. Nominees. I gave word to Troy Bergers that you'd call. He says to ask for Special Agent Ange Wilkie."

Zucker scribbled on a note pad. "Will do."

"So they're going to go for buildings. They're going to bomb the biggest, most expensive real estate they can target," rasped Del Russo, fury roughening his voice.

"Looks that way," agreed Canning grimly. "So we need to identify the possible targets. Then, without in any way alerting them to anything specific, get the word out that they need to beef up security."

He turned back to Zucker. "The put options were six months, by the way."

"So time frame is anywhere between now and Spring," mused Zucker.

"Correct. We need to speed this up. Peters, what's the progress with the private airfields in California?"

"Chief, we're going to have to narrow it down. We have eighteen primary airports in California, there are five notable private-use airports, and there are over one hundred and twenty miscellaneous airports. We cannot have every last one of them surveilled."

Canning thought for a while. "Let's go with a hunch that they won't hijack commercial planes, do a rerun of Nine-eleven. More likely to use a private jet, several private jets. Ali Al Baharna is a fuckin' billionaire! He can throw money at this. They'll either crash them into buildings or use them to drop bomb loads."

"How would they get hold of bombs?" asked Southward.

"Manufacture them?" suggested Peters.

"Let's assume they've got that covered," said Canning, "Chris, take a scroll through any large purchases on the bomb maker's shopping list: ammonium nitrate fertilizer for non-farms, hydrogen peroxide for non-hairdressers, and while you're at it, check out any known C-4 or Semtex trades in any of the badlands." He gave a grim smile, "or in any of the goodlands, for that matter. Check if our guys are missing any."

Furlong nodded.

"Let's further hypothesize," continued Canning, "that the Jihadis will use large private jets if they're using the jets as missiles, medium-size if they have heavy bomb loads. So let's look at all those airports with sufficiently long landing strips for large private jets to take off from. Then let's look at all the large private jets that sit around those airports, see who they're registered to."

"What about some estate somewhere that has its own runway?" suggested Furlong, finally getting into it. "If they're going to be loading bombs they might want some privacy."

"There might be official runways on estates, and there might be an under-the-radar private runway, as it were," said Canning. "Good call, Chris. Get an aerial survey from NASA."

Canning got to his feet. "People, this is top priority. I am going to have to take this to the president right now. Let's get these fuckers before they pull a West Coast Nine-eleven."

61

THE LAB, TUESDAY MORNING

Gwen parked her Mustang. She swung her long, denim-clad legs out, grabbed her bag, and headed into the Lab. In the light of day, the terror she had felt the night before had burnt off, replaced by simmering fury. She felt half sheriff, half maverick, wholly out to get whichever bastard was fucking with her seventy-eight-year-old neighbor and friend, not to mention fucking with her. Whichever bastard had the blood of two women on his hands. Whether that was the mysterious Haas/Hans, or Gabriel Messenger, or one and the same.

She flashed her key card at the reader, input her PIN, pushed through the glass doors, and strode through the central atrium. Preoccupied with the visions in her head, she didn't notice that her office was occupied.

She swung through the open doorway and froze. Gabriel Messenger was sitting at her desk. Her desk drawer was open and the laptop he had given her was on the desk, open and running.

Gwen felt her heart slam against her ribs. She just stood and glowered at him, willing herself not to speak, not to say something irrevocable.

Messenger leaned back in her chair, raised his hands in a gesture of surrender.

"Whoa, stop there! What'd I do?" A faint smile played on his lips, but his eyes were wary.

"Don't you have your own office?" demanded Gwen. "I mean, this is the second time I've come in to find you just sitting at my desk as if—" Gwen cut herself off. She was sounding ridiculous, she knew, but that was a cover of sorts.

"As if I owned the place," supplied Messenger, amused now. "Goodness Gwen, I had no idea you were so proprietorial."

"And how'd you get into my desk drawer? I suppose you have some kind of *master* key?" she continued, hands on hips.

"I do, as it happens. Goes with owning some of the place."

"But not the people!" declared Gwen.

Messenger got to his feet. He kept his distance, noted Gwen, skirted around her. He stopped at the doorway.

"Better now?" he asked.

Gwen said nothing. She moved past him and sat at her

desk. Her body ached from the collision of the night before. Now her head pounded. *Had it been Messenger?* She needed proof, one way or the other.

"What rattled your cage?" asked Messenger. "I do not think I own you or anyone else here."

Gwen blew out a breath. She was going to have to get a serious grip on herself if she wasn't going to blow everything.

"Bad night," she replied. "Sorry. And yes, I am proprietorial, I guess. I'm an only child. We don't do sharing." She nodded to the laptop.

Messenger's eyes hardened. He was running out of patience, Gwen noted.

"I wanted to see what you had done to the model," he replied, voice clipped, clearly unused to having to explain himself. "I didn't have much time," he continued. "We've been summoned. You and I, and Peter and Kevin. Sheikh Ali Al Baharna, who I suppose you could say really does own the place, has requested our company this morning aboard his yacht. He wishes to hear about Project Zeus, and so I was updating myself." Messenger paused, tilted his head to one side like a hunting dog, listening.

"And if I'm not much mistaken, that's his helicopter approaching. So get your bag, bring your laptop, and if I might suggest, find and bring some good humor. Sheikh Ali is not the kind of man you want to offend."

62

Gwen had seen big yachts before. You couldn't live by the sea and spend half your life working on it and surfing it and not see some whoppers. But she'd never seen anything like this craft before. It was gunmetal gray, for a start, not a pretty anodyne white, and there were no gentle angles. This craft was clearly built for speed, whilst being big enough, huge enough to offer serious home comforts.

Gwen had a chance to eye it from all angles as the helicopter approached, did a circle round, then came in to land on a demarked *X* on the deck at the aft. *Zephyr* looked ruthlessly futuristic, almost military. It was too gentle a name for such an aggressive-looking craft. Should have been *Hurricane,* thought Gwen, or *Typhoon.* So this is what billions bought you, she mused, wondering if the Sheikh himself were as lean and mean-looking as his yacht.

During the forty-minute flight, she had forced herself to calm down. She had sat in silence, gazing at the sea, trying to empty her mind of all thoughts, all incriminating thoughts anyway. It was a dull, energy-sapping day: low skies, low pressure. An unbroken layer of dark gray stratocumulus blocked off the sun.

Two tall, well-built, Middle Eastern–looking men wearing polo shirts, tan shorts, and deck shoes met them as they exited the copter, ushered them across the deck and into the yacht itself.

Gwen noticed the heavy door closed behind her with a hiss, as if air- or watertight. She wondered if the yacht could withstand a three-sixty. She guessed it could.

The interior was radically different from the exterior. Outside was pure functionality, but inside was lavish, sensuous almost. The walls were paneled with a rich, dark wood. The carpets were so deep you felt yourself sinking into them. There was a heady smell that seemed to permeate the hallway; a sweet, spicy tobacco. Someone smoked the same cigarettes as Peter Weiss. She padded along, silent on the thick carpets, following behind Messenger, Weiss, and Barclay. One of the large men led, another fell in behind her, shepherding, she realized.

They were shown into a large stateroom.

"Could I have your bag, please?" asked one of the men in chino shorts.

"I'm sorry?" queried Gwen, holding onto her bag.

"Security," replied the man. "We check everyone who comes aboard, apart from family."

"Don't take it personally," said Messenger, a warning note in his voice.

No one asked him or Weiss or Barclay for their laptop cases, thought Gwen.

"We've been checked a hundred times," said Weiss, as if reading Gwen's mind. "Just hand it over."

Gwen handed over her bag. She didn't like it. Clearly didn't have a choice, save getting back on the helicopter and getting the hell out.

The man opened her bag, juggled quickly through its contents, then took out an airport-like scanner, moved it over her bag and back again.

Gwen stared at the ceiling, waiting for him to finish. He handed it back.

"Thank you, ma'am," he said.

"Please, take a seat," said the other man. "Can we bring you some refreshments? We have most things here aboard *Zephyr.*"

Gwen asked for a coffee, and water. One man disappeared on his errand, the other stayed, hovering in the background. No one spoke.

A few minutes later, the door opened, and in walked a man who could only have been Sheikh Ali. He smiled with the quiet munificence of the proprietor. He moved with an athletic confidence, swishing toward them in his flowing white robes, hand outstretched, murmuring greetings.

He greeted Messenger first, then Weiss, whom, Gwen noted, exchanged an Arabic greeting with the Sheikh, then Barclay, who did likewise. Then the Sheikh came to her.

"Ah, the Oracle," he declared, shaking her hand firmly. "It is a pleasure. I have heard much about you and your ingenious work."

Gwen smiled back. She enjoyed the way he rolled the *r* of Oracle. It made her company sound exotic and special to her own ears.

"Thank you," she said.

"Please, sit," murmured the Sheikh, gesturing at the leather sofa.

The refreshments arrived. The coffees were served in tiny gold cups, then, at a signal from the Sheikh, one of the men disappeared. The other moved away, to the far end of the stateroom, where he stood, feet firmly planted, eyes on the visitors.

Gwen sipped her coffee. She felt a welcome jolt as the caffeine hit her system. She hadn't slept much the night before. Dan had insisted on staying until she had left for work. He had slept on the sofa. Painfully aware of him, just feet from her on the other side of the wall, Gwen had lain in bed, the ceiling fan turning softly above her, going over the events of the evening, playing out endless *what if* scenarios. She had fallen asleep just before dawn.

"So, I am very interested to hear about your model, Dr. Gwen," the Sheikh was saying. "About Oracle and about Zeus. I am told you have had a very beneficial impact on that."

"She has," cut in Messenger. "She's done a lot of work; I checked her input this morning. I'm confident her adjustments will materially boost the rain yield."

"Excellent! Excellent!" repeated the Sheikh, bringing his hands together as if in prayer.

"So sad, about the death of the inventor, but so useful that you have come along in our hour of need," Al Baharna added softly.

"Well, I'm sure Peter Weiss has more than held the reins since then," said Gwen. "I'm a latecomer to the model. I've just tinkered a bit."

"Ah yes, Peter has been most helpful. But two brains are better than one, don't you think?"

The Sheikh was eying her intently, thought Gwen, feeling a tad discomfited. The man was charm himself, but there was acuity to his gaze. She could see why Messenger described him as someone you would not want to offend. Something else lay below the charm. Probably the ruthlessness that had garnered him billions. Perhaps he *was* like his yacht, lean and mean.

For an hour, the five of them spoke about Oracle and Zeus. Gwen quickly gathered from his questions that the Sheikh was extraordinarily well informed. By no means a passive investor. He turned to them all with questions. Ever polite, ever the diplomat, it seemed to Gwen, he was solicitous not just of Messenger but of Barclay and Weiss and herself, keen to elicit all their opinions. There was nothing of the brash billionaire about him, nor the lordly Sheikh. The man was a listener, one of the best Gwen had ever met.

Gwen watched her colleagues. Barclay, perhaps impressed, or oppressed by the Sheikh's wealth, had reined in his inner jock and was thoughtful, studious, low key. Weiss seemed on edge. He kept flicking glances between Messenger and the Sheikh, perhaps keen to impress both, gauging how well he was doing. Gwen was sure Messenger's metrics included impressing the Sheikh. Messenger himself was guarded, old-world European correctness to the fore. He sat, straight-backed on the sofa. Gwen got the impression he had himself under lockdown. It wasn't as if he felt the Sheikh were above him, just that he seemed unduly wary of the other man. Was that what billions did, as opposed to tens of millions? If money was your metric, then Messenger was the underdog.

"So, final questions, then I must let you all get back," murmured the Sheikh.

"Dr. Messenger, do you think you have more progress to make with Zeus, that you can increase the rainfall further?"

Messenger turned to Gwen. "Gwen, this is your department, really. I think Peter and I have gone as far as we can with it."

Gwen thought of the model, of how Messenger was planning to use it to ramp up an ARk Storm, to nudge a big winter storm into one. Or could it have been Sheikh Ali? Could he be Haas/Hans? It seemed unlikely. Gwen couldn't imagine him grubbing around at a private equity conference. And he was not likely to have a Germanic name.

"There was a big storm here, back in June," mused Gwen. "Do you remember it?" she asked the Sheikh.

He looked at her quizzically.

"I'm afraid I don't. I spend all of June in Saudi, attending to business there so that I can come here and escape the worst of our heat over July, August, and September. Why?"

"Oh, because I learned a lot from it. Lessons I still want to apply to Zeus," improvised Gwen. "I reckon I can get the yield up still further. Materially higher."

There had been no such storm, but at least it had answered her question. Sheikh Ali had been out of the country during the conference.

The Sheikh nodded. "That is excellent news. Please apply those lessons. I am keen to hear the results. Now, just two more questions for you, Dr. Gwen."

"Sure. Ask away," responded Gwen, flip with relief that her ruse had worked.

"What I would particularly like to know is when do you think this ARk Storm might hit? And how much notice do you think we shall have that it is approaching?"

He seemed to caress the word as he spoke, rolling his *r*s over it. Arrrrk Storm.

"Well, we're in October already," started Gwen. "Earliest would be November, latest April. But there are no guarantees that it will hit."

"Your percentage," said the Sheikh, sitting forward, arms braced on his robed knees. "What percentage likelihood would you give it?"

Gwen looked at the man opposite, at his eyes, shrewd, calculating, waiting. He wasn't smiling anymore. Gwen had a feeling, just fleeting, that the man could see right into her, could see her secrets, fluttering like moths.

She blew out a breath. This wasn't academe, *on the one hand this, on the other that*. This was what commerce looked like, thought Gwen, glancing around. This is what commerce built. And commerce needed answers it could work with, answers it could parlay into a bigger fortune. Sheikh Ali'd be shorting the markets, Gwen was sure, along with Messenger and Falcon. And, however distasteful, it was her job to help him.

"I'd say ninety percent," she replied grimly. "Does that work for you?" she couldn't resist adding.

Messenger's eyes flared, but the Sheikh didn't seem offended.

"Thank you," he replied thoughtfully. "That does work for me." Then he smiled, a big open smile, revealing white teeth, brilliant against his brown skin.

"As you can see, I like living here at sea, I spend a lot

of time off the coast of California. But I'd like to put some distance between myself and this storm when it comes," he added.

"We'll know some days in advance," said Gwen. "At least I think we will. Remember, this has never happened in living memory, so we're all operating on assumptions here."

The Sheikh got to his feet. Weiss, Barclay, and Messenger all jumped up as one. Gwen rose.

The Sheikh took her hand. "Here is my business card," he said, slipping a small gold case from his pocket, extracting a stiff card. "Please be sure to call me, keep me personally informed."

Gwen took the card, nodded. The Sheikh said his good-byes to the others, escorted them all out onto the deck where the helicopter waited. She moved to go, but the Sheikh caught her arm.

"Just one second, Dr. Gwen."

She turned back to him. He smiled at her, dark eyes intent. The others were already getting into the helicopter, couldn't hear what he was saying to her.

"Please feel free to call me at any time. Not just to update me, but if you have any worries, any concerns that I might be able to help you with. . . ."

He let his offer float. Gwen swallowed. Had she been that transparent?

"I'll remember that," she said. The Sheikh nodded back. He let her go, turned, disappeared back inside his yacht. The door hissed shut after him and closed with a heavy thud.

63

Back in his stateroom, the Sheikh turned to Ashgar, the handbag checker.

"Did you plant the transmitter?"

Ashgar nodded. "Inside her pocketbook, under all her coins, in the lining. It looks like any normal stud."

"Well done. Nimbly done."

Ashgar smiled. For an instant his face transformed, the hardness left him, revealing echoes of the sweet boy he had once been. "Thank you, my Sheikh. The benefits of a misspent youth. I picked pockets on the West Bank from five years of age."

"Yes, but you took, not planted."

"I've done my share of planting since."

The Sheikh nodded.

"Women take their pocketbooks everywhere," said Ashgar. "We'll have a very good idea where Gwen Boudain is, twenty-four/seven." Ashgar had spent the last three years in the US, either onboard the yacht, or else in San Diego. He had learned to blend in. His English was flawless.

"Good. Then arrange to keep having her followed. With the tracker in place you can afford to be extremely discreet."

Ashgar nodded. "And the battery life of the tracker is at least a month, so it gives us plenty of time," he added.

The Sheikh's eyes narrowed and his voice dropped to the ominous murmur Ashgar knew so well. "No more accidents. No more interrupted house entries, no more midnight collisions."

Ashgar bowed his head. "I am sorry, my Sheikh. Their errors are my errors. Their failings are my failings."

"We cannot afford errors, not whilst waging jihad."

"I can atone. I can join the ranks of the Shuhada'."

"You are too valuable to me to blow yourself to pieces, no matter the rewards, the seventy-two virgins who would await you. I need you here on earth."

Ashgar looked up, met the Sheikh's eyes, nodded. "Thank you." He paused, gave the moment its full respect before he spoke again. "You just want her followed? Nothing more?"

"Nothing more, for now. This is the day of second chances, for you and the onshore team. This is the day of stayed executions, for Dr. Gwen Boudain too. She is too valuable to kill just yet. By her own words, she is improving the model. Has some way to go. And, if my calculations are correct, she won't go to the police or the authorities yet. She's keeping herself busy on the trail of *justice*," intoned the Sheikh, contempt lacing his voice. "We'll hear from the device in her little house if she is planning to go to the authorities, and if she is, then, and only then can you act."

Ashgar nodded. "I'll brief The Man. I'll tell him to let her live. For now."

64

THE LAB, TUESDAY P.M.

Gwen stared at the card Sheikh Ali had given her. Did the Sheikh have a Haas/Hans aboard who knew enough about Zeus to plan to ramp a winter storm into an ARk Storm? She doubted it. This was the stuff of masterminds, not minions. Messengers . . .

She played with the Zeus model, looking at how else she

might get the rain yield up. Then, in the name of scientific testing, she reversed many of the inputs, discovered, theoretically at least, that while the model could increase rainfall, it could also reduce it. Messenger *had* mentioned that, but she was impressed to see how it worked on the model. She filed that one away as a potential lifesaver all of its own.

Her phone rang. She snatched it up. Dan.

"I've got your stuff," he said by way of hello.

"That was quick."

"I'm a quick mover, Boudy. Given half a chance."

Gwen smiled to herself.

"When shall I bring it over?" Dan asked.

Gwen paused. "I'll come and get it, if that's OK. Haven't seen how you live, Dan. Want to make sure you're not still living at home with Mama." Truth was, she wanted to get out of her cottage too, away from Hurricane Point, if only for a while.

He laughed. "And if I were?"

"Then I'd have to find someone else to fantasize about."

A slight pause, a lowered voice. "Don't you get bored, Boudy, just fantasizing? I grant you it can be good, very good if you fantasize about the right person, but I'm a reality guy by choice."

Gwen felt her blood begin to pound.

"Can't always get what we want, Dan," she drawled, affecting nonchalance. "Didn't your mother ever tell you that?"

"Can we leave my mother out of this?"

Gwen laughed. "What's your address?"

"127A, Seventeen Mile Drive."

Gwen blew out a silent whistle. How the hell did he afford to live there on a journalist's salary? She said, "You and Gabriel Messenger are neighbors."

"In a manner of speaking."

"So when's good?"

"I'm around all day today. All night too."

"I'll bear that in mind."

Gwen hung up. She allowed herself just a minute to think of him, to imagine standing face-to-face, body-to-body, holding each other. She felt the heat, even from a distance. With a supreme act of will, she forced her mind onto the weather.

65

DOJO, MONTEREY, TUESDAY AFTERNOON

At five prompt, Gwen quit the Lab, drove to Monterey through the rush hour traffic to train with Dwayne.

Her trainer stood, head angled, eyes sharp, subjecting her to his usual scrutiny as she walked from the changing room in her shorts and tee. He was seeing, she knew, into her head.

"Something's happened. Vent or leave it outside lest you get hurt."

"You know, you should retrain as a shrink. Honest to God," said Gwen, doubling over into the first of her series of stretches.

Dwayne burst out laughing, a big rolling belly laugh that had Gwen smiling along.

"Nice diversion. True or false?"

"True. Shit's flying around." Gwen straightened up, eyed Dwayne right back.

"Work me hard, Dwayne. Make me strong. Help me to hurt someone if I need to. Really hurt them." She spoke softly, her usual drawling intonation making her words strange and sinister.

Dwayne was unusually silent. He just stared right back at Gwen, pondering. "You sure you don't want to talk about this."

"Another time. Over a bottle of tequila."

Dwayne nodded. "You can bring one to my house-warming. We'll do it then."

"You moved?"

"Got me a fixer-upper." He smiled, breaking the tension, reeling off the address, an up-and-coming area on the out-skirts of Monterey, with a first-time homeowner's shy pride. "Move in next week." His hands framed a shape in the air. "Got a big-ass peacock cut into my hedge!"

"That I *have* to see," said Gwen.

"Any time, Boudy." Dwayne paused, looked thoughtful again. "This hypothetical person you want to hurt . . ." he mused, hands on hips, gazing down at her. "Just to get it straight. You want to hurt them so bad they don't get up again?"

Gwen nodded. "Call it a terminal pain."

Dwayne glared at Gwen in a sudden flash of protective temper. "Jeez Boudy. What the fuck you got into?"

Gwen glared right back at him. "Don't go there."

Dwayne shook his head, a look not of refusal, but res-ignation.

"I'll do what I can. You're the strongest woman I ever met, Boudy, stronger than many men, but you know the score. You gotta be meaner and faster."

"So help me get there."

Dwayne danced back. "You ready?"

Gwen smiled. The remnants of her sedition, long bur-ied, came bubbling up. Anger was a wonderful thing. And fear, channeled right.

"Oh yeah. I'm ready."

Dwayne pushed her harder than he ever had. When they sparred he hit her hard, punished her for not deflecting or anticipating his blows. He was merciless, making her repeat again and again the new moves he was teaching her: the lethal moves—fingers to throat, chop to throat; the disabling moves—fingers to eyes, the kick to the side of the thigh, the kick to the knee, not terminal, but enough to bring your opponent to his knees, to buy you some time. When Gwen got them wrong, she had to hit the deck with twenty push-ups. She'd done over two hundred by the end of the hour. Bruised, muscles trembling, she felt near her limit when mercifully the timorous teenager she'd first seen three weeks ago pushed through the door and into the dojo.

"Charlie, my man!" called out Dwayne.

"Hey Charlie," breathed out Gwen. "Perfect timing! I think you just saved me!"

The boy grinned, walked on over.

Dwayne greeted him with a gentle knuckle punch.

"I'll just get changed," said Charlie, flicking a sweet, shy smile at Gwen. She gave him a dazzler back. She pulled on a thick hoodie and flopped down on a bench.

"Dwayne, can I ask you a favor?" she said, still breathing hard. Her body ran with sweat. It dripped down her face. Her hair was soaked. It fell in tendrils to her waist. She looked, thought Dwayne, every inch Boudicca the warrior queen. He tossed her a towel. She rubbed her face in it. Dwayne sat down beside her.

"Depends what. You askin' me to kick someone's ass? My buddies and I are always here."

Gwen reached out, laid her hand on his huge one. "Thanks Dwayne. I know it. I hope I won't ever have to call you on it. It's information I want. Er, I have this friend—"

"Uh, uh, here we go. And she has a problem . . ."

"It's not me, Dwayne. It's a he. A former Marine. I get the feeling he also did some kind of Black Ops. Truth is, I'm not sure what he did."

"He the one scaring the shit outta you?"

Gwen shook her head. "No. He doesn't scare me." Although not quite true, she told herself. There was something about Daniel Jacobsen that frightened her. It just happened to excite her at the same time.

"You want me to dig the dirt?" asked Dwayne, moving off the bench, squatting down before Gwen so he could eyeball her.

"There might not be any dirt."

"*Everyone* has dirt, you dig deep enough," said Dwayne expansively.

"That's a wholesome vision of mankind."

"You saying different?" asked Dwayne, eyes narrowing. He loved verbal fighting with Gwen nearly as much as he did physical. She played dirty on both counts and could take insults as well as dish them out.

"No," she conceded. "Anyway, can you do this?"

"He your boyfriend?"

"No. Not yet anyway."

"What's wrong with him?"

"Nothing."

"Then why you asking me?" asked Dwayne, straightening up, shaking his legs out.

" 'Cause that's it. Everyone has something wrong with them. He's too perfect."

"Now who's got the screwed-up worldview?"

"Fine!" Gwen threw up her palms. "Me."

"Must be something about him got you bothered."

Gwen's eyes went distant, pondering. "Money, maybe. Flash car, house on Seventeen Mile Drive, on a journalist's salary." She looked back up at Dwayne, towering above her. "And it's just a feeling I get, that there's a lot more to him than what's visible."

"Sounds like a dude!" exclaimed Dwayne, hands on hips, eyes beaming approval.

Gwen gave a soft chuckle. "He *is*. I just don't want to make a mistake."

"Life's not worth living, in my view, if you're not ready to screw it up time to time."

"Enough with the homilies. Can you do it?"

Dwayne, looking thoughtful, ignored the barb. "No, but I know a man who can. Gimme the guy's name."

"Jacobsen. Dan Jacobsen."

Dwayne nodded. "Gimme a few days. Now beat it."

Gwen got to her feet as Charlie came out, immaculate in his *gi*. A few sessions with Dwayne seemed to have already put a spring into his step, lit his eyes with some new confidence. Gwen knuckle-punched him.

"Hey Charlie. Give him hell."

The boy laughed. "Maybe in another life!"

"Hey, this one's good. You got time on your side. Big, bad Dwayne doesn't. Believe it!"

She left Charlie laughing and Dwayne cursing. She walked out to her car, shivering in the evening cool. Late October mists were swirling in from the sea, bringing with them the smell of the fish plant and the ocean: salt, with just a hint of putrefaction. Gwen put her car in gear, turned on the heater, and drove off for Seventeen Mile Drive. To Dan. She felt suddenly grubby, disloyal. Why couldn't she just take Dan for what he was? Gorgeous, irresistible, and just let herself fall headlong into bed with him. Why did she have to look for monsters under that bed?

66

SEVENTEEN MILE DRIVE, TUESDAY EVENING

Gwen paid her nine-dollar entrance fee and drove through the gated entrance to Seventeen Mile Drive. It was now seven in the evening and the sun was setting. Amber light flowed through the trees, dappling the road as she accelerated away from the security kiosk.

She had always loved this place for its beauty and drama, for the just-glimpsed mansions which lay behind the high hedges, beyond the long sloping grass lawns. All that manicured elegance just yards from the cliffs, from the Restless Sea, as it was officially named. The whole place was pure poetry. She loved it for the forests of Monterey cypress. She drove through them now, the gnarled branches reaching up in a desperate but slow-fought race with their neighbors for the touch of the dying sun.

It was amongst those same cypress trees that Elise Rochberger had met her death, had been buried, had been unearthed. It was here too that Gabriel Messenger lived. And Daniel Jacobsen.

She found the driveway to his home. It was on the higher elevation of the seventeen miles of drive, on the sea side of the road. Gwen bet the views would be spectacular. Again she found herself wondering how a jobbing journalist had the means to live here.

She followed the driveway as it arced round a circular drive before veering off, away from a huge Spanish hacienda-style house to come to a stop before a small, two-story structure of stone and wood, built in a more modern, angular style.

Gwen exited her car and walked to the cottage. 127A. The heavy wooden door had an old brass knocker and an electronic doorbell. She tried the knocker, tried the doorbell. No one came. She tried again. Still no answer. She tried the handle. The door opened.

"Dan?" she called out, feeling a flash of apprehension. "Are you home?"

Her voice reverberated away to silence, to the silence of an unoccupied house, it felt like. But he'd said he'd be here. Gwen walked into the narrow hallway, flagged with wood, and out into a room flooded by light. A floor-to-ceiling window looked out over the foaming ocean. Gwen strode up to it and gazed out. The view *was* spectacular. The cottage was only a hundred feet or so above the sea, and from its perch it seemed as if every thundering wave would shake it to its foundations. The lowering sun gilded the frothing waves. Above them seagulls dipped and squalled, an aeronautic riff to the day's end. A distant bank of clouds meeting the fading horizon of sea seemed to mark the edge of the world. There was an air of enchantment to the place, to the evening. A tremor ran through Gwen. All her senses felt supercharged.

She turned her attention to the interior. On one side she could see a cozy, eat-in kitchen. On the other, a spiral staircase led to the upper floor, which she supposed housed the bedrooms.

The house was neat, clean, warm, and lived-in. Books crammed the bookcase that lined one wall. Papers were stacked neatly in an in-and-out tray on the small desk that faced the other wall. The faint smell of coffee lingered, a paperback lay closed with a marker extending from its curling pages: Korda's biography of Lawrence of Arabia.

Gwen smiled as she sighted a simple wooden-framed photograph. She picked it up: three men in army fatigues, desert DPM, arms draped over each other's shoulders, tanned, dusty-faced, smiling like they were immortal—Dan and two friends. Was one of them the friend who had been blown up, right next to Dan?

"Dan," she murmured, softly replacing it. "Where are you?"

She walked on through the house, through the yellow-painted kitchen, out through the back door and onto the deck.

Immediately she saw another building off to her left, a small wooden barn. She could see that the big double doors were thrown open. And she could hear grunts coming from it. Rhythmic, guttural grunts. Two sets of them.

She walked toward them, mind racing. She stopped before the open doors, and just looked.

Dan Jacobsen stood naked from the waist up, the wicked scar daggering up his side. He was clad in shorts and he was hefting weights. Huge weights. His body glistened with sweat, and, obviously well into his workout, his muscles were pumping. Next to him stood another large, well-muscled man, hefting weights of his own. Gwen recognized him from the photograph. They both seemed utterly intent on their exercise. Gwen wondered if they'd noticed her.

They finished their circuit and in unison laid down their weights and turned to her. They'd noticed.

"Gwen," said Dan, on a heavy outbreath that made his voice deeper than normal. He gave her his crooked smile. Gwen smiled right back. He leaned in, kissed her. She could smell his sweat: salty, musky. It smelled good. Some men did. Some men didn't. Maybe it was a hormone thing, a gene thing. If their genes were good for yours, then they smelled good to you.

"This is my buddy, Spence."

"Hi, Spence," said Gwen, shaking his hand.

"Gwen." He smiled briefly, gave her an appraising look. Gwen got the feeling he knew exactly who she was.

"Care to join us?" asked Dan.

"Already worked out."

"Another time then."

"Sure. You've got some good kit here," said Gwen, eyeing the free weights, the pulley system, Bosu balls, the VersaClimber and rowing machine. And by the evidence before her, he clearly made use of it.

"We'll be another fifteen minutes, give or take. Make yourself at home. Cold drinks in the fridge."

Gwen was glad to get away. She didn't think she would have been able to stand there just watching him without wanting to take a bite out of him. *And that is a bad idea,* she murmured to herself. *Let me count the reasons . . .*

She opened the surprisingly well-provisioned fridge:

steaks, salads, berries, six pack of something called Liberty Ale; BREWED IN SAN FRANCISCO, said the label. She popped one open and ambled back onto the deck. She leaned against the table, sipping the ale, enjoying the yeasty hop flavor, gazing at the sea. She caught the flare of red, the briefest flash of green as the sun slipped below the horizon. Then the color leached quickly from the sea, all blue gone, leaving dark turbulence. She stared at it, sipping and thinking.

The men sauntered up through the gloaming. Long, easy strides, loose limbed and relaxed. They'd pulled on t-shirts and sweatshirts against the chill that fell with the quickening dusk. Gwen could hear the ocean and the crickets starting up in the grass, then the slosh as Dan opened two more ales. He carried out the bottles in one hand. In the other he held a small bag.

Spence drained his ale in one long draft. He was acting all casual, but Gwen could feel him scrutinizing her. There was something about him that made her wary.

He set his empty bottle on the table. *What, was she supposed to take it in for him?*

"Shower time," he declared in a slow, Southern drawl. He nodded to Gwen, smiled at Dan, then ambled past, a rolling athletic gait.

"One of my best buddies," said Dan, as his friend disappeared into the kitchen.

"I saw the photo. Three army boys."

"Marines. We were in the Marines. Did three tours together."

"Afghanistan?"

"Hm," Dan's eyes went distant for a moment. Gwen wondered if he were seeing the images that flashed across her TV screen: the sand, the rocky mountains, the flashes of gunfire, the thud of explosions. His eyes came back to her. Hard. Unreadable.

"Quite a place you have here," observed Gwen, suddenly

ill at ease, looking for a subject change, clumsily grabbing one.

"Not bad, is it? Seems we both lucked out on the real estate stakes."

Gwen caught the edge in his voice, tilted her head to contemplate him.

"Your point being?"

"We both live in multimillion-dollar properties without the apparent means to afford them."

"Ah."

"You were digging, Boudy, in your oh-so-subtle way."

Dan said it with a smile, but still the edge was there. Gwen remembered the sense of honor she had picked up when she'd first met him at Stanford with Reilly. *I don't need threats to keep secrets;* honor and sedition, cocky grin and hard eyes, openness and secrets, surfer and Marine . . . she still didn't know who he was, couldn't get a handle on him. Most people she could peg, could figure out who they were and what they wanted, but not him. Was it her desire that stopped her seeing or was it that Dan did not want her to see?

She shrugged, affecting indifference. "So call me the Curious Cat."

"I'd rather not. We all know what happened to her."

Gwen smiled. "I got no plans to die for a while yet."

"My grandfather died," said Dan, startling Gwen. "Six months ago. He left me this place."

Gwen felt herself scrambling to keep up. There were too many undercurrents swirling around: the slightly hostile friend, the edge in Dan's voice, the warmth and the cold, the desire . . .

"You were close?" she asked.

"Very. Closer than to my parents."

"I'm sorry," said Gwen softly.

Dan frowned. Gwen noted that, like her, he disdained sympathy.

"My father's a lawyer, my ma does the whole society shtick. Grandpa was an entrepreneur, made a ton of money. The big house you drove past was his main residence. This place belonged to his staff." He smiled. "Hell of a perk."

"So did your parents inherit the big house? Is that where they live?" Gwen glanced in the direction of the mansion. She really wasn't in the mood to meet Mama.

Dan gave a grim smile, softened by a glint of amusement.

"They expected to. The old man left it to a veteran's charity. They've put it on the market. The vets can do a lot with the cash from that big old place."

"So he wasn't close to your parents?" asked Gwen.

"Not really. They were very anti my going into the Marines. *Not the kind of thing a boy from our sector of society does,* I quote. I thought *fuck that.* Grandpa thought *fuck that,*" Dan laughed. "He told 'em so too. He was behind me. Totally supportive. Remember, he'd lost his other son on Nine-eleven."

"You miss him," stated Gwen.

Dan turned his eyes on her. For once they were unveiled, no cockiness, no hardness, just pain.

"Yeah, I miss him," he said simply.

Gwen knew how that felt, didn't offer any homilies about it getting easier. The rawness went, the longing never did. "Where do your parents live?"

"San Fran. Nob Hill, of course."

"You see them?"

"A little. We're cordial."

Gwen winced.

Dan drained his bottle, got to his feet. "I'm gonna get another. Can I get you one?"

"Thanks."

Dan returned with two more ales, set them down on the table.

"First off," he said, "Messenger's middle name bears no relation to Haas/Hans. It's Kurt."

"Ah. Kurt. So Haas/Hans could be a false name then."

"Could be."

Dan took hold of the paper bag, pushed it across the table to Gwen.

"Your present," he said. "This might help you find out more."

Gwen raised her eyebrows, opened the bag, pulled out two small black objects, one the size of a matchbox but half as deep and the other the size of an iPhone.

"A bug? Two bugs?" asked Gwen.

Dan shook his head. "One GSM bug." He held up the one that looked like a thin matchbox.

"We activate this by phoning it. It has its own normal phone number and access code that you have to type in to listen to it. We switch it on, we switch it off at will. That's part one. Armed, it acts as a microphone, and is voice activated so it will only transmit when there is activity in the room. It picks up all sound in a twenty-meter radius. I can listen to this live whenever I want to. Part two is the store-and-forward recorder." He brandished the black box the size of an iPhone, wiggling it at Gwen. "It can be placed anywhere in the room and has two microphones for extra sensitivity; both have their own battery power. It's our backup for when we're not listening to the bug live. This will just sit and record all activity in the room and store it until we call it up and download from it."

Gwen, chin propped in her hands, leaned across the table toward him, listening intently. One thing she had always been a sucker for was expertise.

"Cool tool," she murmured.

Dan paused, took a long draft of ale, wiped his mouth with the back of his hand.

"There are lots of reasons why this is a cool tool," Dan agreed, "but the main one is that as it's not transmitting till we ask it to, it's very hard for bug sweepers to detect it.

"Wow!" said Gwen. "Pretty amazing." She picked up the two small, innocuous-looking devices, wondering at this strange, parallel world where your conversations could be hijacked, sent spinning around the globe.

"And before you quiz me on how I know all this stuff, Spence, as well as being one of my best buddies, is a security consultant. He got me the kit."

"Useful friend. What do I owe him?" asked Gwen, putting down the devices, taking her bottle by the neck, drinking deeply. She felt a buzz warming her, ale on an empty stomach. . . .

"He is. And we'll figure that out down the road." Dan took a swig of ale, continued. "I'd recommend that all conversations be relayed back to me here. One, because as sheer luck would have it, I'm less than a quarter mile from Messenger's house, so it works perfectly." He stood and gestured to his right. "He's just along the way. I took a run past last night. Although the GSM device has unlimited range, we need to be this close to download from the store-and-forward device."

"How fortunate," observed Gwen, running her forefinger down the side of the bottle, condensation making it wet. "And two?"

Dan leaned toward her, eyed her with a glint of mocking humor.

"Do you really want to risk listening to your boss potentially discussing you, or making dirty phone calls to his lover?"

Gwen grimaced. "You may have a point."

Dan took his seat again, voice businesslike once more. "So I'll listen in, wade through it, get you over to hear any juicy bits."

"You happy doing all the listening-in bit?"

"I'll run the GSM device through my iPod when I'm

working out." He gave the crooked smile that Gwen liked so much, added: "Who said men can't multitask?"

"Some idiot," replied Gwen.

Dan laughed. Night had fallen as they spoke, and the first of the stars emerged glittering and distant, like watchful eyes. For a while the two of them just sat, relishing the night, being together.

"I'll position the devices this Sunday," said Gwen, breaking the spell. "Messenger's throwing a party for Falcon staff. It couldn't be better."

"Be careful. If he, or anyone catches you at it . . ."

"I will be careful. Don't worry about me."

Dan leaned forward, took Gwen's fingers, twined them with his. "But I do," he said softly. "I do worry about you, Boudy." He kept his eyes on hers. She felt the heat punch through her, just looked right back at him.

Spence appeared silently, like a wraith, despite his size. He saw the two of them, moved on by into the garden, toward the cliff. He stood staring out into the darkness, backlit by the rising moon.

Gwen broke contact, got to her feet. "I'd best be going. Leave you to quality time with your buddy."

Dan nodded. He got up, pulled Gwen in close, spoke into her ear. She felt his breath warm on her skin.

"Will you come here to me after the party, after you've planted the device?"

Gwen looked back at him. She ached with wanting him. She could see his own desire in his eyes. *What are you so afraid of Gwen?*

"I don't know, Dan," was all she could answer.

He kissed her lips. "You're killing me, Gwen. You know that, don't you?"

She smiled. "Yeah, I know it." And you're killing me too, she thought.

67

Gwen drove off through the darkness of Seventeen Mile Drive, past the nighttime cypress trees. With their gnarled branches they looked like something out of a horror movie. For Elise Rochberger, they had been.

Back at the cottage, the two men stood in the darkness, staring out to sea. All that was visible was an endless void, defined in the foreground by the moon-silvered spume of breaking waves.

Spence turned to Dan.

"She's gorgeous. Beautiful. Defiant. Sexy as hell."

Dan nodded. "All of that."

"Dangerous too, for you my friend."

"That I know."

"So what you gonna do?"

Dan turned away, spoke to the night.

"Trapped between a rock and a hard place is I think the expression that fits."

"Maybe. You still haven't answered the question."

Dan gave his friend a tight smile. "I haven't, have I?"

Spence barked out a laugh. "Hoping to play both sides, the old double-agent trick, Danny Boy? We all know what happens to them in the end."

"We're a long way from that, I hope," said Dan as the memories flooded back. The knife, the exposed neck, the blood gushing onto the sand. He felt the breeze chill his skin as it washed over him. He wished, as he had many times, that he was able to wash his mind.

68

Andrew Canning was in a pacing mood. He felt like he had swallowed fire. Burning fingers probed his guts. Last night's barbeque and today's frustrations were an inflammatory mix. Up and down he went along his office's windowed walls, glowering through the glass. He paused, turned to Moira Zucker, who sat immobile on the far side of his desk, following his progress with her eyes.

"Where are we with those nominee companies and the puts?" Canning demanded.

"Nowhere, sir," replied Zucker grimly. "All I got is the three counterparties who put on the trades on behalf of the nominee companies. I've rung all three. They're big banks. They won't spill. They're all citing client confidentiality and—"

"Fuck client confidentiality!" erupted Canning in a rare show of fury. "Which banks, exactly, put on the trades? Please tell me it was US banks."

"Yes, sir. As it happens." Zucker reeled off three US banks.

"Let's give them a choice," mused Canning. "They can cooperate, offer up whoever they are acting for, the identity beneath the nominees, or we get a court order, force disclosure." Canning gave a broad smile, teeth gleaming. "Trouble with a court order is that it's messy. Might even leak to the press that they're acting for terrorists. . . ."

He hit his intercom. "Coop, get me Richard Bull on the line. He's CEO of—"

"I know who he is," cut in Coop. "I see his and his wife's pictures in all the glossy magazines, at charity things."

Coop's Southern accent made it come out "theeangs." Canning smiled, waited. Five minutes later, Coop buzzed him. Bull was on the line.

"Mr. Bull, thank you for your time. I need a little information here, sensitive information," intoned Canning.

"If I can give it, appropriately, it's yours," replied Bull in a tone of deep distrust.

Canning paused. "Mr. Bull, Dick, you're a busy man. I'm a busy man. Wall Street might not sleep, but neither does terrorism. And me? I know which one I'm more afraid of . . . so let me make things simple for you." Canning leaned forward over his speakerphone. He spoke softly, conversationally, his level tone quietly sinister. "I am investigating a planned terrorist atrocity. We have evidence that a financial transaction undertaken by your bank is directly related to that potential outrage, so, one way or another, your bank will need to divulge the identity of the organization or individual for whom you placed that trade."

Canning waited, imagining his words spreading like the force field from a grenade. Even a desk warrior got to lob a few.

Bull gathered himself quickly. "All of our clients and counterparties are vetted, Mr. Canning. You must know that," he replied, with rote-like monotony, deliberately omitting Canning's title.

Canning smiled nastily. That just made his job even more enjoyable.

"So, let me get this straight, Dick, you are assuring me that there is zero possibility that any of your counterparties could ever be involved in a terrorist outrage, one that might cause thousands of deaths. You want to go on the record with this? You'd be happy with all that blood on your hands. . . ."

There was a silence on the other end of the line. Canning imagined the fury contorting the other man's features. The aptly named Bull was a bully, as were many investment banking CEOs, and similarly unused to being on the receiving end.

"Give me ten," grunted Bull, then the phone went dead.

Bull rang back after twelve minutes. Through what sounded like clenched teeth, he offered up the name behind the nominee company.

Canning wrote it down. "Thank you, Mr. Bull," he said crisply, terminating the call.

Canning called the other two banks, applied the same pressure. Two hours later, both had yielded up the same name.

A beaming Canning called in Zucker.

He nodded at a chair. "Sit."

He leaned forward toward her, smiling still. "Bull spilled!" he announced. "As I knew he would. So did Hackman and so did DelAcardia. Amazing what an appeal to naked self-interest can achieve."

Zucker raised her eyebrows speculatively.

"Broke through the nominee walls, got the name," announced Canning. "The same name in all three cases: one Ronald Glass, aged thirty-five, resident of Manhattan." He reeled off the address.

"Way to go, *sir!*" cried Zucker.

Canning gave a mock bow. "Apply for a FISA warrant," he instructed.

Zucker nodded. She scribbled the name down on her notepad. "Consider it done. Think he's a terrorist?"

Canning stroked his bald head, looked intently at Zucker. "Probably not. But he's gotta be connected in some way. Whoever he is, and whatever his agenda is, we're gonna rock his world."

69

Gwen had just returned from dinner with Lucy in Carmel when her landline rang. As she was unlocking her door, it started trilling. She hurried in, pulled the door shut, double-locked it behind her. Her new habit.

Leo was waiting for her, calmly, which meant all was well. No intruders. She ruffled his neck with one hand, grabbed the receiver with the other.

"News for you, Boudy," boomed Dwayne in his deep voice.

"And?"

"Friend of a friend has high clearance, as in real high. Your man was in the Marines, but that's all he could find out. Just plain vanilla stuff. Nothing at all of interest."

"Good. That's a relief."

"No it ain't."

"Meaning?"

"Too neat, too clean, too boring. My friend reckoned his real identity had been moved to a cover identity to hide him from all but the most connected of searchers."

"And this in turn means?"

"He was Black Ops, Boudy."

Gwen fell silent. Did this change anything? Should it?

"You still there?" asked Dwayne.

"Yeah, I'm here. Just trying to process."

"The dude's retired, Boudy. Been out of it for two years."

"OK. Still knows a hell of a lot of stuff."

"What kind of stuff?" asked Dwayne sharply.

Gwen couldn't tell him about the bugs. "Just stuff," she answered.

"Fine. Move it on. So what's your problem, Boudy?"

"I just don't know what I'm getting into with him. I keep feeling he's hiding things from me."

Dwayne's laughter boomed down the phone.

"Girl, listen up! We're all hiding stuff! And he's got plenty to hide that's just plain none of your business. Not relevant. And, *FYI,* when did we ever know what we're getting into when we take a roll with someone?"

"True, to a degree," conceded Gwen.

"Cut the crap. This ain't Stanford. This is life. You like the dude?"

Gwen paused. *Like* was damning him with faint praise, didn't come close to what she felt.

"Yeah, Dwayne. I like the dude."

"Then stop being a scaredy-cat, Boudy. Big bad, surfer girl. Go get him!"

70

SEVENTEEN MILE DRIVE,
THE FALCON ANNUAL PARTY, SUNDAY

In a rare departure from her beloved jeans, Gwen wore a black sleeveless linen dress, cinched in with a Navajo-style leather, silver, and turquoise belt, a present from Lucy. She wore leather flats on her feet and threw a turquoise-colored pashmina over her shoulders. She got into her Mustang and drove to the Falcon Capital Annual Party. She had deliberately driven her own car, intended to drive it back rather than take the promised limo service. If she got tanked up on Messenger's fine wines, God only knows what she'd come out and say. Her "stop" switch was faulty, she reckoned. Once she had started, she liked to go for it, and tonight was not the night. She couldn't afford to say the wrong thing or get caught planting the devices.

Inside her usual capacious bag was a present for Dr. Messenger, a fine Cabernet Sauvignon, and the usual assortment of female paraphernalia: a hair brush, a packet of tissues, a lipstick, a packet of Advil, a tube of Life Savers, a small bottle of scent, and a bottle of water. Nestling alongside this, concealed in a makeup bag bought specially for the purpose, was one GSM bug, one store-and-forward recorder, a pot of dental paste, a palette knife, a chopstick and a saucer, carefully wrapped in a hand towel, and three screwdrivers. Not easily explained away if Mandy, Mel, or Atalanta tried to raid her makeup bag, she thought wryly.

She drove down Seventeen Mile Drive, past the turnoff to Dan's house, on to Messenger's. She pulled up outside a monumental iron gate.

There was an intercom system and a CCTV camera angled down on her. She pushed a button, but before she could speak, a voice came back at her.

"Come on in, Gwen."

Randy Sieber. On home security detail today. Did the guy not get a day off?

The gate swung open silently. Gwen arced the Mustang down a tree-lined drive, parking in a large turning circle.

She deemed it unnecessary to lock her car. She got out, eyed the house that stood before her.

Built of timber and glass, all hard planes and angles, it was a monument to minimalism. But not to brutalism. There was something beautiful in its angularity. It stood gazing out to sea, planted defiantly on the land, almost challenging the elements, it felt to Gwen. Would the steel repel the water that would come, slicing through the air if the ARk Storm did hit? Could the dark wood planks withstand it?

"Pretty cool, isn't it?" said a voice behind her.

Gwen turned. "Hi Randy. It's *amazing!*"

"Sixty million dollars gets and builds you a lot of amazing," Sieber added, nodding as if at his wisdom.

Gwen blew out a low breath. "Messenger commissioned it?"

"Bought a knockdown four years ago. Built this baby."

"The house that private equity built," murmured Gwen.

"They're all through in the garden, out front," said Sieber. "C'mon, I'll walk you. You were the last. Everyone's here now." Sieber checked his watch.

"Am I late or something?"

"Just in time. Dr. Messenger's going to give a speech."

There they all were, Falcon Capital's disparate group of employees, gathering to hear the word of Mammon. But Luke and Narissa were absent, noted Gwen. Perhaps Dr. Messenger was not quite the egalitarian his party suggested.

Mandy and Mel were glammed up in fluttery summer dresses and heels. Gwen could see them mincing across the grass together, champagne flutes in hand, trying to keep their stilettos from bogging down. Peter Weiss wore his habitual uniform of black. He saw Gwen and gave her a hesitant wave. Kevin Barclay, Curt, and Jihoon wore dress-down uniforms of polo shirts and khakis. Atalanta wore a skimpy black sleeveless tee and a full-length green silk skirt that billowed beguilingly as she walked across the garden, effortless on flat sandals, chatting earnestly with Gabriel Messenger. She looked, as always, sensational. Kevin Barclay was watching Atalanta over the rim of his champagne glass, his measuring eyes and the forward thrust of his body unveiled and vulpine.

Gwen noticed two strangers, each quaffing champagne, looking around with undisguised curiosity. A man, about thirty, with sandy wavy hair and freckles, and a Latina woman about the same age, bursting out of a pink sheath dress.

"Who are they?" she asked Sieber, confident that he would know.

"Journalists!" he declared portentously.

Gwen couldn't have been more surprised than if he'd said prostitutes or priests. She glanced across at Messenger in puzzlement.

"Why?" she asked. "I thought this was a private party."

"They're only here for the first hour. It's good PR for Falcon," explained Sieber.

As if conscious of Gwen's scrutiny, Messenger glanced up, audibly said "Excuse me" to Atalanta, and strode over to them.

"Gwen, hi. Glad you could make it. Welcome to my home."

Gwen smiled. "Wouldn't miss it for the world, Dr. Messenger."

A uniformed waiter bearing a laden circular silver tray approached.

"Champagne?" he offered.

Gwen shook her head. "Something soft please."

"Water, or sparkling elderflower if you want something a tad more interesting," declared the waiter, almost disapprovingly.

Gwen took a sparkling elderflower, smiled her thanks.

"Not drinking?" asked Messenger.

"Detox," improvised Gwen.

Messenger wrinkled his nose. "How boring!"

"Call it penance," said Gwen. "This is for you," she added, reaching into her bag, careful not to dislodge the devices. She handed over the bottle of Stags Leap Cabernet Sauvignon, wondering suddenly if it were a major solecism. It really wasn't a bring-a-bottle type party.

Messenger took the bottle with a delighted smile.

"Very kind of you Gwen. Very thoughtful. 1997! Great vintage."

Gwen felt a guilty pang, summoned the youthful pictures of the murdered Al Freidland, burned off the guilt.

"I'll go and put this somewhere safe," said Messenger. He turned and marched away with the bottle.

Kevin Barclay sauntered up, eyed Gwen speculatively.

"My God. Gwen Boudain in a dress."

"It's been known."

"Who are you hoping to impress?"

She thought of Dan and his question: *will you come to me later?* She smiled.

"Me, of course," cut in Peter Weiss, who'd just joined them. "Gwen knows I dig black."

Gwen smiled. "Got it in one, Peter. How are you?"

"I'm good. I—"

"Good afternoon," declared Gabriel Messenger in a projectile voice, silencing Weiss.

He was standing on the steps that led down from the terrace that flanked the house to the garden below.

"Welcome to Falcon Capital's Fifth Annual Party! Our first at my new home."

Fulsome applause broke out. Messenger raised his hands, graciously acknowledging then quelling it.

The journalists had pens and notepads poised.

"It's been an interesting journey here, in all senses. I'd like to thank you all for coming and I'd like to say a few words too about why I and why you are here." He paused, looked around, taking in his guests, his garden, the sea. Then his eyes seemed to go beyond all that was visible. They took on the look of the visionary that Gwen had first seen in him.

"Capitalists, such as I, such as you, have taken a bit of a knocking recently. I'd like to set the record straight. Some

people say Greed is Good; I say the urge to accumulate is
good. That urge is hard-wired into our brains. It is part of
the promptings of the old brain, the brain that guided us
when we were lumbering around accumulating firewood,
berries, roots, fruits, vegetables, sharp stones, prey . . .
whatever we could to ensure we did not starve or freeze."
Messenger gestured to his garden as he spoke, linking in
the gesture Neanderthal Man with all those who stood now
on his lush grass.

"Now the survival of economies depends on the human
desire to accumulate, to buy goods and to buy services. And
where do those goods and services come from?" Messenger
took one step down, closer to the gathered listeners. "They
come from the men and the women with ideas. They come
from the men and the women with money to finance those
ideas and the guts to turn them into reality. In short, they
come from venture capital." This was met with whoops
and claps from Kevin Barclay and Mandy.

"If we choose right, we make money. If we choose
wrong, we lose it. *That* is the morality imposed by market
forces." Messenger turned to the journalists now.

"And I make no apologies for that. Over the past five
years, Falcon Capital has paid over one hundred and
seventy million dollars in tax to the federal and local
governments. If we make money, we can contribute. If we
fail, we contribute nothing."

A roar of approval met this.

"But here at Falcon, we are succeeding! I have made
millionaires of every one of my staff."

Gwen glanced around at this, saw Mandy reach for another glass of champagne, muttering something inaudible,
while Curt, Atalanta, and Jihoon looked on hopefully.

"So, I repeat," continued Messenger, "I make no apologies for capitalism. We take risks. And for our vision and
our ability to stomach those risks we are rewarded. Without rewards, the incentives to take risks would evaporate.

They are two sides of the same coin. Those who try to tax our rewards to hell might do well to remember this."

This was met with loud hand clapping by Falcon employees and with frantic scribbling by the journalists.

"I shall leave you with a great quote from George Bernard Shaw. *"You see things that are and ask, 'Why?' But I dream things that never were and ask 'Why not?'"*

Messenger bowed. "Welcome to Falcon Capital!"

A round of tumultuous applause broke out.

Was he dreaming of ARk Storm, wondered Gwen.

71

Gwen mingled, eyeing the house, eyeing Messenger, wondering when to make her move. Every time she wanted to peel off, someone collared her. Mel, Barclay again, Randy Sieber, Peter Weiss. An hour passed.

A shrill whistle made everyone freeze. Mandy stood on the steps, swaying slightly.

"Listen up! Listen up!" she trilled.

"Uh oh. Lookee here," murmured Weiss. "The poster girl for moderation."

"Does she make a habit of this?" asked Gwen.

"Every year," replied Weiss. "That's why Dr. M. supplies the limos. She tried to drive home last year. He had to haul her out of her VW."

"Bet that dented her metrics."

Weiss snorted.

Mandy glowered at him, wobbled back on her heels, then began to declaim.

"Well, speaking as one of the Falcon millionaires, though God himself only knows where all that dough has gone, probably on my ass and on my back," she giggled.

"Ah well, anyways . . . what I got up here to say was this . . . I'd just like to ask every a one of you good people to put your hands together and say a heruuuge thank you to Dr. Gabriel Messenger for this here party, for Falcon and all of that good stuff."

Everyone clapped, thanked Dr. Messenger, but Mandy hadn't finished.

"And when's the guided tour I wanna know?" she yelled.

Messenger materialized by Mandy's side. He took her arm gently.

"How about now? What say you we stick to the garden though?"

"Yeah, sure," said Mandy. "Garden's good."

Damn! thought Gwen. A guided tour of the house was what she needed.

Messenger said a determined good-bye to the journalists, then he began to lead a chain of Falcon staff through the five-acre garden. Mandy, clearly a gardening buff, fell behind. Gwen noticed her snipping off branches of shrubs with her fingers. She turned, saw Gwen.

"Cuttings, for my own little patch of green."

"Plenty to go round," said Gwen. She stayed behind Mandy, worried that the other woman would fall over. Mandy's place beside Messenger had been taken, adroitly, by Atalanta.

It was when Messenger led them off the edge of the grass onto a stairway carved into the cliff that Gwen really started to worry.

They snaked back and forth. Toting her heavy shoulder bag, Gwen followed one step behind Mandy. A rope hand-rail separated them from the rocks fifty feet below. Gwen could see a wooden raft, moored a hundred meters out. Did Messenger swim to it, she wondered? He must do. It was opposite his property.

Around it, the Restless Sea lived up to its name. It bubbled and boiled and heaved. The swell was big today. Gwen could feel the mist off it bathing her face as she followed the path down. She could taste the salt.

They got to the bottom, Mandy and Gwen left behind by the others who were striding along a natural rock platform that jutted out into the sea.

Messenger was already leading his followers on up another cliff-carved path to what looked like a small viewing platform that abutted from the cliff. Like the Pied Piper, thought Gwen.

She saw Mandy try to speed up. The woman was teetering close to the edge.

"Hey, Mandy," Gwen began to say, broke off as she saw the other woman's heel snap, saw her beginning to fall. Gwen lunged toward her but she was too far away. Mandy toppled into the sea.

A wave picked her up, sucked her back and in seconds she was twenty feet offshore. She screamed, swallowed water.

Shit! Gwen kicked off her shoes, dumped her bag, eyed the waves, didn't have time to pick a pattern.

Aware of shouts and screams behind her, Gwen stood at the edge, arrowed her body, and dived.

She felt the sea grab her, kicked, came up twelve feet from the jagged cliff. The current and the breaking waves pushed her back toward the cliff. She kicked out, swam as hard as she could to where she had seen Mandy. There was no sign of her now. She sucked in a breath, dived down. Underwater, she opened her eyes, saw a flailing limb below her. She dived deeper, grabbed it, kicked hard, hauled Mandy upward. Mandy was heavy, not just dead weight but one hundred and thirty pounds of panicking weight, flailing against her. Gwen got her to the surface, sucked in a breath, saw with horror how close they were to the cliffs. One slam from the waves and they'd both be unconscious, or dead.

Gwen kicked back, away from the impact zone, dragging Mandy with her. She wanted to time her approach, ride a wave in if she could, hauling Mandy with her, but Mandy wasn't cooperating. She was climbing on Gwen, pushing her down so that she could stay higher.

"Cut fighting," shouted Gwen. "Go limp!" she screamed, but Mandy was driven by terror. She flailed, pushed down on Gwen.

"You're gonna kill us both, you stupid bitch!" shouted Gwen. "Go limp!"

They washed closer to the cliff. Gwen tried to kick out, to get distance, but dragging Mandy and fighting her to stay afloat, she made no progress. There was nothing for it. She pulled back her fist, punched Mandy in the head. The other woman went limp.

Gwen kicked, dragged her back, but it was too late. A huge wave was roaring up. All Gwen could do was try to cushion Mandy. She stuck her arm between the woman and the rapidly approaching cliff. At least it would raise them up, she calculated. Messenger seemed to be thinking the same, for he threw himself to the ground and stretched out an arm, reaching down. Randy Sieber grabbed his feet and held on.

The wave carried Gwen to the cliff. She felt the impact. Pain seared down the entire length of one side of her body. Miraculously, her head had not hit the rock, but she must have bitten her tongue for she tasted blood in her mouth. She was aware of arms grabbing Mandy, of the other woman being hauled up. Arms free, Gwen scrabbled at the rock, found a foothold, propelled herself up, felt Randy Seieber grabbing her, hauling her to safety.

"Fuck!" breathed Gwen.

"Fuck," agreed Sieber.

"You OK?"

"Yeah, I'm fine," said Gwen. "Let's get the hell off this platform before we all get swept in."

She grabbed her bag, silently grateful that it hadn't been washed away.

"Here, let me take that," offered Sieber, reaching for it.

"Not your style," retorted Gwen, gripping it tightly.

Up on the lawn, high above the Restless Sea, everyone gathered.

Gwen walked up to Mandy, who was sprawled on the grass.

"You OK?" she asked.

Mandy rubbed her head, and glowered at Gwen. "I got a sore head. Why the hell'd you hit me?" she demanded.

Gwen blew out a breath, contemplated hitting her again.

"To save your life, and to preserve mine," she answered.

"She did what she had to do, Mandy," said Sieber. "You would have drowned the both of you! Should have listened to her and stopped panicking!"

In response, Mandy vomited all over his shoes.

Sieber threw his hands up in despair. "This just gets better and better."

Gwen burst out laughing.

"Thank God the journalists have gone," muttered Mel.

Messenger exchanged a look of mild horror with her, then he turned back to Gwen. "We need to get you seen to."

"I'm fine."

"You're bleeding. You need treatment."

Gwen followed his glance. Her arm was pouring blood.

"You're lucky the sharks didn't come after you, bleeding like that," said Barclay.

"Thanks for that cheery thought," replied Gwen, wishing Mandy had thrown up on his Tods, not on poor Randy Sieber.

She turned back to Messenger. "I'm fine. I'll just wrap it in something."

"It's a big cut."

"Not really. Jeez, stop making a fuss."

"You need stitches or you'll get another scar."

"Look, I'm covered with scars from the sea, from my fin hitting me or me hitting coral or whatever. It's no big deal. What I really need is a change of clothes." She shivered as she said this, the first sign that she had been affected.

Messenger took her arm. "Come with me and I'll get you one."

She walked with him across the grass. Barbieri was helping Mandy to her feet. Everyone else stood round, waiters and guests, each uncertain of their roles.

"Listen Gwen," said Messenger firmly. "Say what you want about your scar collection, that cut needs treatment. It could get infected."

"Look, I'm not going to a hospital to be stitched up. More likely to pick up an infection than prevent one."

"What kind of hospitals do you frequent?"

Gwen laughed despite herself. "Ones in dodgy out-of-the-way places in the back of beyond."

"My case rests."

"I don't like your fancy hospitals here any better. In fact, I hate them." She sounded about seven, she realized.

"You don't need to go to a hospital. I can stitch you up right here if you like."

"You?"

Messenger gave a forbearing smile, like a parent to a trying child. Gwen realized she had never thought of him as a father until confronted with the evidence. Was he a good father or did he forever torment his children with metrics?

"Yes, me. I *am* a doctor. Not a plastic surgeon, admittedly, but I've always had good stitch work, or so I'm told."

"Oh God, go on then. Do what you must."

They walked into the house. She'd wanted access. . . .

72

Gwen felt a wave of tiredness begin to wash over her. She recognized it as the aftermath of adrenaline. Now that danger had passed, her body and her mind just wanted to switch off. She glanced around as Messenger led her through his home. Polished wooden floors. Persian rugs. A huge, stone fireplace dominated a room with a soaring roof and floor-to-ceiling windows. Modern art decorated white walls. Not her style, but striking. Gwen bet it was Messenger rather than some tony art adviser who picked the pieces.

He led her upstairs into what looked like a guest bedroom, on into the en suite bathroom.

"I'll just get my bag. And a chair. And some dry clothes."

He came back carrying a pair of jeans and a t-shirt and sweatshirt. "These should fit. My wife, my ex-wife," he corrected himself, "she was near enough your size."

"Thanks," said Gwen, as Messenger strode out.

She pulled off her wet and bloodstained dress, dropped it in the bath, pulled on Messenger's ex-wife's clothes. The jeans were tight, Gwen's thigh muscles were not designed for skinny jeans, but they were dry and they were warm. Tee and sweatshirt were fine. Gwen looked in the mirror. The eyes that looked back at her were not as cocky as she'd have liked. *Silly Mandy,* she thought. *Nearly fucked us both up big time.*

A knock at the door made her jump. Messenger stood there carrying an armchair and a traditional doctor's bag. Gwen looked at it curiously.

"I thought they only existed in old movies."

"A present from my ex," he explained. "It's quite useful, actually. Sit."

Gwen suppressed a smile. There was just one thing more dictatorial and God-like than a private equity guru and that was a doctor. She sat.

Gabriel Messenger extracted a somewhat disturbing collection of instruments and set them on a plastic sheet he took from his bag. He then took out a bottle of what must have been a sterilizer and washed his hands, then his instruments.

"Do you want a local anaesthetic?" he asked, brandishing a needle. "Most people I would simply stick and not ask, but I wouldn't dare do that with you."

Gwen chuckled. "Why not?"

"You'd bite my head off and tell me you didn't need it, that all your limbs have been torn off and reattached without it."

Gwen grinned. "Well, now that you mention it . . . But thanks for asking, and no jab. I'll anesthetize myself at home later."

"It'll hurt, you know that."

"Get on with it. Please."

Messenger sat on the edge of the bath, bent over her arm, face wrinkled with concentration. Occasionally, he would glance up, look into her eyes, check that she was fine. It was oddly, discomfortingly intimate. The healer, the murderer . . . Involuntarily, Gwen shuddered.

"You OK?" Messenger asked, concern etching his brows.

"Mm. Sorry."

"Delayed shock, maybe."

"No. Just cold still."

Five minutes later, Gwen's wound was swabbed, cleaned, stitched, and bandaged.

"Get your own doctor to check it and rebandage in a few days. You know the drill; any undue pain, any fever . . . straight to A and E."

"Yes, Doctor. Thank you, Doctor."

"My pleasure." Messenger stuck out his hand, took Gwen's, and pulled her to her feet.

"Thank you for saving Mandy. She was too drunk to appreciate the risk she was in, the risk she put you in."

Gwen gave a rueful look. "Maybe you should have a bowling party next year. In Utah."

Messenger barked out a laugh. "Maybe I will. But right now I need to go back out and salvage what I can of my party."

Gwen nodded, felt like a heel again. "Mind if I lie down for a few minutes. Just want to gather myself."

Messenger gestured to the bed. "Please do. Take as long as you need. You took one heck of a bang."

Gwen nodded, watched him go, closed the door behind him. She lay down on the bed, ruffled the cover a bit, then got up and edged over to the window. A few moments later she saw Messenger striding from his house, down the steps, onto the emerald grass.

Quickly, she got up, grabbed her bag, and tiptoed out into the hall. Where was his study likely to be? Upstairs with a killer view, or downstairs with a great one? She trotted down the stairs, tried a few doors, found his study on her third attempt. Her heart was pounding. She pulled the door closed behind her. A desk, a computer, a six-screen Bloomberg Terminal. A huge window, covered with drawn blinds to frustrate prying eyes, no doubt. Gwen imagined the party outside, perhaps just yards away. The glass window was too thick to allow any sounds of normal volume to penetrate. No sounds issued from the hall.

On the desk there was also a phone and four silver picture frames: ex-wife and three sons, all fine looking. Healer, murderer, husband, and father.

Gwen searched the room. Desk light, hollow base of, Dan had suggested, or the underside of a desk, far enough in to avoid knocking anyone's knees. The desk was a single sheet of cherrywood, thin, attached to metal stanchions. The bug, small as it was, would stand out a mile if anyone looked. She checked the Anglepoise on Messenger's desk. Flat base. Strike two.

She looked around. There was an antique filing cabinet in one corner. She hurried up to it. There was a lip on three sides that protruded an inch and a half, leaving a gap between it and one wall. She inserted her fingers, probed the gap. Enough space, if she were dextrous enough to stick it there. She got out the GSM, held it in place, hand trembling. Perfect fit. She smiled, felt the adrenaline pump.

Quickly, she took out the dental paste, the palette knife, the chopstick, her bottled water, and the saucer, which she unwrapped from the hand towel. Mercifully it was unbroken. She shook out some dental paste in powder form, added water, stirred with the chopstick. It thickened quickly. She took the palette knife, smeared it with paste and quickly smoothed the paste under the lip and as far back as her fingers were able to reach. She smeared some more dental paste onto the device, then pushed it against the filing cabinet, holding it in place.

She counted to sixty. Each second seemed to have been elongated. She could feel the blood pounding in her head. No way to explain this away if Messenger walked in. She counted to sixty again then gingerly released her fingers. The device stayed put. She blew out a breath. Now for the store-and-forward device, which was bigger, harder to hide.

She checked the Anglepoise lamp again. The base comprised a large plastic disk, attached by screws. She dug out the screwdrivers. The second one worked. Quickly she unscrewed all five screws. There was a gap, several inches high. Plenty of room for the device. Again she mixed up dental paste, stirred in water, smeared it on the top of the hollow space and on the device, held them together till the device adhered, then quickly, fingers still trembling, she reattached the base and replaced the screws. She put the lamp back, stashed away all her tools, turned three-sixty, made sure she had left nothing she hadn't intended to leave. Then she stood by the door, ear cocked to the hall, listening. No sound, but she had an irrational fear that someone was there.

She held her breath, cracked open the door, peered out. The hallway was empty. She edged round the door, slipped out, softly closed it behind her. She was sweating. She drew her hand across her face. A new wave of tiredness hit her. Now she genuinely needed to lie down. She hurried back upstairs into the guestroom, dragged back the covers, lay down, her bag beside her. She yanked the covers over her, felt her body subside in relief. Just five minutes was all she needed, then she'd get the hell out, go home. In less than a minute she was fast asleep.

73

She awoke in darkness, a knock at the door echoing in her consciousness. She sat up, fumbled for a light, found the switch, flooded the room with a soft glow.

"Come in." She swung her feet over the side of the bed.

Messenger pushed open the door and stood in the doorway with a cup of what looked like milky tea in his hand.

"Like one?"

"Love one."

He crossed the room and handed it to her. She sipped gratefully.

"Doctor's remedy: hot sweet tea."

"It's working. Thank you. Can't believe I fell asleep."

"Shock, exhaustion."

Gwen shook her head. "I've been through worse and—"

Messenger smiled. "I'm sure you have. But you're

human, not superhuman, Gwen. However much you try to convince yourself you're the tough surfer girl, your body knows when it comes close to death. Sleep is what it needs to recover."

"You exaggerate. I wasn't that close to death."

Messenger looked thoughtful. "If you insist."

He walked over to a curved window seat, sat down, leaned toward her, arms braced on his legs, eyes earnest.

"Have you ever wondered how many times we come close to death and don't even realize?" he asked.

Gwen stood up, felt the undercurrents swirling. Shit, he hadn't discovered the bug, had he? Was this a veiled threat?

"What do you mean?" she asked, tilting her head to one side in a show of casual inquiry.

"A truck careens out of control just after you've passed by on the highway. A loose brick falls from a building just after you've walked by. A maniac walks the path you've just jogged down. And today, in your case and in Mandy's, you got close. As you well know. When a wave breaks on top of you, you are hit by hundreds of tons of water. If that water meets resistance, say, a rock, and you are between it and the rock—" Messenger scissored his hands together.

"Enough!" said Gwen. "You make life sound like a constant hazard."

"I don't mean to. Just that death is not so far away as we think. It's all around, could come and get us at any unguarded moment, so better to make our accommodation with it."

If this were a coded message, she had one of her own. She walked up to him, drained her tea, handed him back the cup and saucer.

"Have you ever read Dylan Thomas?" she asked, all casual surfer drawl.

Messenger frowned. "A little. Why?"

"How about 'Do not go gentle into that good night'?"

Messenger shook his head.

" '*Do not go gentle into that good night, rage, rage against the dying of the light*' " she recited. "Well that's me. I shall not go gentle. I shall kick and scream and fight to stay alive. I shall take down anyone who tries to take me down," she added softly, with just the hint of a smile. She glanced at her watch.

"I need to go. Thanks for the party, for the stitches."

Messenger made no move to get up. He sat, watching her curiously, like a puzzle he was determined to solve.

74

Outside on the lawn, tastefully arranged uplights revealed a party that looked like it was winding down. A close knot of bodies was crossing the grass. Peter Weiss spotted Gwen.

"Hey, here's the heroine of the day!"

"Hey, Gwen," echoed Kevin Barclay. "Perfect timing."

She walked up to them; the three grunts were part of the group too. Mandy and Mel and Randy Sieber had gone.

"Join us. We're going to hit the beach bar in Carmel."

Gwen eyed them. They weren't drunk, but they were on their way. She had the feeling if she ever wanted to slip in any discreet questions about Falcon and Messenger, this would be her chance.

"Sure," she replied.

The bar was heaving with people. They spilled out onto the sand. Gwen sipped on the Coke Peter Weiss had bought her. Everyone else was on tequilas, save Weiss, who announced he was sticking to beer. Gwen thought he looked oddly guilty drinking even that. He kept looking round as if expecting censure. He wasn't saying much, just sipping and lapsing into song. More R.E.M.; "Everybody Hurts," this time.

The limos lined up on Scenic Road, further incitement, if any were needed, to a liquid night.

Gwen half listened in to the conversations, eyes on the sea, on the breakers silvered by the full moon.

Weiss moved closer to Gwen. "That was amazing, what you did today," he murmured over the rim of his beer bottle.

Gwen shrugged. "Instinctive, really."

Weiss gave a slight shudder. "Not for me. I wouldn't have jumped in there."

"If someone you loved were drowning . . ."

"Yeah, well maybe then, but hell, please don't tell me you love Mandy."

Gwen laughed. "No, Peter. Rest assured, I do not love Mandy. In fact you could say I am severely pissed with her."

"I'll bet." He sipped, paused. "So, who do you love then, mysterious Dr. Boudain?"

Gwen looked at Weiss, standing before her, eyes sad. She thought for a while.

"Truly love, rather than care for?"

Weiss nodded.

"My parents."

He nodded again. "Bit sad, isn't it, to love the dead best."

Gwen shrugged. "At least it's love. How 'bout you?"

"My mother. My dead mother." He gave her a wry smile.

Gwen nodded. "No one since?" She saw her chance. "Like a substitute father figure?"

Weiss looked at her sharply. "Meaning?"

"Dr. Messenger?"

"Shit! I don't love him!" he said angrily, slopping beer over the sand as he gesticulated.

"He's my boss. That's it!" he declared, face reddening.

"A kind of mentor?" suggested Gwen. "Like he said,

he's made you all millionaires. He's made you all part of something."

"That's what he thinks, with all his speeches and his grandstanding. There are bigger things, Gwen," intoned Weiss, with a mixture of what seemed like bitterness and portent.

Still angry, he turned and headed for the bar. Did he mean religion, wondered Gwen? There had been a brief flash of a manic light in his eyes.

She'd get no more out of him, she realized. He'd joined Jihoon and Curt at the bar. They made way for him, but it was obvious he was the odd man out, the permanent outsider, thought Gwen, feeling a flash of sympathy.

Atalanta and Kevin Barclay had disappeared. Gwen was alone. She felt oddly calm. Her hands dangled by her sides. She stood quite still.

Her normal restive energy was all burnt out. She was only truly relaxed when she had felt the catharsis of fear, all adrenaline spent on the waves, or when she had had truly spectacular sex.

She smiled to herself.

With the calm came a kind of super clarity, where she felt as if she could have seen individual blades of grass, seen through pretenses to the core. It was as if all the extraneous noise in her head and outside had faded away to insignificance. It was a kind of addiction, this feeling.

Now she was left with one clear image, one clear want: Dan Jacobsen. Messenger was right. You could die at any moment. So she might as well really live. She could imagine the smell of Dan's sweat: honey, musk, and salt. She craved him. With her body, with her mind. If she fell in love with him, if she got hurt, then it was a price worth paying.

75

Gwen detoured along the beach, wanting to make sure neither Weiss nor Jihoon nor Curt saw her. On one side was the ocean, on the other a line of cypress trees. She had to do a big loop to get to her car. She was fine with that. She pulled off her shoes. The sand was cold and soft underfoot. As she walked further from the bar, the darkness deepened, relieved only by the pooling glow of the streetlamps on Scenic Road. She was about to head up toward the road when a sound stopped her. A sort of grunt, half protest, half fear.

She stopped, foot poised, toe to sand, like a ballet dancer at the barre. The sound of movement, of breathing, a word cut off: "N—"

Eyes straining, she caught movement behind one of the cypress trees. She walked closer, on silent feet. Closer still, she could see limbs thrashing. A man, on top of a woman. She wanted to turn away, but something told her to stay. The woman was thrashing her head back and forth, trying to evade the mouth of the man on top of her. Long black dreads. Atalanta.

"Get off her! Now!" said Gwen, loud, but calm.

The writhing bodies froze. Kevin Barclay rolled off Atalanta, who sat up and spat.

"What the hell are you doing here?" demanded Barclay.

"You bastard!" shouted Atalanta, scrambling to her feet, backing away from Barclay.

Barclay stood slowly, hands on hips, eyes dark with fury, mouth sneering, as if none of it mattered.

"You weren't saying that a minute ago," he drawled.

"I was saying *No!* Until you stuck your fucking hand on my mouth."

Gwen took a step closer to Barclay. "So what's your

problem Barclay? You think *no* means *maybe*? That it?" asked Gwen softly.

"Her body language, her come-ons all night. All that meant *yes*."

"Maybe in your eyes. But *no*'s kinda unequivocal, don't you think." Gwen walked closer, put down her own bag, picked up Atalanta's, which lay on the ground. She turned, handed it to the woman, who was watching her with big eyes. Atalanta took her bag with shaking hands.

"You really would have raped her, wouldn't you Barclay?"

He barked out a laugh. "And she would have loved it, sucked it right up. Anything to squirm up the ladder. If you hadn't fucking come along." He took a step closer to Gwen. "Now why don't you just fuck off and leave us alone." He shot his hands out to push her.

He didn't see it coming. Gwen didn't see it coming, just acted out of instinct, and training and anger. With her left arm she blocked him, sweeping away his hands while she shot out her right palm, hand rigid, and smashed it onto the end of his nose. Barclay yelped with pain, lashed out his hand. Gwen dodged easily, caught his hand, turned it palm outward until the pain bit, then pushed him down to his knees; an aikido hold, one of Dwayne's, a favorite of Special Forces who had to subdue someone without damaging them. Barclay knelt on the sand, nose gushing blood.

Gwen stood over him. With her free hand, she grabbed his hair, pulled up his head so he had to look at her.

"You try anything like that again, then I will really, truly hurt you. And if you do anything, and I mean any tiny little thing in the office to cause trouble for Atalanta, I will tell Messenger about this. And then I will hurt you again."

Barclay said nothing. His breath rasped in and out.

"Do you understand me?" asked Gwen.

Barclay tried to nod.

"Not good enough," said Gwen.

"Yes!" spat Barclay. "I understand you."

"Good." Gwen released him and backed away, keeping her eyes on him until she was a safe distance. She turned to Atalanta, who was staring at her, mouth open. She picked up her bag and her shoes.

"Let's go, Atalanta."

The other woman nodded. As they walked away, Barclay spoke again.

"You psycho bitch," he muttered.

Gwen paused, turned, laughed. "Yeah, that'll cover it." They left him on the sand.

"That. Was. Truly. Amazing," breathed Atalanta.

"Had it coming. Fuckwit," said Gwen.

Atalanta sucked in a breath. "I did flirt, I grant you—"

Gwen turned to her. "Not you! Him!"

"Ah. Yeah. Sorry. And you gave it to him, my God! I got you wrong, girl. I owe you a grade-one apology. And the biggest thank you. How can I?"

Gwen smiled. "You can buy me lunch one day. Might want to give the Cupcake Café a rain check for a spell."

"Just say the word! Anytime."

Gwen walked Atalanta back to the limos, saw her safely in, watched the limo drive off down Scenic Road, through the orange pall cast by the streetlamps.

Then she got into her own car and drove. It was 1:00 A.M. She should have been tired. She wasn't. She'd gone to the party hoping to learn more about Messenger. She'd learned that Mandy was a drunk, Barclay was a rapist, and Messenger had a hidden streak of kindness. She'd made two new enemies. Not altogether useful for her purposes. Fate had dished out the shit twice to her that day. She didn't believe bad luck would come in threes.

76

Gwen parked outside Dan's house. Rang the bell. No reply. Following instinct, she walked round to the lawn overlooking the sea.

As if he'd known she were there, he called out: "Over here." His voice was low. The faint huskiness tightened something in her stomach. The full moon lit the night. Gwen saw him, his back to her, standing at the edge of his land near the cliff top. She stopped by his side, gazed out with him at the moon-silvered path that cut across the ocean.

He turned to look at her. His eyes held hers. His lips quirked into a smile, but still those green eyes just looked at her, revealing nothing.

Gwen wanted to see the desire she felt reflected back at her, but all she saw was control. She smiled her own smile. I'll break that into a million pieces, she vowed.

She turned to look out to the sea. "I used to imagine walking along that path when I was a little girl. Wondering where it would take me," she said softly.

Dan remained silent for a while. "Funny thing, so did I."

They turned back to each other.

"Your path seems to have brought you here. To me," he said.

Gwen laughed softly, moved away, five paces, ten, twenty. She stood, the moon glowing off her, smiling across at Dan. He gave a smile of understanding, moved across the silent grass to her.

"And my path has brought me to you," he said. Still they didn't touch. The air between them felt alive. Gwen could feel him even though she wasn't touching him. She could feel the force that was him, the energy pumping out of him. And she throbbed with the energy and the desire pumping out of her.

"I wasn't sure you'd come to me," he said.

"Neither was I. I tried to hold back, for the longest time."

"Why?"

"Because I've known from the beginning if we do this there is no holding back. At least not for me."

Dan raised an eyebrow. "Why would I hold back?"

"Because you do. Because underneath that dude exterior you're as controlled as anyone I know. Whatever's hidden inside, that's what I want. All that power, all that loneliness and stillness, all that contained violence I feel in you. I want it all. I want to feel it all."

"You want me to lose control?" Dan asked, his voice raw-edged.

As she spoke, his eyes turned hard and wild; that look she had glimpsed, seen in her dreams, wanted above all else. His body seemed to be vibrating with tension.

Gwen took a step closer. "Can you do that, Dan?" she asked softly. "Can you lose control with me? No holding back?"

"Jesus, Gwen. I'm catching fire here."

Gwen laughed. "Let it burn."

"Here?"

"Yeah, right here. I don't want a bed and sheets and pillows, safe and sanitized in your bedroom. I want you here, outside, under the moon, on the grass, the night air on my skin."

Any remaining control snapped. Dan grabbed Gwen in one swift move. He pulled her into him, chest to chest. She could feel the armor of his muscles. He bent his head, mouth on hers, kissing her with all the violence and the yearning she had sensed in him. Abruptly, he broke away, held her at arms' length.

"You want it all, I'm gonna give it to you. Every last bit."
Then he pushed her down onto the grass. Gwen pulled him
onto her, felt the weight of his body pressing down on her.
She kissed him back, pulling him to her as hard as she
could grip. Unnoticed by either of them, her stitches began to bleed, all pain subsumed.

77

NATIONAL COUNTERTERRORISM CENTER, MONDAY MORNING

Rain pattered against the bulletproof windows of Andrew
Canning's office. Dead leaves scuttled along the ground
outside, dank and depressing. He hated the slow prelude
to winter. Slow death. It made him feel old, and he was
only fifty-three. He sat defiantly in his shirtsleeves, scowling at the weather. He had his weekly golf game scheduled that evening.

He turned away from the window. The core of what he
regarded as his Sheikh Ali team sat before him: Del Russo,
Peters, Furlong, Zucker, and Southward, whom he had co-
opted to CTC for as long as he needed her. By special
arrangement, she traveled back and forth between Fort
Meade and Tyson's Corner.

Canning could see Southward was pleased with the
arrangement. NSA must get a tad dry, and the woman was
flourishing here at the sharper end. She seemed to be on a
mission to get Sheikh Ali. Canning liked that. A zealot
with brains. A rare combination, in his experience.

He eyed his team in turn.

"Briefing at the White House tomorrow at five," he declared. "I'll need to talk about Sheikh A. Give me something to take to POTUS."

Del Russo, Peters, and Furlong all came up with versions of *nothing new,* some wordier than others. Southward shook her head, lips pursed in disappointment.

"We haven't lucked out on the algorithms again. We're trying, but no more successful intercepts."

Moira Zucker gave Southward a pitying look. Displaying the big-game temperament that had accelerated her rise up through CTC, she had waited till last.

"As it happens, sir, I have something. It's to do with the puts. I've been following the markets, seeing what gets registered, using some real useful software which flags up these specialized trades. More have been put on over the past ten days. And some shorts. Someone's doing it with finesse, not wanting to overload the market. But it's systematic, and it's huge. This is the Big Player."

"Excellent!" declared Canning.

"The trading pattern is extremely intricate," continued Zucker. "Layer upon layer of nominee companies. I've peeled some more layers back, only to find yet more. Cunning sonofabitch, whoever put them on."

"Recognize any of the nominees? Got anything real under the layers?" asked Canning.

Zucker curled her lip. "Yet again, Wall Street's finest," she replied, reeling off a list of specific names.

"*Reallllllly . . .*" Canning rolled out the word, stroking his shiny pate thoughtfully. He smiled. His desk warrior would get to play again.

"I might be able to help," he said musingly. "In the meantime, I think we should get SEC more involved in this. At the small end. Let's see what they have to say about our little player. They might have some extra insights. I got the feeling Bergers was holding back. We got the FISA warrant on Ronnie Glass?" he asked Zucker.

"Up and running as of nine a.m. this morning," she replied. "I'm gonna start snooping soon as we're through here."

"And I'm gonna ring Troy Bergers at SEC," replied Canning. "Might just make his Monday."

78

THE SECURITIES AND EXCHANGE COMMISSION, NYC, MONDAY MORNING

Troy Bergers liked Mondays. He loved his weekends, rich with sport, food, and sex, but when they were over he was more than ready for the battle of the week. This particular Monday would go down as one of his all-time favorites.

He'd only been in the office three minutes, his takeout cappuccino was still hot, when the phone rang. Andrew Canning himself, the head honcho at Counterterrorism Center on the line. Bergers gripped the receiver hard. Canning had news and a request; an order, effectively. Bergers was more than happy to accede.

"I'll get my people onto it as of now. Keep me in the loop," Bergers said, listening in for a few more moments of mutual pleasantries, before thudding the phone back into its cradle.

He hit his intercom. "*Bret!* Get Wilks and Rac in here, would ya?"

Wilkie and Rodgers appeared within the minute. Rac, noted Bergers, looked darker-eyed than ever. Wilkie glowed like the star in an ad for middle-aged vitamin supplements.

"Sit," instructed Bergers. He stayed behind his cluttered desk, wearing his best poker face.

He watched them sit, waited a long moment, ratcheting up their interest, ever the showman.

"We got something big here. We got something nasty here," he intoned, leaning forward, head lowered like a bull about to charge.

"And this is good?" asked Wilkie, head tilted, one eyebrow elegantly raised.

Bergers sat back. "Very good for us. Very bad for Ronald Glass."

He cracked a smile, benevolent father to favored child.

"I happened to overhear you saying, Ange, that you would like to listen in to Ronnie's cell phone, and to his home."

"Yeah, well, a girl can dream."

Bergers' smile grew even bigger. "Sometimes dreams come true."

"We can *listen in?*" asked Ange, springing to her feet.

Bergers nodded. "Home. Cell phone."

"How?" asked Rodgers, suddenly wide awake.

"I think it was you, Ange, who said that it would take evidence of terrorist activity to get approval to listen in to his cell phone and his home. You even added that the Counterterrorism Center would be able to get approval and access," mused Bergers.

"I did," replied Wilkie, not quite believing where this seemed to be going.

"You must be psychic."

Wilkie laughed. "Oh I am. You're giving me a pay raise tomorrow!"

Bergers belted out a laugh. "Maybe I just will."

"Guys! Put me outta my misery here!" cried Rac, raising his palms in the air. "What the hell's going on?"

"CTC just rang!" declared Bergers. "Andrew Canning, no less. They connected two pieces of your intel. One of the buyers of the puts on California real estate casualty property companies happens to be none other than our Ronald Glass."

Ange shouted, *"Whaat?"*

Rac blinked rapidly. "Well, I'll be . . ."

Bergers grinned. "My reaction too. Dirty Ronnie was using nominee companies and all that shit, but CTC would appear to have just blown through those walls like a house fire. You should know that Canning told me there are other buyers of the puts too, but the identity of that buyer or buyers they don't know or aren't sharing."

Ange stared at Bergers, mouth open in amazement.

"And get this," continued Bergers, fisting his hands, drumming them on the table. "What is evident is that the buyers of these puts are suspected of being involved, directly, or possibly unwittingly, in potential terrorist activity. CTC's already got a FISA warrant out on Ronnie, enabling them to get access to *all* his comms; *all* his electronic intel; audio, text, and e-mail. The whole friggin' lot!" he exclaimed, raising his meaty arms in a triumphal salute.

Ange let out a whistle. "Pay dirt!"

Bergers nodded. "Damn right! Guys, your contact at CTC is Moira Zucker; I believe you've already spoke with her, Ange. Zucker'll copy you both in on all the intercepts."

Ange and Rac exchanged a look: thrill, determination, delighted shock.

"For our part," Bergers continued, more soberly, "we have been asked real nicely by the CTC guys to keep digging, to find out what the hell is going on. And to help interpret the intel that comes down."

"Christmas and birthday all at once," said Rodgers, beaming.

"Freakin' miracle!" exclaimed Wilkie, beaming back. "Oh Ronnie, what the hell have you gotten into?"

"That's the question, ain't it?" retorted Bergers.

"Doesn't seem like a terrorist to me," mused Wilkie.

"All the more dangerous, then," noted Rac.

"Maybe he's the bag man?" suggested Wilkie.

"That's what CTC wants to figure, like yesterday," replied Bergers.

"Did you pass on my contact's thoughts about why someone would buy California casualty prop puts?" asked Wilkie.

"Because of the earthquake or this fabled ARk Storm?" asked Bergers. He shook his head. "Too far fetched."

"Can we afford to make that call?" pushed Wilkie.

Bergers stopped grinning. "I'll think about it. Keep digging."

"Until I hit China," promised Wilkie, striding from the office. "Ronald Glass, you are going *down!*"

79

NATIONAL COUNTERTERRORISM CENTER, TYSON'S CORNER, VIRGINIA

At Tyson's Corner, the weather built. The rain sluiced down, weaving a series of rivulets on Canning's windows, snaking, crossing, merging. Golf would have to be postponed, but Canning was bolstered by the warm feeling in the pit of his stomach that came with progress. Ronald Glass was their first break. It often took just one, then the chain could build, link by link, taking you right to the end.

Technology was a wondrous thing, and he had at his disposal an arsenal of toys that would have been deemed science fiction just a few years ago. Asymmetric warfare, another way of saying *play to your strengths* . . . the US had money, still, and technological tools at the razor end of cutting edge, but, just as important, it had agents with skills and brilliance and just the right measure of larceny in their souls. In this case, it was a measure of his own larceny that had served up Ronnie Glass in quick time, but it was technology that would slice and dice him, show all his hidden angles.

And in the meantime, a tad more larceny was called for. There were times when Canning felt like a mere administrator, a paper pusher, not even a desk warrior. The excuse to rattle some cages delighted him.

Through the morning, he made a series of further phone calls to a number of Wall Street CEOs. At noon he called in Zucker again.

He could sense her own larceny, see it in her eyes, veiled and proper, just occasionally unveiled for him in the safe sterility of his office. Every boss had favorites, couldn't help it. Zucker was at the very top of his favorites list, seemed to know it too.

"Close the door," he instructed.

"Sure," she answered carefully. She folded herself into the chair, sat demurely, hands in lap, face uptilted like a child awaiting a favorite story.

"Amazing how cooperative Wall Street can be when the pressure's really on," Canning began, smiling broadly at his analyst. "Helps that we're on the side of the angels tho," he conceded.

"Always," agreed Zucker. "So, tell me, sir," she urged throatily.

"They sold out the next layer. Three names cropped up repeatedly. Canning named the banks.

"The Far East," mused Zucker. "I'll bet those banks are another layer in the cake. There'll be yet another level of nominees underneath."

"I'm with you. It'll be harder to make *them* talk," observed Canning, running his finger up and down his nose. "Might have to get creative," he concluded.

Zucker nodded slowly, conveying with her eyes that she

had taken his meaning perfectly. "There's more than one way to peel an onion, I believe."

The word hovered unsaid between them: hacking. The Chinese weren't the only ones who excelled at it.

Canning nodded sagely. He didn't say a word. *See no evil, hear no evil, speak no evil.*

As if to underline her point, Zucker removed her red-framed spectacles, laid them on Canning's desk.

"Depending on how successful I am, we might have to get someone on the ground if it does turn out to be Singapore or China, depending on how fast you need answers," she added.

"Let me think about it. We do not want to alert Mr. Big, whoever he might be, not until we're ready to close him down. Time and discretion, usually enemies," cautioned Canning.

Zucker smiled. She put on her glasses.

"I'll tread softly," she said, proving her point as she rose smoothly, turned, and glided noiselessly from Canning's office, high heels soundless, even on the carpets worn thin in the corridor beyond.

80

THE LAB, MONDAY MORNING

Gwen arrived at Falcon at 11:00 A.M. Two hours later than normal. Two of the best hours of her life. She smiled at the CCTV as she swiped her pass, keyed in her PIN. She walked toward her office wondering if Kevin Barclay had come in to work. She glanced toward his office, saw him sitting there. She gave him brownie points for that, at least. He looked up, met her eye.

Two minutes later, he joined her at the coffee machine. His nose was heavily swollen, bruised blue, black, and red. His left eye was also swollen and bruised from where Gwen's palm had also hit. Collateral damage, thought Gwen, veiling her smile.

"So, what happened to you, then?" she asked him, of necessity, as Peter Weiss ambled up beside them.

"Ran into some trouble when I left the bar. Couple of punks," he said neutrally, eyes on Gwen.

Weiss angled his head. "Looks even worse than when you came in," he observed in a voice richer in glee than compassion.

"Surprised you can see to focus," Barclay replied, his normally smooth voice nasal and piqued. Gwen almost felt sorry for him. Weiss looked rough too, she noted: red-veined eyes, bloated face; hungover.

"What you put away last night would sink a football team," continued Barclay. "Thought you'd given up the hooch."

"I don't touch it. As a rule," Weiss replied tightly.

"Now now, children. Play nice," murmured Gwen. She took her coffee, walked away, leaving them to their sparring.

She sat at her desk, sipping her coffee, body humming. She tried to work on the model of Zeus running on the laptop before her. Her mind strayed repeatedly.

"So how's the arm?"

Gwen looked up. Gabriel Messenger, resplendent in gray trousers and electric-blue shirt, stood in her doorway, smiling at her.

"Oh, seems fine, thank you. Doesn't hurt."

"Of course it hurts. Unless you're dosing yourself with morphine!"

Gwen tried, and failed, to suppress a smile. No, something much more powerful, she thought. She wore a long-sleeved shirt to cover the grass stains. She hoped Messenger wouldn't ask to see it.

"You're the tough surfer girl, of course. I forgot. You feel no pain," he said with an ironic smile.

"Correct."

"Keep an eye on the stitches. Get your dressing changed tomorrow."

"Yes, Doctor." Gwen smiled, felt the burn of her betrayal as she thought of planting the bug after Messenger, with surprising gentleness, had cleaned and stitched her wound.

"How's Mandy?" she asked.

"In bed. Recovering." Messenger gave a pained smile. "Every year she gets tanked and pulls a stunt. Can't imagine what she'll get up to next year." Messenger raised a hand in farewell, turned and left her.

Gwen swiveled in her chair, looked out of the window, gazed over the sandy scrub toward the hills, pale blue in the shimmering distance. She could not imagine being here in a year. The fluttering in her stomach wasn't just because of Dan. Under the euphoria there was still fear, and the gut awareness that something, the unseen wave that seemed to be heading her way, would break soon.

81

SEVENTEEN MILE DRIVE, FOUR DAYS LATER,
FRIDAY, LATE AFTERNOON

Dan put down the weight, picked up his shrilling cell phone, grimaced when he saw the caller ID.

"Yeah?" he said.

"You haven't been into the office all week," declared MackStack acidly. "You avoiding me?"

"Nope."

"I'm getting a kinda disappointed feeling here, Jacobsen."

"Why? Couldn't get it up last night?"

"Cute. Nothing on Falcon, nothing juicy on ARk Storm. Professional failure kind of disappointment."

Dan glanced at Gwen. She was lying on a bench, pressing 140 pounds. Sweat ran down her face and she was breathing hard. Her hair fell from the bench, tumbling toward the floor. Her muscles bulged and shone. Her bandage covered half her forearm. She wasn't supposed to be working out. Had a blithely contemptuous attitude toward personal injury, which he shared, and loved. She looked to him like a warrior princess. She looked magnificent. And oblivious.

Foreigner pumped from the speakers: "Dirty White Boy." That was how Dan felt right now, and not in the good sense. He walked from the gym onto the lawn.

The sun was setting and the air was chill. Dan hunched in on himself.

"I get the feeling you're getting sweet on the meteorologist," murmured Mack, as if psychic. "It would be a shame," he added silkily, "if she knew how you stage-managed your meeting with her. She might think you only got close to her to get close to her boss, to get yourself a story. Makes you a kind of prostitute in her eyes. Not to mention making a dupe of her."

Dan stayed silent. Thought of fifty different ways to kill his editor.

"Stay on the job, Daniel. Deliver us what we need."

"Adding blackmail to your box of tricks now, Mack?"

"What d'you mean, *adding*?"

Dan ended the call. He gazed out at the ocean: cool, blue, pure. It offered no comfort this time. He felt the darkness creep, remembered too much. The memories flooded back. No matter how hard you tried to wash your mind after a task, you never could. He shut his eyes. It would be so easy to pick up that mantle again, to do what he had done so effectively in years gone by for his country. He could do it for himself without a qualm. And, most likely, get away with it. What difference would it make to spill a little more blood?

82

Sheikh Ali sat with Gabriel Messenger in the large stateroom. A wind had blown up and the yacht pitched slightly. Sheikh Ali had instructed the captain to motor downwind, minimizing the disruption to his guest, who he knew suffered from seasickness. Despite that kindness, Messenger looked pale and his face was pinched. In his black trousers and black shirt, he looked more ascetic priest than venture capitalist.

The golden coffee cups lay before them, empty, sides stained dark. The sweet smell of the *shisha* pipe hovered in the room, almost alive, like a visiting spirit borne round the room by the air conditioning that the Sheikh loved.

They covered much Falcon business before the Sheikh asked his main question.

"Zeus. And the meteorologist. What news?"

Messenger nodded. "Gwen Boudain is proving invaluable," he replied, enthusiasm overcoming his latent queasiness. "I'd say she has boosted our rain yield by close to six percent. That's very sig—"

"I know it's significant," cut in the Sheikh in a rare show of temper. "It's more than significant. It's impressive."

Messenger sat in silence, his wordless reaction to the insult.

The Sheikh looked away, calculation in his eyes. It was

a full minute before he turned back to Messenger. The German was used to his silences, and to his very occasional outburst of temper. He had seen much worse. He knew just to wait, to let the storms pass.

"We need to press on with the next parts of the plan," Al Baharna declared at last.

"Gwen thinks she can get more still out of Zeus," Messenger said quietly, steepling his hands. "She says there's one input she's still struggling with."

"Keep pushing her."

"I will."

"In the meantime, I think it's time to start acquiring farmland. Marginal farmland wherever we can, subject to the minimum humidity requirements."

"What's our budget?" asked Messenger, eyes quickening.

The Sheikh paused, brain scrolling through his assets. He should call Marcel, get a current tally. He gazed out at the sun, which was dipping into the water in a blaze of red, setting fire to the waves. He knew to the closest fifty million. That would do.

He turned back to Messenger.

"Let's start with one billion US," Al Baharna said levelly.

Messenger kept his face impassive. Inside his blood raced.

"I'll get Kevin and Peter identifying the targets," he replied equally levelly. He wondered if the Sheikh had so much money that it merely bored him, or if like many of those who dealt in astronomically large sums he depersonalized it for rationality's sake, reduced it to a number so that the power of it would not seduce, so that the emotions of it would not cloud clarity.

"Is she happy, with you? Satisfied?" asked the Sheikh.

Messenger frowned, tilted his head, wondered what he'd missed.

"With Falcon!" exclaimed the Sheikh. Messenger further wondered what had upset Al Baharna. The Sheikh seemed unusually febrile.

"She seems to be. Been smiling a lot recently, so yes, I think she's happy. Sometimes she looks like she's just sucked a lemon, like she doesn't want to be there, in Falcon, but it passes. She's unused to the constraints of corporate life. But her work is excellent and I tell her as much."

"Good. Keep her happy. She is essential to our plan."

Messenger nodded. "Perhaps I'll give her a bonus . . ."

"Do that. And please allow me to add one of my own." The Sheikh paused. "Let's say a million dollars. Five hundred from each of us."

Messenger thought that the Sheikh threw money like punches.

"That's a big kickoff," he said. "We don't want her to get enough money to want to leave."

The Sheikh laughed, a mirthless sound. "She won't leave! You know how it is with money, Gabriel. The golden rule, I call it. You hook someone on an amount they had previously only dreamed of. Then they get used to it. They need a bigger dose. So you feed them a bit more, and they get used to that. Once they take the first hit they keep on coming back for more. It's a very rare person who can break the habit. I've never met one who could."

Messenger felt a twist of distaste. The Sheikh had no compunction in using his wealth to corrupt. Messenger had seen it too many times firsthand to doubt.

"She has her Oracle to be financed, does she not?" continued Al Baharna. "That will keep her on the leash."

"Yes," replied Messenger frowning. "She does. She's been working hard on that too."

"What's the latest prognosis on the Niño?"

"Roaring in. Far as I can gather."

"Excellent!" exclaimed the Sheikh, clapping his hands

together. He rose to his feet, signifying that the audience was over.

Messenger rose too, shook the Sheikh's hand, and headed for the helicopter and his ride home.

Sheikh Ali watched him go. He paced the deck in the falling night, seeking to walk off his restlessness, the source of which he had tried and failed to identify. The pacing did not work.

"Hussein!" He yelled to one of the polo-shirted patrollers. "Meet me in the gym."

Hussein, a fellow Saudi Shia, was known for his ruthlessness, whether in training his master or in following his orders to kill. The Sheikh knew Hussein could assuage his restlessness, at least for a while.

One hour thirty minutes later, Al Baharna finished his grueling exercise regime. He nodded a curt farewell to Hussein, then he left the cool grays of his customized gym for the warm splendor of his cabin.

He stripped, dropped his clothes on the heated marble floor of his bathroom, eyed his naked body in the mirror; privation and rigorous exercise had honed him to a wiry strength. He was pleased, even though he recognized in it the sin of vanity.

"*Zakharf ad dunya wasawis ash Shaitan*," he murmured to himself—*the adornments of the world are the whisperings of Satan*. But the feverish training was prompted by more than mere vanity. As the days neared what Al Baharna thought of as Nemesis for the Californians, he trained as if he were personally going to war. It made him feel connected, not just the mastermind with the money. He smiled. It would seem it was all going according to plan.

It was time for a woman. The workout had charged his physicality, replaced one form of restiveness with another. He felt the urge, the warmth in his belly going lower. He thought of the pretty meteorologist, wondered how she would be lying under him, naked. Might it be worth an attempt to seduce her, before she became redundant? Of course, if there were any question of her talking, of her going to the police with what she knew, or thought she knew, then seduction too would be redundant, but the Sheikh disliked coercion, it was inelegant and usually beneath him.

He pulled open the glass shower door, suddenly froze. His own complacency hit him. He knew enough of the affairs of commerce, and of jihad, to be aware that whenever you thought things were going according to plan, they rarely were. Things seldom went according to plan.

He closed his shower door, pulled on a heavy toweling robe, padded through to his private sitting room, took a seat at his desk. He would normally have preferred to have the ensuing discussion face-to-face, but the urgings of his instinct allowed no delay.

He picked up his phone, the one with the Telsey encryption, and dialed The Man. They exchanged codes by text message. The background beeping on their handsets ceased, confirming the encryption was in place. Only then did they speak. The algorithms rolled, shrugging off all attempts of interception as they had been designed to do. For the first fifteen seconds of the call, they worked. Then, due to a mixture of skill and the plain luck that furnishes many triumphs, they failed to work and the call was intercepted.

At the National Geospatial-Intelligence Agency, the intercept was downloaded and saved.

83

Gwen lay in Dan's bed, swathed in a thick duvet, the warmth from Dan's body heating her right side, suffusing her whole body. She had spent five of the past six nights with him. Being with him, having sex with him in her own home with a listening device capturing it all, was unthinkable. And she did feel safer here with him. That made her annoyed, made her feel like the feeble female she had resolved never to be, but there wasn't a hell of a lot she could do about it. Or wanted to.

Beside her, Dan slept. He had made love to her, they had walked on the lawn before the sea, wrapped in dressing gowns. Then they had come back in, and he had fallen asleep. She looked at him, his profile lit by a shaft of moonlight cutting through the gap between the curtains. It was getting harder to keep her feelings in check, to deny what she had felt from the first time they had been together.

Finally, she fell asleep, dreaming of waves, of huge monsters screaming in, breaking on her, holding her down, keeping her down. Those dreams segued into visions of storms, or rivers running through the skies, of a Ferrari speeding through the Carmel Valley, scything down all in its path.

She woke at four thirty, shivering, alone, the duvet on the floor. She pulled on one of Dan's shirts, padded through the dark house. He could, she had noticed, navigate very well in the dark. Before they went to bed, he turned off almost everything electrical save the recording stack.

Gwen found him sitting before it now, in his study, his back to her, headphones clamped to his ears. He turned before she got close, his own internal alert system warning him as it always seemed to do. He smiled up at her, flicked a switch, and removed the headphones.

Gwen leaned over him, kissed his mouth. "Couldn't sleep?" she asked.

"I like waking early, as you're getting to know. I like the dark."

Gwen nodded. He did seem to love darkness, like some kind of a nocturnal animal. He loved sunshine and blue skies and blue seas too, but he was, unusually, equally at home at night. One of his favorite things was to run late at night, after the streetlamps had dimmed. She'd gone with him a couple of times. It had spooked her, but Dan came alive. There was still inside him, for all her brave demands, a side that was utterly unreachable. It made her all the more determined to probe it, even though she felt subconsciously that it was better left alone. She still got the feeling that she had never seen Dan completely lose control. She did when she was with him, when he was deep inside her, almost torturing her with a pleasure so intense she felt it would brand her. But he never did.

"What news from the bug?" she asked.

He shrugged. "Still nothing incriminating. A bit of business, a bit of pleasure. Nothing that paints him as a killer. No mention of the elusive Haas or Hans."

Gwen nodded. "I don't suppose he'd ring a friend and rehash the details."

"Exactly. I'm just looking for an aberration, a phone call or a meet with someone out of his pattern, any conversation that's just a bit opaque, a kind of coded speech."

"And?"

"And still nothing."

"At what stage do we go to the cops?" Gwen wondered.

"We'd get laughed out of town with what we've got now. We need proof. It's all just hearsay this far. We'd blow our chances of getting the real proof if we're premature."

"Are we looking in the wrong place, d'you think?" asked Gwen.

"You mean with him, or geographically?"

"Either? Both?"

"Give it more time. It's not even been one week. Get digging in the office. I can always plant a device in Falcon if we don't make any progress in the next few weeks."

Gwen raised an eyebrow. "With all that security?"

Dan looked at her, a level gaze, and gave the slightest of shrugs. He said nothing, didn't need to. That he could get in if he wanted to was evident.

"It's been weird in the office this week. Seems to have gone quiet."

"How so?" asked Dan. His editor's voice echoed in his head. *Get the dirt on Falcon. . . .*

"Oh, Atalanta's quit bitching at me, she's become a bit of a buddy, Barclay's keeping his bruised head down, Peter Weiss has been working like a fiend, whistling away to himself, stuck in his own little world, getting paler by the day, Messenger is as quietly driven as always. Mandy came back to work on Wednesday claiming to have given up the booze." Gwen shrugged. "No backgammon tournaments, no hissy fits. All's quiet."

"Let's just hope it's not the quiet before the storm," mused Dan.

In Dan's thin cotton shirt, Gwen gave an involuntary shiver.

"That is exactly what I think it is."

Dan got up, stood before her. "Come on, Boudy, let's go back to bed, shall we? We've still got a few hours before dawn."

Gwen saw the intensity in his eyes. One thing she did know, he wanted her just as much as she did him. It was still a craving that never went away for either of them for more than a few hours. And for the next few hours, they would revel in it.

84

The leaves had fallen from the trees, save for a few shrunken stragglers. They lay like decaying corpses in the fields, in the valleys, blowing into streams engorged from the recent storms. The trees were bare and seemingly barren. For many, it would be their last summer. When the earth had turned another year's rotation, there would be no visible traces of many thousands of them.

Around two and a half kilometers up in the sky, the Pineapple Express roared northward. The super-Niño in Peru had increased the evaporation of water at the equator, raising humidity levels, feeding the atmospheric river, which tapped into the water with a ruthless efficiency. This river in the skies, a band of moisture over 900 kilometers wide and 2000 kilometers long, was carrying more water than forty Mississippis. And it was racing through the skies toward the west coast of the United States at close to eighty kilometers per hour.

The storm system that traveled with it ate up the miles of sea that kept it from the shore. It almost seemed hungry to make landfall. It was accelerating; slowly, but determinedly, it was getting faster. Its circumference sucked up the warmth of the sea and just kept getting bigger. It wasn't huge, not like Hurricane Floyd, which was bigger than the entire state of Florida, or Ivan, which at its peak was bigger than Texas, but it was big enough. It registered on the satellites that monitored the world's weather. They could see it coming, but they had no idea how long it would last. A lashing of one day was very different to a biblical storm of forty days. The meteorologists were not shamans or seers. They could not say if the storm would make landfall at this stage. They could just say that a storm was heading their way: a big one.

And banked up behind the first storm system, separated by days, by a few thousand kilometers, there followed another storm, with its arsenal of winds and waves whipped up by a swirling low pressure. The sea raged and boiled, half fighting the winds that lashed it, half driving them on, until sea and wind merged in a mass of towering waves. They had done this before, here on this ocean, but not like this, at least not for a long, long time, before the record keepers began recording the power of the elements that surrounded them. It had been too long.

Since then, too many buildings had been built in ignorance; the architect-designed houses of wood that the wind, like the three wolves, would huff and puff and blow down, their beautiful plate glass windows gazing out at the ocean, mockingly, tauntingly, fatally inviting; all those grand houses on Seventeen Mile Drive, with their fine art; all the power and the glory that money could buy—all standing in storm tracks that had been long forgotten, long forsaken, until everything came together, possibly with this storm, possibly with the next one—the winds, the currents, the pressure differentials between the poles, the humidity in the skies, the myriad seemingly invisible factors that make up the weather—to create the perfect storm.

85

They sat round the gleaming table, coffees and waters to hand. Canning held his mug like he was warming his hands over it. He held it to his lips, but took no sips. He really shouldn't drink it. Not even one sip. His dyspepsia was getting worse. Like some kind of warning level, it had gone from code pink to code red. That meant zero coffee, so he just inhaled, wet his lips. Agents Del Russo and Peters flanked him, drinking their coffee with the carefree abandon of the untroubled, noted Canning with a scowl. Moira Zucker sipped a Diet Coke. Chris Furlong fiddled with a nicotine patch. Pauline Southward took neither coffee nor water. Ramrod straight, she sat with a small black box before her.

She turned to Canning.

"I have another Sheikh Ali intercept!" she announced, failing to keep down the excitement in her voice. "It's in English this time."

She hit a button. A disembodied voice filled the room, rich, smooth, languid.

> "What have they found, the Pattern of Life team?"
> "New person in her life. Perfect insurance policy."
> "Really? Who?"
> "Her new lover. Daniel Soren Jacobsen."
> "And who exactly is Mr. Jacobsen? Someone powerful from what you imply."
> "Power sex. Out in the open. Whole world could have seen. I saw."

"Really?

"At it the whole time. His place. Inside and out. All over."

"He sounds like the perfect insurance policy. You see, our clever doctor is turning out to be quite invaluable. I would like to keep her alive if at all possible."

"Yeah, well then what I would advise is that I work up an extraction plan for him."

"Meaning?"

"Work out how we would kidnap him. The how, the where, and the where we would take him. Just in case she decides to go to the cops. We'd get warning of her plans from the bugs. We could move in, get him, keep her sweet. No need to kill her. Not yet anyway."

The voices fell silent. Southward clicked off her machine.

Canning forgot his code red and rapidly drank his coffee, half of the cup in four quick gulps.

"So we have an unnamed party, acting on behalf of the Sheikh, surveilling someone, this 'clever doctor,' who knows something dangerous," he summed up. "And we have a kidnap plan. Against one Daniel Soren Jacobsen." He rubbed his hands over his bald head, mused.

"This is the first concrete proof that the Sheikh is more than the legit businessman he purports to be. Good job, Southward." He threw the analyst a brief smile. Involuntarily, she let her formal demeanor crack and flashed him a big smile back.

"Let's assume this is connected with the terror threat," continued Canning.

"OK, Chief," said Del Russo. "So we find out all we can on Daniel Soren Jacobsen, find out the identity of the clever doctor at the same time."

"Let's start with that," agreed Canning.

"What, just watch him?" asked Southward.

"We can't go in and protect him, warn him off," replied Del Russo. "There's too much at stake."

"What, we throw him to the wolves?" demanded Southward.

Zucker pursed her lips, her disapproval patently directed at what she regarded as Southward's undue squeamishness.

"Who is he anyway? Ol, go run his name," said Canning.

Five minutes later, Peters came back into the room.

"Er, sir, I think you need to make the request."

"Why? You too busy, Ol?" scowled Canning.

"I don't have that level of access. The guy's file is beyond Top Secret. He's Special Access Program."

"Shit, who is the guy?" murmured Canning. "Clear the room," he instructed. He logged on, got access, read the file, whistled quietly. He logged out, called the team back in.

"You need to hear this, but your ears only, or I will personally see to it that your balls are removed." He glowered at Furlong, Peters, and Del Russo, then turned to Southward and Zucker. "You too. Your balls are just as big as these guys'."

"Yes, sir," Southward nodded, concealing a smile.

Zucker, to Southward's astonishment, gave Canning a wink.

Canning spoke slowly, in his low guttural voice.

"Guy's a freakin' hero. Awarded the Medal of Honor! Silver Star. Purple Heart. Afghanistan. Three tours of duty." He fell silent. The rest he would not share. He looked out, beyond the gray skies of Virginia, saw instead the dusty valleys and craggy badlands thousands of miles away in the east. Where Daniel Jacobsen went in to the most extreme situations, targeting the most dangerous, most wanted individuals from the pack of cards. Kill or capture, it was called; sometimes it was both. One of the other side's best makers of IEDs came to an unfortunate end. And there was more. A lot more. Jacobsen had saved probably tens of dozens of lives in Afghanistan.

Canning dragged his gaze back to the room. "Let's just say, these guys go in to try and take him, they'll end up dead."

"Black Ops," mused Southward.

"Doesn't make him superman," said Peters. "He might be the one who winds up dead and we'll have just thrown one of our guys to the wolves," he said, unconsciously echoing Southward. "We could warn him," he added with a flash of defiance, locking eyes with Canning.

"Too much at stake," said Canning, revealing the political ruthlessness that ran through his veins. He was ex-army, had risen to four-star general. His loyalty was no longer to the tribe but to the anonymous cruelty of the big picture and the exigencies it demanded.

He leaned forward, gave Peters a hard-eyed scowl, shared it round the room.

"If we extract Jacobsen, any chance we had of getting close to these fuckers and preempting a West Coast Nine-eleven gets blown out the window, so we say nothing, we do nothing."

"Leave him to his fate," said Peters, jaw clenched.

Canning eyed his team. "His fate's in his own hands. I guess we're gonna find out just how good Daniel Jacobsen really is."

86

At mid-altitude, almond-shaped altocumulus lenticularis clouds drifted across the sky in the lee of the coastal ranges like a squadron of UFOs. They were white at the top shading down to gray at lower levels. Packed with small droplets of rain, the clouds looked solid and had on many occasions been mistaken for alien spacecraft. They were a rare sighting, often believed by the ancients to be a portent of some kind.

Far below in the Carmel Valley, dead leaves blew across the sandy scrub, skittering like rattlesnakes. Gwen Boudain, alone in Falcon's thirty-meter outside pool, did not hear them.

The weights dragged her down, as intended. Panic was near, always, but she sought the calm that had saved her life many times. She ran through the water, feet pushing off the tiled floor of the pool, fighting the weight, fighting the panic, pushing on. She couldn't see much, just the cool, cruel, blue. She ran on, farther and farther, back and forth, back and forth until she felt her lungs would burst, then on, and on again. Only when the flecks of black started speckling her vision did she reach for the rail, drag herself out. She lay on her stomach on the tiles, gasping like a landed fish.

"What in holy hell are you doing?" asked a voice.

Gwen flipped over. Gabriel Messenger stood, hands on hips, eyeing her with a look of mystification.

Gwen waited until she could speak. It took half a minute.

"Training," she replied, slipping out of her weight vest. "Trying to increase, or at least maintain my lung capacity."

"Is that what big wave surfers do?"

"Some of them. You have to be able to survive a two- or sometimes three-wave holdown, several minutes without breathing, getting the shit kicked out of you in what feels like a giant washing machine from hell. Doing this stuff could save my life."

Messenger nodded. "You ever come close?"

Gwen laughed. "More times than I care to remember." She muscled back into her weight vest. "Now, if you'll excuse me, I need to get back in there." She nodded to the pool.

"When you're done here, please come to my office," he intoned.

Gwen felt a flutter of fear.

"Why?"

"Why not?"

"Something specific?" asked Gwen. "You're looking kinda intense there."

Messenger laughed. "I am. We're ready to kick off the next stage of Project Zeus. I want you in on it."

Gwen nodded. She felt a roaring in her ears. The next stage . . . the calm before the storm was over.

"Winter waves'll be coming soon," said Messenger, softly, almost, thought Gwen, with a hint of menace. "Train hard, Gwen."

Gwen closed her eyes for a moment. A vision came, the vision from her dream, of huge, relentless monsters, banking up, crashing down, holding her down, keeping her down.

"Give me half an hour," she said. She breathed, long and slow and deep. She felt Messenger's eyes on her as she slipped back into the pool. As she ran along the bottom once more, she could see his outline, distorted by the dancing water, just standing on the side, watching her.

87

Forty minutes later, Gwen knocked on Messenger's door. She'd lingered longer than planned in the shower, warming up. Despite the exercise, she'd felt chilled when her pulse had slowed and her breathing had returned to normal.

"Come!" bellowed Messenger.

Gwen walked in, closed the door. Messenger was sitting at his desk, leaning back in his chair. He had the quizzical expression he often wore when looking at her. Gwen had a fleeting but unpleasant sensation that he could peer into her brain. She frowned at him. This made him smile.

"Take a seat, Gwen. And don't veil your feelings, will you?"

Gwen stopped frowning, sat down opposite him. "Stop scrutinizing me with that laser look then."

Messenger raised his hands in surrender.

"I've stopped. Look, I got you in here for several reasons. One was to discuss the next step with Project Zeus, but another was to say thank you for all your work on it. I tested the model last week, sent up the drones. You've got the yield up close to nine percent."

Gwen blinked. "Wow! It worked."

"And some," beamed Messenger. "Sheikh Ali and I would like to thank you."

"Just doing my job," replied Gwen.

Messenger slid an envelope across the desk. Gwen stared at it.

"Take it," said Messenger. "It's not booby-trapped!"

Gwen took it.

"Go on then," urged Messenger. "Open it up." He was smiling.

Gwen felt uneasy.

She tore open the envelope, pulled out a check.

"Holy hell!" she exclaimed, echoing Messenger's earlier words.

"One million dollars! That's insane!"

Messenger burst out laughing, but Gwen saw anger in his eyes.

"I swear you are a one-off! I just do not get you. Every other person in this office would be whooping with glee, but you . . . you look almost outraged!"

Gwen felt like she was being bought. She wanted to hand back the money, or at least demand why, really why, she had been given it. But her warning bells were clanging and she pushed down her defiance. *Act, you silly fool!*

"I'm overwhelmed, that's all," she stated. "You have to remember a few months ago I was flat broke. Now I am a millionaire many times over. It's a leap."

She forced a smile. "Sorry, I'm being ungracious." She leaned across the desk, offered Messenger her hand to shake. Messenger gripped it in his customary clench.

"Thank you," said Gwen. Messenger held on past the time of release. Gwen felt his scrutiny again. Finally he released her.

"My and the Sheikh's pleasure. Now go and put that in your pocketbook before you lose it, or before someone sees it, and would you please call in Peter and Kevin and come back in here?"

"Sure," murmured Gwen. Heart pounding, she stashed the check in her pocketbook. It nestled in the bottom, against the lining, touching the location transmitter.

Peter Weiss and Kevin Barclay sat at the round table. Gabriel Messenger paced. Gwen took a seat beside Barclay, gave him her bright, slightly mocking smile. His bruises had almost, but not quite faded. His wariness had not gone. He looked away, met Weiss's eye. Weiss frowned at Gwen, puzzled by the undercurrents.

"We are at the next stage of Project Zeus," announced Messenger, steepling his fingers, voice slow and low as he glanced between his three employees. "Thanks in part to your efforts, Gwen, we have got the rain yield of Zeus up to where we can make a significant economic difference to agricultural yields on farmland." He leaned forward, eyes gleaming. "Kevin and Peter have identified the best potential land areas to buy. I wanted to run them past you, Gwen, get any weather observations you might have."

Gwen just nodded. There was a visceral, tangible hunger in the room. She saw it in the three men's eyes.

Messenger pointed to a map he had pinned up on his cork board. In it were stuck ten red pins.

"To back up a bit, here's the initial thinking. In the initial stages, we wish to limit the risks. I told Kevin and Peter not to go for Africa—too unstable, huge corruption, poor transport infrastructure, political instability. Much better to go for Australia—serious water problem, huge marginal semi-arid areas, and Anglo-Saxon law, not to mention easy access to the enormous Asian markets." Messenger swept his hand across the map, shot a smile at Gwen.

"And right here on our doorstep in the US Midwest there are extensive areas of marginal farming territory which could be bought for a song, but which crucially have the transport infrastructure, as would Australia."

Barclay and Weiss were nodding enthusiastically.

"We are also planning to buy, build, and own storage, transportation, and port infrastructure, both at the exporting as well as the importing ends, as well as grain trading companies. The idea being, once we have the entire supply chain sewn up we can make a fortune."

Messenger sat back, folded his arms across his stomach, beaming at his own brilliance. Weiss and Barclay gazed up at their boss like the acolytes they so clearly were.

Gwen nodded, said nothing for a moment, finally found her voice.

"Wow. You've got it all planned out."

"That's why we're here. That's what we do," replied Messenger, looking hard at Gwen, as if seeking out any hint of sarcasm in her words.

It was like a military campaign, thought Gwen, or a kind of modern-day colonialization by capitalism.

88

Half an hour later, her input given for the sake of her cover, Gwen walked from the office, out into the gray November afternoon toward the Cupcake. It was empty, save Narissa and Luke.

"Late lunch. Gimme anything, please," said Gwen. She ran her hands over her face. Low blood sugar and a feeling that she could not go on like this gave her the slightest of trembles.

She sat, wondering how much all the farmers who would so gratefully sell their land to Gabriel Messenger would be shortchanged. Zeus would change the economics of their land totally. Zeus could have kept the land in the hands of the family who had owned it for generations. But Zeus was a private tool for making money, not an instrument of public good. The metrics of moneymaking. The metrics of morality had no room there. Gwen felt sick.

Her cell phone rang. Joaquin.

"Hey, flaco. What's up?" she asked, injecting some lightness into her voice.

"Hell has come to Punta Sal!" declared Joaquin theatrically. "Seriously, it's like an inferno and we're getting rain like it's the end of the world. All over Peru. Five villages in Huaraz have been swept away by landslides, over four thousand people killed, just washed away in an ocean of mud. There've been three fatal shark attacks in the last ten days. No food. Water's too hot. The upwelling's dead and the nutrients are all stuck deep in the thermocline. The food chain's going to hell and the sharks are going after humans, anything. Two kids, just down the coast, then a surfer a day later," he announced, voice sorrow-tinged.

"Shit," murmured Gwen.

"Yeah, shit covers it."

"It's a mega-Niño, Joaquin," Gwen said softly. "We always knew it would be ugly. They always have blood on their hands," she added.

"There's numerous outbreaks of typhoid and cholera," continued Joaquin, "caused by all the flooding, the stagnant waters."

"All we can do is what we're doing," Gwen replied with lame comfort. "Report and warn."

Only that was the hell of it, thought Gwen. She wasn't allowed to report and warn. Her information was too valuable. Everyone knew now it was a mega-Niño, but not two months ago. Back then, flood defenses could have been prepared, sandbags ordered, terracing fences dug into mountainsides above villages. But none of that had been done because Gabriel Messenger wanted to make money. And because she was on a mission to prove him guilty of murder. And because she was employed by him? Because she had taken the thirty pieces of silver? To the tune of first, ten million dollars. Now another million sat burning a hole in her pocket book. . . . How much blood is on your own hands, Gwen? she asked herself.

89

The setting sun filtered through a dome of high cirrocumulus clouds, the rippled clouds known as "mackerel sky." It gilded them red gold. Gwen and Dan stood on the back lawn near the cliff edge sharing a bottle of beer and admiring the display. They stood hip to hip, finding reason to touch, as they so often did. Dan wasn't saying much. Gwen could sense his preoccupation, felt it cloud her own mood. Dressed in jeans and a short-sleeved t-shirt, she gave a sudden shiver as a gust of wind pulsed over them.

Dan put his arm round her, pulled her closer, gave her his heat.

Gwen molded to him. He had the quality that no other man but her father had had: the gift of making her feel safe. When he held her, she could feel in that moment that all was right in her world, never mind whatever was going on outside the circle of their arms. She knew it was transitory, partially illusory, didn't care.

"Storm's coming," she said, gazing up at the clouds.

Dan frowned. "How can you tell? It looks so peaceful up there. Those clouds are downright beautiful."

Gwen looked into his eyes, smiled. "Beautiful things can be lethal too."

"Oh, I know it," he answered with a smile of his own. "But you haven't answered my question."

"Well, firstly, the large area of high cloud tells me there's a lot of moisture up there at the top of the troposphere," said Gwen, swinging from play to serious, enthusing about her passion.

"In temperate regions like here, this can be an advance

warning of a depression coming in, bringing rain. And those ripples we see? Up high they're real big choppy clouds, like big waves on a rough sea. That means the winds up there are strong."

"I'm impressed, Doctor Boudain. Let's go in and light the fire."

"Is that code?"

Dan laughed, the tension he had carried breaking. He gave her his crooked smile.

"Both."

Inside, they lay together on the sofa, staring into the fire that jiggered and played in the stone fireplace. Neither spoke. After a while, Dan got up, opened a bottle of Carmel Road Chualar Pinot Noir, poured out two generous glasses, drank a good sip, and handed one to Gwen. He lifted her legs, sat on the sofa, drawing her legs back over his lap. Gwen noticed his tension had returned, furrowing two vertical lines between his eyes.

"I'm being surveilled," Dan said slowly. "Four different guys over the past week. It's a Pattern of Life study. The full works."

"Shit!" replied Gwen, spluttering into her wineglass. She knew better than to ask if he was sure. His eyes said he was. They were oddly dispassionate.

"The question is, why would anyone want to surveil me?" Dan continued, his voice thoughtful, empty of the outrage Gwen would have felt.

"Messenger's bad guys?" she suggested.

"Yeah, but here's the weird thing. They're not surveil-ling you."

"And you know this because?"

Dan gave a grim smile. "Because I returned the favor, slipped them without appearing to try to do so, surveilled them. They didn't follow you. I checked several times. No one's on your tail, unless you're with me."

"Wonderful," declared Gwen, taking a big swig, swallowing with a gulp. "So what do we do about it?"

"We appear to do nothing."

"You think they've bugged you here?"

Dan shook his head. "Not in the house. I've checked. It's too well protected for them to get in anyway. But my car's bugged. The driving mirror has a little fucker stuck behind it."

"Nice. You leave it there?"

"Of course, so we have to watch what we say in there. Listen, Boudy, do something for me, please try to stay away from situations where you find yourself isolated, or alone. I have a real bad feeling about this. I'll be with you a good chunk of time, but I can't protect you twenty-four/seven and I know you wouldn't want me to."

Gwen sipped her wine. She kept the glass pressed to her lips, gazed over the rim at Dan.

"We can't go on like this, just you and me, a two-man investigation team."

Dan said nothing, just swirled his wine in the bell glass, gazed thoughtfully into the viscous red.

"Let's just give it a bit more time," he said, looking across at Gwen. "We get the FBI in, we scare the bad guys off and we'll never get the bastards. I get the feeling things are accelerating. Some kind of move is gonna be made. Let's just keep our nerve."

"I guess we can give it a bit more time," said Gwen thoughtfully. "It's beginning to get a bit out-there on the mad-and-scary spectrum tho."

Dan nodded. "We need to keep alert, keep our radar on, keep to crowded places."

Gwen thought of the faceless men, perhaps watching Dan's house even now, beyond the curtained windows, out there in the darkness.

90

In the early hours of the next morning, the first big storm of the season roared in and hit California. Gwen and Dan lay in their usual tangle of limbs, warm, languid, fast asleep. And then the night seemed to deliver a punch to the house. Gwen sat up. Dan woke with her. Outside, the wind roared. Dan jumped from their bed and closed the window they both always loved to have open.

"Wild out there," he said, climbing back into bed. "You were right, Guru." He took Gwen in his arms, held her. The punch came again. Gwen felt it in her lungs, like an explosion.

"Gotta be gusting near a hundred Ks per hour," murmured Gwen, sleepy, waking up fast. "Your house built strongly?" she asked.

"We'll see, won't we? One thing I did do last weekend was cut down the overhanging trees."

"Good plan. Don't fancy being squashed in my bed by an oak."

Still, the wind roared. As the hours passed, the pitch rose to a scream. Gwen lay awake, surprised by the ferocity of the storm. She listened in a kind of rapt thrill and fear, as if by staying awake she could somehow keep the worst of the storm at bay. Then the rain started, a hissing sluicing sound, relentless, torrential, too extreme to be comforting in any way.

It slammed into the roof, pouring in torrents from the gutters, waterlogging the grass. This was not the gentle rain of a fantasy, enjoyed from the safety of a warm dry bed. It felt to Gwen like rain with *intent*.

91

It rained throughout the weekend. On Monday morning it was still raining. The sky was slate gray, seemingly liquid. Gwen sat at her desk sipping from a mug of coffee, warming her hands around it, reading the *San Francisco Reporter,* drying off. The dash from car to entrance had soaked her in five seconds.

She found Dan's byline, read with a smile.

THE SAN FRANCISCO REPORTER
A Warm-up Act?
BY DAN JACOBSEN

The storm that has visited death and destruction upon California from Friday night through the weekend and at time of press is raging still is the first storm of the winter resulting from the atmospheric rivers that course through the sky like giant fire hoses. The National Oceanic and Atmospheric Administration, NOAA, issued a statement late yesterday saying that a landfalling AR caused the disastrous high winds and rains that have led to the deaths of 14 people. Two people were killed when a tree fell onto their car in Salinas, three more when two cars collided in treacherous road conditions in San Simeon and a total of nine more lost their lives when a landslide washed away five homes at the foot of the Coastal Ranges near San Miguel. The questions ordinary citizens, and the panel of experts at NOAA are asking themselves is: *Is this a warm-up act for the much feared Shake Out ARk*

Storm? Might it even be the beginning of the ARk Storm 1000 itself?

What is it about atmospheric rivers that makes the storms they can create so dangerous?

Most of the water vapor transported within the ARs (75%) takes place within the lowest 2.5 kilometers of the atmosphere, well below the highest altitudes of the Sierra Nevada. The combination of strong horizontal winds, large water vapor content, and what the scientists call lower-tropospheric-moist-neutrality all combine to create "ripe conditions" for heavy orographic rainfall. To the layman, that means heavy rainfall on the coastal side of the Sierra Nevada.

This occurs as a result of the Sierra Nevada mountain range and the Coastal Ranges forcing moisture-carrying air upward. Daytime heating of the mountain barrier surface forces the air farther upward. As the air rises it expands and cools. This cooling of a rising moist air parcel may lower its temperature to its dew point, causing the water vapor within it to condense and form a cloud. If enough water vapor condenses into cloud droplets, these droplets may become large enough to fall to the ground as rain.

The rain then slams down the mountains, causing landslides and flooding in the plains below.

ARs are laden with water vapor, some of them carrying as much water vapor as does the Amazon in liquid form. With the right preconditions, just one intense atmospheric river hitting the Sierra Nevada mountain range east of Sacramento could bring devastation to California. Expanding urban centers lie in floodplains where flooding could result in extensive loss of life and hundreds of billions of dollars in damages.

With what threatens to be a mega-Niño kicking off across the Pacific, meteorologists predict we are in for a season of wild weather. Niños typically bring a wetter-than-average winter season to California. The NOAA's official advice is to stay tuned in to your local radio stations for weather alerts. They declined to comment when asked if they thought yesterday's storm was "a warm-up act."

"The storm we've just had occurs perhaps once a decade," spokesperson Abby McVeil stated. But that may be premature given that it's still raining.

"It's like Texas Hold 'Em after the first four cards," joked a research scientist who wished to remain anonymous. "We're still waiting for the final cards to be dealt."

92

Fair summary, thought Gwen, though she reckoned the cards for this storm had been dealt, and it wasn't the big one. She folded the paper and placed it thoughtfully on her desk as Mandy teetered in on her four-inch heels.

Messenger's PA swiveled her pencil-skirt-encased ass and perched on Gwen's desk. Gwen had a fleeting desire to raise one booted leg and push her off.

"I just read that too!" exclaimed Mandy, nodding at the article.

"Whaddya reckon?" she asked, leaning across the desk conspiratorially. "It looks like it's gonna keep raining forever. This the big one?"

Gwen looked over Mandy's shoulder as Gabriel Messenger appeared. He paused in the doorway, tucked his hands into his trouser pockets, and raised a questioning eyebrow.

"Rain'll stop soon," announced Gwen. "This isn't the big one. Call it a warm-up act if you like," she added, eyes on Messenger as she spoke, almost by rote, knowing what he wanted to hear, giving it to him in the easy sound bites that allowed her to think other thoughts, to scrutinize him, to wonder why he was having Dan surveilled. If it was him who was responsible. She and Dan were still infuriatingly short of evidence.

"Why?" asked Messenger, taking a step closer. Mandy got up from the desk and moved to the side of the office, her scowl showing she was all too aware she was just a sideshow now. "What makes you so sure?" Messenger continued.

"Just wait. And watch," added Gwen with a gnomic smile.

"For how long?" asked Messenger, glancing at his watch.

Gwen got up, walked to her window, peered out, studying the clouds.

"It'll stop raining in an hour. Two max. That do you?"

Messenger barked out a laugh.

"Thousand dollars on it stopping by ten a.m.?"

Gwen turned to him, amused. "You and your metrics . . ." But she shook his outstretched hand.

"Done," she said.

"Accepted!" declared Messenger. "So, now tell me why I'm going to lose."

"OK. Those thick, gray nimbostratus that have set in over the past two days are breaking up," said Gwen, pointing at the sky.

Messenger moved up to her, stood alongside her, peering out. Gwen could smell his citrus cologne, could feel his body heat. Mandy had come up on her other side, stopping her from inching away.

"The sky is lighter," continued Gwen. "A pale gray. Not a slate gray. That's 'cause the darker gray stratus fractus clouds, which often sit below the nimbostratus, they're the result of falling rain, well they've blown away overnight. That tells the story you can see with your own eyes. The rain's lessening." Gwen took a breath, continued at a sharp clip. "The nimbostratus have dropped most of their load. They're almost, but not quite, purged by the storm. They're still moving at a good nick, so they'll be over the mountains and out of our way soon." Gwen gestured like a weather girl.

"Blue skies are coming." She turned to Messenger, gave him a wry smile. "Meteorologically speaking."

One hour and five minutes later, followed by Mandy, Gabriel Messenger appeared at Gwen's office fighting a smile. He stood by Gwen's window, staring out at the brightening sky. From which no rain fell on Carmel Valley.

"Well done, Miss Oracle," Messenger announced, turning to Gwen, lips twitching. He reached into his pocket, removed a wad of notes. He counted out ten hundreds. Gwen watched Mandy's eyes, narrow with avarice, as Messenger handed them over to her.

Gwen took the money. It was still warm, alive almost.

93

Pauline Southward sat in the library room of the NSA. She read and reread the article, feeling a mixture of excitement and anger. She grabbed up the paper, ignoring the PROPERTY OF NSA stamped on it. She rolled it into a baton and squeezed it into her handbag, then she hurried down the stairs to the underground car park.

She called ahead on her cell as she drove from Fort Meade in her black Porsche 911. Ten years old and it still drove like a dream. It was her indulgence, her reward, her greatest love, she thought with a wry smile. It made all her brutal economies more than worthwhile. It made the commute from Fort Meade to Tyson's Corner a pleasure. She knew where the speed cameras were and where they weren't. She drove like a pro, accelerating into open space, feeling the car surge forward, hugging the road, cornering like it was Velcroed to the tarmac. She wove through the traffic, slowed just before she came into the camera's range.

She got Chief Canning's PA, Cooper. "Coop, I got something for the Chief and the Project Oscar team. I'll be with you in twenty."

She walked into Canning's corner office twenty minutes later, exactly. They were all waiting for her, save Chris Furlong: Canning standing staring out of his window; Zucker sitting, hands folded primly in her red-trousered lap; Del Russo and Peters standing like sentries, gripping the backs of hastily pulled-up chairs, one to either side of Zucker. To Del Russo's left, a chair stood empty.

"Chief Canning," said Southward, addressing Canning's back.

He turned. "Ms. Southward. Please, take a seat."

Southward stayed standing. She threw down the copy of the *San Francisco Reporter* on the polished desk. Her normally pale face was flushed. She glared at Del Russo and Peters.

"Did none of you do the most basic check, the A part of the A to Z?" she asked. "Or were you all searching around the sexy end of the alphabet?"

Canning stared from the newspaper to Southward, then at the vacant seat. Southward sat. Del Russo and Peters stared at her. As if by common consent, they angled their chairs and sat, each facing Southward.

"All you needed to do was Google the guy!" Southward declared.

"ARk Storm!" she said, pointing at the newspaper. "He's writing about an ARk Storm, a calamitous winter storm that sooner or later is predicted to hit the US West Coast, causing biblical flooding. Read the article!" She jumped up, reached forward, picked up the newspaper, still rolled, brandished it like a weapon. "Today's *San Fran Reporter*. It's the second article he's written on ARk Storm. It's the link we've been looking for. The method. The delivery system, if you like."

Canning held up his hand. "Whoa, with the greatest respect, Ms. Southward, are you trying to tell us that somehow Sheikh Ali is plotting to produce an ARk Storm, that he can control the weather?"

Collegial male laughter bumped round the room. Zucker was frowning and regarding Southward speculatively.

"That's exactly what I'm telling you," insisted Southward.

"Jihad by weather," drawled Del Russo, leaning back in his chair, stretching out his long legs, inadvertently kicking Southward's ankle. She kicked back, with a stilettoed heel.

"I don't think so, Ms. Southward," cautioned Canning. "Be careful," he added. "Seems to me like you've got target fixation. Losing clarity. I know you want to get Sheikh Ali, have from the get-go, but pinning the absurd on him ain't gonna work."

Southward jumped to her feet. "Absurd is it? You're all so pleased with yourselves, you can't see what's in front of your own noses. Sheikh Ali is planning jihad on the West Coast of the USA. Sheikh Ali sets up a 'contingency kidnap' of one Daniel Jacobsen, who just happens to be writing about a devastating event possibly hitting the West Coast, incidentally justifying the short sales and the put options on California real estate casualty insurance companies." She shot a look at Zucker, who was watching her with a kind of hyper-alert fascination. "And you guys cannot connect the dots . . ." she added with quiet finality.

Zucker said nothing. She had never heard anyone talk to Canning in this immoderate, overly emotional way.

"Coincidence," said Peters. "It does happen and it's not always sinister or relevant when it does." He spoke gently, as if trying to calm Southward.

Southward took the time to glower at each of the four occupants of the room.

"Go fiddle then!" She spun round and stalked from the room.

Canning watched Southward half amused, half annoyed. He winced as a shot of acid stabbed his guts. It was a long time since anyone had spoken to him like that. Maybe too long . . . everyone was so keen to tell him what they thought he wanted to hear.

He pursed his lips, wondering. . . . The woman was passionate, brilliant, thought outside the box . . . as did the

Jihadis themselves. His stomach gave another squirm of disquiet. He leaned back in his chair, ran his hands over his bald pate, asked himself, just for intellectual completeness, *What if you could control the weather? Or worse, what if the wrong person could control the weather?*

94

THE SECURITIES AND EXCHANGE COMMISSION
REGIONAL OFFICE, NEW YORK CITY,
TUESDAY MORNING

Manhattan had received its first somewhat unseasonably early snow that morning, a good two inches that freshened the city, at least for the few hours before it turned to slush, filling the air with its clean, crystalline smell. Rac Rodgers' nose glowed red in tribute. He had taken to getting off a few subway stops early, speed marching the last twenty minutes of his commute, come rain, shine, or snow, in a desperate attempt to regain some of the fitness he had lost since his daughter had been born. Watching Ange Wilkie flex her muscles all day long, going out for lunchtime workouts or runs, got dispiriting. He wanted to level the scores, just a little. And his belt was already one notch tighter.

Ange, in deference to the snow, wore slim-legged black trousers, some kind of tough-girl combat boots with ridged soles, and what looked like a cashmere turtleneck in triumphal red. Bergers, by contrast, made no concession to the weather. He wore his white shirt with sleeves rolled up as always, as if ever ready for a fistfight. A downy parka did hang from his door hook, draped with a scarf that looked like it had been knitted by one of his children, but

Rac imagined he wore it only because his wife insisted. The man seemed impervious to the elements.

Ange sat in the very self-contained way that Rac knew by now presaged news, big news. She had her excitement under lockdown. She glanced at him and Bergers, who was just finishing off an e-mail.

"I just love CTC," she announced. "I get to listen to Ronnie and his shit all day long."

Rac eyed her, wondering if she was being sarcastic, realized she wasn't. She was on the hunt and she *did* love it.

"Something came in yesterday," Wilkie added. "And about friggin' time. Two weeks since the FISA warrant came out and Ronnie's been the proverbial clean whistle."

Rac raised his eyebrows. "Nothing clean about his whistle. He's been blowing it round at least two women besides his wife," he declared indignantly.

"Yeah, well much as I might like to, I can't arrest a guy for that. Cells would overflow," observed Wilkie wryly. "You finished moralizing? Wanna hear my stuff?"

"Always," replied Rac, sitting back, stretching out his legs.

Bergers glanced up, watched the exchange with an indulgent eye before returning to his e-mail.

"I picked it out from all the daily crap when I was on the treadmill this morning," declared Wilkie. She glanced at Bergers, fiddled with her nails.

Bergers pressed SEND, glanced up, shot her a big smile. "Hit me!"

Wilkie hit PLAY on her iPod. She'd attached it to a speaker. Two voices issued forth, ebbed and flowed: blue-collar California female; white-shoe East Coast male — Ronnie Glass.

"Shit, R, it's been raining super-size cats 'n' dogs out here. There was an article 'bout it today, saying 'is

it the big one?' And in here they think it is coming,
the big one. ARk Storm 1000. Our nice lady doctor
says this storm that just hit was like a warm-up act.
Her words to the big doctor, a 'warm-up act,' for the
big one."

"*I got the puts already. Could buy some more, I guess.*"
"*How much?*"
"*Don't stress. I'll cut you in. Fifteen percent of profits,*
as always."
"*Oh I know you will, R. I know you're straight.*"

The sound of high-pitched laughter made them wince.

"*Well, straight as a crooked sonofabitch can be.*"
"*Thanks,* Auntie. *That's cute. Gotta go.*"

Wilkie switched off her iPod, gazed across the desk at
Bergers and Rac. The silence seemed to echo as Bergers
stared into space.

"Holy Hell," he murmured, eyes coming back to them.
"So they *are* betting on an ARk Storm."

Neither Wilkie nor Rodgers said anything, just exchanged a glance.

"Yeah, yeah, you guys were right," declared Bergers.
"And I told you to lay off the drugs. I remember. No need
to do these cute little long-suffering looks." He spoke with
affection. This was why the man was loved by his people.
He was big enough to see when he'd been wrong, and
gracious enough to say so.

"So will you ring Andrew Canning now?" asked
Wilkie.

"Oh, he'll know about it. But I'll ring him anyway. He
can throw resources at this *aunt,* whoever she is, and
these two doctors, find out who the hell they are and why
they think they have a hotline to God. Don't suppose we
can trace her phone?"

"Pay as you go. Disposable. Can't trace her through her cell phone," replied Wilkie.

"Good job, you guys. Clear off and find this article about 'the big one' and let me call Canning."

95

Andrew Canning glanced round at his team: Southward, Del Russo, Peters, Zucker, and Furlong, who had just hurried in nursing a swollen cheek courtesy of a root canal. Canning did not smile, scarcely bestowed recognition. His eyes were devoid of expression. He rose to his feet and began to circumnavigate the meeting room. All those sitting at the conference table had to turn and watch his progress, or else sit with their backs to him as he passed, an uncomfortable sensation that made their skin tingle or their nape hair bristle.

Canning paused at the head of the table. He leaned over it, fists braced on the polished wood. Again he cast his eyes over his team, measuring.

"So, people, let's sum up where we are, shall we?" he asked in the smoothly rhetorical voice his subjects all knew spelled danger.

"We have prior knowledge, have had prior knowledge for close on six weeks now, that Sheikh Ali Al Baharna is planning a terrorist atrocity. We have spent several thousand man hours attempting to identify his plan. And have we identified it yet? Have we a tame airfield, planes at the ready, bomb loads, pilots with recently shaven beards training for their licenses in Miami?" He paused, allowed his words to settle.

"No," he answered himself softly. "We have none of that."

He began to circumnavigate the table again, talking as he went.

"Is that A) because you are all incompetent and have failed to find these leads, or is it B) that you have been looking in the wrong place all along?" He paused behind Pauline Southward, making her swivel in her chair to look up at him, neck cricking.

"Apologies to you, Ms. Southward. You would seem to have been a lone voice in the wilderness, possibly looking in the right place all this time. Even though, of course, that was not your principal, nor original job."

Southward tried and almost succeeded in keeping her face expressionless.

Canning scanned the other faces again, lingering long enough on each for them to feel the full weight of his judgment. He moved on.

"How predictable. You think because they flew planes once into the Twin Towers that's the model going forward? God help us when the Jihadis are more creative than us. That's when we lose this war."

He walked to the head of the table, resumed his seat. His face lost its masklike quality, softened just a fraction.

"So let's join the dots. We've got, at the bottom of the food chain, one woman, this *aunt,* still un-ID'd, in California, tipping off Ronnie Glass that an ARk Storm is increasingly likely, she and these doctors believe. We have the two doctors. . . . We have a number of still un-ID'd nominees." He flicked a glance at Zucker, who had lost her customary cocky air and sat shifting uncomfortably in her seat. "God Damn the bankers and the lawyers they rode in on," continued Canning, "taking out huge bets against California casualty insurance companies. Then, at the top of the food chain, sits Sheikh Ali Al Baharna, planning an atrocity. So let's start with the insane premise that you *could* make an ARk Storm . . ." Canning paused, let his words settle. "How would you start?" he asked softly.

Canning's four CTC agents glanced around at each other, the politics of ridicule no longer open to them, the possibility of catastrophic error looming.

Southward sat motionless, apparently calm, but Del Russo, sitting next to her, could almost feel the tension vibrating through her body. Vindication?

"So let's think the unthinkable, people," mused Canning, steepling his fingers as if in prayer. "We've come up with zero on any other front. Let's just say, Ali Al Baharna *is* planning an ARk Storm."

"This is insane, sir," said Chris Furlong, his words bursting out, thickly sibilant due to his swollen cheek. "He is not God! He cannot *make* the weather. We go down this line we miss the crucial clue to what he really is planning."

Canning scowled at him. "I'm well aware that it's insane. That's what people would have said on Nine-ten about flying planes into the Twin Towers. So we have two task forces here: one looks at the ARk Storm scenario, as in how do you make an ARk Storm. That task force is headed up by you, Furlong, so you'd better buy into the idea and fast. Two, headed by you, Ms. Zucker, looks at everything else."

Zucker nodded, chewed off a corner of one red-painted nail, mind already scrolling through a plan.

"Timing is in critical phase," declared Canning. "Remind us of the sensitivities please, Ms. Southward."

"The Festival of Ashura falls on November twenty-fourth; that's in two weeks. Milud un Nabi is January twenty-ninth. The intercept suggested the attack would go down any time from the twenty-fourth of November."

Canning got to his feet. "Two weeks and counting. Ms. Zucker, I want you to turn up the heat on all those nominee companies. Do what you need to break through the walls . . . you got me?"

Zucker looked thrilled. "Oh yeah! I gotcha."

Southward watched Zucker, exchanged a complicit smile with her; zealot to zealot.

"I think it's time one of you went to California," continued Canning, "paid the legendary Dan Jacobsen a visit. Del Russo, you go. You're an ex-Marine. One of his kind, or near enough."

96

SINGAPORE, WEDNESDAY 6:00 A.M.
SINGAPORE TIME

Marcel Caravaggio was starving, one of his least favorite sensations. Instead of waking to the gentle ministrations of Jeannette, his mistress, with whom he had contrived an overnighter, he woke to the shrilling of his cell phone. It was Xu Ling, one of his mules, as he thought of them, the private bankers who helped orchestrate his cascade of nominee companies and trades.

"We need to talk," Xu Ling had said. "Right now."

And so Marcel found himself seemingly going for an early morning walk around the Botanic Gardens, skirting the silent, almost-ghostly figures practicing their tai chi—five separate groups; God, it was like a contagion—while he listened to Xu Ling, who strode out beside him, skinny legs encased in green lycra.

Xu Ling played with his beard, glanced up nervously at Marcel.

"Yesterday someone got in our system. I'm not hundred percent. More a feeling. I did some stuff, saved my work, switched it back on later, and it was up. It was live. I'm sure I shut it down, man." He shot another nervous glance at Marcel.

"What exactly are you saying?" demanded Marcel, coming to a dead stop, rubbing his bleary eyes, blinking at Xu Ling.

"I have feeling, no firm evidence, but strong feeling someone they hack in my system."

"Which bit of it?" asked Marcel. He felt sick.

"The trading records. All the US trades we done, the special trades . . ." Marcel's head began to swim. Worst case. If someone were looking, then they had burst through all his layers of nominees, right down to the source. It would only be a matter of time before someone came knocking at Xu Ling's door, and then at his. Best case, Xu Ling's system was leaky.

"Get a security expert in. Build up your firewalls. Now. Anyone comes knocking, you say nothing!" He gripped Xu Ling's arm, his long fingernails cutting into the flesh.

Xu Ling shook off his grip.

"The cops, if they come calling," wailed Xu Ling, "If they knock on my door, I gonna tell them 'fuck off,' but if they looking, man? If they looking, they not gonna go away. Sooner or later they'll peel back the skin, get the onion. What shit you got going on, man? What you brought to my door?"

"Hold your nerve," hissed Marcel. "This is Singapore. You do not have to disclose anything. Anyone comes knocking, you just keep telling the guy to 'fuck off,' and smile when you say it, like it's no big deal. Don't use the cell phone for any kind of related conversation. We go into lockdown mode now. You need to see me, you invite me for a walk."

"No more of this. I'm done now," said Xu Ling heatedly.

Marcel gave a soft laugh. "Too late for that. You're too far in! You asked me what I'd brought to your door . . . it's more a question of who," he said softly. "You really, really do not want to upset this man. If you do, you and I and whoever you love will be dead. And it won't be a good death. It would be the death of your worst nightmares."

97

SEVENTEEN MILE DRIVE, TUESDAY EVENING

Dan sat Gwen down at his kitchen table. He'd led her there, his hand warm on hers. With grave eyes, he'd asked her to sit. The pine was rough under her fingers. Outside the sun had set and darkness was coming on fast. Clouds massed, black and purpled like the legacy of violence. The wind lashed the windows. Another storm was coming. Gwen sipped on a beer. She wore jeans and one of Dan's cashmere jerseys. Leo lay in the sitting room, basking in front of the fire smouldering in the hearth. Gwen remembered all the details later. Everything, however minor, seemed etched.

"Had a shit day today," Dan said slowly, ignoring his own beer. "There's stuff I need to tell you."

Gwen tensed. There was always stuff hidden, she knew that, had come to accept it, not to ask questions, though it almost killed her curious nature. Black Ops and something else hovered in the air. Gwen lifted her chin, faced him.

Dan met her gaze. His eyes were cold.

"So tell me," Gwen said, her voice quick. No surfer drawl.

"First, you need to know something I have never said to you. You need to know that I love you. That I am in love with you. I didn't want to be. I don't want to be. But I am."

Gwen felt as if she didn't dare take a breath. His words

did not fill her with the euphoria she would have imagined in another context. They filled her with dread.

"But I have also used you, or to be more precise, I set out to use you. When push came to shove, I didn't actually use you. Couldn't do it. So my editor fired me today."

Gwen pushed up out of her chair. She could not stay still, could not sit, felt the need to run, not to hear more. She walked to the window, looked out in the last of the dying light, at the gray sea churning. It was never still here, the Restless Sea, but for the last week it had been not restless, but tormented. She gave a bitter smile, turned back to Dan.

"Get it over with, Dan. Tell me quickly."

"I'm a specialist in a few things, back from my time in the Marines. As you will have gleaned, electronic surveillance is one of them. My editor knew a bit about my background, hired me straight from my diploma. He wants a shortcut to stories. Hardly unique in the newspaper world. I was his tool. He wanted dirt on two things: Falcon and the ARk Storm story. So I bugged Falcon. I heard all your first pitch. Next I bugged Riley's office. Then I started to follow you, staged the first meeting in the sea, staged the meeting at Riley's."

Gwen felt her mouth fall open. She clenched it shut. She stared at Dan as he spoke, a cascade of emotions pummeling her: betrayal, fury, humiliation, disbelief.

"I pulled the devices from Riley's the same day. I'd pulled the bugs from Falcon as soon as you went to work there. My editor kept pushing me for stories, for the real, back stories." He gave a bitter laugh. "He knew something was up, the man has a nose for a story like a fuckin' bloodhound. The real story would have blown him away, got me a Pulitzer," he added ruefully. "But after that day I spent with you at Hurricane Point, surfing, eating, and talking, I was never intending to tell that story. Or any other story involving you."

Gwen listened, nodded. She was clinging to calm now, summoning it from the deep, channeling it over the roaring of blood in her brain.

"Why now? Why are you telling me now?"

She saw Dan give an infinitesimal flinch. Her voice was ice.

"Because we had a showdown. I refused to give him any stories. He fired me, told me he was going to ring you."

"Ah, I see. So you thought you'd get your pitch in first."

Dan glanced away, then back at Gwen. "You could put it like that. Sounds cold though."

Gwen laughed, a bitter, curdling sound. "Cold it is." She walked to the door. She did not allow herself to turn back to him. "Good-bye Dan."

She called out to Leo. The dog was at her side in seconds, drawn by her voice.

Gwen grabbed her keys from the sideboard, walked out. One foot before the other. *Keep walking* said her mind. Keep it together.

Her surfboard was still in his car. She opened the door, pulled it out. Dan appeared from the house, silhouetted against the light.

"Gwen. Please don't go. For any number of reasons, please don't go. You're not safe out there on your own."

"I'm not safe here with you, either. And don't worry about me. I'm going to go to the cops. I'm gonna tell them everything. It's over Dan. It's all over."

Leaving Dan's car door open, Gwen took her board, carried it to her car, slid it in. Leo jumped into the passenger seat. Gwen started up, drove off. She saw Dan standing on his drive, looking after her.

In their high emotion, each of them had forgotten the bug in his car.

98

The yacht *Zephyr* rode the rising waves. Sheikh Ali paced his stateroom. A wind had kicked up in the last two hours and *Zephyr* was rocking softly, well able to deal with the waves, but registering their presence. Outside, the wind had built to a roar. Even through the reinforced glass, Sheikh Ali could hear it as he paced. His starched kandoora snapped against his legs.

He turned to the man before him. The man who had adopted the name *Hassan*, even if able to use it only highly selectively.

The Sheikh veiled his distaste. Hassan was a tool. You didn't have to like your tools, just know that they did their job efficiently and effectively. Hassan did both. He would be off the yacht soon enough, up in the helicopter, homeward bound.

"Update me. Please," he added, a sop to Hassan's ego. These Westerners with their sensibilities, their innocent inability to grasp the realpolitik of power . . . they could be tiresome. Decades of living in a feudal theocracy had schooled him well in the subtleties of power. Those reared in a democracy thought they had recourse to a larger power. A larger power that was not even God. But he knew that power came with a family name or with money or with a weapon or with the name of God as worshiped by the right sect, he thought bitterly.

"The drones are all ready," replied Hassan with a quick smile. "I ordered twenty extras too, so we're all set up."

"Good," the Sheikh smiled back. "I do like the drones. They are almost poetical to me."

Hassan ignored this comment. He never knew what to do with the Sheikh's odd bursts of whimsy. He stuck to the details.

"I've got two takeoff strips ready so we can get as many drones airborne as quickly as possible."

"Good thinking."

"And I reckon the model's all ready too. As good as it's ever going to get."

The Sheikh sat down, took a sip of his cardamom-flavored coffee.

"All we need now is the right storm," he murmured, glancing out of the windows.

Hassan followed his glance. "A good one's powering toward us right now." He stuck out his arms, allowed the yacht to pitch him gently from side to side. He dropped his arms to his sides, took out his iPad, scrolled through until he came to the National Weather Service site.

"They've issued a warning, the NWS. Not a high alert, but a storm warning nonetheless. The ARk Storm people are quiet. Nothing from USGS or FEMA or CalEMA."

The Sheikh held up his hand, scowling.

"Who the hell are that lot? I know USGS, but FEMA and CalEMA?"

"Federal Emergency Management Agency and California Emergency Management Agency. If they thought an ARk Storm was on its way, they'd be bleating to all hell."

"But their silence isn't definitive, is it? They wouldn't want to be accused of crying wolf, warning prematurely, reducing their credibility. . . ."

"Exactly!" agreed Hassan enthusiastically. "Who knows," he added with a big smile. "It could be the big one. We've just got to be ready."

"And are we?"

"If we think this is it, we need the model here on board."

"You haven't got it with you?"

"Falcon rules. We keep it under lockdown. It's not easy to take it out discreetly."

The Sheikh got up, walked back to the window, looked out.

"I think maybe you should come back tomorrow with the model, don't you?"

"Whatever you say. If you want to go live. . . ."

"I want to be ready," intoned the Sheikh. "Choice is, after all, the greatest luxury of all."

99

SEVENTEEN MILE DRIVE, 7:00 P.M.

Dan Jacobsen watched Gwen drive off. He wanted to shut down, to feel nothing. Then he saw the open car door and his face turned white.

Gwen's declaration, her intention to go to the cops, every word she had spoken as she was removing her board from his car, would have been picked up by the bug. If someone were listening in real time, they'd be on Gwen's trail right now. These guys had an infrastructure, they had numbers, and they had a clear intention: to protect their operation. They would have no hesitation in killing Gwen to do that. He had to find her first.

He slammed the car door, hurried back into his kitchen. He saw that she had forgotten her pocketbook. It lay under the table, abandoned. He grabbed it, grabbed his keys, ran down the stairs into his basement, spun the combination on his safe, opened it, took out a kit bag, chose his weapons. He took his favored SIG Sauer 226, grabbed three fifteen-round magazines, loaded one in the weapon and two in the covert magazine holster that he clipped on the sturdy belt that he still wore out of habit. He slid the SIG into its covert holster and pushed the holster and weapon down the inside of his jeans against his right kidney with the spare magazines pressing onto his left kidney . . . uncomfortable but reassuring. Next he took out the stubby Heckler & Koch MP5K submachine gun, slapped on the dual 30-round magazine clip and slipped the weapon into a leather shoulder holster. The H & K would be his main firepower. Secured in its holster, it fit snugly between his inner arm and the side of his chest. He hauled on a light rainproof jacket to hide the holster and weapon.

Tooled up, he felt the old surge of purpose flooding back. Every sense became hyperaware. Time seemed to slow as he moved, methodically, as if by rote. Training and experience kicked in. A lethal muscle memory. He grabbed the kitbag and Gwen's pocketbook, locked up, alarmed his home, and sprinted for his car.

Gwen couldn't have gone far. She had three minutes' lead, maybe four. He should be able to catch up with her easily enough. She'd go home, he was sure of it. And probably walk straight into a trap.

He raced through the gears, driving as fast as he could without risking the cops stopping him. He'd have to lose the surveillance on him too, and that would cost him more time.

He rang her. In her bag, on the passenger seat, her cell phone trilled.

Daniel said nothing. He called on his training, on all his reserves. And then he prayed. *Don't go home, Gwen. Please don't go home.*

100

Sheikh Ali Al Baharna reached inside his kandoora pocket, removed his cell phone, frowned, and took the call. It was The Man. His phone beeped, indicating that the encryption had not been activated. He saw the three-digit code, sent it back, waited until the code came back and the beeping stopped. He walked from the stateroom into his private quarters.

"Speak," he said.

"Gwen Boudain has just announced she is going to go to the cops. Device on Jacobsen's car picked it up."

"*Yakhrab baitik,*" swore the Sheikh. *May Allah destroy your house.* His face tightened into the harshest juhayman look as fury punched through him.

"When exactly?"

"Five minutes ago. I was listening in real time."

"You did well. Where is she now?"

"We're trying to locate her. She drove away from Jacobsen's place just after she made the comment. But it'll be easy to find her. We have the tracker still active in her pocketbook."

"Good. Find her and kill her. And kill Jacobsen too. Is the team still surveilling him?"

"Yes. Four guys, but they need hardware. One team of two will follow him, the other will peel off, meet me, get the tools. That'll take an hour."

"I want them both disposed of tonight. Do not under any circumstance allow Boudain to get to the police."

"If we have to take her down in public?"

"Do it. Make it look like a robbery. Dress it up if you have time. Either way, make sure she's dead."

101

It had started to rain, slowly at first, but now it came down heavily, sluicing over the road. The Mustang's headlights reflected back off the slick blackness. Gwen's wipers were wholly inadequate, batting back and forth like flickering eyelashes. Nighttime, heavy rain, visibility was crap. Gwen needed to stop, get the top up, but she drove on, heedless of the rain falling on her, falling inside her beloved car, falling on her dog, who cowered in the footwell casting baleful looks at his mistress.

She swore loudly as she took a corner at speed, felt the Mustang wallow and skid. She brought it back under control but it had given her a fright. She was lucky there'd been no car approaching. She slowed. No car crash would claim her. Daniel Jacobsen wasn't worth dying for. She parked, caught her breath, did what she should have done first off—pulled up the roof. It'd still leak in the corners in rain this hard, but it would dry out in a day.

Dan would follow her. She knew that. She needed a bolt-hole, somewhere he wouldn't find her. The answer came to her as she swung out of Seventeen Mile Drive. Dwayne Jonson had recently moved. Finally, he had moved out of his rented studio apartment into his own home, a fixer-upper on the wrong side of Monterey. Gwen found it easily enough. The topiaried peacock cut into the laurel hedge was a bit of a giveaway.

His Harley Low Rider was parked outside. The lights were on inside. Gwen blew out a breath of relief.

She parked, shut off the lights, got out. Leo jumped out after her, whined as the wind and rain whipped him. Gwen slammed the door, heedless of the keys she had left in the ignition. She walked up the path, Leo trailing her. The door opened. Dwayne stood framed, almost filling the whole space. He looked at Gwen, taking in the streaming wet hair, her eyes, huge in the darkness, desolation, fury and a silent plea for help flickering across them.

"Come on in." He eyed Leo, let him pass, though he wasn't keen on dogs at the best of times. Gwen and Leo, he knew, though, came as a package.

He didn't touch her. She seemed to be vibrating with pain and the effort to keep it in. He knew any overly demonstrative display of kindness would undo her, shred her pride.

She told him in staccato bursts as she sat on a packing crate hugging her knees. Her dog sat at her feet, gazing forlornly at his mistress, all too aware of her pain.

Dwayne listened, nodded, but said nothing.

When she'd told him the basics, Gwen released her knees, got up, walked around the dusty floor. Her boots left imprints.

"I left my pocketbook there," she finished miserably. "And my phone."

"He'll bring it to you. Kind of thing he would do, from all you've told me," said Dwayne, breaking his silence.

"I don't want to see him again."

"You say that now."

"Now's all there is. Can I stay here?"

"To hide from him?"

Gwen nodded.

"You can't hide from yourself, Boudy, but you're welcome to crash here for as long as you want." Dwayne glanced at Leo. "And your mangy dog."

She managed a smile. "Thanks, Dwayne."

102

Dan lost the surveillance team with little effort. One car had peeled away, leaving just one vehicle following him. They weren't first rate, but they weren't bad either. He added that to the equation. How much time did he have before the intercept was listened to, acted on? A few hours, he hoped. Enough time to get into position. The darkness helped. He gave a grim smile. He had always been best in the dark.

He wished he'd had time to scope out the terrain; he wished he'd anticipated this. Too late for regrets. There was a small dirt track a few miles north of Hurricane Point. No one was tailing him. He had watched all the way, made sure, so he yanked the wheel, swung the Cougar off the road, bumped down the rough track, smiled as he saw the bend, followed it, out of sight of Highway 1. He came to the end of the track, maybe fifty feet above sea level, two hundred feet from the beach. He turned the car, parked tight against a huge bush, heedless of the scratches to his paintwork. Now the car was pointed ready for a quick getaway.

He got out his cell, rang Gwen's house. No answer. He prayed it was because she wasn't there. He shut off the engine, shut off the lights, rolled down his windows, listened and looked.

The wind roared, the rain hissed down, help and hindrance, but he heard nothing suspicious. It took two minutes for his eyes to adjust.

He stepped from the car, reached for his kit bag. Still scanning the night, he pulled out a pair of black, toughened leather gloves, thin enough to allow maximum feel for the trigger. He pulled these on. Next he took out his Kevlar knife. This normally came into its own in getting through airport security undetected. It worked well too. He bent down, strapped it to his lower leg under his jeans. He took out the single night-vision goggle, secured it in his jacket pocket. He ignored the Kevlar vest. It was too heavy to fight in effectively, and he reckoned the fighting would be close quarter, unless he were lucky.

Next he took out a stick of face camo. *Roughie-toughie makeup* his Brit friends in the SAS called it, so dubbed by their girlfriends. He dabbed the stick onto his face, rubbed it in streaks, secured it back in the kit bag. Last, he took out a condom, stashed it in his pocket. Then he locked the kit bag in his car. On a hunch, he grabbed Gwen's pocketbook, slipped it into the large inner pocket of his rain jacket. Next he locked his car and zipped his keys into his jacket pocket. The rain had soaked his jeans already and slicked his hair to his head. It was cold and he shivered. He needed to get moving, but first he had one more job.

He moved into the undergrowth, gathered an armful of branches. The shoulder holster dug into him as he bent and stretched, but he found the pressure reassuring. He arrayed the branches over his car, starting with any areas that reflected light; windscreen, lights. Quickly he covered the Cougar. It helped that it was black. He would only ever drive black cars.

He straightened up, checked the job from a number of angles and distances, satisfied himself. The wind would blow off the branches sooner or later, but he'd done what he could.

The visibility was poor. Thanks to the cloud cover and rain, the darkness was almost total. A haze of light pollution from San Francisco and Monterey provided just a hint of light.

He unzipped his pocket, pulled on the single-eye night-vision goggle. He knew well enough the problem with

NVGs was that if there were a flash of light, like from a gun barrel, he'd be blind for about four seconds. By choice, he always used a single goggle, leaving one eye uncovered.

No turning back now. If he were found by any law enforcement types who happened upon the scene he was beyond any doubt equipped to kill. He unzipped his jacket, took out his Heckler & Koch from the shoulder holster, opened the condom and slipped it over the barrel. He probably didn't need it, the weapon wasn't going to get submerged in water, but just in case . . .

He moved from the scrub, H & K held securely, an extension of his arm. Out into the open, he stopped, listened, and looked. Again nothing.

He had a rough idea of the topography. He should be able to walk an unimpeded course to Hurricane Point unless the tide were very high. He cast his mind back to the last time he had surfed, worked the calculations since, smiled. He headed for the beach. Luck was on his side; the tide was out. But when he walked onto the sand he thought he must have miscalculated. Huge waves were breaking and shuddering and racing up the beach. There was room to walk, but a rogue wave was a distinct possibility.

He hugged the contours of the cliff, not just to avoid the raging sea, but to stay hidden, to blend his own outline with the rough bushes that clung to the sloping land that edged the sand.

He couldn't afford to linger, to move as slowly as he would have liked. Gwen could be at home right now with the killers closing in. He moved at a lope, long legs covering the ground. His kit was not as silent as he would have liked, but here the raging seas, the rain, and the rising wind were his allies. He moved through the dark, armed like a knight of old, and with the sole intent that the knights would have found worthy. He went in defense of someone he loved, futile though that love might be. It would be him against however many men Messenger or whoever was behind the operation decided to throw at them: four, five, maybe more. Certainly not less. Those weren't great odds. He'd faced better. He'd faced worse.

He didn't want to die, but like the Shuhada', he was ready to if need be. Difference was, he knew there would not be seventy-two virgins awaiting him in Paradise. He didn't know what there would be. A void, or a something . . . a Heaven or a Hell . . . and with what he had done and seen, even if Heaven existed he doubted he would be admitted.

He ran on through the darkness. He slowed, stopped as a detail in the rock caught his eye. Mostly the beach was bounded by rough ground sloping down to the sand, but for stretches there were rocky cliffs. He stopped beside one now, noting the indentation, a cave of sorts. He moved in, out of the rain, glanced around. It was about fifteen feet deep. He filed it away, moved out and on along the beach.

He rounded a contour, saw above him the light shining in Gwen's house. He felt his pulse quicken. He paused. No room for impulsive dashes, no room for mistakes. Now he had to slow, to move undetected.

He approached as close as he could on foot, veiled by the darkness, any slight noise he made covered by the waves. Then he had no choice but to fall to his stomach and leopard crawl, yard by yard, H & K extended in front, closer and closer, stopping, listening, straining all his senses to pick up anything human.

He got close enough to observe the front of the house. Gwen's car was not there. He let out a slow breath of relief. He prayed she had some bolt-hole neither he nor the surveillance team knew about. No other car was there either, but then he hadn't expected the killers to roll up and park in full view. He waited, watched. The rain sluiced down on him and the wind chilled him as the minutes ticked by, but he stayed where he was. He'd waited hours in far worse conditions. He'd forgotten the misery of it, told himself the special ops mantra: pain, discomfort of any kind, is just a sensation. It has no power beyond what you choose to give it.

Ninety-five percent of his mind was utterly focused on waiting, watching, on readying himself. The other five percent wandered. He froze suddenly. He had forgotten to turn off Gwen's cell. He heard his trainers' voices dripping scorn. *Amateurs die. You cannot afford a single mistake.* Feeling a flush of shame, he set down the H & K, reached into his pocket, took out the pocketbook, felt around for the cell phone. It seemed to have hidden itself. His fingers probed. In the night, all the senses were heightened in normal times, and as his fingers brushed over a stud, one in a row, larger than the others and out of sequence, his senses leapt. Keeping his finger in place, he pulled the bag up to his goggled eye, carefully wiped the rain from the lens, scrutinized the stud, smiled slowly. He let it go, found the phone, switched it to silent, as was his own phone. He rapidly made a new plan.

He picked up his weapon, turned, crawled forward until the scrub shielded him, then he ran at a crouch back down to the beach. It took him four minutes to get to the cave. He took Gwen's pocketbook from his jacket pocket, stashed it in the furthest corner of the cave, then moved out, looking for cover closer to Gwen's house.

If his calculations were correct, the tracker beacon he'd found in the bag would lead the killers straight to the cave. They might wonder what Gwen Boudain was doing in a cave, they might be suspicious, but they would have no choice but to check it out.

He found the perfect spot, another small cave about two hundred meters from where the pocketbook was stashed. He settled down just inside, lying on his stomach. He switched the goggle to the other eye so that he could just peek round the edge of the cave and watch the approach from the house. He felt fairly sure that the killers, when they came, would come that way.

He switched off all other thought, just focused on the night. He heard the surf roaring in. The tide was turning, he could hear it, could see the waves encroaching. They were getting bigger, propelled up and in by the growing wind, and by a storm, a bigger storm, far out to sea. Coming his way. He had maybe two hours before he would be forced to move. In his mind the images flooded back, the killing moves. He had tried for years to keep them at bay; now he called them up, reveled in them, felt the blood flow.

103

THE SUPER-YACHT, *ZEPHYR*, 9:30 P.M.

Sheikh Ali stood in his stateroom, feet braced against the pitching and tossing. The windows, uncurtained, gave out onto unrelieved blackness. Rain lashed the glass and he could hear the wind roaring. His yacht was still in control, but the storm was challenging her.

He was speaking on his encrypted cell phone with The Man. He was on the edge of control. "Have you found Gwen Boudain?" he demanded, voice fast and clipped.

"We've not closed with her. Not yet. But we know where she is."

"Then go in and eliminate her. Every second passes she could be on the phone to the cops."

"I don't think there'll be a signal where she is."

"Meaning?" Sheikh Ali bent down, took a mouthful of hot coffee, slammed down the cup. The contents lurched over the side of the golden cup and dripped from the mahogany low table onto the handwoven carpet.

"She's in a cave, hiding out, on the beach one mile north of her home."

"Since you know where she is, why the delay?" The Sheikh's voice rose with disbelief.

"We think it could be a trap. We cannot find her car, nor Jacobsen's, just the signal coming from her pocketbook."

"How many men are out there?"

"Five."

"And you are hesitating, with five men up against one woman, possibly with a man at her side. A meteorologist and a journalist. *Have your men killed before?*"

The Sheikh held the cell phone in a death grip. His fury, his disbelief was threatening to overwhelm him. He struggled to control himself, not for the sake of The Man, but for his own clarity. Loss of temper was a weakness he despised.

"You know they have. They are your men. Handpicked."

The Sheikh nodded slowly. "They have the blood of many on their hands, and you hesitate to use them against these amateurs. Send them in *now*. Kill them. Leave no trace of the bodies. Do you think if they had called the cops they would be hiding in some cave on a seashore?"

"No. I just don't know why they would feel the need to hide. Doesn't make sense. That bothers me."

"They probably spotted your surveillance guys! Maybe old Freidland told them something new. *Khalas!* Enough! It's their time. Send in the men. Now!"

The Man nodded. What choice did he have? And as the Sheikh pointed out, even if Jacobsen were there with Gwen, the man was a journalist. Neither of them posed any real threat.

104

It had been three years since he'd been active, since he'd last killed, or been in the theater, as they called it. He knew he must have been rusty, but he didn't feel it. Every sense was screamingly alive. He felt them coming. He felt it before he saw them. Some animal instinct that went beyond training. You just had to silence the noise to let it speak, to hear it. He heard it now. He held the SIG in his left hand, the Heckler in his right. He would prefer not to use his own weapons in case they were traced back to him, but he would if he had to. He had used them in Iraq, had them smuggled back to him. Were they traced back to him, there would be a furor that would stretch from the Pentagon to the White House; the trained killer gone rogue on home soil. . . . No, better he killed by knife, or hand. If he had the choice.

He waited. He saw the party split, saw two men aim off, up the hill. They would come at the pocketbook, at where they thought he, or Gwen, or both of them were, from left and from right. That would have made it harder, had he not foreseen it, had he not moved. They weren't complete amateurs. He still didn't think he would die. He never did. It was always an academic possibility, but he never allowed it to feel real. Never allowed himself to imagine the bullets slicing into his own flesh, or the knives, or any of the weapons he had used on others.

Two came forward from the south. They should coordinate with the two coming from the north, to the second, if they were good. He waited in the shadows, breathing, listening, feeling. The roar of the surf and the growing storm drowned out most sound. But not all. He could hear the soft fall of their feet as they closed on him. He could smell them. Aftershave, coffee, cigarettes. And adrenaline. Not fear. That was a rank smell, deeper and harsher and stronger. They didn't fear him. They didn't know who he was.

One followed the other. He holstered his weapons. He let the first man pass, so near he felt his heat. Then he straightened, grabbed the second man's head, twisted. The click of the broken spine was immediate. The man slumped. Dan laid him down, took his knife from the ankle holster. Two strides and he got the man in front. Some instinct made this man turn at the last moment. He locked eyes as Dan plunged the dagger into his throat, deepened, slashed, watched the eyes roll back, heard the futile attempt as the man tried to cry out, drowned in his own blood. Dan laid him down, pulled him out of sight. The man's blood spurted over him. He felt the flare of revulsion, brutally shoved it down. He hid the other man, then took both sets of weapons: one a Škorpion machine pistol and the other a Makarov pistol, both Soviet weapons.

The two other men should be nearing the cave now. Dan moved slowly. He could feel his blood throbbing in the pulse points: throat, neck, temple. He could feel it coursing through his veins, in protest, in thrill, in horror, and in screaming, defiant life.

He saw them ahead, creeping along the cliff wall, glancing right and left, unaware. He waited until they had entered the cave, then moved closer. He wanted to get them in a range of ten meters or less.

He heard them crashing around inside. Heard the dismay, unmistakeable, even in Arabic. He could decipher their repeated questions: *Where were Ashgar and Jaffar?*

The first one rushed out, the second close behind. Dan fired the Makarov, taking down the first man with two shots to the body, another to the head, rolling as he fired, aiming at the second man with the Škorpion. He fired off three head shots. The Škorpion had a far smaller caliber round than the Makarov, making it more accurate. Dan wanted instant death and that meant hitting the cerebral cortex. All three shots hit and the man crumpled. Neither man had moved fast enough to fire back a single shot. But there should be another man.

Dan moved back into the cover of the cave, hunting him. There should always be a fallback guy. If he were good, he would come after Dan now. But there *was* no fallback guy. Most likely he was in a depth position further away. If he had guts he would come now, slowly hunting Dan. Most likely he would run. Dan waited in the cave. He heard the waves roaring nearer. He couldn't stay long. Fifteen minutes later, the spray from the waves gusted in, lacing his face with brine. Time to go. In a fight with the waves, the waves would win.

He edged out. The NVG showed no sign of a human crouching or retreating. He bent over the bodies, went through the pockets. No IDs. Pros in that respect, anyway.

He eyed the waves. They would reach the cave that night. Of that he was sure. He moved up to the other two bodies, dragged them into the cave, pulled in the second two. He returned the Makarov and Škorpion to their dead owners. Then he grabbed Gwen's pocketbook and moved silently and quickly away from the cave and its carnage.

He ran through the darkness, cautious, hyperaware, but he saw no one. When he got near to his parked car, he stripped off his bloodied clothes, turned them inside out. The rain sluiced down on his body, chilling him to the bone. He felt it rain on him, washing away the blood, knowing that nothing would ever wash his mind.

He pushed down the images and ran for his car. He removed the cover of foliage, unlocked the door and grabbed his kit bag. He stashed his bloodied clothes and leather gloves in a special sealable bag, pulled on the sweatpants and t-shirt he kept spare and slid into his car.

He took Gwen's pocketbook, fingers probing, removed the tracking device concealed in the stud. He threw it into the bushes.

All he had to do now was find Gwen. He drove up the track, heating on high, hands steady on the wheel, mind numb.

105

Ijaz stood before the Sheikh. He was covered in dried blood. The Sheikh eyed him with disbelief.

"All dead? All four of them?"

Ijaz bowed his head. He might as well have gone after them, died on duty, but sheer terror had made him run. When all comms had gone silent, he'd hidden in a hollowed-out space under a bush, waited, finally crept out from the foliage toward the cave, seen the carnage within, and run again. The pilot had picked him up a half hour ago, battling the winds to get him.

"And no sign of who did it?"

Ijaz shook his head.

The Man had been picked up too. He looked on grimly, and in disbelief.

"So neither Jacobsen nor Boudain were there," he said, voice dripping scorn. "Just four dead bodies." He paused. He sounded almost admiring now, but not of Ijaz. "One neck broken, one throat slit, the other two shot with Jaffar and Ashgar's own weapons." He held up his fingers as if ticking off an inventory.

"Correct," replied Izaj hoarsely.

The Man turned to look at Al Baharna. The Sheikh

stood rock still. The rage pumping off him was palpable. A vein was pulsing in his right temple. The Man subtly moved backward.

With a spasm, the Sheikh seemed to crack. "Who the fuck is this guy?" he screamed, whirling round, pacing from The Man to the blood-soaked Ijaz. Neither answered. They both just stood still, inuring themselves to whatever would come. On the rare occasions when the Sheikh lost his temper, he could and did strike out with whatever weapons came to hand—fists, bottles . . .

Al Baharna turned away. He circled, came back, but stood more than arms' length from the two men, visibly attempting to control himself.

"A *journalist* did this?" the Sheikh continued, voice lowering. It came out like a hiss.

The Man thought this was no time to say he had thought all along that the cave was a trap.

"It would appear that Jacobsen is more than he seems," he said.

"And that you did not research him deeply enough," said the Sheikh, voice dipping as though he were passing sentence.

The Man nodded. That much was true. And fair.

The Sheikh paced away. He stopped at the black windows, braced his palms on the glass, stared out into the darkness. The yacht was really beginning to pitch and toss now, despite its huge length. Baharna picked up his walkie-talkie.

"Get the captain down here."

Blaine Shaffer appeared one minute later. He was stocky, dark, competent-looking. He wore wire-rimmed glasses and a crisp white uniform. He studiously avoided looking at the blood-stained man.

"Sheikh Al Baharna," he said with a slight bow.

"This weather . . ." posed the Sheikh. "Is it getting worse?"

"The forecasts suggest it is. The National Weather Service has issued an updated Advisory winter storm warning in the last hour; it's in effect until further notice, which means they think it'll be a storm of some duration." Shaffer was South African. He spoke in a staccato rhythm, emphasizing the last word of each sentence. It made his words portentous at the best of times.

The Sheikh nodded. "What do they say, *exactly*?"

The captain consulted his log, an old-fashioned leather-bound book, which he carried everywhere. He looked down, read from his notes. His glasses slipped a fraction down his nose. He ignored them.

"Fast-moving Pacific storm; wave warnings, precipitation warnings, wind warnings . . . They've added a 'precautionary/preparedness warning.' "

"Meaning?"

"It's related to coastal areas, warning of extra-high waves, of potential wave damage, to stay out of the sea or to exercise extreme caution if at sea. They're also warning of heavy rains making driving conditions hazardous. They're saying, stay off the roads, and stock up on any essentials."

"Do you think they are covering themselves?" asked the Sheikh.

"No. If anything I think it'll be worse than the forecast," the captain replied definitively, ramming his glasses back into position on his nose. "I would like to motor south through the night. With all dispatch," he added crisply.

"How bad do you think it will get?"

"It's early in the season for a really big storm, but I don't like what I'm seeing. I didn't like the color of the sky today, the color of the sea."

"Not very scientific," observed The Man.

The Sheikh shot him a speculative glance. He looked away.

The Captain ignored him, spoke just to the Sheikh, his voice milder than his words. "I could give you the scientific parameters if that would make you happier. I find, that in thirty years of experience on the seas, that personal observation is often as valuable as the science."

"And sometimes much neglected," added Al Baharna, looking levelly at The Man. "Do you think?" he continued, "that this could be the fabled ARk Storm 1000?"

The captain waited a while before replying.

"USGS and the National Weather Service do not think so. They would have gone into Major Alert mode if they did."

"That doesn't answer my question," replied Al Baharna, spacing his words.

"They could be wrong," conceded the captain. He shrugged. "As I said, it's early in the season for a huge storm. But it could be. It'll be a big storm, an ugly one. Of that I am sure. Whether it will develop into an ARk Storm, let alone *the* ARk Storm . . . we shall have to wait and see. Preferably from hundreds of miles away."

"We stay here. For now," declared the Sheikh. He felt, along with the fury at a mission botched, the soar and the pulse of adrenaline. Standing in the path of a storm was an almost sexual feeling. Delaying, staying not running, was the sweetest kind of self-denial, like choking off oxygen prior to an orgasm. It intensified the feeling when you did run. Besides, they couldn't run. They still had outstanding business.

"With our top speed of sixty-odd knots we should have time to outrun any storm, no?" the Sheikh asked the captain.

"In theory. Perhaps. But I would rather not put it to the test. And in these conditions we cannot go that fast. A lot can happen at sea."

The Sheikh smiled. "We are all in God's hands. If he

wills it, and if the power of our engines allows it, we shall
escape. *Insha'Allah*," he added, palms raised, eyes glancing upward to the only power he recognized as greater than
his own.

106

STANFORD UNIVERSITY,
WEDNESDAY MORNING, 6:00 A.M.

Art Graffenburg threw up his hands in despair. His two
co-heads, Bridget Riley and Jon Hendrix, were going at it
like cats and dogs, as always. They'd all come in ultra-
early. Big storms did that. The weather didn't sleep.

Lack of sleep had done nothing for their sense of diplo-
macy. They'd started fighting at the get-go. Co-heads never
worked. Bad idea, bad execution. Egos, philosophy, inter-
pretations, and visions clashed and it was ugly. Graffenburg had left the meeting. Now he stood silently outside
the door, like a bodyguard.

"The parameters aren't there," Hendrix was insisting. "Yeah it's a big AR, but the variables suggest it won't
precipitate when it makes landfall."

Inside the meeting room, Bridget Riley and Jon Hendrix
faced off across a Styrofoam-laden conference table.
There were no windows and the heating was set high. Both
were sweating. Their faces were red with the heat and mutual exasperation.

Riley jumped to her feet and began to pace the conference room, taking short staccato steps that matched her
voice.

"Look, Hendrix, let's recap, shall we, see what we got?"

Hendrix folded his arms across his chest and leaned back in his chair, attempting a look of nonchalance.

Riley kicked off. "Right! We have Sat images of an atmospheric river hurtling toward us at speeds estimated to be upward of eighty kph. If we could get one of NASA's Hawks up there we could make better estimates *re* speed and severity. So first off, I want to put in the call, if you're amenable?"

Hendrix nodded. "Go for it. It's their dollar."

Riley hid her distaste, just nodded back. "Will do. This AR is scheduled to hit, at its current speeds, tomorrow, maybe at noon, let's say around twenty-four hours from now, give or take. The rain we're seeing now is just the outrider of the storm. This is the warm-up."

"Maybe this rain is all there'll be," countered Hendrix. "The AR might not precipitate when it makes landfall," he repeated, scowling.

"Then again, it just might. I want to up the severity of the warning. I want us to issue a Special Weather Statement."

Hendrix shook his head. "No need," he declared, pursing his lips.

Riley walked up to the man, bent over him, lowered her voice.

"You a gambler, Hendrix?"

"No. I'm a scientist."

Riley cocked her head. "Really? 'Cause it seems to me you're more than happy to gamble with people's lives."

"Really? And it seems to me that you forgot to take your medication." Hendrix spoke mildly, the barb so sharp a soft delivery still drove it home.

Riley did literally see the legendary red haze of rage. A dozen, terminal retorts rocked through her head. Instead, using up almost her last reserves of will power, she blinked, turned, and walked from the room.

107

The Man pulled over at the viewpoint, got out his cell, rang the Sheikh. He rubbed his hands over his face. He was exhausted. The chopper had flown him to Monterey at midnight and he'd spent the hours since driving around. In vain.

The Sheikh answered. They both completed the encryption process, and only then as the background beeping died did they speak.

"I take it the cops haven't visited, or called?" asked The Man.

"They have not, so we can hope that Boudain did not make good her threat. Please tell me you've found her," said the Sheikh, voice impassive, emotions under lockdown.

"I'm sorry, but we have not. No sign of Boudain or Jacobsen, not at their own homes, and nowhere else we've looked, and we've looked. No one slept last night. But we did find Boudain's car."

"Where?"

"Out by the airport in Monterey. I tuned into the cops' frequencies, heard a concerned citizen call it in. It was crashed. Burnt out."

The Sheikh raised an eyebrow. "As in fatally?"

"As in trash crashed. And burnt out. My guess it was stolen."

"Maybe by Boudain's and Jacobsen's design, to lead you off the scent," said the Sheikh.

"That's my thinking."

"Get the other guys to keep looking. I have another job for you. The main extraction. Get what you need to get.

Silence the target. Make it look like an accident. Go now.
Get him at home."

The Man sucked in a breath. The endgame. "I'm ready."

"You'd better be. This is your chance to redeem yourself. You do understand that, don't you?" the Sheikh said
softly.

The Man looked out across the gray sea. He knew. You
supped with the devil, sooner or later you had to pay. He
just needed a bit more time. If he could pull off this last
big job for the Sheikh, pull off the endgame, then he'd get
out his fake passport, the best his money had been able to
buy, and head for Brazil, far from the reach of the Sheikh
and his Shuhada', or so he had to believe.

"I'll send the copter now," said the Sheikh. "It'll be waiting at Monterey Airport."

"I'll get there as soon as I'm done. Should be ninety
mins, max."

The Sheikh clicked off the phone. They had got Jacobsen and Boudain wrong. Fatally underestimated them.
Nothing seemed to be going to plan. Apart from the
weather. That at least was promising to deliver Hell. And
if the extraction plan worked, then Hell would be delivered.

108

MONTEREY, TUESDAY, LATER THAT MORNING

Gwen woke with a wicked hangover and the sense that
something was very wrong. She lay still, listening to rain
drumming against the window. The wind punched the
house like percussion. Alarmed, she sat up and looked
around blearily: Leo lay on a blanket in the corner, one

eye open, regarding her carefully; Dwayne's spare bed-room. His new crib. She pushed up, hair streaming down her back. She was wearing a huge black t-shirt and yes-terday's underwear. It all came flooding back through the tequila haze. Dan, his confession, her running, Dwayne's house; the bottle, shared.

"Urggh," she groaned. Knuckling her hair from her eyes, she swung her legs out of bed, walked unsteadily over to her dog. She bent down, ruffled his fur, then went to the window. She drew back the curtains to a vista of sheer gray. Rain sluiced down from a gunmetal sky. There was a big old oak filling most of Dwayne's backyard. Its dark branches, stripped of all foliage, danced to the wind's discordant tune. An array of small, broken branches lit-tered the lawn. The weather mirrored her mood, and for that she was oddly grateful. She couldn't have dealt with blue skies today.

She headed for the bathroom, turned on the shower. No hot water. After two minutes standing in a stream of freez-ing cold water, she felt half human again.

She pulled on her jeans and, reluctantly, Dan's cashmere jersey. It smelled of him.

"Damn him" she muttered, "and the surfboard he rocked up on."

She found Dwayne in the kitchen making coffee. He turned, smiled at her.

"You look surprisingly alive."

"Miracle of plumbing," she mumbled. "Cold water cure."

"Yeah. New boiler comes next week."

"Hey, softie, who needs hot water anyway?"

"This one," replied Dwayne gruffly, handing Gwen a steaming mug.

Dwayne scraped out a can of tuna and sweet corn for Leo. The dog gave the man a grateful look and fell to eat-ing with slobbery enthusiasm.

Gwen sipped her coffee. "Two of these and I should be fit to drive."

Dwayne took the cup from her, held her arm. "About that . . ."

"Hey, don't fuss me! I'll be fine."

"Sure you will, Boudy. Always are. Car's gone."

"What?" Her voice had shot up an octave. "What the hell d'you mean?"

She pulled free, rushed outside into the slanting rain, let loose a tirade of swear words Dwayne hadn't heard since he was in the SEALs.

Gwen turned, hand on hips, wild eyed, water streaming down her face and body. "Whichever fucker took my car is gonna have a short life. I swear to God!"

"Call it in," said Dwayne, squinting through the rain.

"Yeah, call it in. My parent's car," she said, her voice breaking. Tears burned her eyes. She blinked them away furiously. Dwayne came, took her in his arms, and walked her indoors. He kicked the door closed behind them and stood with her, both of them dripping onto the bare linoleum. He said nothing. Just held her.

"I'll put the word out. Get it back. You call it in. I'll call in some favors. Street and cops. We'll get it back."

109

Gwen and Dwayne sat on packing crates in the empty den, making their calls. Gwen used Dwayne's landline, he used his cell phone. She missed her cell, felt ridiculously incomplete without it. It took Gwen five minutes to discover that her car was trashed. A burnt-out shell found on Via Malpaso.

She turned to Dwayne, fists clenched.

"Joy fuckin' riders. Trashed it. I swear to God if they were in this room I would kill the fuckers."

Dwayne gave her a gentle pat. "Real good thing they are long gone then, Boudy. Not worth doing time for."

"You know what that car meant. . . ." She felt the tears threaten again.

"I know. Nothing can replace it. No amount of money."

She nodded. Swallowed. She drank another coffee, mind seesawing through emotions and plans. Dwayne left her. He started work upstairs. Over the wind and rain she could hear him working with a power saw. It was a curiously reassuring sound. Life went on. Good things happened.

Where to now? Gwen pondered. She didn't want to go home. Dan might be there waiting. The fuckers surveilling him might be there waiting. She didn't want to hand it over to the police either, not that there was anything concrete to hand over. Now she wanted a measure of personal vengeance. She wanted to go to Falcon. She wanted to confront Messenger, to bring this whole fucking charade to an end. She wanted to tell him what she knew, throw it in his face, read him for the truth or for the lies, the cover-up she thought would follow. She wanted to smash something, to right the wrongs, today's, yesterday's. She'd heard tell of the red haze, the killing haze of fury. She felt it now. Contained, but burning. She was a danger, she knew it. To herself as much as to anyone else.

She used Dwayne's phone again, called a cab. It came ten minutes later. Standing in the open doorway, rain sweeping in, Dwayne saw Gwen off with a hug and a loan of a fifty. All her cash was in the pocketbook she'd idiotically forgotten at Dan's.

"See you later?" Dwayne asked.

"Yeah. Got some business to see to first, but if it's OK I'd really like to crash here for another day or two."

"Mi Casa," said Dwayne with an extravagant sweep of his arms.

Gwen grinned, reached up, kissed his cheek.

"*Hasta Luego,* Buddy."

"Where to, lady?" asked the driver, eyeing Leo with a frown. Afghani by the look of it. Good looking, educated. Probably had a doctorate, like her. Christ the world was fucked up.

"Carmel Valley Road," she said. "Ten dollars extra for my dog."

The man smiled, nodded to his backseat.

Gwen and Leo got in. Gwen strapped herself in, rolled down her window. Leo hunched at her feet. The cab pulled out of Dwayne's side street onto the main drag. It lurched as the wind pummeled it, making the driver swear in some low, guttural language. Gwen leaned against the door, looked up at the sky. All she could see was rain.

110

THE LAB TUESDAY, 9:30 A.M.

Gwen swung shut the taxi door and strode to the entrance of Falcon Capital. Leo ran with her, head down, tail down, a picture of misery. The wind whipped at Gwen's hair, lashing her face. She paused outside the building. Her pass was in the pocketbook she'd left at Dan's house. Sooner or later she'd have to get it back, but not yet. She reached out to ring the bell, paused as Atalanta rushed up behind her, braids flying.

"I'm late! I'm late!" she cried. "Hey, Dog!" she said, glancing at Leo.

"Not the end of the world," replied Gwen, making way for Atalanta and her card with relief.

"Feels like!" cried Atalanta, fumbling for her card. "It's *wild* out here."

Gwen rubbed her arms, nodded.

Atalanta swiped her pass, the door clicked open, and they both found themselves propelled inside by a huge gust. Leo stepped inside, looked around cautiously at the unfamiliar place. Gwen leaned back against the door, forcing it closed. She pushed her hair from her face, saw Atalanta observing her with a frown of concern.

"What's with bringing your dog in?"

"Long story," murmured Gwen.

"You OK?"

Gwen waited a beat. "No, honey. Not really."

"Anything I can help with?"

Gwen saw the sincerity, wished she could say *yes,* that a solution were so easy to grab.

"I don't think so, but if you can, I *will* let you know." Atalanta's kindness cut through her anger. Below the rage, she felt raw, exposed. It wasn't just the theft of her parents' car, it wasn't just Dan's betrayal. It was the sense of threat that dogged her, had all her instincts firing.

Atalanta laid a hand on Gwen's arm. "*Do* that."

Gwen nodded, cut through the atrium to her office, Leo trailing her. She half expected to see Messenger there, invading her space, but there was no one. She glanced around, almost as if seeing it for the first or last time.

She watched Leo examine her office, sniffing the corners, before he circled three times then sank down onto the floor in the corner, nose on his paws, lugubrious.

Gwen reached down, ruffled his neck. "Hang on in there, boy."

She switched on her desktop, logged on, and checked the satellite images of the approaching storm. The atmospheric river showed up as a green swath cutting across the

Pacific. She wondered when it was due to make landfall. Couldn't be long. She didn't have much time.

She walked from her office, closing Leo in behind her. She glimpsed Kevin Barclay in his office. He seemed to be packing up, removing things from his desk drawers, placing them in a large briefcase. Running from the storm, thought Gwen.

She strode up to Mandy, eyed Messenger's empty office.

"Where is he?"

"Well *Good Morning* to you too, honey," responded Mandy archly.

Gwen paused a beat. She wanted to chew up Mandy. Fought it down. It would be like savaging a sheep.

"What happened to you?" went on Mandy. "Look a tad wild this morning, if I may say."

"You may not say, Mandy," said Gwen, bracing her fisted knuckles on Mandy's desk. The other woman shrank back.

"Where's Dr. M.?" repeated Gwen.

Mandy's forehead creased. "Didn't come in. Not answering his phone. If you gotta know, I'm kinda worried."

Gwen straightened. "Don't be. I'm sure Dr. M. can take care of himself. Look, I forgot my desk keys at home. Is there a master key? I need to get the laptop that Dr. M. gave me to work on." Get it and take it to the cops, she decided.

Mandy eyed her with a look bordering on suspicion. Then she seemed to relent.

"I have the masters. Wait in your office."

Mandy appeared a few minutes later.

"Holy Hell, what's that?" she cried, eyeing Leo.

"He's friendly, don't stress," replied Gwen, moving between her dog and Mandy as if to protect one from the other, unsure who needed protection more.

"Taking liberties, Gwen."

"Unavoidable. The key?" she asked crisply, nodding at the jailor's selection Mandy brandished.

Mandy rifled through the bunch, selected a key, un-locked Gwen's desk drawer. Gwen pulled it open.

"Shit!"

"What's up?"

"The laptop's gone. I locked it in here yesterday."

Mandy crossed her arms below her large bosom. "Maybe you gave it back to Dr. Messenger and forgot. Bite my head off, but you don't look yourself," she added truculently.

Gwen eyed Mandy. Her heart was thudding in her chest. She felt sure that Mandy must be able to hear it. She forced a smile.

"Yeah, that must be it. Thanks M."

The other woman nodded, withdrew, a thoughtful look on her face.

Gwen sank into her chair before the empty drawer. She just sat there, staring into space, wondering. Someone had removed the model. It had to have been Messenger or Mandy.

She heard the whistling before she saw Peter Weiss. "Everybody Hurts" again. Didn't he get sick of it, Gwen wondered? Everyone else did, silently putting up with it through gritted teeth.

Weiss ceased whistling. He stuck his head theatrically round her door.

"Whassup, Weather Girl? Hey, you got a dog!" Weiss reached down, stroked Leo. "Sweet!"

"He is."

"Why's he here?"

"Long story," Gwen said for the second time. "Whas-sup with you?"

Weiss angled in, perched on her desk. "Same old, same old."

"Know where Dr. M. is?" Gwen asked.

Weiss frowned. "Why should I know?"

Gwen shrugged. " 'Cause you know him. You're one of his 'intimates,' the inner core. That's why."

"Maybe. Maybe not."

"And?"

"Maybe he's scared of the storm. It's a biggie already," declared Weiss, nodding portentously, as if at an adversary's accomplishments.

"It is."

"You reckon it could be the one?"

"As in ARk Storm 1000?" asked Gwen, leaning back in her chair. A pulse of pain flashed across her temples. The hangover's last stand.

"It *is* slated to be an atmospheric river storm," acknowledged Gwen. "That much we already know. Several of those hit every year. We've just had one. The National Weather Service has a Warning issued—'dangerous storm' and all that—but the Hazard people haven't said anything about this being the Big One."

"They know everything?"

Gwen gave a bitter laugh. "Who does?" She got up, brushed past him, headed for the coffee machine. She wanted another caffeine hit. When she got back to her office, Weiss was gone and only the rich, sweet scent of tobacco lingered.

111

THE LAB, 9:40 A.M.

Gwen drank her coffee. It roiled through her stomach. Caffeine was the last thing she needed. She was jittery enough. She had that sense of acceleration, of events moving beyond her, way out of control. She was reacting, desperately trying for a control that she had long since lost, and she knew it. Half of her wanted to run. The other half wanted to finish this thing, whatever the fuck it was, to see all the hidden, missing parts, dig them out, almost whatever the cost.

She got up, closed her office door, something she rarely did. She didn't care if she looked instantly suspicious. It was way too late to care. She picked up her phone, put in the call.

Riley's assistant, Art, answered. "Hey Gwen. She's kinda busy at the mo. They're all looking real close at this storm. She and Hendricks are having a real donnybrook. Kicked the rest of us out of their meeting. Shoot, sorry, shouldn't have told ya that."

"Art, listen, please go and get her. Drag her out if you have to. Tell her it's me and tell her it's urgent."

She could feel Art conjuring a flip response but something in her voice must have stopped him.

"Sure Gwen. I'm gone."

The roar of wind and rain blended with another, lower throb. A helicopter was flying in. Gwen angled out of her chair. She peered through the window but she could see neither the copter nor whoever was arriving or leaving. Maybe it was Messenger, showing up at last. She wanted to get up and check, but forced herself to wait for Riley.

Her friend came on the line two minutes later.

"Gwen! Thank God. I've been trying to get hold of you. This storm's looking ugly. I'm trying to upgrade the warnings. Fuckwit Hendrix is blocking me. I want you off Hurricane Point. Over the hills and far away."

"You 'n' me both, Riley."

"Now what's up with you? Art got all serious. Demanded I talk to you."

"Get those warnings upgraded all the way, Riley. And listen up. Don't interrupt, however far-fetched this is gonna sound." Gwen took a breath, glanced round the office. No one in sight. It seemed oddly quiet.

"This storm," she said in a low voice. "People I know have the technology to ramp it up. You guys're probably debating whether the AR will produce rain when it makes landfall. . . ."

"Got it in one!"

"Well, these people can *make* it produce rain. Via ionizers. I've seen it Riley. I've seen them make it rain and God help me I've helped them fine-tune the model so that they can increase their rain yield. They're gonna ramp up a storm sooner or later, trying to make a monster, and I have a horrible feeling it's sooner."

"What, you're telling me some people think they can *make* an ARk Storm?" Riley whispered, her voice faint with disbelief and horror.

"That's exactly what I'm telling you. They have an army of drones all ready to go up and do just that. I'm gonna try and stop it, Riley, I might not manage it. I have a horrible feeling it's too late."

112

THE LAB, 9:45 A.M.

Gwen jumped up, went to see who had arrived. Or left. There was no sign of Mandy. And none of Messenger. She hurried round, checking the offices, the restrooms. Weiss and Barclay had left. Only Atalanta, Curt, and Jihoon Lee remained. They were working at the communal workstation, a long table jammed into one office.

She walked up to them. "Guys, you should leave. Get outta here. This storm's only going to get worse."

Curt shrugged. "Grew up in Tornado Alley. Reckon it can't get as bad as that."

Gwen bit her lip. "Please. Curt, now's not the time. Please, just go. All of you. Drive to Reno."

They laughed. "I don't gamble," said Jihoon.

"Jeez, you work in private equity, you gamble," retorted Gwen. "But that's not the point. What's coming is going to be bad. People will die. I'd rather you grunts didn't."

They shifted and looked uncomfortable at that one. "OK," declared Atalanta. "Soon as you go, we go. How about that?"

Gwen blew out a breath, saw it was all she was going to get. She just had one more thing to do and then she could leave, snag a lift from one of the grunts and get the hell out. "Deal."

She walked back to her office, closed herself and Leo in again. She sat at her desk, feet up, forced her racing mind to slow, to analyze like an academic. She slowed her breathing, found reason.

No sign of Messenger; a huge storm brewing. Could this be what he was waiting for? Could he be trying to make an Ark Storm of it even now? Was it pure coincidence that today, of all days, he hadn't come into the office, he couldn't be contacted?

"I don't fuckin' think so," murmured Gwen.

If an ARk Storm were coming, she would have to act now. The technology could be used to increase rainfall, or to decrease it. Falcon's resources could help avert a disaster, marshaled in the right hands. She opened her desk drawer, took out the card, picked up her phone.

"Sheikh Ali? Gwen Boudain. I need to talk to you."

There was what sounded like an intake of breath, followed by a long pause. Gwen wondered suddenly if the Sheikh had been sincere in giving her his card. Maybe she was breaking some undefined rule of etiquette by calling him.

"Dr. Gwen," came his voice. "How nice to hear from you. It's been a while."

"It has," said Gwen, offering nothing more. This was no time for small talk.

"How can I help?" asked the Sheikh. He sounded slightly less slick than normal, thought Gwen. She must have caught him at a bad time.

"There's stuff I know. About Falcon. About Dr. Messenger. I need to talk to you about it."

Another pause.

"I would be happy to talk to you. Please, allow me to send my helicopter."

"I'd really rather not fly," said Gwen. "If you don't mind. The weather's not exactly conducive to jumping in a helicopter."

That wasn't true, exactly. She knew choppers could fly in high winds. Rescue helicopters routinely flew at big surf competitions, in big winds, ready to spot surfers in distress and help pluck them from the waves. One of the rescue pilots who had bailed her out on a horrendous wipeout at Mavericks had told her that, unlike fixed-wing aircraft, high winds could even help the helicopter to fly as the wind increased the relative speed of the air over the blades giving the chopper more lift while using far less engine power.

"Oh, please don't worry. My pilot is trained to fly in far more hazardous conditions than this," replied Sheikh Ali with the blithe confidence of the super rich.

"Even so. I'd actually like to get out of here and head way inland. I really don't like the look of this storm," continued Gwen. "Can't we just talk on the phone?"

Another pause. Gwen could feel the cool calculations running on the other end of the line.

"Dr. Gwen, I do understand your reticence, rrrreallly," murmured the Sheikh, sounding back to full charm with those wonderful rolling r's.

"But please trust me," he continued in his mellifluous voice. "My pilot can be with you in forty minutes. He'll bring you to me, we'll talk, then he can fly you anywhere you want, well, within reason. He can shortcut you straight to where you want to go, far inland if you really want. . . ."

Gwen glanced out of her window. The trees were bending sideways, small branches were beginning to snap off and fly through the air. She made up her mind.

"Fine. Let's do that. I'll be here waiting."

"Excellent. See you soon, my dear Dr. Gwen."

She said good-bye, hung up.

Her phone rang almost immediately. She checked the number. Dan. She ignored it, walked from her office. There was nothing he could say she wanted to hear.

113

STANFORD UNIVERSITY, 9:50 A.M.

Riley walked up to Hendrix's office, knocked on his door and opened it simultaneously. He was keying instructions, his fingers flying over his keyboard, his face turned to the satellite images on his screen. He glanced at Riley, continued typing. Riley waited, impatience simmering. She counted to ten. On eleven, at boil point, she opened her mouth just as Hendrix turned to her.

"Bridget. Ten minutes on. What's changed?"

Riley blew out a breath. "Everything. Listen up. Don't interrupt." Verbatim, she told him everything Gwen had told her.

Hendrix listened in silence. Halfway through he picked up a pen and twirled it like a baton. His face went from displeasure to disbelief to fury. He pointed the pen at Riley.

"You just don't quit, do you, Bridget? You don't get anywhere with the science so you bring me this fantasy scenario, some whacko science I've never heard of. You have target fixation. You're seeing what you want to see. You're in your manic phase and everything's magnified."

Riley slammed her palms on Hendrix's desk. She angled toward him, voice quivering with rage.

"Don't you dare use that against me you bastard! I'm a damn good scientist and you know it!"

"We all know it," Hendrix retorted. "It's why you're here. The bipolar's why I'm here. To keep you grounded."

A scientific straightjacket, thought Riley. She closed her eyes. Behind her lids she saw the images of her nightmares. The rain falling in torrents, the people and homes washed away, the waves crashing into coastal homes, the landslides drowning everyone and everything in their path in a river of mud. She opened her eyes, blew out a breath. She would not give up.

"You think I made this up?"

"No, I think you consort with whack jobs."

"Yeah, a meteorologist. Just as well qualified as you. And because you've never heard of this science it cannot be real, is that it? Not invented here? Christ, this is all about your ego, not my target fixation. You think I want to see a monster come and eat up California? You're out of your mind."

Hendrix exhaled slowly. His face was several shades redder. His control on his own legendary temper was tenuous.

"No, I do not think you *consciously* want to see ARk 1000 hit us. But maybe subconsciously, from scientific curiosity, you do. Like the pyromaniac firemen who start fires so they get to fight them. You seem to me to be suffering from a kind of scientific Munchausen by proxy syndrome. That and your condition have put you on a hair trigger. We cannot jump at every bump in the night. The state of California is close to bankrupt. You know that. The cost and the disruption of declaring this ARk 1000, both in terms of dollars and potentially of lives, is too big to undertake on your obsession and some lunatic's tale."

Riley found the urge to step forward and strike the man almost unendurable. She knew the only chance she had to convince him was to maintain an icy calm.

"It's not a lunatic's tale," she said, forcing her voice down the register, slowing her words. "I only wish it were. And it's not an obsession, Jon. It's called dedication. Stop hurling my *condition,* as you so squeamishly call it, at me. Everyone's got *something*! Haven't you learned that by now? There *is* no normal. And stop playing the politician here."

"Someone has to!"

"There are *lives* at stake, thousands of lives! You *know* what's at stake if this is ARk 1000."

"Of course I fuckin' know what's at stake!" thundered Hendrix. "We're scientists, or we're supposed to be! We analyze the data, we make the call! We don't have this data! Just the word of someone who thinks another someone is gonna ramp this storm, send up an army of drones, God help us. For fuck's sake!" The genie was out of the bottle; Hendrix's temper was running free.

Still Riley did not give up. Art had sauntered up casually and now stood outside the office, rolling his shoulders, as if waiting for a word.

"Jon, listen. Please," urged Riley. "Knowing what I know, I think we have no choice but to push the button, call this an ARk 1000, get FEMA and CalEMA to issue the evac orders. Jeez, if this thing is ramped up either by these people or by nature itself what're we gonna do? Wait until the rain's so heavy that FEMA orders people to stay in their homes saying driving's a hazard? Just how do you think you are gonna organize the evac of one and half million people?"

Hendrix got to his feet, came round his desk toward Riley. He looked as if he were about to physically eject her. He stopped a foot from her. In her space. His face jutted toward her and his voice was artificially low.

"We cry wolf on this then when the real ARk 1000 comes rocking through no one'll believe us. No one'll go."

"That's what compulsory orders are designed to cover," said Riley, holding her ground despite the urge to step back. "Are you really ready to bet that this one isn't the Biggie? Shouldn't we involve FEMA and CalEMA in those calls?"

"Not on this evidence, Riley. I will not put my name to it," said Hendrix. "Therefore Hazards will not put our name to it. Now go. I have a storm to monitor."

Mechanically placing one foot ahead of the other, moving like a marionette, Riley returned to her office. In her own sanctuary, she gazed out of her window into the gray world beyond, waiting for her breathing to slow. Trees stood. Buildings stood. The odd brave soul ran hunched through the rain, the wind grabbing at their clothes. If the storm hit, she and the Hazards team had a safe underground bunker from which to operate. Windproof, flood proof, earthquake proof. But the rest of California just had normal buildings. The storm would come with deadly intent and it would huff and it would puff and it would blow their homes down, or rather wash them away, and there wasn't a damn thing she could do about it.

114

The Sheikh turned to Ali. Of all his security team, he was closest to Ali. He saw the same fire in the younger man's eyes, the same vision, the same yearning, the same disgust with the West and its incontinent excess, its neo-colonialist trampling over sacred lands. Ali was far more than mere brawn. He had a brain and a heart, and he had spirit. He had the *Hilmun yaruddu bihi jahl aljahil* of his desert-dwelling Bedu ancestors—a commanding forebearance and serenity in the face of ignorance and adversity.

"Life never ceases to surprise me," murmured the Sheikh. "That, as you will have gathered, was Gwen Boudain. She wants to come here! To talk to me."

"Or to kill you?" posed Ali with a delicate raising of one eyebrow.

"Here, on the yacht, with protection all around me?" countered the Sheikh.

"She, and/or Dan Jacobsen, killed four men, one of whom they killed with their bare hands," replied Ali, his voice unnaturally calm.

The Sheikh looked away, not through delicacy or pity. In his eyes there was only calculation. He looked back.

"You go with the pilot to pick her up at Falcon. Frisk her before she gets on the copter."

Ali nodded. He moved to go, paused as the Sheikh laid a hand on his arm.

"Then, when Gwen Boudain has told me whatever she has to tell me, if indeed she does have anything to say and this whole thing is not a ruse to come and attempt to kill me, we will kill her."

Ali thought of his murdered friends.

Sheikh Ali eyed him, read his thoughts.

"You will be avenged, Ali. We will all be avenged in ways we cannot even begin to imagine. Nine-eleven succeeded way beyond all the greatest expectations of Sheikh Osama. They never thought the iron girders would melt. They never thought the towers would collapse. When we unleash ARk Storm there'll be the death toll, but beyond that, who knows? The storm might just be the final blow for the bankrupt state of California. It is after all the eighth biggest economy in the world," he added, as if debating some arcane point at an academic conference. "If it were devastated, it could tip the Great Satan into a depression." He smiled. "And Gwen Boudain and the Zeus model will have helped!" He squeezed Ali's arm. His dark eyes were hard.

"An eye for an eye. The justice of the desert will be ours."

115

SEVENTEEN MILE DRIVE, 9:52 A.M.

Dan slammed his hands on the desk in frustration. Gwen *was* at Falcon. That metallic-voiced woman had said as much. He pulled on his leathers, grabbed his keys, Gwen's pocketbook, and alarmed his house. He still wore his holstered weapons. The danger was in no way over. It was only just beginning, and Gwen had no fuckin' idea.

He exited the back way at a run, scanning his garden for surveillance. The PIR alarms had not gone off, which told him that no one was in the inner perimeter, but he looked anyway; they could be hiding out beyond. He saw no sign but he still ran fast, zigzagging in a crouch.

A branch snapped off and stabbed his face, cutting him below his left eye. He laughed. He had emerged unscathed from the killing spree last night only for a twig to mark him.

He wouldn't use the Cougar, it was too identifiable. The surveillance team, if they had managed to regroup, knew nothing about his bike. He sprinted through the rain, round to his garage, swung it open, uncovered the Ducati. He swung his leg over and started it. It growled back at him, the perfect foil for his mood. He revved the throttle. Roared out, closed and alarmed the garage with his remote control. Motorbikes were prohibited on Seventeen Mile Drive. Too bad. He knew the booth guards, they'd turned a blind eye for him before, would again. And with the storm roaring in, the cops would be preoccupied elsewhere.

The bike screamed along the wet tarmac. The wind slammed into man and bike. Their combined weight and the skill of the rider kept the bike upright. Just.

Fifteen minutes and he'd be there. And he would make Gwen Boudain see sense.

Only it wasn't fifteen minutes. A Monterey pine had been blown across the road. Dan got off his bike and maneuvered it off-road into the forest and back onto the road, adding seven tortuous minutes to his trip. The bike was heavy. In his leathers, Dan sweated; half exertion, half fear for Gwen.

116

THE LAB

Gwen called all her friends, starting with Dwayne and Lucy, gave them the same message: *get the hell away from the coast. Immediately.* Best thing to do was get on a flight, but failing that they could drive to Nevada, hit the casinos for a while.

Dan would know about the storm. In his capacity as a newspaper man, even a fired one, he couldn't not know. And he was a big boy for God's sake. He could take care of himself. All she could do now was wait.

She glanced down at Leo. She couldn't take him with her. She got up, headed to the Grunts' office.

"Atalanta, I'm gonna call in that favor," she said.

Atalanta looked up, big eyes wide and sincere. "Sure. Shoot, honey."

"Leo. Can you take him with you? I've got some stuff to do. . . . I can't take him with me and I can't leave him here."

"Don't sweat it. He can come with me. We'll do the handover if 'n' when."

Gwen bent down, kissed the other woman's cheek. "Thanks, hon."

On her way back to her office, she snagged another coffee, warmed her hands on the mug. She glanced into the gray mayhem outside. Her guts gnawed at her. She got up, paced to the window, peered out, paced back to her chair and sat down. The minutes inched by. Just as her patience was about to shred, she heard above the rough percussion of the wind, the deeper thud of an approaching helicopter. She grabbed Leo and hurried to Atalanta.

"Here he is." She bent down, hugged her dog, straightened up. "Stay!" she said. "Be good for Atalanta."

Leo looked from his mistress to the other woman, who was bending down, petting him, her fingers gripping his collar.

"Go," said Atalanta. "I'll take good care of him. I promise."

Gwen nodded.

"Where you going then?" Curt asked.

"Long story. Another time," replied Gwen. "Now get gone! Time to hightail it, guys."

"OK, OK, we're going," said Kurt.

She eyed the three of them, and then looked at her dog, gazing up at her with worried eyes. "See you around," she said. She felt a sudden pang as the thought leapt into her head that she never would.

She pulled open the glass door. The wind hit her with a punch. The same chopper as last time was waiting for her, rocking slightly. A man stood beyond the orbit of the blades, catching the full force of the rain, seemingly oblivious, just watching her. He was one of the unsmiling men who patrolled the Sheikh's yacht. He ran toward her, leaned in, yelled at her over the twin roars of the helicopter and the wind.

"I need to frisk you."

"To *what*?"

"Pat you down." He mimicked frisking himself.

Gwen shivered in the rain and wind. She raised her arms. "Get on with it then!" she shouted, wondering what the hell was going on.

The man patted her down, thoroughly, his hands urgent and rough. Some unspoken hostility close to rage seemed to pump from him. Gwen swallowed back the urge to bring her knee up into his groin.

Then he was finished. He gestured for the copter and they both ducked down, ran for it.

As soon as they were buckled in, the pilot pulled back the joystick and the chopper lurched up into the sky. Gwen just had time to see a motorbike roaring in, stopping, the helmeted rider gazing up, then the copter twisted in flight and crabbed away toward the ocean.

117

THE LAB, 10:38 A.M.

Straddling his Ducati, feet braced on the soaking earth, Dan gazed up at the sky. He saw the helicopter rise above him and fly off. He couldn't see who was inside. Visibility was bad. He ran to the intercom, buzzed repeatedly.

The door was opened by a beautiful black woman with long braids. She was holding onto Leo. She stood with two men. They all seemed to be leaving.

"Is Gwen here?" asked Dan. "Is she *here*?"

Atalanta eyed him coolly.

"Gone," she said, nodding at the sky. "In the helicopter."

Dan swore. "Any idea where it's headed? Who she's with?"

"You some jealous boyfriend?" quizzed Atalanta.

"If only," said Dan, trying to tamp down his impatience. "Why've you got Leo?" he asked, reaching down to stroke the dog, who wagged his tail in enthusiastic greeting.

" 'Cause Gwen asked."

"So, where's she going?" Dan asked again, "and who with?"

"I know not," replied Atalanta. She turned to the men. "You guys know?" They shook their heads. "She just told us to hightail it out," said Curt. "Didn't say where she was going, said it was a long story, then she upped and left."

Dan thanked them, returned to his bike, analyzing, processing what little he knew.

Perhaps the bug in Messenger's house might reveal something. He hadn't listened in for over twenty-four hours. The wind was roaring and he could scarcely hear outside. He headed off to Roy's Deli in Carmel Valley Village. The roads were almost empty. He angled the Ducati, leaning into the curves, accelerating along the straight stretches. Carmel Valley felt like a ghost town. But the Deli was still open, Dan noted with relief, despite the weather warnings.

A man he guessed to be Roy himself was realigning a wall full of black-and-white photos of local landmarks. He turned as the door chimed.

"What can I get for you?" he asked with a gruff smile.

"Black coffee and a haven for twenty," said Dan with a smile of his own.

"You got both."

Dan took a seat on a red padded banquette at a clean wooden table. He dialed up the device, got it to relay back to him. Earphone in his ear, he listened. Roy brought over his coffee. Dan nodded, sipped distractedly. The device only recorded when there were voices. It took twenty minutes to wade through Messenger's anodyne conversations of the previous evening on the phone, conversations with his three sons in Germany by what little Dan knew of German. Then the recording moved to six fifty that morning.

Dan froze, coffee mug to his lips. He listened, switched off the relay, pocketed his earphones, took out a ten dollar bill. He leapt to his feet, leaving the note on the table.

He ran for the Ducati, calling the cops on his cell as he went.

118

Frank Del Russo stood in the driving rain, frowning at the house. He skirted round it, seeking any means of entry. Metal blinds covered every window. He couldn't see in. He'd already speculatively pushed his shoulder against the doors, front and back.

There was no give on the upper or lower parts of the doors, which indicated to him the presence of multilevel bolts set into the frame. The door was also very well fitted, so that the option to card the five-pin tumbler locks was out. And he didn't fancy his chances trying to wire-pick the lower mortice locks; they looked to him like Chubb 110s, not the ones you want to try if you were in a hurry unless you were a master locksmith. Which he was not.

He'd already noted the PIR lighting surrounding the house. This made it impossible to approach the building at night without a laser defeat attack on the sensors. Then there were the light patches, just very slightly depressed, in the well-kept lawn. They appeared innocuous, but in this context they indicated to him the presence of ground sensors. A very discreet and sophisticated alarm system designed to allow you to walk into the trap well announced. The man had style.

Del Russo hurried back to his car, called Canning at Tyson's Corner.

"He's not there, Chief. Not answering his cell."

"Break in."

"Get me an order."

"Oh for fuck's sake, just get in there. Use your skills!"

"I'm outclassed here, Chief." Quickly he told Canning

about Jacobsen's security. "It'd take me hours to get in and I'm not even sure I could manage it at all."

"Then sit tight. Wait for the guy to come home."

"That's just it. I'm not sure he will. There's a big storm brewing and his place is near enough on the cliff edge. The local radio's telling those on the coast to evac out."

"Jesus! Is this the ARk Storm?"

"They're not saying that, Chief. Just that it's a big storm."

"Stay tuned. Keep me posted."

Across the continent, Canning hung up and said a quick prayer.

119

THE SUPER-YACHT, *ZEPHYR*, 11:35 A.M.

Gwen looked down as the helicopter strained through the air, the engines screaming against the onshore winds. Whitecaps littered the ocean like debris. She could practically taste the brine. In the leaden sky, the cumulonimbus were racing in. They angled forward, the top anvils leading the lower-hanging darker base of the clouds. So many were grouping they looked in danger of forming one massive supercell. That meant thunderstorms. Huge ones.

Gwen suppressed a shudder. She knew from her pilot buddy that the violent conditions in and around thunderstorms could exceed rotorcraft structural limits and bring a helicopter down in seconds. The extreme updrafts and downdrafts could toss you hundreds, if not thousands of feet up or down. The pilot would rightly refuse to fly and she would be stuck on the yacht with Sheikh Ali and an even bigger storm bearing down on them. She had to get in and get out quickly.

Through the gloom she made out the gray hulk of *Zephyr* a quarter of a mile ahead. In the big seas the huge yacht looked like a child's toy. Super wealth, super yacht meant nothing to a big storm.

The helicopter lost altitude, coming down into a hover above the pitching yacht. Gwen could see the pilot casting his eyes back and forth, trying to time the landing. The cords in his neck stood out in stress. Beside her, the other man said nothing. He just looked on with the kind of stoic resilience and stillness of someone who had experienced real fear and survived it.

Sometimes during the half hour flight, Gwen had felt his eyes on her. The scrutiny had felt like more than mere curiosity. She had shrugged it off, evaded his gaze, focused instead on what she was going to say to the Sheikh.

After a few false starts, the pilot brought down the helicopter. It slammed onto the deck, jolting Gwen and the silent man. She watched three men emerge from the yacht and run to the helicopter with what looked like guy ropes, to anchor it.

Once it had been secured, Gwen forced open the door, jumped out, and ran across the deck. The rain fell like sleet, arrowing into her face, soaking her. A door opened as she approached. She felt herself blow in, braced herself on the wall opposite. She let out a breath, laughed, half in alarm, half relief.

The majordomo type she'd seen before gave a slight bow, then led her into the stateroom. The silent man followed behind her.

Sheikh Ali stood with two of his men, one to either side. It almost looked to Gwen as if they were guarding him. They eyed her with hard, unsmiling eyes. Gwen could feel their hostility pumping across the room. Their presence, the frisking, Gwen wondered if they all thought she was going to attack the Sheikh.

She frowned, it didn't make sense. She caught a look of uncertainty in the Sheikh's eyes. He was regarding her with more than his usual intense scrutiny, but then the moment passed and he smiled.

"My dear Dr. Gwen! Thank you so much for coming, for braving what appears to be a growing storm."

Gwen gave him a brief smile. This wasn't a social visit.

The Sheikh beckoned and Gwen approached. Ali Al Baharna held out his hand, shook Gwen's warmly, grasped it with the other and led her to the sofa. His two shadows followed.

"Please, sit. Coffee? Tea? Water?"

"No, thank you," said Gwen. She wanted to get on with it then get the hell off the yacht onto dry land somewhere far away.

"Just a water then," the Sheikh said to the majordomo. He turned back to Gwen.

"Please forgive my insistence. It's a Bedu tradition. It is incumbent upon us to offer refreshment to any and all who come visit. Even our enemies," he added, eyes no longer smiling.

"How inconvenient," replied Gwen. She pursed her lips. This was going to be awkward, but she had no choice.

"Sheikh Ali, please forgive me but I need to talk to you in private."

She kept her eyes on his, but remained peripherally aware of the men who flanked him. A small pulse of energy seemed to go through them. They widened their stance, loosened their limbs, exchanged a look. What the hell did they think she was going to do, she wondered?

The Sheikh paused for a moment. He turned to the majordomo, who had returned with a glass of water.

"Go," he said sharply. The man set down the water and went. The Sheikh dismissed the other two men.

"Ali, wait at the other end of the room will you," he

said, adding something in machine-gun Arabic. The other
man moved away, stood by a door, perhaps forty feet from
them.

"He won't hear us, and his English is imperfect too, so
please," his dark eyes warmed, "do not worry."

Gwen nodded. At that moment, if anyone was worried,
she thought it was the Sheikh. A current of tension seemed
to flow through him. His body was restive, his fingers
made small movements, shifting on his kandoora, smooth-
ing it down, then adjusting his headdress. His glance flickered too, from her to Ali, to the windows behind her.

"OK, you have a problem. A major problem," said
Gwen. As the Sheikh sat forward in the sofa opposite,
Gwen told him all about Gabriel Messenger, about her suspicions that he was Hass/Hans, and about his plans to
attempt to ramp up a big winter storm into an ARk Storm.

The Sheikh listened in perfect silence. Only the arch-
ing of one eyebrow and the shifting fingers betrayed any
reaction. Only the roar of the storm punctuated Gwen's
silences. When she had finished speaking, the Sheikh's
eyes ceased flickering and locked onto her. For the first
time, she felt a flicker of alarm.

120

SEVENTEEN MILE DRIVE, 11:35 A.M.

The Ducati screamed round the corners, wheels kicking
up plumes of spray. In his head, Dan replayed what he had
heard:

Messenger, the note of surprise in his voice. "Good
Morning. What a surprise! What brings you here?"

A male voice. "Need to talk to you about something. You mind?"

"Well, I was just about to have my breakfast, but please, come in."

Silence for a few beats, save the padding of shoes on hardwood floors.

"Sit, please."

"I need the laptop," said the unidentified man. His voice was brusque.

"What?" Messenger had asked, indignation sharpening his German accent.

"The laptop, with the Zeus model," replied the man, almost conversational now. "We only have one. We need the second, the one with the authorization codes. The one you have."

"What are you talking about?" demanded Messenger. "Have you—" His voice trailed off abruptly.

"Let's make this civilized, shall we?" drawled the other man, enjoyment in his voice.

"You point a gun at me and you want to be civilized?" asked Messenger, creditably calmly. "*What* is going on?"

"Long story. Get the laptop. Now. Don't try anything."

Silence, then what sounded like the rattling of a safe's combination, a breezy whirring. Dan could imagine the wheels spinning, then there was a whoosh as the heavy door of a safe was opened.

"Here. One laptop. Now perhaps you could tell me what the hell is going on?"

"Too late for that," came the reply. "You underestimated me. Never *saw* me. Now I'm the *last* thing you'll see." The mocking words were followed by a low pop and a sickening thud—Dan could visualize the scene—the shot from the silenced pistol, almost certainly to the head, instant death as it hit the cerebral cortex, Messenger's body crashing to the floor.

Dan swore. He and Gwen had the wrong guy. Haas/Hans was someone else all together. He suspected Gwen was with him now.

He couldn't ring her, he had her phone. He angled round the bend, his knee almost touching the slick tarmac. He slowed as he saw the ambulance and the cop cars on the road outside Messenger's drive.

He came to a stop, pushed up his visor. Rain lashed into his eyes. He rubbed a leather-gloved hand over his face.

"What's going on in there?" he asked a Patrolman.

"Who the hell are you?"

"Neighbor. I live at number 127." He knew the cop'd ask him that, drew goodwill by offering it up.

"Name?"

"Dan Jacobsen."

Cop wrote it down. "You hear anything?"

"Like what? Storm's kinda loud."

"Gunshot."

He'd heard it all right. He kept his eyes bland.

He shook his head. "Gunshot? No, sorry."

"Move on then. Get outta here. Storm's getting worse. We're getting evac orders coming in for coastal residents. Get in a car if you have one and head inland. And hurry. Shouldn't be on a bike in the drive anyways."

Dan nodded. "Can't use my car." That much was true. He and the patrolman glanced up at movement. A stretcher was being run out of the house, a body lying prone. Messenger. Dan said a quick prayer, slammed down his visor and roared off. The body count was rising.

121

Dan needed to make a phone call, but no one would hear him over the roar of the storm. He headed for the Pebble Beach Club. He wasn't a member, but his grandpa had been and the staff knew him. They were closing up as he arrived, boarding up.

He propped up the Ducati, jumped off, ran to one of the handymen.

"José!" he shouted. "I just need to make a few calls. Can I go in for five?"

"Go. Then get. We all gotta move."

Dan raised his hand, called out a thank you as he ran for the entrance, let himself in. The door closed heavily behind him, sealing out some of the noise. He pulled out his cell, paused for a moment, recalled the number he had never had to use. The line rang. SOCOM, Special Operations Command, based at MacDill Air Force Base. This was the central US command for all Special Forces stateside. The underground secure Operations Center had a dedicated team to deal with non-active personnel and incoming information. They would get SOCOM himself, Dan's old friend Jack Meade, in touch with him.

The phone was picked up at the third ring. An impassive voice said a flat "Hello."

This was a standard security practice so that the caller would have no idea who he has rung until his identity was verified.

"Hello. 4157BQ," replied Dan with equal flatness.

"XT279" replied the other man.

"Swordfish2" responded Dan. There was a pause. Dan could feel the pulse of interest on the other end of the line.

Swordfish2 was the code that indicated information relating to terrorist activity from a currently nonoperational ex-special-ops guy who still held clearance or was at risk of reprisal action. In the world of special ops, Dan had just thrown a big bright flare into the sky.

"I need to speak to SOCOM himself. ASAP."

"Wait out!" came the voice.

Dan hit END. *Cry Havoc, let slip the dogs of war.* He just hoped it wasn't too late.

122

Dan scrolled through his contacts, made another call.

"Dr. Riley, please."

"Dr. Riley's a tad busy at the moment," replied a camp but officious voice. "Can I take a message?"

This wasn't the SEALs, Dan had no chain of command. He issued an order and Mr. Camp would hang up. He blew out a breath.

"Please tell her it's Dan Jacobsen, that she needs to call me *urgently*."

"Yeah, yeah. Everything's urgent today. Storm's urgent."

"It's about the storm I'm calling."

"Yeah, well, I'm her deputy. You can try me."

"It's Dr. Riley I need to speak to. Please get this message to her, like *now*!"

There was a pause for a moment, then the guy seemed to relent. "Okaay. Okay!" Dan heard the scratch of pen on paper. The guy writing down his number.

Dan thanked him, hung up, paced. The wind was smashing into the windows. José would be in any minute, throwing him out, and he couldn't place or take a call in the storm. Neither side would hear a word.

He eyed the wooden furniture, the framed images hanging on the wall, old black-and-white prints of the pristine Big Sur shoreline, of the clubhouse in which he sat, of members raising glasses to celebrate victory. He wondered if the clubhouse would still be here in a day or two.

Five minutes later José blew in. "Mr. Dan, you haveta go. Now! Real sorry but we all gotta leave."

"Just a few more minutes, José. I'm down on my knees here, amigo. I have to wait for a—"

The trilling of his cell interrupted. Dan glanced at the number. Riley!

"Just let me take this. One minute. I promise!"

Jose opened his mouth to say something. Dan took the call.

"Dr. Riley. Thank you. First up, d'you know where Gwen is?"

"She rang me this morning from the Lab. Don't know where she is now. Why?"

"She's disappeared."

"Whaaat?"

"Long story. No time. Dealing with it. Listen up. You won't believe half of what I tell you, but it's all horribly true."

"Art said it had something to do with the storm."

"Everything." Dan gave her the sixty-second version.

"Boudy told me. That's why she rang me. I've told my cohead. He won't listen to me. Says it's science fiction."

"*Shit!* He has to listen."

"You're a journalist, Dan. Pond life to him. Not a source he would ever entertain."

Dan swore under his breath. He hated to use his past as a calling card. Now he had no choice.

"How about if you told him I'm an ex-Navy SEAL. Three tours of duty in Afghanistan."

"Fuck me! Come on in here and tell him yourself Dan."

123

The Sheikh got to his feet. His face was hard-planed, all the muscles tight.

"We have no time to lose. Allow me to take care of this," he intoned, his voice grave as he took Gwen's hand, squeezed it warmly between his. "Thank you for trusting me. For bringing this to me."

"I really didn't know what to do," replied Gwen. "I thought of going to the cops. Then I reckoned if *you* can get control of the laptops, *I* can program the drones to try to reduce the rain, to lessen the storm, maybe stop it tipping over into *the* ARk Storm."

"I'll get my pilot to fly you wherever you want to go now, and I'll send one of my men with him. He can go and try to find Dr. Messenger, get hold of his laptops. Then he can fly them to you."

"Good plan," said Gwen, getting to her feet.

The Sheikh bowed. His eyes were sharp with purpose. He called out to the man at the end of the room, Ali, gave him instructions in his rapid-fire Arabic. Ali approached Gwen. Then the Sheikh turned and walked away.

Gwen watched him go, still troubled.

She turned to Ali.

"I need to go to the can, powder room," she added when he looked mystified. He nodded, grudgingly it seemed. He led Gwen from the stateroom, indicated another door across a corridor. He leaned back against the wall, eyes speculative.

Gwen was opening the door, was almost inside, when she heard the bustle of feet then a snatch of a song. "Losing

My Religion." Being whistled. She froze. A voice called out:

"Hassan! Wait!"

She turned, body shielded by the door, saw Peter Weiss crossing from one room to another at the end of the corridor. He didn't look her way.

Her blood beat in her ears. Hass, Hassan, Peter Weiss. The convert with the Islamic name; the drunk who hated alcohol, who abused it and rebuffed it in shame. The answer hit her like a breaking wave: *Weiss* was the builder of ARk Storm, and Sheikh Ali was the architect.

124

Weiss, carrying a laptop, sauntered into the control room, still whistling. He was followed by the majordomo, bearing a glass of Coke. Sheikh Ali turned slowly, looked at him. Weiss stopped whistling. He took the Coke, nodded his thanks.

The Sheikh turned to The Man, laid his hand on his muscled forearm. The Man looked vaguely queasy, thought the Sheikh. He was not a natural sailor, and the conditions were testing many of those aboard. It seemed to him that only he, the captain, and Hassan were truly immune.

"I would like you to escort Dr. Boudain into the helicopter. Ride with her a while. She loves the sea. Let it make a fitting grave for her. Burial at sea, like Sheikh Osama," he added with a smile. "I see an open door, a gunshot to the head, a little push. Pfff! Game over."

The Man nodded. "Why did she come here?"

"To warn me about Gabriel Messenger. She thinks he wants to start an ARk Storm."

"Messenger?" The Man angled his head in disbelief. "She thinks it's *him*?"

"She appears to. She appears to have no idea what she's walked into."

"So she didn't kill our men?"

"I have to believe that Jacobsen did that."

The Man shook his head in disbelief at their luck.

"It wasn't luck!" observed the Sheikh, reading his mind as he so often did. "It was God's will."

Because he had to, The Man nodded. Only a billionaire zealot would spit in the face of luck.

"Maintain the pretense that you are flying her out of harm's way. That way you can take her by surprise when the time comes."

"I'll do my best." The Man walked from the room, feeling the thrill of incipient action for the second time that day.

He checked his weapon, hidden in the holster inside his loose chinos, concealed under the long leather jacket. He had two spare magazines concealed too. More than enough firepower to do the job. He didn't like killing but sometimes there was no other way. And if he were to live, it was the only way. A life for a life. A fair trade.

The Sheikh turned to his protégé.

"Hassan. Our time has come. Is all ready?"

Hassan, Weiss, glowed in the look the Sheikh bestowed, in the complicity, in the momentousness of their creation. He registered the death sentence he had just heard issued on Gwen Boudain, but felt almost unmoved by it. In war, there were casualties. Jihad demanded them, welcomed them.

"Everything is *perfectly* ready," he replied, eyes fixed on the Sheikh.

"Then get all the drones in the air. Every last one. Make sure the program is set to maximum yield." The Sheikh smiled. "Let us give California the flood of our Holy Quran. Let us give them the ARk Storm of their nightmares."

Hassan smiled. All it took was one click of a button. He set the laptop on the desk, sat before it. He had already wiped the blood off it, but a small smear remained. He ignored it now. He turned to the neighboring desktop, clicked in a command. A four-way split scene shimmered into life: one image showed a tarmac strip on which two runways were marked in yellow paint, another a huge hangar, the third and fourth just showed rain-sluiced sky.

Hassan turned back to his laptop. He glanced up at the Sheikh. "Ready?"

The Sheikh angled his body forward. "Go!"

Hassan's finger hovered over the command. Then he hit ENTER.

His program sent its instructions to the drones, which waited for his command, massed like a private army. Hassan pointed to the desktop. The quarter-screen image showed the massive door of the hangar, designed to look like a grain silo, slowly retracting back into its groove. Then when fully open, the next image showed drone after drone after drone come to life, engines whirring. Obeying the commands sent to the GPS each one carried, they moved slowly from the hangar, accelerated along the landing strip, then rose into the air.

A few didn't make it. Hit by gusts of wind as they prepared to take off, they were hurled to the side and tipped over, but the resources of the Sheikh allowed for redundancy. Forty percent of the drones could crash and still the model would work, still the rain yield would be ramped up, maybe by as much as twenty-five percent.

Fifty drones could cover a massive area, perhaps ten thousand square miles. Up and off they went, aiming for their preordained orbits where in groupings of five they would fly round and round, gaining and losing altitude as programmed. Ramping the storm.

The Sheikh watched the live feed, saw the drones nosing into the turbulent air. His own private army. His jihad.

"Live by the drone, die by the drone," he murmured.

125

Gwen stood in the restroom. She braced her hands against the sink, blew out a long slow breath. She wanted to kill Peter Weiss, to take his head in her hands and snap his neck. Thanks to Dwayne's training, she could do it too.

The scale of Weiss's, *Hassan's*, betrayal was beyond her understanding. But, more than murder and revenge, she wanted escape. She straightened, turned, looked for any kind of weapon. Nothing. *Think! Think!* The toilet paper dispenser, the metal inner tube! She pulled it free, loosened her shirt, stuck it into her waistband. She ducked into the next cubicle, grabbed another one. Rammed into someone's eyes, they could do some damage. All she could do was go along with the charade, pretend she didn't know. Still. Then what? Dive off the yacht, swim for it? The engines would suck her under, chew her up in seconds.

She heard the guard, Ali, rapping on the door, calling her.

She eyed herself briefly in the mirror. She saw fear. And fury. *I'm not ready to die,* she thought. She blew out a breath, cast her mind to the dojo, to Dwayne. To all the dirty fighting tricks she knew. Then she pushed open the door and walked out.

Randy Sieber was waiting for her. Gwen gasped, tried to recover.

"Randy! What a surprise! What are you doing here?"

"Sheikh had a threat issued against him. Needed some security advice," he answered gruffly.

"Well, that explains why I was frisked then," Gwen replied, mind racing, trying to maintain her mask of calm.

"Let's go," said Sieber. "We need to fly you outta here. Outta harm's way."

Gwen smiled. "I'm ready."

The pilot was furious. "Flying in *this*?" he shouted at Sieber. "It's beyond marginal, man," he yelled, his South-African accent strengthening with his fury.

"Sheikh's orders," repeated Sieber. "Let's go."

They buckled up. Sieber sat next to the pilot. Gwen sat in the row behind.

The pilot handed Gwen a set of headphones. She wondered if he knew what was planned for her. She didn't believe for a second that Sieber would fly her to dry land. She got the feeling that the pilot wasn't in on the plan. She could use that.

They lifted off. Straightaway, before they had even gained twenty feet, they were almost slammed back on deck. Gwen could see the pilot muscling the joystick, fighting to get the chopper up again. Maybe the wind would do the Sheikh's bidding. Crash the copter, kill them all. Takeoff and landings were always the most dangerous parts of the flight, but when a storm was raging the risks went up exponentially.

Gwen focused on her breathing: deep, smooth, calm. She wriggled her fingers and toes, imagined strength suffusing every inch of her.

The pilot won the first battle with the wind, got the chopper up, maybe a hundred feet above the waves.

"Where to?" Gwen heard the pilot ask.

"Head toward the shore," replied Sieber. "And don't argue. Just do it!" he yelled, as the pilot started to shout.

The pilot fell silent, set a course, flew with the wind behind him. It felt as if the helicopter were surfing the wind.

"Go higher," Sieber told the pilot.

"I'm not gonna go too high. System's coming in at altitude. Don't want to get caught in all the crap up there."

Senses straining, Gwen sat, waiting, wondering when and how Sieber would make his move. She drifted her fingers up inside her shirt, felt the metal tubes, saw in her mind how she would use them. Below her she could see the swell building. The wind speed was high enough to blow the spume off the waves in trails of white, feathery spindrift.

"Go higher," Sieber said again.

"What don't you underst—" the pilot began to say. He paused abruptly. Gwen leaned forward to see why. Sieber had a pistol out, was pointing it at the pilot.

"What don't *you* understand?" asked Sieber.

Gwen guessed the plan. *Breathe slow, build the oxygen in your blood, slow your pulse, stay calm.*

She felt the chopper rise, felt it hit a buffer of wind, slew suddenly to the right.

"It's too high. We need to come down," shouted the pilot.

"OK. OK. Just a bit, take her down."

The pilot brought them down. He brought them down a lot, unnoticed by Sieber, who was undoing his seat belt, getting up, moving back between the seats to her row.

Here we go, thought Gwen. She felt her pulse begin to race as adrenaline pumped her veins.

"Unbuckle. Get up," Sieber ordered her, pointing his pistol at her. She looked in his eyes, tried to reconcile this man with the one she knew at Falcon, failed. There was no fellow feeling in his glance, just a void. Gwen unbuckled, got up. As Sieber fiddled with the door, glancing between her and it, she edged forward so that she was between

Sieber and the pilot. Holding on to the side, Sieber threw open the door. The chopper lurched again. Christ, they were going to crash at this rate.

"What the fuck are you doing?" yelled the pilot. He slowed their flight, Gwen noticed. Quickly, he had brought the chopper to a near stationary hover. Gwen looked down at the waves, rising, falling, huge. But huge was better than flat. Flat meant concrete. Waves meant a chance of surviving the fall. Even if a small one. She grabbed one of the metal tubes, held it behind her as she grasped the seat back to hold steady.

The chopper was still tilting dizzily. Sieber was off balance. Gwen slammed forward, rammed the metal tube at Sieber's throat. The lurching of the chopper meant she hit his chest. Sieber roared, lashed out at Gwen. She ducked, pivoted, grabbed him from behind, hauled backward. She had the advantage of surprise. He seemed to realize too late what she was doing. He roared out, hauled back, tried to get his arm behind his back, fired off two shots. The pilot screamed in rage or pain—Gwen couldn't tell.

The helicopter listed wildly, losing altitude as it went into a death spin. *Get out, get out.* Still holding Sieber, Gwen jammed her feet against the seat, pushed off into space, arced into a dive, letting go of Sieber. Below her the waves loomed. How high was she? Two hundred feet. Maybe one-fifty. The water'd be like another element, almost a solid. Streamlined, body hard, she arrowed down into the sea.

126

Eight miles away, *Zephyr* pitched violently as a huge wave hit. In the control room, the Sheikh, Ali, and Hassan were watching The Weather Channel. The pitching yacht threw them against one another.

The door flew open and in strode the captain, Blain Shaffer. The South African balanced perfectly on his stocky sea legs, honed by over thirty years working at sea.

Captain Shaffer addressed the Sheikh. "Sir! Sheikh Ali, with the greatest respect, I insist we depart now. This storm is building. We are not invulnerable. If we stay here, I fear we shall be sunk."

The Sheikh turned to him, contempt in his eyes. He despised fear—in himself, in others—but knowledge he respected and he knew his captain was correct.

"Even if we run now at full speed, I am not even sure we can evade the storm. We should have left hours ago," the captain added.

For a second, the Sheikh wanted to snatch the Makarov pistol from Ali's waistband, pull the trigger, end the captain's impudence. Then through the haze, reason prevailed.

"Have more faith, Captain Shaffer. *Zephyr* can outrun this storm." Al Baharna smiled then. "As soon as the helicopter has returned, from what is only a short journey, we leave. Full throttle."

The captain nodded, feeling only partial relief. He did not share the Sheikh's confidence that *Zephyr* could outrun the storm. The winds were accelerating. Storm warnings were being upgraded to severe/extreme by USGS. Their window of escape was narrowing.

The Sheikh watched his captain depart, then he walked to the windows, braced himself against the bulletproof glass, and gazed out at a mayhem of gray.

He took up his encrypted BlackBerry and he called the
ayatollah. When he believed the encryption process was
complete, he spoke.

"Assalam Aleikum. Prepare to watch the wrath of Allah raining down on the Infidel."

127

THREE MILES OUT TO SEA,
NEARLY 12:00 NOON

Gwen hit the water in a bone-screaming collision. She
smashed through the froth of a breaking wave, then plum-
meted into the black. She went so deep she felt her ears
would implode. And she kept going down. She was desperate to stop her descent, could do nothing but go with it.
When at last she began to slow and stop. She jackknifed,
arrowed up, desperate for the breath smashed out of her
by the impact.

She came up to a heaving, desolate world. Fifty feet
away the helicopter, rotors thrashing the waves, slowly
sank. Of the pilot, there was no sign. Rising and falling
with the waves about ten feet from her was Randy Sieber's
body. He lay face up. Eyes unmoving. Gwen looked at him
without pity. He had fought. He had lost. He had got what
he deserved. She turned away. She had another battle to
fight.

What way was home? How far away were they? Which
way to swim? Around her the waves were cresting, breaking
on her. She worked her arms and legs, treading water, staying afloat, just. She was beyond lucky. Nothing broken,
just hideous bruising. She pulled off her boots, struggled
out of her jeans and shirt.

Her watch, her Garmin with its GPS system, was still strapped to her wrist. It was waterproof. But crash proof? It had survived enough surf wipeouts, but nothing like this. Gwen said a small prayer, flicked on the GPS. It worked! The shore was indicated by an arrow. It was three miles away. She'd swum that far before. Easily, but never in seas like this. And not after a slamming fall that had bruised every inch of her and had killed a man. What choice did she have? Stay here with Sieber's body?

Shit! He moved.

"Help me," he called, thrashing suddenly. "My legs . . . they're broken."

Gwen didn't say a word. Just looked at him for a moment, checking there was no pistol in his floundering hands. There wasn't. In water your body could cool twenty-five times as fast as in air. Unable to swim, to move to keep warm, Sieber wouldn't last long before he succumbed to hypothermia. That was if he didn't drown first. Justice for Al Freidland, for Elise Rochberger, and for whoever else Sieber might have killed.

Gwen turned and swam away. Sieber's cries soon faded.

She fought through the water, doing a slow front crawl. She couldn't look back, couldn't stop to check over her shoulder for looming waves that might crash on her. All she could do was swim, and keep swimming.

Her body rose and fell with the waves. Water gushed in from all angles. The air was saturated with water, spume, and spray. The spindrift spooled like shredded white ribbons. It looked pretty, in pictures. It was deadly to swimmers.

Gwen breathed through clenched teeth, careful not to suck in water. When she did, she had to stop, cough, grab at a slice of calm, carry on.

The minutes passed; the waves grew bigger still. Up and down she went, riding the waves, propelled forward, but too often down, underwater. The wind screamed with an almost personal savagery. The rain sluiced down. Fighting to stay afloat, to move forward, Gwen felt her muscles begin to burn. Oxygen, she needed more oxygen. She sucked in more breath, told herself, over and over, *you can do it, you can do it.* She checked her Garmin to ensure she was swimming as straight a line for shore as she could. She had covered one mile. Two to go.

Hope flared. She imagined arriving at the shore. Somewhere near San Luis Obispo, if the currents didn't push her north or south. She tried to see it in her mind, saw herself feeling sand under her feet, saw herself on dry land. The images of the truly enormous waves that would be breaking on the shore, should she even make it that far, she blanked from her mind. Arm over arm, leg kick, leg kick. On she went as the storm built and the sky darkened.

128

THE SUPER-YACHT, *ZEPHYR,* 1:00 P.M.

Sheikh Ali stared through the glass at the thrashing sea. The helicopter wasn't coming back. He had to accept that now. It had been gone for an hour. Gwen Boudain had exacted her last measure of revenge. He was stuck aboard, stranded at the mercy of the storm. *Zephyr*'s top speed was approximately 60 knots, but the storm was coming in faster and on a broader front than they had all thought. He took out his iPad, consulted a map. Then he rang the pilot of his private jet, a Boeing 767, currently in Los Angeles.

"Fly to Tijuana, Mexico. Await me there."

"It's, er, getting kinda rough here, Sheikh Ali. Not sure we'll be allowed to take off," the pilot replied after an awkward pause.

"I don't think you can have heard me," shouted the Sheikh above the roar of the winds. "Be in Tijuana. Contact me when you are in the air."

He didn't wait to hear the pilot's reply, just rang off, Googled the distance. 338 miles. 541 kilometers. At 60 knots, nearly 70 mph, he would get to Tijuana in just under five hours. But *Zephyr* couldn't hit that speed in these seas, so more likely he would be there in five and a half hours. The storm wasn't forecast to hit as hard there and he should be able to take off, fly straight to Saudi, watch the havoc unfold from the safety and the sanctity of the Kingdom.

He buzzed the intercom.

"Captain Shaffer."

The captain bustled in moments later. He planted himself, eyed the Sheikh expectantly.

"We leave now, for Tijuana," dictated the Sheikh.

The captain exhaled with relief.

"The helicopter?" he asked warily.

"They went to shore," answered the Sheikh.

The captain saw the lie, merely nodded. He was paid to ignore lies.

He gave a half salute, turned and hurried back to the foredeck. The storm was roaring in, making even his seasoned crew sick as *Zephyr,* moored like a sitting duck, took the full impact of the waves. He set the coordinates, marked their course on his paper map, as he always did, then he programmed the yacht, fired up the engines, accelerated forward. Running was always better. He just hoped they could run fast enough.

129

Dan arrived at Stanford, parked up the Ducati in the lee of the building, out of the worst gusts of wind. He rang Riley. Her assistant, Art, butch in tight t-shirt and jeans, met him and led him into the underground facility.

He checked his cell. Three missed calls. All from the same number. He rang it. He saw Riley barreling toward him as the call went through. He leaned forward, kissed her cheek, held up a hand, mouthed "wait up!"

His call was answered.

"Dan?"

"Admiral."

"Old friend. What's up?"

Dan felt the flood of memories wash over him. SOCOM. That voice, surprisingly soft; it conjured sand, flies, snow-capped mountains, blood and camaraderie.

Moving out of earshot, talking softly, Dan reported what he knew, omitting to mention the dead bodies. All evidence would be washed away by the storm; always a silver lining, he thought ruefully.

SOCOM, Jack Meade, listened, blew out a breath as Dan finished.

"You're a lightning conductor, Dan. Always were. A magnet for trouble."

"Yeah, and not for babes sadly."

"And a bullshit artist! You'll have a plan. What is it?"

"Plan A, capture the bastards. My guess is that they'll be on this super-yacht my source mentioned. Don't know its name. Owned by Sheikh Ali Al Baharna. Get on board, get the computer, shut down the operation. Plan B, get the Air Force in and shoot down the drones. Shoot the yacht to hell."

"Nice. I'll make some calls."

"Oh, and I might have a favor to ask. I'm here at ARk Storm Central in Stanford. Might have to convince one of the coheads that I'm not a certified lunatic. Think you can do that for me?"

"You're mad as a coon, Dan," laughed the man, adding, "put me onto the bastard right now."

130

Hendrix was bent over his set of terminals, head swiveling like an owl between the monitors. Riley tapped him on the shoulder.

"Hey, Hendrix. Got someone here who has a story for you."

Hendrix swiveled round on his chair.

"Kinda busy now, Riley." Then his eyes tracked up to Dan, standing in his leathers, six foot four of muscle, eyes hard.

"Who the hell are you?" Hendrix asked, going for bluster. And failing. Involuntarily, his body moved back tight against the seat back.

"A messenger," replied Dan, with an amused smile. "I've got someone on the line, wants to speak to you. SOCOM, that's SEAL Command. . . ."

Riley watched as Hendrix took the call. She saw his eyes widen, watched him blink, then eye Dan with extreme circumspection. He said little, just a few *ers* and *yeahs*, then he handed the phone back to Dan.

Dan took the cell, listened, smile still playing on his lips. "Thank you, sir. Will do."

He clicked off the call, pulled out a chair, straddled it, turned to Hendrix.

"Ready to listen, now?"

131

NATIONAL COUNTERTERRORISM CENTER

Andrew Canning's PA, Coop, took the call, buzzed his boss.

"SOCOM on the line, sir. Admiral Jack Meade."

Intrigued, Canning took the call.

"SOCOM."

"Chief."

The men had met, had already undergone the obligatory dog sniff that so often went with their territory.

"You familiar with an individual named Ali Al Baharna?"

Canning sucked in a breath. "We are."

"Information has just come to me that he is planning to ramp up the storm currently hitting California into a major ARk Storm. My source claims he has the technology to do it. Ionizers, sent into the clouds on UAV's. Makes it rain harder. *Much* harder. They're in the air now. In California somewhere. The source, and we concur, recommends we call in the Air Force, shoot down the drones, track and blow up Ali's super-yacht."

Canning stared out of the window. He sat entirely motionless, save the rising and falling of his chest.

"Your source," said Canning. "Dan Jacobsen."

"How the hell you know that?"

"Educated guess, and a long story. In brief . . ."

Canning told Meade what they knew of Jacobsen, and ARk Storm, and the hit squad sent in to kidnap Jacobsen.

Meade swore. "Nice. And you didn't let us know."

"Couldn't. Sorry."

"Well, I'm relieved to say he's alive and well as of five minutes ago."

"Where is he?"

"Why?"

"If it's California, I have a man there. I'd like to hook them up."

"Stanford. Secure ops room."

"Great. Can I call him?"

There was a short silence. "I'll ask him to call you."

Canning smiled. SOCOM protecting his own. He'd expected nothing less.

"Thank you. For everything."

132

STANFORD SECURE OPS ROOM, 1:22 P.M.

Two minutes later, Dan called Chief Canning, told him what he knew.

"I have a man outside your home," Canning responded. "I'll get him to you soonest. Frank Del Russo."

"Fine. Do me a favor, call Jon Hendrix, here's the number," Dan reeled it off. "He's the cohead of Hazards here. He is having some trouble believing the story of the ionizers and the drones. We need him to declare an emergency and he won't because the science wasn't invented here and all that bullshit."

"Let me call Del Russo, then I'll call Hendrix." There

was a smile in Canning's voice. He enjoyed a battle, especially one he would win.

Dan turned to Riley. "Come with me. Say nothing. Just watch."

In two minutes, good to his word, Canning put in the call.

Art answered, called out to his boss.

"Hey, Dr. Hendrix, I've got someone called Andrew Canning here. He's er, he's the Chief of the Counterterrorism Center."

Hendrix jumped to his feet, looked at Art as if the man had lobbed him a grenade. Dan could read the man's mind: *First SOCOM, now this.*

"Put him through," Hendrix said stiffly.

Stifling smiles, Dan and Riley watched as Hendrix listened. They saw him stiffen, then slump.

"Yes, sir. I agree. A credible threat. Yes, I see. New information changes everything. Thank you. I will do that immediately."

He hung up, got up, turned to Riley and Dan. He blew out a breath. "OK, Riley. You win."

133

Riley was not magnanimous in victory.

"Yeah, Counterterrorism Center, Navy SEALs, freaks and whackos, figments of my *condition*!"

"Let's just do this, shall we?" barked Hendrix.

"Let's just," agreed Riley. "Let's try and save a few lives. . . ."

Hendrix studied the satellite images, rebriefing himself. He gathered Art and fourteen other colleagues. He stood beside Riley. Dan sat on the edge of a desk in the background. He was glad for Riley, and for all the people she would save. But he couldn't relax or rejoice with Gwen out there, unaccounted for.

Riley let Hendrix speak, let it be his.

"So here we have it, people. The AR is due to make landfall at around six p.m. Pacific Time Zone, that's somewhat earlier than we anticipated. As we can see it's already raining. We're seeing flooding already. The wind speeds of the incoming storm are high, around 120 kph, not as high as in ARk 1000 but still hurricane force." Hendrix cleared his throat, fought with an imaginary tie. "Er, we have other collateral data suggesting this rain will continue and that from the Total Precipitable Water loads we might expect exceptionally heavy precipitation." Hendrix paused. "And there are other factors which I am not at liberty to share with you that suggest the rain yield will be significantly higher than our models might predict." He paused again, gave a small cough.

"People, I think we have no choice but to declare this an emergency, to call this ARk 1000."

Riley gave an abrupt, heartfelt bow. "I'll ring CalEMA and FEMA, get the word out."

Riley made the call, set the machinery in motion. Her mind turned to the coastal areas, seeing the storm, the atmospheric river as it smashed in at one hundred and twenty k's an hour. The evac orders would go out in minutes. She could only pray it wasn't already too late.

134

She was cold, so cold, never been this cold. Never swum this far in seas and rain like this. She wiped the thoughts from her brain. She had survived three wave hold-downs, she had surfed a forty-foot wave, she had survived a fall from a helicopter. Not going to die now. She'd swum three and a half miles now, the extra half mile a result of the currents pushing her south. She'd made it this far. She thought of her parents, waiting for her, on the wrong side . . . she thought of Dan. Somewhere out there, on dry land. Good to see him again, to be in his arms, held warm and tight. All her training, all her belief, all her stubbornness and her rage for life combined to keep her going, arm over arm, stroke after stroke.

The sky had turned dark. The air around her screamed with sound: the howling of the wind, the crashing of the waves, the slamming of the rain that emptied upon her in a sheet, making it even harder to breathe. Through the maelstrom she saw the waves grow. She could feel them accelerating under her. She knew through the exhaustion what that meant. The seabed was rising, the sea was getting shallower, the waves were being forced up. She was getting closer to shore. She tried to raise herself in the water, to search for the shoreline, but all she could see was the rain sluicing down.

She checked her Garmin. A quarter mile to shore. She could do it! If she survived the waves that would be slamming into the shore, she could do it. No surfboard, no floatation vest, just her, hypothermic and beyond exhaustion. The odds were crap. But she'd never been cowed by odds before, always believed that by sheer act of will you could shift them in your favor.

She swam on. Her skin was blue. Through the unrelieved gray she thought she saw a glimpse of something shiny. She saw it again, moments later. Glass. A window. Buildings on the shore! She felt the surge of hope. She could make it, if she could get through the surf.

She swam on, closer and closer. She saw through the endless monotone, explosions of white. The waves breaking, slamming down on the shore. Thirty feet for sure. Gnarly as hell. She wouldn't surf them on a board, let alone with her body. She'd be slammed to pieces. There had to be another way. So close. She fought down the despair that rose, threatening to engulf her. She peered, left and right, seeking a harbor, a breakwater, anything that might lessen the waves. Something, she saw something. She swam to her right, fighting the waves, which were bunching under her, pushing her closer to shore. If she weren't careful she'd have no choice, she'd be pushed by the waves into the break zone.

It wasn't a harbor, but a breakwater; a long, good sized one. If she could get round to the lee side, the waves would be smaller. She battled the current, the waves pushing her closer to shore on the wrong side. Desperately, she fought, angling round, a hundred meters, then another. The waves so nearly pushed her into their path, into the break zone. She could hear them exploding near the shore, the roar and thud of the sea's artillery. She struggled on, got round the breakwater. The waves *were* smaller. But still a good ten feet. High, marginal by any standards, breaking suicidally close to shore. She would *never* choose to swim these waves, but this was her only chance. Her time and her options were almost up. Her vision was clouding. She could hardly move. Her face, fingers, and feet had long since gone numb. Hypothermia would claim her soon, and exhaustion.

She swam closer to the break zone then she turned, looked back out to sea, tried to spot a pattern in the waves racing in. Too tired, too tired, and the waves were too wild, too ragged. Time to go. She breathed, sucked in more oxygen. Her blood ran faster, she couldn't stop it. The last shot of adrenaline. She kicked, pulled forward, felt the wave lift her up, up, rising, then it curled, fell on her, tumbling her round, pushing her on, and down.

135

Breath! Air! Air! Breathe. She fought up, fought the water, kept shut her mouth, fighting the fatal instinct. Do not breathe, not yet. Only training, and the memory of it, the ruthless drill kept it shut. Then she felt air, of a kind. Wet air, but still air. She opened, breathed, sucked it in before the next wave hit, slamming her down again.

She let it roll her, felt its energy weakening, fought up, breathed again, heard the roar behind her. A big one, she tried to straighten her body, to fly with it. It slammed her down. She felt the shore beneath her. Searing pain as her shoulder slammed into it. The wave rolled over, she pushed up, felt the sand beneath her feet. She ran, pummeling her legs against the shore, racing to beat the next wave. It caught her, smashed her down again. She forced herself up, legs burning, just raw survival, the fumes of it driving her on, then she was out, free of the sea.

The rain and wind whipped her. She was shivering so much she could hardly move. On to the house, to the huge structure before her. Legs shuddering. She struggled to make each step. The commands from her head were only intermittently transmitting to her body. She forced herself on, closed on the house. The wind had done its job. A window was smashed. She stepped in. Cold, so cold. Her whole body was spasming. Phone. She saw a landline. Rang the number her mind gave her.

Her lips wouldn't move. She grabbed them, rubbed them, tried again. "Dan," she managed to say.

"Boudy! Thank God! Where are you? What's happened?"

She tried to speak ". . . choppr . . . ree mi—ou t'sea . . . swam. . . ." The words came out slurred, half formed. She searched on the desk, found headed notepaper, read out the address, the zip code, struggled over the code, repeating it again and again till Dan understood, repeated it back right.

136

ARK STORM OPS ROOM

Dan slammed down the phone. San Luis Obipso! Christ, it would take him forever to get to her. In the ops room TV monitors showed the jams clogging the roads. The scrolling headlines declared that an estimated half a million residents of California were trying to run from the storm. The ARk Storm warning had gone out one and a quarter hours ago. The warnings were apocalyptic, stripped of bureaucratese—basically, *Get the hell out or get washed away.* Dan felt fear coursing through him. Gwen sounded like she was going down. She needed him *now.* And he needed a helicopter. He scrolled through his contacts.

Riley was hovering at his shoulder.

"Was that Boudy?"

"It was and she's in a bad way. I've got to get to her."

He hit DIAL.

"Mack, you bastard. You want a story?"

"Thought I fired you."

"I quit, actually. Consider me a freelance. I'll give you the story of your career if you give me a helicopter. Now."

"What story?"

"The real story behind this ARk Storm. The story of how it is being made, even as we speak."

"Being *made*?"

"No time. Just trust me. And get me the copter."

"Why the *fuck* should I trust you?"

"Because," said Dan through gritted teeth, "if you don't I will come and break your knees tomorrow. Got it?"

The editor laughed. He thought Dan was joking. But he could smell a story, could hear one in the intensity of Jacobsen's voice.

"The chopper's in Monterey, overflying the coast."

"Ring the pilot. Get it to Stanford."

Dan turned to Riley. "Tell me you have a landing pad!"

"We do," she replied, matching his urgency.

"There *is* a landing pad," Dan confirmed, thinking of Afghanistan and what passed for landing pads there. "I'll be waiting."

137

Warmth. Bath. Taps. Hands shaking violently, Gwen struggled with the taps. She got them on, ran the bath. The water that came out of the taps felt cold. Both the hot and the cold faucet felt cold. She knew enough to know she was too chilled to feel the water, might scald herself. Using only her right hand, her left shoulder she knew was dislocated, she turned them off, picked the shower, turned it on, scrolled it to a high heat setting. She stepped in, felt the water gush over her from all angles. One of those high-end showers with multiple heads. She propped herself against the wall. Fifteen minutes and she felt colder than ever. And her shoulder hurt like crazy. She thought she might pass out with the pain. She stepped out, grabbed towels, staggered into a bedroom, ransacked the drawers; a sports nut, a tall man. She pulled on his layers, base thermals, mid-layers, overlayers. She found a ski suit in a closet, mittens, hat. She pulled them all on, shoulder screaming. Food. Tea. Kitchen. One handed, she boiled the kettle, made tea, dumped in the sugar she managed to find, spotted a jar of energy bars, ripped off the wrappers, ate five. In the bathroom cabinet she found Advil. Popped four. Then she got into bed, pulled the duvet over her whole body and passed out.

138

The Boeing CH-47 Chinook flew its precious cargo along the coast to the prearranged site. The evacuation order had cleared the coastal community, making life simpler. The collateral dangers of the weapon meant that no one could be near it when it was fired, but, added to that, the weapon was highly classified. Civilian witnesses were not an option.

The Chinook landed. The three technicians, assisted by three more army engineers, rolled out a trailer, struggling in the wind and rain. They needed line of sight, and by their calculations they should get that in twelve minutes—time enough for them to secure the kit and get the hell out.

They maneuvered the trailer into place, and carefully they unwrapped its cargo: a large object that looked like a TV-shaped lens at the front. It was about two meters long by one meter wide. It was mounted on the front of a similarly shaped box about three meters long. This was in turn mounted on a remote-controlled pan. The engineers worked quickly in the torrential rain, securing the equipment with steel halyards they drilled into the tarmac of the empty road. The technicians consulted their mobile radar screens and identified the yacht *Zephyr,* approaching from the north. They programmed in its coordinates, and the unit tilted like a giant camera.

"Time to go!" called out the commander.

Quickly they all ran back to the Chinook, jumped in, slammed the door, and strapped in. The helicopter lifted off, crabbed up sideways into the throbbing air. In three minutes they were out of harm's way.

One hundred and fifty miles away, in the weapons control center of the warship USS *Comstock*, moored off San Diego, the commands were input and the directional energy weapon was fired. It zeroed in the beam of energy on the yacht *Zephyr*. It blasted it for thirty seconds. Then the beam was switched off and the Chinook flew back to retrieve the delivery system.

139

STANFORD UNIVERSITY, 3:10 P.M.

Twenty-two minutes after he had put in the call, Dan watched the helicopter approach the landing pad. The winds were vicious. The pilot seemed to know what he was doing. He circled once, then came in fast, slamming the copter down. Dan hunched, sprinted toward him, wrenched open the door, and pulled on the safety strap in seconds. The pilot was as keen as he was to get off the ground where gusts could slam them over. *She,* Dan noted, nodded at him, pulled on the joystick, and they soared upward. The wind hit them like a punch and the copter veered sideways. The pilot handled it coolly, adjusting, gaining altitude, face taut but unflinching as if she were dealing with nothing more irksome than Sunday drivers. Dan pulled on his earphones.

"Amelia Holdstone," announced the pilot in an educated British accent. "Must be one hell of a story! Where we off?"

Dan smiled. "San Luis Obispo." He reeled off the zip code, watched Holdstone input it into her GPS.

"Seventy-nine minutes."

Dan nodded, said a silent prayer.

Holdstone flicked him a glance. "You going to tell me the story? Seeing as I'm risking my life flying to the coast." Her voice was droll. The woman was a card.

"You ex-military?" he asked.

"Yup."

"And? What'd you do?"

"Would you understand it?"

"Try me. Navy SEAL."

Holdstone's eyes widened.

"Flew Apaches for the British Army Air Corps."

Dan's eyes widened in turn. "The best of the best."

The pilot smiled.

"Top Gun?" asked Dan, seeing the pride behind the smile.

"As it happens."

Dan felt a surge of relief. They had as good a chance as any of getting to San Luis Obispo, landing and taking off intact. It was marginal, though, and they both knew it.

"I'm going to rescue my girlfriend," said Dan. "I don't

know the details. All I could just about glean is that she fell or was pushed from a helicopter at sea, swam three miles, negotiated the waves, and got into a house. If I'm real lucky, she won't have died of hypothermia in the next seventy-nine minutes."

Holdstone raised her eyebrows. "Wow! Miracle she's still alive. Waves are thirty foot, breaking on the shore." She flicked another glance at Dan.

"And the story?"

Dan gave a grim smile.

Holdstone suddenly flinched. "Holy shiiit!"

"What's up?" asked Dan. Holdstone was staring at her radar monitor. Dan saw what she was looking at. Twelve dots, approaching from behind at high speed. Twenty seconds later, splitting the air, came a series of sonic booms. Dan looked up through the glass roof of the chopper, saw the jets, a half-squadron of F-22 Raptors, scream past. And he smiled: the look of a reaper.

140

THE SUPER-YACHT, *ZEPHYR*, 3:15 P.M.

Unseen from the ground, hundreds of meters up in the sky, the army of drones flew on. "They followed their programmed flight paths, circles at first and then figures of eight, starting each time at a different point of the initial circle so that they could cover all the area inside it, sucking out more rain from the clouds, harvesting the storm. Many had been smashed from the air, but many flew on. They had fuel for another ten hours. They were grouped in teams of five, and in an example of serendipity, or diabolical luck, they roughly spanned the area that the atmospheric river was due to hit.

Peter Weiss, Hassan, monitored their progress, phlegmatic when another of their number was smashed from orbit by the weather. Suddenly all his screens went blank.

"Fuck it!" He fiddled with the controls, finally turning them on and off, trying to reboot. Nothing. The drones had stopped transmitting their positions.

Sheikh Ali frowned at the dark screens.

"What's happening?" he asked.

"Coms're down," replied Hassan. "Satellites obviously are not affected by the weather, but maybe the relay station on the ground's been hit."

"What does it mean for Zeus?" asked the Sheikh.

"Nothing. The coordinates are programmed into the drones. They should keep on flying in their preordained orbits. All it means is we can't monitor them."

The Sheikh shrugged. "We can see their harvest, can we not, on the television screens?" He nodded to the scenes of mayhem unfolding before them. The screens had flickered, gone blank for a minute, but were now flickering back to life.

"We can."

The Sheikh smiled. "They declared an ARk Storm 1000 nearly two hours ago. It worked! Zeus worked." He placed his hand on Hassan's shoulder, kept it there. The weight of it was a blessing, a benediction. Vindication.

Hassan smiled, warmed to his core, magnanimous in victory. "Maybe the storm would have come anyway, made it to ARk Storm without us?"

"You are too modest. We shall never know. It was in God's hands, at the end of the day. But we have our wish, Hassan. We have delivered California the ARk Storm of their nightmares. Or Allah has." He smiled. "And like Noah, we shall escape it."

The Sheikh stopped smiling. He raised his fingers to his temples, frowning. He shook his head as if to clear it of some kind of fugue.

Hassan watched him, puzzled, then he suddenly felt a pain in his head, a kind of searing headache. Worse than any he had felt before, and he had suffered some blinders. He winced, sucked in a breath, wondered insanely if it was his old Nazarene God smiting him for desertion and dereliction, avenging the atrocity that was unfolding, arguably at his hands.

Two minutes later, Captain Shaffer burst in. His façade of control seemed to be slipping. His tie was askew and his face was red.

"A bunch of my systems has been punched out!" he announced, running his fingers under his loosened collar. "No GPS, no radar, no ship to shore. TV's recovered, everything else is dead as Elvis. Engine's working, thank God."

"Something weird happened here too," said Hassan, forcing his words out through the miasma of pain. He tried his iPad, shook his head.

He used the pads of his fingers to massage his temples. It didn't help. The pain just radiated from his skull. He thought he might be sick.

"So captain, are you telling me we are now lost at sea?" asked the Sheikh, pain chiseling his voice.

The captain seemed to swallow back a curse. "No. We are not lost at sea," he replied in a staccato voice, face reddening further. "Fortunately I do not rely exclusively on the electronic tools. I always plot the course on the map. I have our most recent GPS position, as of two minutes ago, plotted. Now we shall sail by dead reckoning."

"Dead reckoning?" queried the Sheikh, his mouth curling down.

"Yes. It's the old school way of doing things; compass, speed, tidal drift, landmarks on the coast. If the skies were clear and it was night I could use celestial navigation. As they are not, I shall have to motor in closer to the coast so I can see landmarks. Visibility's appalling, so I'll need to go in fairly close."

The Sheikh gave way to a full blown juhayman frown. "We need to get out of this as fast as possible, get to Tijuana."

"I am as keen as you are, Sheikh Ali, to escape this storm. But if we wish to arrive at Tijuana, as opposed to getting lost in the middle of the sea or floundering on rocks, we need to move closer to shore and we need to slow down." Shaffer delivered his monologue with his eyes fixed on the Sheikh as if daring his boss to challenge him.

Sheikh Ali glanced at the roof of the control room as if seeking an answer in the sky. Then he looked back at the captain.

"Do what you have to."

The captain nodded, turned, and hurried to the door, anxious to return to his post on the foredeck.

"What caused the burnout anyway, if I can call it that?" asked the Sheikh.

The captain paused, swiveled, shook his head. "Beats me. Never seen anything like it."

Ten miles away, the Chinook was flying with their answer back to its Nellis Air Force Base landing pad.

141

The Squadron of F-22 Raptors scrambled from Nellis Air Force Base in Nevada waited out of range. Only when they got word that the directional energy pulse had gone out, had wiped out any communications between the drones and their controllers, did they go in.

The jets flew on the express orders of the President of the United States. Two Squadrons had been scrambled. Squadron A was armed with AIM-120 AMRAAM air-to-air missiles. The AMRAAMs, commonly known in the Air Force as Slammers, were all-weather, beyond-visual-range guided missiles with a top speed of Mach 4 and a range in excess of thirty miles. The chances of escape from an AMRAAM were minimal.

At close range, the pilot could fire the missile and its own radar tracking system would acquire the target without further input from the pilot. They were known as Fire and Forget. Though none of the pilots operating that day would ever forget their targets. Squadron Alpha was tasked with destroying the drones. Squadron Bravo was tasked with obliterating the yacht *Zephyr*. They had flown out to sea and were busy quartering the ocean in their search for the fugitive yacht.

Squadron B was armed with ship-killing missiles known as Harpoons. Once launched, the Harpoons homed in on their targets with active radar. They could fly low-level, skimming the sea, making them almost undetectable until impact, when the warhead containing 215 pounds of high explosive would explode.

Each Squadron split into hunter packs of two. There were few other aircraft in the sky. Some of Squadron A passed a Helicopter, a Bell, which should have known better than to be out in these conditions, but it wasn't their call. Their mission was to find the drones.

Along the coastal valleys of California, those still stuck in their cars, or stubbornly cowering in their homes, heard above the roar of the storm the scream of jets and the sonic boom as the sound barrier was broken. Glass windows shattered, shards flew into walls, into flesh. The Raptors flew on. The pilots found the drones on radar. The Slammers acquired their targets. The pilots fired. One by one, in a streak of fire, the drones were blasted from the sky.

142

A voice, hands, a face. Gwen struggled to focus. "Dan!" She smiled. "You came."

He smiled back. "I came. Now we're going on a trip." He pulled her to him.

She yelped. "Shoulder. Dislocated."

He nodded. "Want me to put it back in?"

"If you pour half a bottle of whisky down my throat."

Dan smiled. "That would be good for hypothermia."

"Done it before?"

"Several times. And I am a trained paramedic, for what it's worth."

Gwen gave a wan smiled. "Do it."

Dan pulled off the ski jacket, then he braced himself against Gwen.

"You ready?"

"Yeah." She gritted her teeth, clenched her right fist, let out a scream as Dan yanked the joint down, pushed it back in.

Gwen felt a wave of nausea, fought it down as the blood pulsed through to the wound like fire.

Dan helped her back into the ski jacket.

"Time to go, Boudy."

"Where?"

"Out of the path of this storm. It's officially ARk Storm 1000, Boudy. Hazards called it! Due to make landfall in ninety minutes, they reckon."

"Shiiiit," murmured Gwen.

Dan carried her to the helicopter. He could see Holdstone struggling to keep the skids on the ground. He crouched, ran, with one hand opened the door, got Gwen inside, jumped in.

Gwen staggered into a seat, strapped herself in, the pain screaming through her shoulder.

Dan strapped himself in. Holdstone pulled on the joystick and the copter soared. It was hit by gusts, by the wind roaring in from the sea. It lurched groundward. Holdstone muscled it back up. Dan could see the stress now. The veins in Holdstone's temple were standing out. She eased the copter higher, above the battered tree line, up and into the full force of the winds. It lurched again as the winds pushed it faster, and then it seemed almost to surf on the winds, accelerating, racing away from the coast. Dan could only hope they would outrun the incoming ARk Storm. If it hit them, it would drown the chopper like a paper plane.

143

156 MILES FROM THE MEXICAN BORDER,
4:30 P.M.

Bravo Squadron of F-22s tracked the yacht. They stayed out of sight. They didn't have to worry about the yacht's radar. They had been informed that the radar and the GPS had been disabled. If the captain was any good, he would have kept a written log and would be plotting their course the old-fashioned way, with a map and a sextant to sight from landmarks on shore, but many captains, especially the younger ones, had neglected that skill.

The Secretary of the Air Force, SECAF, rang Canning.

"We have the target on radar."

"Good job. What does POTUS say?"

"On my way to discuss that now. The Storm of the Century's heading in and we'd like to do the dirty and get the hell out."

"Let me call POTUS, see if I can expedite," replied Canning, putting in the call.

Canning was put through immediately.

"Sir, I would like to know when you will give SECAF permission to take out the yacht *Zephyr*. This ARk Storm is coming in fast and hard, and he wants to do the deed and be gone. If it's all the same to you."

The president frowned at the phone. "It's not all the same to me. We're talking about the yacht *Zephyr* with a crew of thirty. We're talking about the yacht *Zephyr* owned by a very rich and prominent Saudi. A major strategic ally."

"All of that, sir. All of that," replied Canning, a shot of acid stabbing his guts. "And he's a Shia Saudi, sir, not a Sunni. I think you'll find there's quite a difference in how the death of one would be met to the death of the other."

"Don't lecture me on Middle-Eastern sectarianism, Canning. I'm well aware of the subtleties."

"And so where does that leave us, sir?" Canning persisted. "And the squadron. With the ARk Storm bearing down on them."

"I'll ring you back," declared the president. He hung up and made a call to Saudi Arabia. He mentioned the name, heard the slow machinations, the thought process. The man he spoke to was a Sunni. He made the decision expected by the president.

"We in the Kingdom wish to eliminate extremism wherever we find it," said the man. "Do what you must. You have our support, though of course we shall have to make a bit of a fuss. In public."

"Understood. Thank you."

The president ended the call. He rang Canning.

"Hold off!" he ordered. "For the time being. *Zephyr* might sink. I've had briefings from SECNAV, from the Hazards people. Like you say, the storm's a bitch. Save us from having to shoot a yacht with multi-jurisdictional citizens out of the water."

At the price of the F-22s and their pilots, wondered Canning? "But we have a window," he replied, struggling to keep his voice as bland as the president's. "Sir. We'll have to decide soon before *Zephyr* gets close to the Mexican border."

"And we shall. But I live in hope that fate will intervene," replied the president. "We have three hours, I believe."

"Three hours at the current average speed of the yacht. But the further she runs from the storm, the faster she can go, so we have to assume we have less time. Perhaps two hours thirty or less."

"Perhaps . . . But my point remains. . . . That's the difference between us, General Canning. You get to play War. I get to play Politics. And War. The latter only if I have to."

144

4:35 P.M.

The Bell helicopter fought its way through the storm. Holdstone didn't speak. Gwen could see the pilot was fully focused. Gwen recognized her skill, the single-mindedness that meant, most likely, they wouldn't die today. It would be ironic, she thought, to survive her battle with Sieber and the sea only to die in a crash.

Her shoulder hurt like hell, but slowly the warmth was returning to her body. She still felt beyond weak. It was all she could do to sit upright in her seat.

"How you doing?" Dan's voice came through Gwen's headphones.

"Warming up. And before you ask, I do not want to go to a hospital."

"That's where you should be. You need an intravenous. You're in shock."

Gwen shook her head violently, swore volubly as the motion wracked up the pain in her shoulder.

"I'm not in shock. Not now. I want to go to the ARk Ops Room," she added. "We'll be safe there and we can watch it all."

"We don't have many options. I'm getting warnings," said Holdstone. "*Get out of the air.* This ARk Storm is right on our tail. The atmospheric river is scheduled to make landfall in approximately eighty minutes, and it's steaming in at one hundred and twenty k's per hour. We've got to get down and we've got to hole up somewhere safe once we do."

"Stanford," declared Gwen. "Their secure Ops Room. If that works for you?"

Holdstone nodded. "That works. Don't fancy my chances on the street."

Gwen nodded then abruptly fell asleep. Dan watched over her, twisting in his seat, noting the rhythmic rise and fall of her chest under the metal foil blanket he'd dug out from the chopper's emergency supplies. Holdstone ran a good ship.

Gwen slept through the entire flight, exhaustion trumping terror. She awoke just as they were descending to Stanford. It was 5:50.

"The ARk Storm is due to make landfall any minute now," said Holdstone. "We're two miles inshore. I have two minutes to get us down, then we're going to have to run like hell."

Gwen nodded. Dan looked around. The trees were

blown double, like old men hunkering down from the storm. Branches were scything through the air. He'd been on enough helicopter sorties to know this landing would be at the far end of marginal.

He watched Holdstone, saw her eyes flicker over the controls, then out to the weather, tangible as an enemy force. It wasn't just the speed of the wind, though that was problematic. It was the gusts slamming in from the ocean; unpredictable, deadly. Add to that, the poor visibility. Darkness was falling early, and the sheet rain was an almost impenetrable gray veil.

They were coming down fast. Dan saw the landing spot rushing up toward them. If Holdstone got it wrong, one gust would slam them down and the last thing they would know would be the ball of flame on impact. A gust came then, hit them, knocked them sideways forty feet. Holdstone gripped the joystick with both hands, yanked it right and down. With a crunch they landed. Holdstone kept the chopper going, kept the downward thrust on high.

"Get out!" she yelled. "Get out and run. I'll follow."

Dan knew what that might mean. He squeezed Holdstone's arm, nodded, unstrapped himself. Gwen was already unstrapped and moving out of her seat. Dan muscled open the door, held it firm against the winds trying to slam it back in his face. He jumped out, crouched against the door, keeping it open for Gwen. She bent over, ran past. Dan let the door slam. He ran beyond the thrashing rotors, kept running, turned and saw the copter picked up by a gust, then slam down again. Then the scream of the blades slowed. The door opened, and the crouching figure of Holdstone appeared. She ran hard after them. The door was five meters away. Dan got to it, wrestled it open. Gwen staggered up and through. Holdstone sprinted closer. When she was ten meters away, a gust lifted the chopper straight into the air and propelled it toward them. Holdstone didn't look back, just barreled toward Dan and the open door. He reached out a hand, grabbed her, yanked her in, slammed the door, sprinted for the stairs down to the underground rooms.

145

5:58 P.M., PACIFIC TIME ZONE

The atmospheric river made landfall at 5:58 P.M. in the state of California. It traveled at one hundred and twenty kph. It was one hundred and thirty-five miles wide. It stretched from Watsonville to San Luis Obispo. The storm doors on this river were open. Rain poured down. No monsoon could compete with this. National Weather Service webcams showed what looked like walls of water slamming through the air, smashing away all in their path, masonry and steel, making of them weapons of destruction. The rain fell onto the slopes of the coastal range, then flooded back down in torrents. The rain of the forerunning winter storm had fallen for over twenty-two hours before the ARk Storm hit, bringing with it rain of an entirely different magnitude. Like a blizzard compared to snow flurries. The ground in the Salinas Valley was becoming water-logged, could not absorb all the water, so the flooding began. In the Sierra Nevada, the snow began to fall in a blizzard so dense that all visibility was wiped out. Low-lying real estate lining the coast was deluged by waves.

The sound made by the storm was diabolical. The screeching, hurricane-force winds, the hammering rain. Both called up a chorus of car alarms and human screams.

Wind and rain threatened to smash their way into homes and make off with live bodies. In many cases, they did. Roofs were blown off, sheet rain scoured homes. Pets drowned. Humans drowned. Livestock drowned. And this was just the beginning. The streets ran with water. Storm drains overflowed. The air was rich with the smell of soaked foliage and ozone. The rain and the winds, gusting up to one hundred and fifty-six kph in places, equivalent to Hurricane Force Two, ripped off roofs, uprooted trees, swept them down streets like rough-hewn boats seeking the ocean.

The roads were full of traffic. Many had not believed in the severity of the coming storm. Now they sat in their cars, blinded by rain, trapped. Those stuck near rivers would be washed away when the banks broke. And they called it an Act of God.

146

STANFORD, ARK STORM OPS ROOM, 6:00 P.M.

The Ops Room was a mass of bodies, some bent over monitors, others on the phone, others dashing between terminals. Dan, Gwen, and Holdstone erupted into their midst, causing temporary paralysis.

Hendrix glared at them with disbelief. "Join the party, why don'tcha?"

Dan subsumed the urge to slam a fist into the man's face. Riley ran up.

"Boudy! You're blue."

"Should have seen her ninety minutes ago," murmured Dan. "I need a sofa, pillows, blankets, and intravenous hot, sweet tea. And some heavy-duty anti-inflams."

Art, hovering in the background, spoke up; "Hey, Boudy. I'm on it. You with the muscles, follow me."

Gwen slipped into an empty seat and smiled as Dan hurried off. He and Art returned a few minutes later carting a sofa covered with pillows and duvets. They placed it in an alcove at the back of the room.

Dan escorted Gwen to it, draped her with duvets while Art returned with the first of what would be an endless stream of sugary, milky teas.

Gwen lay back, still wearing her ski suit, and sipped the tea. Riley doled out two prescription-only anti-inflammatories she kept in her cupboard, the legacy of a broken toe. Then she raced back to check her screens and the feed from the webcams dotted around California. She had gone beyond manic and scurried back and forth, her heels replaced by running shoes.

Holdstone sat cross-legged on the floor beside Gwen's sofa, refusing all Gwen's offers to take a seat beside her. "I'm fine here," she said. She pulled out her cell, tried and failed to make a call. The networks were overwhelmed.

Above ground, FEMA and CalEMA orchestrated the evacuation. Those on the coast had fled, or been helped to flee in scores of army transport trucks. Those living in the line of mudslides were the next priority. Transporters took them north or south depending on which edge of the storm was closest. Over two hundred and fifty thousand people were mobilized already. More would follow in the days to come.

The atmospheric river just kept on coming; one thousand kilometers long, banked up with more than enough water to feed forty Mississippis, it wasn't going to run out of ammunition anytime soon. Ominously for the state of California, once it approached the Sierra Nevada, it began to slow and stall.

The Sacramento, Colorado, and San Joaquin rivers were

rising relentlessly. Many stretches of the Southern California coastline were already suffering erosion as ten-foot waves gouged away at cliff and dune.

Frank Del Russo watched the live feeds, biding his time. His attention flickered between the disaster unfolding on the screens to the players who, in their own way, had stood like a doomed Canute trying to hold back the waves, or in this case, the flood. He felt a tad queasy at the thought of the flood. The building he now found himself in was supposedly hurricane, flood, and earthquake proof, but they'd said the *Titanic* was unsinkable. On the screens before him, man's hubris was playing out loud and clear as nature toyed with man and his creations with an unparalleled brutality.

Del Russo noticed the two women, one half dead, clearly in severe pain, the other pulsing with vitality. When he saw the man who had to be Dan Jacobsen blow out a breath, saw his shoulders drop about five inches, he approached.

"Jacobsen?" he asked, extending his hand. "Frank Del Russo. CTC. Have a bit of catching up to do."

Dan shook the man's hand, gave him a smile, half grim, half amused.

As the two men, nearly matched in height, bowed their heads and spoke softly, Hendrix bustled about, trying and failing to eavesdrop. He wore his complaints on his face. "Getting a tad crowded in here!" he would shout every ten minutes as he passed Gwen's sofa or the bulk of Dan and Del Russo, deep in conversation. They ignored him utterly, only adding to his bubbling fury. Beneath her manic movement, Riley was strangely calm: the general in the heat of battle, utterly focused.

Dan finished briefing Del Russo.

"Need a landline," said Del Russo to Art. "If I may."

"Office back there. Private too," said Art, leading Del Russo.

Dan waited until the CTC man had made his call, then he walked into the office and nodded at the phone.

Del Russo vacated the seat and the phone.

"Mind if I listen in?" he asked.

Dan shrugged. He rang Meade.

"Admiral, what's up?"

"Down," came the answer. "Every last one of the 'squitos."

"Great. The yacht?"

"Still going."

"What the—?"

"My thoughts. Politics. Wait out."

"He'll be close to the border by now. Must be. My guess is he'll have a jet ready and waiting to fly out from there."

"We're checking on the jets."

"Mexicans won't cooperate in time. There's no choice but to shoot that yacht out of the sea."

Del Russo smiled. Jacobsen was everything he'd heard about, and more.

Dan asked Meade to keep him posted, then hung up.

Gwen had materialized silently in the doorway. She held onto the doorjamb.

"Will they do that, really? Shoot a yacht from the sea in US waters?" she asked.

Del Russo eyed her in alarm.

Dan turned to him. "She was the one who got the first intel on this. She knows everything," he said. "Risked her life many times over."

Del Russo gave a brief nod, but looked deeply uncomfortable. As a serving member of the intel community, he was restricted in a way that Jacobsen wasn't, but he could hardly silence the man.

Dan turned to Gwen. "I think they will. I hope they will."

"If I could get to the Zeus model, I could reverse the program, get the ionizers on the drones to reduce the rainfall," said Gwen.

"The drones are no more," said Dan. "And there's no time to get anything off the yacht."

He looked beyond the room, his eyes seeing the F-22s, hoping that even now they were closing in on Al Baharna and his super-yacht, the ship-killing Harpoons primed and ready.

147

THIRTY-TWO KMS FROM THE MEXICAN BORDER, 7:00 P.M.

Five miles off the coast, approaching San Diego, the super-yacht *Zephyr* was outrunning the storm. In his cabin, Sheikh Ali watched the devastation play out on his TV screen. He watched cars being washed down streets. He watched houses collapse and sail away in the deluge. He saw desperate people, standing through the sunroofs of cars, holding their children aloft as the flood waters swirled around them. He felt the surge of righteousness. The rain would wash away his old sins, purge him, as it purged the land of the infidel and his possessions. In twenty minutes he would be across the border, in Mexican seas.

148

Squadron B, low on fuel, had been replaced by Squadron C. The new contingent of F-22 pilots watched the clear and distinct thermal image of the yacht *Zephyr* powering toward the Mexican border.

The squadron leader communicated with his commander.

"Target is approximately twenty minutes from entering Mexican waters, sir. Requesting guidance."

"Wait out." The commander rang SECAF, who in turn rang CTC's Andrew Canning, who, guts doing a tango, rang the president, who took the call on speakerphone.

"Sir, we have approximately fifteen minutes left. Target is very much afloat. In my opinion, we need to take action," declared Canning as tactfully as he could manage.

The president turned to his secretary of defense. The man nodded. He turned to the head of the CIA. The man smiled.

"I'll ring SECAF to give the command to fire," intoned the president. He hung up, made the call.

"Here's your order," he told SECAF. "Permission to fire is granted. Destroy and sink the yacht *Zephyr* before she gets near Mexican waters."

The squadron leader got the message twenty seconds later. He passed it on to his second-in-command.

The two pilots primed their Harpoons, two each, and let them fly.

Ali Al Baharna, gazing out of the bulletproof window of his stateroom, saw the darkness pierced by streaks of gray. Coming right at him.

He just had time to intone "Allahu Akbar," then the world turned white.

The yacht took four direct hits. The Harpoons with their combined payload of 860 pounds of high explosive DESTEX blew it apart. Flames billowed into the night.

The F-22s overflew, checking their handiwork. What little was left of *Zephyr* sank in less than a minute. Ali Al Baharna and the whole ship's crew were buried at sea.

149

NATIONAL COUNTERTERRORISM CENTER, TYSON'S CORNER

Canning's phone rang. He picked up the handset, listened intently, said three words: "Good. Thank you."

He hung up, turned to Peters, Furlong, and Southward. In the Eastern Time Zone, it was late, past 10:00 P.M., but none of them were tired. They were fired up on adrenaline, bolstered by caffeine. Paper cups littered the table, along with the remains of a sandwich dinner and an empty tube of Tums. Canning's dyspepsia had gone nuclear, but at that moment he didn't care. Southward sat upright, spine scarcely touching her chair back. Furlong slouched, thin legs stretched out under the table. Peters lounged against the bombproof glass window, gazing into the darkness, conjuring images of his own. He wheeled round as Canning began to speak.

"Ali Al Baharna is no more. The yacht *Zephyr* will be reported as *lost at sea*. A casualty of the storm."

"Live by the storm, die by the storm," mused Peters. He took a seat at the table, eyed his boss keenly. Was this a victory, or a failure? Canning's eyes were cold, revealing nothing.

Canning nodded. "I wonder if Al Baharna really did create the ARk Storm, or whether it would be happening anyway?" he asked.

"Who can know," replied Southward. "What matters was his intention. He *wanted* to create it. And hell, maybe he really did. We won't know the death tolls for days, for weeks if it keeps raining. What we do know is that he has more than enough blood on his hands to justify killing him and the rest of the Jihadis he had on board."

Peters glanced across at Southward. He'd wondered if she would shed a tear, go all queasy, but her hand as she lifted her coffee cup to her lips was rock steady and in her eyes was the glow of triumph.

He reached out his hand, shook hers.

"Your trail," he said. "Good job!"

She smiled.

"In at the beginning, in at the end," intoned Canning, giving Southward the ghost of a smile.

Oddly, it was only Chris Furlong who wondered who else had been on board, who might not have been a Jihadi, but he said nothing, just sat in the still office, hands folded in his lap.

Canning picked up the phone again, rang the number at ARk Storm Ops. Del Russo took the call, listened hard, smiled. He hung up, walked over to Dan, Gwen, and Holdstone.

"Went down," was all he said.

150

While the storm raged on through the night in California, in Manhattan it dawned calm and clear. Ronnie Glass took a spinning class at Equinox, snagged a coffee and bagel, then made his way to his office. He got there a comfortable half hour before the bell rang on the NYSE and trading got underway.

He clicked on his Bloomberg Terminals, scrolled straight to the three California casualty insurers. He smiled. At the opening bell they were already down an average four percent. His Aunt Mandy had rung him last night, 2:00 A.M. his time, raving about the storm.

"Hey, Ronnie!" she'd screamed. "ARk Storm! They called it, officially, at 1:30 yesterday afternoon. It's the real deal. I got me the hell outta there. I'm in Reno on the slots."

Ronnie smiled at the memory. His aunt was a prime-time pain in the ass, but she was useful; as to the true extent of her value, time would tell. If Mandy were right, the storm would go on and on, causing billions of dollars' worth of damage. They'd make out like bandits. He felt the stirring; making money always made him horny. He might just treat himself, some more art, some fresh sex, not in that order.

He scrolled on ArtScene, checking the exhibitions, running quick calculations, scenario-planning on different budgets. Next, he scrolled to the news. Storm warnings flashing red. Hundreds already dead in California. Potentially thousands of deaths feared. The trend was right. All he needed to do now was sit back and watch the devastation.

151

Ange Wilkie checked her reflection in the mirrored elevator. Agent chic, she liked to think of it. The sleek trouser suit, part wool, part lycra, body-conscious and fluid enough to let her wrestle, to let her run if she needed to; the MBT shoes. She wouldn't need to run, though, she reckoned.

She turned to Rac Rodgers. "You ready?"

"Oh *yeah*!"

"Let's goooo!"

She loved the looks of naked curiosity, the rows of swiveling heads, the halted conversations as they strode across the floor accompanied by two of the bank's security men: the human equivalent of a siren and a flashing blue light. The security guys thrummed with excitement despite their poker faces. Ange could feel it. Schadenfreude met the thirst for justice. Who didn't love to see the bad guy go down, especially when that bad guy earned near on a hundred times what you did? Plus, it enlivened their day, broke the monotony. They were keener than keen to help.

Ronald Glass was in his office, Master of the Universe, leaning back in his padded leather chair, feet draped on his desk. He eyed them narrowly as they approached, scowling first, then the scowl faded and the first flicker of fear showed. As Ange had known he would, he pushed it down, turned on the outrage as she and Rac walked into his office, bypassing Romula. Failing to knock, failing to wait.

Glass got his feet off his desk, jumped up. "Who the fuck are you?" he demanded, eyes flicking to the security men standing sentry outside his door.

"Just call us Nemesis, Ronnie," declared Ange, blocking his exit, hands on hips, smiling.

She read him his rights, the smile never leaving her face. Glass cursed her out.

"What the fuck are you doing? What's this about? You cannot storm in here and arrest an innocent man, you *fuckers*! I've done nothing! You've got *nothing* on me!"

Ange held up her hand, stopping the traffic of his words.

"Oh, Ronnie, or should I call you *Stud,* that is where you are so, so wrong."

She nodded to Rac. "Cuff him."

If he'd played nice, no swearing, no outrage, she would have spared him the cuffs, the walk of shame as they escorted him across the floor, the long way to the elevators. But as she had predicted, Ronnie Glass had not played nice.

She winked at Rac as the elevator doors closed, shutting out the crowds who gathered with the speed of hyenas at a kill. *Job done.*

A simultaneous operation in Reno resulted in the arrest of Mandy Hoopman. Within the hour, she was offering up Ronnie Glass on a plate.

152

In Singapore, it was the next day, 1:00 A.M. Marcel Caravaggio was entwined with his mistress, Jeannette. He had taken her out for a celebratory dinner. So far he had made over one point three million dollars on his California real estate casualty company puts and he expected the trade to move further in his favor. Only then would he exercise the puts and realize his profits. Last he heard, it was raining still, raining down catastrophe. The news reporters had been almost trembling with excitement: rainfall measured in feet not inches, landslides, floods, horror, disaster. All great for the share price. For deflating the share price.

It took some time for the ringing of the bell to register. When Marcel did awaken fully, he was furious. He pulled on his silk robe, checked the peephole, saw two uniformed policemen and a man with an immaculate turban standing at the door.

"Open up Mr. Caravaggio," said the man. "I heard your feet slapping on the marble. I hear your breathing."

Marcel was taken into custody that night. He was charged with complicity in a terrorist act. No bail allowed. His accounts were frozen. He lived on three meager meals a day in Changi Prison. Jeannette, ever astute, moved on.

153

IT TOOK JUST OVER FOUR WEEKS FOR
THE RAIN TO STOP.

Gwen's dislocated shoulder was recovering. Not as quickly as she wanted. Dan maintained that she was a lousy patient. Gwen found she needed help with the most basic of functions. Getting dressed and undressed one-handed was infuriatingly difficult. Dan was happy to help.

They rode out the storm in a cottage in Nevada, on the edge of the desert, dry of rain, big of sky, far from the horror. Atalanta visited after five days, bringing with her an ecstatic Leo. She and Jihoon and Curt had managed to

evade the storm, driving for Reno as soon as Gwen had
flown off in the helicopter. They were sharing a condo
there until they all decided on their next move.

Gwen went walking into the desert every day for hours,
sometimes with just her dog for company, other times Dan
came too. He judged her moods closely. She was judging
herself, he knew, for many things. For Messenger's death,
for not alerting the Hazards team earlier.

Hurricane Point House was washed away by the ARk
Storm. Gwen had already commissioned an architect, had
long meetings with him, Dan sitting in, discussing the new
build. The commission was for two houses: hers and
Marilyn's. Miraculously, Dan's house had withstood the
storm, suffering only minor flood damage.

It took a further eight weeks for the floodwaters to
abate, for the water system to be purified. Only then did
they return to California. Gwen moved in with Dan—
temporarily, she maintained.

One week after they had moved back, Gwen was making coffee, gazing out of the window at Leo chasing a
jackrabbit on the lawn against a backdrop of a mockingly
calm sea, when she received a call that made her eyes
open wide. She hung up, slugged back her coffee like a
shot, hunted down Dan, and told him about the call. He
was on his knees, painting the wainscoting, paint-smeared
from his redecoration efforts. Streaks of white lit his
tousled hair.

He stuck his brush in the bottle of turps, sat back.

"Well, I'll be!" He rose to his feet. "You wanna go
now?"

Gwen smiled. "I wanna go now."

Half an hour later, they pulled into the parking lot. Five
minutes later, they were in the room.

Gwen hid her shock behind her smile.

"I know you hate hospitals," murmured the patient, smiling back. "It's good of you to come in."

Gwen nodded. She looked around at the white-painted walls, stark and unrelieved, tried to ignore the Clorox-tainted smell, flicked her gaze from the bunch of yellow roses tumbling from an elegantly plain glass vase to the man in the bed. He was pale, shaven-headed, the skin drawn tight over his skull. He looked like what he was: a survivor. He had that glint of triumph in eyes buffeted by shock.

"Look, I want to get this out of the way right up," said Gwen, fidgeting with her jade ring.

The man leaned back on his stuffed white pillows. The remnants of his smile played on his lips.

"I got you wrong. I made a horrible misjudgment."

The man nodded. "You thought I was a murderous megalomaniac. . . ." He shrugged. "People make mistakes . . ."

Dan made a strangled sound. He brushed his hand across his mouth, desperately trying to hold in his laughter. Gwen glared at him, then turned back to the man in the bed.

"Yes, in short. And as a result, you were nearly killed. It is, I know, a miracle you are here. I am truly sorry, Dr. Messenger."

The man nodded again. "The miracle is largely thanks to your friend here, who I understand rang the cops. When they came I was near dead. Another five minutes and the docs say I would have been. I spent three weeks in a coma." He paused and his eyes lightened. "And then I came round."

"Thank God," breathed Gwen.

Dr. Messenger eyed Dan. "What's puzzled me is, how did you know I'd been shot? The cops traced the emergency call to your cell, but then, instead of you being a suspect, as you might well have been, you were quickly removed as a, and I quote, 'person of interest.' Privately, the cops told me they reckoned you were some kind of operative. . . ."

Dan shrugged, said nothing.

Messenger smiled as if this did not surprise him. He turned to Gwen.

"I must also thank you, Gwen. The cops found a listening device and a forwarding device in my study. I have been wracking my brains to think who could have planted it. My favorite candidate is you."

Gwen's color rose.

Messenger waved his hand magnanimously through the air. "Think nothing of it. It is after all largely thanks to you and your foresight in planting a bug in my home that I am still here. I have to presume that you, Dan, were listening in to the bugs and heard me get shot."

Messenger and Dan were exchanging looks; both of them appeared to be enjoying Gwen's discomfort hugely. Finally, it was all too much, and Gwen started laughing. Soon all three of them were laughing, so long and hard that two nurses hurried in. Tears streaked down Messenger's face.

"We're fine!" he declared breathlessly. "Just fine."

The nurses glanced suspiciously from their patient to his visitors, decided on reflection no harm was being done, and went back to their stations.

Gwen pulled up a chair. Dan leaned on the window ledge. Messenger took a long drink of water. His face sobered then.

"What I don't get is why Randy hated me enough to try to kill me. I've gone over and over all our dealings, what I thought I knew of him. . . ." Messenger shook his head, disbelief and hurt showing in his eyes. "I'm not mad at him now, waste of energy." He looked surprised at himself. "My best guess is, he did it for the money. And because the conspiracy thing would have appealed to him. Being a kind of double agent. He would have thought himself so smart to outwit me."

"Nobody expects to be betrayed," said Gwen. "If we do, we kinda cut it off at the pass before it happens." She paused. "What about Weiss?" She could hardly bring herself to say the man's name. *She* felt mad. That feeling hadn't waned.

Messenger frowned. "Dead, I heard. Cops said, 'drowned in the storm.'"

Gwen and Dan exchanged a glance.

"What?" asked Messenger, the ghost of his old impatience showing.

"It was Weiss, or should I say *Hassan*," Gwen spat out the name, "who stood by and let Sieber do the dirty work. Weiss has plenty of blood on his hands. He was Sheikh Ali's creature. Ali Al Baharna was the architect of the ARk Storm that ravaged California. Weiss was the builder."

Messenger looked as if Gwen had just slapped his face. He turned even more ashen. He slumped back on his pillows. "Tell me," he said simply and plaintively.

Gwen told him. The whole story of how they first heard about Hass/Haas at the Ritz-Carlton, Half Moon Bay, to her last, near fatal visit to Sheikh Ali aboard *Zephyr,* to seeing Peter Weiss being hailed as Hassan, to the helicopter ride, to her escape and Sieber's death, to her swim to shore and Dan's rescuing her.

Messenger lay back on his pillows, eyes widened. He muttered curses, exclamations, twined his fingers in an endless, nervous dance.

It took half an hour and two cups of tea brought in by the nurses for Gwen to tell the story.

Dan said little. A large chunk of his part of the story wasn't for telling. Messenger drained his tea. He looked exhausted.

"If I'd only thought," he said. "I thought I could control everything, everyone. Randy, Peter . . . I thought I knew their agenda: money, progress in Falcon, acknowledgement. . . . I didn't have a clue," he added with a flash of bitterness.

"How could you know it all?" asked Dan. "What I don't get is why Weiss/Hassan converted to Islam. What was the trigger for *that* leap? And what made him Ali's tool? He had a great job, plenty of money, success on that level. . . ."

"And a great big void, ready to be filled, even by a horrible purpose," said Gwen. "He was lonely. You could feel it a mile off. He was an outsider, never one of the boys, never one of the team. I've had small doses of Ali Al Baharna's charisma. He could lay it on when he wanted. He would have sucked Weiss right in. He was the father figure Weiss never had."

"Knowing what I know, it makes a horrible kind of sense," said Messenger. "Did he ever tell you about his mother?" he asked Gwen. "I know he looked up to you."

"He told me she left her homeland, gave up everything to marry his father. I know his father beat on them both, left them, then she killed herself."

Messenger nodded. "All true, but there's more. He told me several years back when I suppose *I* was the substitute father figure. Before I gave Kevin Barclay a bigger bonus and Peter took that as a rejection. Looking back, I can see how his behavior changed from then. Just last Christmas." He batted an arm through the air. "I'm rambling. Seems to happen now. So, Weiss's mother. She was from Indonesia. Met his father when he was working as a contractor over there, for Exxon I think it was." He paused, eyed Gwen and Dan. Dan was still leaning against the windowsill, Gwen was still sitting on the chair by the bed, leaning forward, arms on her knees.

"His mother was a Muslim." said Messenger softly.

"Who gave up her religion," said Gwen. "Losing my religion! Weiss used to whistle it all the time in the Lab."

"He had been brought up as a blue-collar Christian. That he told me," Messenger said. "He lost Christianity, gained Islam."

"And his ma did the opposite," noted Dan. "That makes her guilty of apostasy. Punishable by death."

"Is it?" asked Messenger."

Dan nodded. "She would have been at risk of an honor killing. At best, her family would have disowned her."

"How d'you know so much?" asked Messenger.

"Spent three years in Afghanistan. Picked up a bit about Islam. . . ."

Messenger seemed to glean that Dan didn't wish to elaborate. He just nodded, absorbed it.

"And with all the Islamophobia here he couldn't mourn her as a Muslim, maybe felt he couldn't publicly convert, so he kept it all quiet. Save the beard, save the giving up alcohol. Not that he mastered that one," Gwen added. "So it all went inside, got twisted up. He was avenging his mother, in a totally sick kind of way."

Messenger nodded. "In Sheikh Ali he found religion, he found a father figure."

"He found jihad," concluded Dan.

154

Messenger and Gwen said nothing. Silence stretched through the small white hospital room as all three thought of the consequences.

"So," said Gwen at last, resting her hand gently on Messenger's arm. "What's next for you?"

He smiled at her. "They say brain injuries can change your personality. Seems half of Falcon is dead. I have no wish to bring it back to life. I'm winding it up." He smiled.

"I'm taking a leave of absence from myself." He paused. "And I'm donating Zeus to the United Nations Famine Relief Fund."

Gwen took his hand. "You know, for a murderous megalomaniac, you're not so bad."

He grinned back. "Seems my wife might be persuaded to think so too. I'm flying to Germany as soon as they allow me. I'll recuperate there, with her and my boys."

Gwen felt a surge of joy.

"And what of you? What will you do?" Messenger asked Gwen.

"Rebuild my house. Honor the spirit of the naturists who built the original. Maybe even thrill their ghosts." She turned to Dan and winked.

EPILOGUE

It rained for thirty days straight in California. Three million acres of the Central Valley were flooded. The total damage was estimated to be $870 billion. Four hundred billion dollars of flood-related damage was done to real estate, much of it uninsured. One quarter of all homes in California were flooded, many washed away. Over one million people were left temporarily homeless. Cars were washed out to sea. Boats sailed down streets. The wind itself did another five billion dollars' worth of damage. Landslides added another billion dollars to California's bill. Tens of thousands of animals drowned. Many of their carcasses, drifting on the swollen waters covering the flood plains of the Central Valley, entered the water supply, contaminating it. The share prices of the real estate casualty insurance companies fell by over fifty percent. The interruption to business in the world's eighth largest economy was in the hundreds of billions of dollars. It would take the State of California years to recover.

And the human cost . . . Nearly four thousand people lost their lives. More would have been lost were it not for the efforts of the ARk Storm team and the warnings they had received from Gwen Boudain and Dan Jacobsen.

In the wake of the ARk Storm, as the flood waters began very slowly to recede, rumors abounded. There were reports of F-22s in the air, of UAVs being shot from the sky. The Air Force made no comment, taking the line that to do so would only add oxygen to the wild stories proliferating. Some of those stories said that the ARk Storm had been created deliberately. The weather service did not dignify that one with a comment.

Dan Jacobsen never did write the promised article for his editor. Some stories never can be told.

INTRODUCTORY
AND EXPLANATORY NOTE

The History

I have long been fascinated by the weather. Some years ago, I lived in Peru. Every so often I would escape the mayhem of Lima for Punta Sal, a little fishing village on the border with Ecuador. Hemingway used to fish there for marlin. Framed photographs of him grinning beside his huge catches adorn the walls of the ramshackle bars.

I went not to fish but to swim in the sea, bodysurfing the huge Pacific rollers. Normally you could only stay in for ten or fifteen minutes without a wetsuit because the Humboldt Current kept the waters cold, but one Christmas the waters were balmy! I stayed in for two hours, marveling at the difference, emerging nut brown and slaked in salt. El Niño had come, bringing with it warm waters. That's where it is first felt, in the seas off that remote and underpopulated border. Typically, the Niño phenomenon is felt around Christmastime and hence acquired its name—El Niño—the Christ Child.

The fishermen's children, playing in the unusually warm waters, knew El Niño had come. As did I. But none of the world's media seemed to have picked up this event and did not do so for months.

It made me think: What if you had a weather-prediction system superior to the competition's? You could make out like a bandit using weather derivatives. . . .

One gruesome note that bears witness to the devastation weather can bring and mankind's brutal response:

Two thousand years ago, the Moche civilization of Peru, master potters who lived along the northern coast of the Punta Sal area, sacrificed hundreds of their own people to assuage the weather gods during El Niño years. Massed skeletons were found at the bottom of cliffs in the surrounding areas. Archaeologists studied the depictions on the pottery and dated the skeletons and analyzed the soil and rock and pieced together the story of the Niño sacrifices. The warm waters that El Niño brings devastate the fish supplies and often produce heavy rains that wash away harvests. El Niño meant starvation for the coastal dwellers.

And human sacrifice.

Seeing the pottery of the Moche, swimming in their seas and walking their cliffs, brought home to me the power of the weather and its role in shaping human history. I've been fascinated by weather ever since . . . the roots of *Ark Storm* went down many years ago.

The Science

It's a leap from prediction to manipulation of the weather. We're familiar with cloud seeding, but the ionization technology in this book is a much more powerful tool/weapon than seeding. Making it rain, breaking all records, in the deserts of Arabia has a doomsday biblical slant to it. The science/technology is already here—just google rainstorms in Al Ain, United Arab Emirates, in July and August 2010 (i.e., when rain is nigh on impossible) to see its power. And this technology has moved on some since then.

ARk Storm 1000 is a real and much-feared scenario. Personnel from multiple agencies in diverse locations would play key and active roles in the forecasting and emergency management of the scenario as it hits California, and for simplicity's sake I have gathered the key players together and given them a fictional HQ at Stanford University. Otherwise, the facts, subject to the limits of my brain-power and comprehension, are as I state them.

—L. D., Suffolk, 2013